The Queen of Sleepy Eye

The Queen of Sleepy Eye

Patti Hill

Nashville, Tennessee

Printed in the United States of America

978-0-8054-4750-7

Published by B&H Publishing Group
Nashville, Tennessee

Author is represented by Books & Such Literary Agency,
Janet Kobobel Grant, 52 Mission Circle, Suite 122, PMB 170,
Santa Rosa, CA 95409-5370, www.booksandsuch.biz.

Dewey Decimal Classification: F
Subject Heading: ADVENTURE FICTION \ BEAUTY
CONTESTANTS—FICTION \ MOTHERS AND
DAUGHTERS—FICTION

Publisher's Note: This novel is a work of fiction. Names, places, and incidents are either products of the author's imagination or used fictitiously. All characters are fictional, and any similarity to people living or dead is purely coincidental.

1 2 3 4 5 6 7 8 9 10 • 11 10 09 08

To the dads who have loved me
through every season—
Abba Father
Bill Kegebein
John Kretlow
Jack Hill

It is very unfair to judge of anybody's conduct, without an intimate knowledge of their situation. Nobody, who has not been in the interior of a family, can say what the difficulties of any individual of that family may be.
Jane Austen, *Emma*

A saint is not someone who is good but who experiences the goodness of God.
Thomas Merton

To be alive is to be broken. And to be broken is to stand in need of grace.
Brennan Manning, *The Ragamuffin Gospel*

I was no bigger than a bug in my mother's womb when the two of us drove away from Sleepy Eye, Minnesota, toward our lives as a duet.

Mom had no destination in mind. The Kaskaskia River wound through the trees like a silver ribbon. The scene reminded her of a photograph that had hung over her parents' bed, so she parked the Pontiac and slept for the first time in three days. Months later I was born at St. Margaret's Hospital within a stone's throw of that parking space. The sisters cooed over my young, recently-widowed mother, a Madonna-like vision with her newborn daughter. Mom named me in the Portuguese tradition with two surnames, my father's name listed before my mother's. That was how I came to be María Amelia Casimiro Monteiro. Amy, for short. This was the goodnight story Mom loved to tell.

At my first awareness, sometime around the age of four, I remember hearing the fairy-tale beginning of my life, born to the Queen of Sleepy Eye as I was. Unjustly dethroned after only twenty-three days as the 1958 Queen of Sleepy Eye, Mom refused to return the tiara and the sash. Her larceny seemed justified since her only crime had been a secret marriage to my father. Whenever one of Mom's girlfriends visited the house, Mom brought out the velvet box. With her fingers poised to lift the lid, her eyes lucent, and her smile shamelessly demure, she paused until her audience gushed, "Oh, Francie, for goodness' sake, open the box."

By age ten, I yawned and stretched as she ceremoniously set the box on the coffee table. By the time I turned thirteen, half the rhinestones had fallen from the tiara's settings. Never mind that I'd buried the ratty thing under coffee grounds and potato skins in the kitchen trash more than once, only to retrieve the tiara before my mother discovered it missing. The story was a droning fly I batted away, but it always came back. My apathy went unnoticed. Mom told her story to anyone willing to listen. She worked conversations like a fisherman angling a fighting bass—reel, slack, feed the line—until she hooked the opportunity to tell of her stolen royalty. Grocery lines. Intimate apparel sales. Parent-teacher conferences. The world was ripe for a hard-luck queen story.

Today, Mom rarely speaks of her summer in Sleepy Eye. That was fifty years ago. As far as I know, the tiara and sash lie buried in a landfill with petrified hot dogs and Twinkies. She and my stepfather have retired to travel.

Three years ago, Mom called from New Zealand, and the line between today and yesterday grew decidedly fuzzy. "Amy, honey," Mom yelled as she did when she called from more than ten miles away. "You have to help me find the Pontiac."

I'd spent my early years loathing that car. Mom demanded it be kept in showroom-floor condition. That meant weekly washings, vacuuming, and massaging a special cleaner on the dashboard to keep it from cracking, as if Mom ever parked the car in the sun. Scuffed door panels were scrubbed immediately. The ashtray went unused. If I wore shoes with buckles, off they came before I was allowed to sit on the seat.

Once a month, Mom polished the leather seats while I waxed the car from stem to stern. For that car I missed birthday parties, grand openings of the A&P and the Dairy Queen, and the very first showing of *Chitty Chitty Bang Bang* at the Egyptian Theater. Honestly, a little brother would have been a more tolerable evil, especially since Mom only drove the car when the mood struck her. All of this for the 1958 Pontiac Bonneville Sport Coupe Jubilee Edition, a car that without equivocation, outranked every other car in pure gaudiness. Chrome accentuated every line and arched like drowsy eyelids over twin headlights and taillights. The grill was a chrome waffle. But most unsettling of all was the green-on-green paint that soured my stomach.

Still, the Pontiac was the only artifact of my father I'd known.

"The Pontiac?" I asked her. "You sold that—what, thirty years ago? What's this about?"

"This phone call is costing me a fortune." Mom blew her nose. "*Fofa,* honey, I'm desperate. You're so good at finding things. How hard could it be to find a few thousand pounds of metal with four wheels?" The line went quiet for a long time—on my end, because I was wondering why the Pontiac had reemerged as an object of Mom's devotion. From countless other conversations, I'd learned silence on her end meant she was sifting her memories for leverage. Her effort proved unnecessary. Graham, our youngest, had thrown up grape juice on Mom's white sofa last Thanksgiving. I owed her.

"Do you even remember the name of the man who bought the car?"

"You're such a good daughter, my honey, *meu fofa.*"

While Mom and Chuck took culinary tours of Tuscany and visited the Northern Baltic countries, the search consumed me for three years. I followed hunches and faded memories to heaps of rusted car bodies in tired cities and townships. That's how Mom and I have come to be in Barstow, California, standing in the dust and scanning the ground for rattlesnakes.

"THIS HAS TO be the car, Mom. Look at it."

"I just want to be sure that this is *our* car." Mom reads the vehicle identification number from the car's firewall while I scan the numbers written in the family Bible, something I'd already done over the phone with the car's restorer. Mom sighs and a flush of relief washes over me—and something else unexpected and harder to name. Foreboding? Suspicion? Nausea? I look to Mom to confirm or dismiss my tumbling gut, but she is digging in her purse for her checkbook.

The restorer of the Pontiac waves a hornet away from his sandwich with a greasy rag, but a half dozen more marauders hover around the man's head. From the slump of the man's shoulders, I don't presume him to be ambitious, but his asking price could retire the national debt.

"Ladies, you have to understand, this car is in primo condition. The original owner ordered all the available technology of that time. The sliding Plexiglas sun visor. The Wonderbar AM radio with an automatic power antenna. Power windows. Memo-Matic power memory seats. And they don't make reproduction parts for this baby. Oh no, I hunted down *new* old parts from vendors all over the country. Make that the world. I got an authentic GM resonator from a parts guy in Ireland."

"We're going to the Bay area. Will the car get us there?" I ask.

"This car is better than the day she came off the assembly line. The twos of you could drive her to China and back," he says, backhanding mustard off his chin.

"I better take the car for a test drive, just to be sure," Mom says.

The man eyes me up and down. "You leavin' your daughter as collateral?"

"I'll be accompanying Mom." I open my wallet to the man. "Take a credit card. Take two or three." My feet itch to get off the snake-infested ground, also a true haven for scorpions and tarantulas and speed-of-light lizards. I hate the desert.

The man fingers the American Express Card, stops, pulls out the MasterCard. "I forget. I don't take American Express."

Mom starts the car, and the rumble of the engine thrums against a raw place in my heart. I blink away the tears.

"Let's go," she says and slides the transmission into drive. Her chin trembles. We turn onto a road that curves through a subdivision of tightly packed stucco houses with postage-stamp lawns. The green is startling through the shimmer of heat off the pavement.

I ask, "Are you okay?"

"I will be."

"Is it the money?"

"Memories, mostly."

She slows for a dip, and the Pontiac rolls like a boat riding a swell. The car is heavy, substantial, nothing like the Prius—a bantamweight by comparison—I drive between our home in Carpenteria and Westmont College in Santa Barbara.

"You were conceived in this car," she says.

I glance toward the backseat and shiver. "So, how's she handling? I remember the steering being a little loose."

"Amy, honey, we have to talk." Her hand covers her mouth to staunch a flow of emotion. I watch her, not breathing. Her chest rises and falls. "I know you're expecting a weekend of pampering at Bodega Hot Springs. That's what I promised, and more than anyone I know, you deserve to be treated like a queen. You persevered, Amy. You found the car. But, Amy, *fofa*, we aren't going to the spa." She kneads the steering wheel. "That was a lie."

"Mom? What? You're scaring me. You're not sick, are you?"

Her eyes glisten with tears. "The time has come to set some things right from my past." She glances at me before fixing her gaze out the windshield. "I'm not proud of this, but I stole this car from your father years ago. He left me no choice. I've lived in a state of terror all of these years. Every time the phone rang, I feared the police had found me. A knock on the door? Who else? A detective and his partner. You know, like *Dragnet*? I lived in dread of opening the newspaper to find a picture of the Pontiac and me with a caption, 'Have you seen this car or the car thief named María Francisca Montiero Santos?'"

No one is more melodramatic than Mom.

"You're not making sense. You were married. As his widow, the car became yours."

"The truth is . . . we were never actually married."

"Never?"

Her knuckles pale as she grips the steering wheel. "And he isn't exactly dead either. He's retired and living in Sleepy Eye."

My high school American history teacher, Mrs. Lund, had once told a story about a World War II paratrooper who had been hidden away in occupied Holland by a seemingly benevolent Dutchman. The paratrooper lived behind painted windows, knowing only what his host chose to reveal. Maybe it had been an episode of *The Twilight Zone*, the one with a very young Robert Redford.

All the paratrooper knew to be true about the world had been the fabrication of his host. Finally released, the paratrooper walked a narrow, cobbled street filled with housewives carrying bundles and merchants arranging produce. Children chased each other, laughing and taunting. This wasn't the war-savaged scene his benefactor had described. Bewildered, the paratrooper stumbled along trying to reconstruct his reality.

I know how he felt.

"You should pull over," I say.

She continues driving down the middle of the street. "Maybe I should have told you sooner."

Now I'm angry, which makes me cry. "*Maybe?* I thought my father was dead. I cried for him. I prayed for him. When other little girls asked for ponies, I pleaded with Santa Claus to bring my daddy back. And you think *maybe* you should have told me?" Tears flow down Mom's cheek too. Wounding her deflates my anger. "Please park the car."

The front wheel jumps the curb, and the car lurches to a stop. Mom lets the car idle in front of a fire hydrant as she flexes her hands on the steering wheel. "I wanted to tell you, and I will tell you everything, but I'm sure that greasy man—"

"I think his name is Bob."

"Bob *schmob*." Mom sighs.

My penchant for detail drives her crazy. Too bad. "Mom, please . . ."

"Okay, okay. Chuck and I were snorkeling in this amazing place—"

"I know this part. Tell me about my father and why you're buying this car."

"I was getting to that."

From the crease between her eyes, I know I will hear the story she wants to tell, not necessarily the one I want to hear. Hasn't it always been this way?

"Anyway, we were snorkeling in this amazing spot on the Coromandel Peninsula on New Zealand's north island called Gemstone Bay. Oh, Amy, the kelp swayed with the surge of the water. I startled a manta ray, followed a red moki as he swam through the amber forest. A whole new world—"

"Stop! Tell me about my father."

"*Querida*, please don't cry." She reaches for me, and I lean into her shoulder.

Good heavens, I'm fifty years old! I sit up. "Mom, tell your story."

She hands me a wad of tissues from her purse. "There I was, thousands of miles from home. I hadn't thought about the Pontiac since . . . I just haven't thought of the car in a long time. And there I was, immersed in amazing beauty, and God spoke to me. He said, 'It's time to right a wrong, Francisca. Take the car back to Carl.'"

"Carl? Who's Carl?"

"Carl Swenson is your father." Mom shifts into drive and heads back the way we came. "We have a long journey before us. We'll have lots of time to talk."

"Then who's Fabio Casimiro?"

She winced and expelled a long breath. "I was scared. The sisters asked for the father's name. You don't know what being pregnant and unmarried was like back then. A widow was respected, treated with great tenderness. A single mother was a slut, a whore. I'd made up a name for your father. I used the name to curse him every time my heart dared to long for him. The name isn't so nice."

"But nice enough to give to your daughter?"

"I had no choice." Mom pats my knee. "It's not that bad. *Fabio* means bean and *Casimiro* means great destroyer. Carl, he . . . he . . ."

"He what?"

She shrugs. "Carl farted a lot. I swear he could fart on command. Once he asked me to pull his finger, and when I laughed, he asked me to go for a drive."

All I knew about my father was what Mom had told me, that he was handsome, sweet, and very, very smart. She convinced me he couldn't wait to be a papa. My throat tightens around this new truth. My real father wooed Mom, age sixteen, with a coarse joke. The muscle that connects my left eyebrow to the back of my head cramps. Although doing so won't stop the migraine, I knead my aching eyebrow anyway. "I was really looking forward to Bodega Hot Springs."

"Maybe next year for your birthday, *querida*."

"This long trip you're talking about. Tell me we're not going to Sleepy Eye."

Mom sighs.

What makes her think I would want to meet a man known for passing gas, a man who falls a billion miles short of the father I dreamed about, a man whose lasting contribution was DNA for a large nose and unruly hair?

I don't think so.

"Mom, I'm sorry, but I don't have time for a road trip down memory lane. Remember, I'm the faculty rep for new-student orientation this year. I have to be in Santa Barbara by Tuesday. Sam expects me back Sunday afternoon. Micole hasn't registered for classes. And Rocket—"

"We'll be back in plenty of time for student orientation. We fly out of Minneapolis on Sunday. I called Sam. He's quite capable of helping Micole with her classes. And the dog? Really, Amy, would you put your dog's well-being above your own flesh and blood?"

"You called Sam? He knows about this? Does this Carl Swenson person know we're coming?"

"Not exactly."

By all rights, I should demand Mom return me to the airport where we rendezvoused only hours earlier. But I'm curious. More than that, seeing my father is a clarion call I must answer. Is this the same irresistible urge that pulls a female salmon from the Gulf of Alaska to hightail it back to her birthplace, a stream too shallow to cover her hump? Ravenous bears. Fishermen. Mutilating leaps up rocky waterfalls. She's doomed. At the end, her flayed flesh dances in the current as she gulps her last breaths of life. Who can explain such a drive toward self-annihilation?

Not me.

Back at Bob's Classic Cars & More, Mom charms Bob down two thousand dollars because of a crack in the slide-down Plexiglas sun visor. "You best write that check before I change my mind," he says. "This baby was headed for Hot August Nights in Reno. Collectors pay top dollar for workmanship there."

Mom uses the Pontiac's hood to write the check while I return to Bob's air-conditioned office to retrieve our suitcases. I'm tempted to call Sam to come get me. The telephone hangs on the wall behind a glass counter filled with trophies, all topped with facsimiles of classic cars. I work to untwist the telephone cord. The receiver spins wildly.

What good would come of calling Sam?

My husband is Mom's coconspirator, convinced, no doubt, the trip into my past will be good for me, a kind of slap to the face to break the cycle of hysteria Mom ignites in me. I hang the handset up hard, and the mouthpiece breaks free of the receiver to dangle by two slender wires. Out on the lot, Bob eyes Mom up and down while leaning against the Pontiac. I repair the broken receiver with two

Band-aids from my purse. I write a hasty note of apology on a gum wrapper and prop it on the telephone.

The glare from the Pontiac, resplendent with its chrome and garish exterior, makes me wince behind my sunglasses, and the muscle over my left eye cramps again. My migraine medication lies deep inside a suitcase. I don't remember which one. Mom helps me lift the suitcases into the trunk. Bob chews his lip, looking too much like a man rethinking a decision.

Mom loads her matching leopard-print valise and garment bag on top of my tattered suitcases. "Come on, Amy. We're burning daylight."

"I need to use the restroom."

She slides behind the wheel. "For goodness' sake, we'll stop at the McDonald's."

I hesitate.

Mom starts the car and revs the engine.

I talk to Bob over the roof of the car. "You did a great job on the car. Thank you. I'm sure your craftsmanship will mean a great deal to the original owner." But I'm not sure, not one bit. My heart races at the thought of meeting my father, then deflates at the thought of his possible indifference. This is going to be a long trip.

The McDonald's in Barstow is three railroad cars side by side like sardines in a can, a bit of architectural whimsy meant to coax people out of their air-conditioned vehicles and into the 107-degree heat. The restaurant is disappointingly warm. There's a line into the bathroom. With my bladder complaining, I take my place in line. Mom waits for me in the cool car. This is my last chance to bolt, but I wait my turn.

MOM PRESSES THE accelerator to merge with traffic traveling to Las Vegas and beyond. I wince when a semitruck and a black BMW speed past us. Mom eases the Pontiac to 60 mph. Cars, delivery vans, and semitrucks pass us like we are parked on the shoulder.

"Can this car go any faster?"

"People drive like idiots along here. How can they be in such a hurry to lose their money? Who do they think pays for all those bright lights and fake volcanoes?"

"It's safer to go with the flow of traffic, Mom."

A sun-scorched Toyota full of boys wearing their caps backward pulls alongside us, and a passenger shakes his fist when the driver accelerates to pass.

"What did I tell you? They have to be going ninety."

We pass the Zzyzx Road exit. Who or what would live in a place that is gray and beige and riddled with glass shards? My question goes unanswered because the road dips and disappears around a mound of rock.

I hate the desert.

Mom looks over her sunglasses at me. "You'll never guess how you're supposed to say that road name."

And I hate Mom's guessing games. "How?"

"You have to guess."

I sigh like she has given me a difficult task to ponder, but I'm making plans to call my husband from the next gas stop. Sam will rescue me. He's had tons of practice, but this is the craziest thing I've ever let Mom drag me into.

My desire to meet my biological father is waning. What's the point? I like my life. It's full. I have a family. My husband thinks I'm the sun, the moon, and the stars. He brings me coffee in bed every morning. I'm truly blessed. My second daughter, Micole, has emerged from the black tunnel where she cocooned during her teenage years. She's nice. She calls me from work to hear my voice and brings me dainty pastries when she thinks I need a boost. I could die happy, only I wouldn't see my granddaughter—the most brilliant and beautiful child on earth—grow up to be a woman. Her mother, my oldest daughter Steph, expands my heart like a balloon. She made me the woman I am today—in a good way. And then there's Graham, our youngest, born an old man and way too much like me. One of us must loosen up, or the tension will truly break us. When I talk about him like this, most assume he's a Goth with enough metal in his head to recreate the Eiffel Tower. Far from it. He's earnest and analytical, a people pleaser. But I can crush him with a single word or a sideways glance, although that has never been my intention. As the baby, he is the child whose milky breath I can still feel on my neck. I'm crazy about him. And as alike as we are, he dresses like his father, thank goodness. A good life with good people, that's what I'm living.

Who needs to add a complication to their life? Not me.

Whatever vignette Mom has imagined about meeting Carl Swenson won't come close to reality. I don't need a father. I have one. In fact, I have two—a stepfather who demonstrated amazing tenderness during my greatest disappointment; and all those times I thought I was raising my mother, the Father of the fatherless, God, watched over me. You might think I'm arrogant or mentally challenged to say so, but I believe he moved heaven and earth to my advantage. Sometimes I appreciated his involvement, and sometimes I resented him bitterly. I know this sort of yin and yang between daughter and father is normal because I've watched Sam with Micole.

Until she turned thirteen, Micole was Sam's shadow. High school introduced angry and distrustful friends. Despite our warnings, Micole was determined to help them until, not surprisingly, she became one of them. When she disappeared for over a week, Sam slept in fits and spurts. He finally found her in a downtown hotel with her much older, devil-in-a-blue-shirt boyfriend, Cody. Sam still won't tell me what he found her doing, but decay wafted from Sam's clothes.

The Pontiac grumbles up a long grade that crests only to draw us farther into the institutional beige of the desert valley. On the far horizon, gray mountains dance in the heat. Two stripes of black asphalt score the desert with nothing resembling a destination in sight. This is Nebraska, only someone has forgotten to turn the sprinklers on. I dig a pad of paper and a pen out of my purse to write the word *Zzyzx*.

"I think you'd pronounce it *Zay*-ziks."

Two

1975

Mom honked the horn in the driveway. Lauren and I leaned over the toilet bowl, heads pressed together, as I pushed the birth control pill through the foil backing. We watched the pill sink to the bottom of its porcelain grave, and I flushed the pill out of sight.

"You're doing the right thing," Lauren said.

"Gross. I can't believe Mom thinks I'll need these wretched pills."

Mom honked the horn again and yelled, "Amy! Lauren! Say good-bye already! We're burning daylight."

We embraced, wet cheeks together. Lauren squeezed me hard. "Promise you'll write."

"Every day. I will. I promise."

"Tell me everything. I'm going to miss you so much."

"At least you'll have Debbie."

"Deb's a spaz."

"And I'm not?"

"Yes. Maybe. Just a little."

She was right. I was a spaz. An egghead. A shapeless spear of a girl. I released Lauren to splash water on my face. The towels had been packed away, so I dried my face on my T-shirt.

"I got you a present," she said.

My stomach roiled. "I wish you hadn't."

"No, really, I paid for it and everything."

"Are you sure?"

"What do you mean, am I sure? I used the money I made baby-sitting the Weston twins. What brats." Lauren dug something small out of her pocket. She held my hand and released the weightless gift into my palm. "Do you like it?" she asked.

In my palm lay a delicate cross tangled in its chain. No matter how bratty the twins had been, the Westons weren't known for their generosity. "Lauren, you're going to get caught."

"This was the last time, I promise. I didn't want you to go away empty-handed. Honest, thanks to you, I'm completely rehabilitated. Let me help you with the clasp."

I worried about the kind of hell that awaited a person who wore a stolen cross, but honestly, I hated the idea of hurting Lauren's feelings more. Who knew when I would see her again, if ever.

Mom pressed the car's horn.

"I better go." I looked around the bathroom. Vacant window sills. Clear counter. Towel bars empty. My eyes burned with tears for the hundredth time since I'd accepted the scholarship to Westmont College, my ticket away from Mom that I'd prayed for day and night. How crazy was that? I turned off the light for the last time. One more hug with Lauren, and she walked away from me and out the door, her head down, her hands to her face.

Outside, Mr. Cochran, our landlord, his forehead corrugated with determination, strode toward Mom. They had clashed before over leaky faucets and utility bills and loud parties. Poor Mr. Cochran, he always lost. Her biggest victory allowed Mom to paint her bedroom lavender and mine yellow, a color she'd hoped would rid me of melancholy, which was completely unnecessary. I was plenty positive. I just wasn't my mother, the bloomin' bluebird of happiness.

Mom slid out of the car, and with one swipe of her hand slipped her sweater off her bare shoulders to reveal the low cut of her blouse. "Good morning to you, Henry," Mom said with a friendly wave. "I think summer has finally arrived, don't you?"

"Going somewhere?"

"Amy and I are moving to California. I hope you saw her picture in the paper. Not her best picture by far, but the story was real nice, even mentioned that I raised her by myself. She was the only one in her class to get a full-ride scholarship. I'm so proud of her." With a nod of her head, she directed me toward the car.

Mr. Cochran folded his arms over his paunch, like Mom would ever be intimidated by Mr. Clean. "I gave you two extra weeks to come up with this month's rent, Mrs. Monteiro. I hope you weren't thinking of leaving without paying what you owe."

Mom tossed the sweater onto the boxes in the backseat and leaned through the open window to dig through her purse. My stomach tightened watching Mr. Cochran ogle her rear end, but more than likely she'd planned on him doing just that. She handed him her tip envelope. "That's what I love about you, Henry. I've never known a man with a more generous heart. Go ahead, count the money. Make sure it's all there, minus the rest of this month's rent, of course."

Mr. Cochran shoved the envelope into his pocket and whistled, this time admiring the Pontiac. "Is this *your* car? My younger brother bought one of these babies off the showroom floor when he landed his high-and-mighty job in New York City. How long have you had it?"

"Forever. I don't drive much. Walking keeps me in shape, Henry." She said his name like butter melting on a hot biscuit.

My face warmed. I opened *Pride and Prejudice* and pretended to read.

"How old is the car? Fifteen? Twenty years?" he asked.

"Only seventeen. Amy helps me keep it looking nice."

Every Sunday after church, Mom packed a picnic and we drove the car to a shady place along the Kaskaskia River where we turned the radio up to sing along with the Captain and Tennille and the Eagles and all things Motown. Mom changed the station if they dared to play disco. When I paste-waxed the car, I used toothpicks to remove excess wax between the chrome and the car's body. Mom made popcorn for dinner those nights as a special treat, or she let me use her Tabu foaming bath lotion. Otherwise, the car stayed in the garage no matter how much I complained about walking everywhere. Blizzards. Rain. Wind. Sleet. I threatened to join the Foreign Legion where they treated their soldiers with respect. Mom never explained why we only drove on Sundays. That was our normal.

Two-stepping, Mr. Cochran said, "I wouldn't have hurried over here. It's just that when Edith Zolatel called . . ."

Across the street, Mrs. Zolatel's drapes snapped closed.

"Don't worry, Henry," Mom said. "Edith has a habit of thinking the worst of people. She's very lonely."

And she has breath like rotting fish, I thought.

Mr. Cochran took a long look at Mom, the way you would before walking away from, say, the ceiling of the Sistine Chapel, knowing you would never be back to St. Peter's Basilica in your lifetime. My mother, María Francisca Santos Monteiro, born of Portuguese immigrants in Chicago, had creamed-coffee skin with black, aqueous eyes full of innuendo. When she wanted a man to see things her way, she parted her pouty lips to reveal her white teeth. The men faltered and acquiesced immediately, and when they did, she bestowed a Sophia Loren smile on them. I'd seen the display many times.

Mr. Cochran counted bills out of the envelope and pressed the cash into Mom's hand. "Here you go. Consider this a graduation gift for Amy. Gas is expensive, and you'll be eating in restaurants. California is a long ways from Gilbert County, Illinois."

"Henry, you're the sweetest thing," she said and kissed his cheek, leaving a smudge of Midnight Passion lipstick.

He'll have a hard time explaining that *to Mrs. Cochran.*

I LEANED MY forehead against thc window and watched the rows of knee-high corn and black earth rush by. All that I'd ever hated about Illinois now pulled at me to stay. Biting cold winters morphed into Currier and Ives scenes. The severe flatness of the land reassured me. The pungency of hog farms tendered memories of shadow tag and firefly ballets. Even with Lauren's assurances that California was perfect for me, I struggled to picture myself walking among bronzed coeds with my fuzzy hair and large schnoz. Instead, I saw my hair bouncing with every step along a palm tree-lined path, and students parting to let me and my hair pass. That was why I kept my mass of curls in a bun, à la Lizzy Bennet, the heroine of Jane Austen's *Pride and Prejudice.* Doing so enhanced my literary mystique.

And Lauren. We'd been friends since first grade and suffered through first pimples and first periods together. She taught me how to use tampons. You can't replace a friend like that.

Mom lit a cigarette.

I lowered the window.

"Amy, close the window. I have the air conditioner going."

"I can't breathe when you're sucking on those things."

The Pontiac skidded to a stop on the highway's graveled shoulder. Mom shifted toward me in her seat and extended her little finger. "Pinkie pledge."

"Pinkie pledge? I haven't pinkie pledged since . . ."

She took a long drag of her cigarette and blew the smoke in my direction. I hooked my pinkie with hers. "California is a long way," she said. "I won't have you sassing me about smoking the whole way. Repeat after me: I pinkie pledge I will not make hateful smoking comments until we find an apartment."

"Fine. I'm living in the dorms."

She squeezed harder.

I matched her grip. "I pinkie pledge I won't make anti-smoking comments until Mom finds an apartment to live in . . . *alone.*"

She relaxed her grip, but I held tight. "A pledge for a pledge. Remember? Repeat after me. I pinkie pledge to have nothing to do with men until I dip my toes in the Pacific Ocean."

"I pinkie pledge . . ." A station wagon hauling a trailer whizzed by, then a delivery van, and a stock truck.

"Go on," I urged.

"I heard Frank Sinatra gases up his Ferrari in Las Vegas. You wouldn't want me to pass up such a—"

"Without a pinkie pledge from you, mine is null and void."

I watched her consider the empty miles before us. Corn fields.

Plains. Mountains. Desert. And more desert. Concrete and glass. "Okay." She squeezed tighter. "I pinkie pledge to have nothing to do with men until I dip my toes in the Specific Ocean."

"Pa-cific Ocean."

"That's what I said." Her eyebrows lifted. "Another pledge. This time I want to hear you pinkie pledge no come-to-Jesus sermons."

"For how long?"

Another cluster of cars and trucks sped by. "Until I'm on my death bed."

"I can't promise—"

"All right, until we stand at the corner of Hollywood and Vine."

That night we would be in eastern Kansas; the next day we would cross the Rockies. Las Vegas was our goal for the third day. If Mom saw Frank Sinatra at the gas station, we'd never make Hollywood and Vine, only a day's drive away from Las Vegas. I prayed Frank Sinatra would gas up early in the day, and we'd arrive in California without delay. The last thing I wanted on my conscience was Mom's eternal soul.

"Okay, but a pledge for a pledge."

"Shoot."

If I asked Mom to stop talking about being queen of Sleepy Eye, would she dissolve into a heap of ash? "No telling me to stop slouching."

"No complaining about the time it takes to put on my makeup."

"No complaining about how much I read."

"No groaning when I sing along with Barry Manilow."

"You can't tell me how to wear my hair."

"But Amy, that bun makes you look like Grandma Moses."

"I guess Barry will be singing alone."

"All right! You win. You can wear your Elizabeth Barnetta—"

"Bennet, Mom, her name is Elizabeth Bennet, *the* most endearing character in English literature."

She threw up her hands and checked traffic over her shoulder. "Fine. Wear the bun, but when we get to California, I'm taking you to a salon for the stars."

Besides a minor slipup on Mom's part—she worked her wiles on an old geezer at a gas station for a map of Nebraska—the trip was peaceful. From Omaha, Nebraska, to Kennesburg, Colorado, I read *People* magazine out loud cover to cover, the story about Clint Eastwood twice. We skipped an article about dreams improving creativity.

"Your grandfather, God rest his soul," Mom said, crossing herself, "told us about his dreams every morning at the breakfast table. We were not allowed to speak. He spoke of monsters chasing him, and claws scratching on the door, and people digging out of their graves. I still can't eat breakfast without thinking of dead people."

We passed cars stalled along the highway that wound through the Rocky Mountains. "Vapor lock," Mom said. "Say a prayer the Pontiac doesn't do the same."

Typical. Fear knotted her daughter's stomach, but she wanted me to pray for the car. I slipped onto the floor to sit with my head on the seat and my eyes squeezed tight against the towering mountains. I prayed for the Pontiac. I prayed my mother could keep the car on the narrow road. I prayed my breakfast would stay in my stomach.

We sang every Barry Manilow song Mom knew and a few Frank Sinatra ballads. Still, my hands trembled and my stomach bounced.

Mom leaned over to stroke my hair.

"Are you watching the road?"

"The pill could be causing this," she said. "I was sick for weeks. Let me tell you a story. Maybe you'll go to sleep."

I swallowed hard against the bile that crept up my throat. "Please, Mom, keep both hands on the steering wheel."

Her hand left my head. "I'll tell you about the summer my family moved to Sleepy Eye."

"I know that story."

"My father took a job at the Del Monte plant, processing corn and peas. We lived on the north side near the Catholic church. I was sixteen, and my brothers made my life a living hell."

"Could we stop for some Dramamine?"

Three

I woke up to a twangy country song playing on a radio beneath the car. *Hmm?* I wiped the drool off my cheek and rose slowly to sit on the seat, afraid any sudden movement would send my stomach cartwheeling again. Through the windshield, tin signs touting Sinclair motor oil and genuine GMC parts hung near the ceiling. A small grocery store filled the side mirror. My heart thumped a warning. This wasn't right. Before my eyes registered where I was, the smell of oil and rubber placed me on a car hoist in the service bay of a gas station. The ding of an air hose confirmed my predicament.

"Mom?" I said cautiously, not knowing if movement would tip the car off its perch.

A man with a voice like an idling lawn mower said, "That was real smart of you to downshift into low. Not many women know it's possible to lose a gear and still be able to drive. I'm impressed."

"Is this going to be expensive to fix, Tommy?" she asked, her voice a syrupy mix of helplessness and pleading. Without seeing her, I knew she had pushed her bottom lip out just so and widened her eyes to catch the glint of afternoon light.

Before Tommy could propose marriage, I called out. "Mom, I'm awake."

"Just a minute, *querida,* sweetheart, Tommy and I have to talk business."

"I can let her down, ma'am," he said, and a motor hummed as the hoist lowered the Pontiac to the ground. Tommy matched his voice, broad-chested and frayed. He pocketed the screwdriver he used to clean his fingernails and buried his hands in his armpits.

"Parts are gonna be hard to come by," he said. "I'll start calling around, probably have to get a new tranny from the Front Range. You know, Denver? I'm alone here today, and tomorrow we're closed. I'll have more time to do the calling when Artie gets back from visiting his mother in Glenwood on Wednesday."

I pushed the car door open. "That's four days from now."

"Oh, I wouldn't expect parts to get here before the end of the month."

"The end of the month? Where are we?"

"This here's Cordial, Colorado," Tommy said.

I didn't remember a Cordial, Colorado, on the map. "How did we get here?"

Mom hooked me around the waist and squeezed. "Isn't this a lovely town with a lovely name?"

I turned to Tommy. "How much is a new transmission going to cost us, mister?"

"Well now, that's hard to say. There's the time and the phone calls to find the parts. This car ain't exactly fresh off the assembly line. Then, depending on where I find a good transmission, the shipping is another expense."

"Could you make a guess?"

Mom and I groaned at his estimate.

"Don't worry now," Tommy said, obviously distressed by female emotion. "That's the very highest the bill could be. I've never had a transmission cost that much. I wanted to prepare you if worse came to worse, and the final cost was up there somewhere."

Mom ran her hand over the fender. "This car has special sentimental value only I can truly appreciate." Oh boy, here came the queen story. I looked around the garage for the restroom sign. Mom said, "I rode on the hood of this car as the queen of Sleepy Eye. I was only sixteen."

"Do you have a restroom?" I asked.

Without looking at me, Tommy pointed to a key with a hubcap fob hanging on the garage wall. He motioned with his head and said, "Around the side. Can't miss it."

"One of the judges told me later that he thought I was eighteen," Mom went on.

"You don't look much over that now."

"You're so sweet."

I stepped out of the garage and stopped, overwhelmed by the imposing presence of a mountain. Wounds on its side, like a lion's swipe, gouged through its shrubby hide to expose rocky flesh. I longed for the comfort of a reclining prairie. I looked right. More mountains scraped the horizon. To the left, plateaus like broad stairs led to the base of a rocky peak with crevices still packed with snow. I dared not look behind me. My heart pounded against my ribs.

Trucks rattled by. A mother pushed a stroller toward the double doors of the grocery store, and a train's whistle blew long and insistent. I sank to the curb to behold the mountain and the bluebird sky. I felt small. Weak. Humbled. Defeated. I'd allowed Mom to weasel her way into my college life. California was huge, I had reasoned. We could both live there without seeing one another for months, maybe years. Now I was stuck in some hapless hamlet with my tormentor. As I wallowed in the bilge of self-pity, questioning my cognitive abilities seemed appropriate. What if my teachers hadn't taught me what the kids in California already knew? Perhaps my new peers had pushed themselves to take trigonometry and physics while I'd settled for geometry and chemistry. Maybe I was too stupid for college. Maybe I would have to beg for my job back at Tom's Bait and Bite Shoppe.

I'd rather die.

When I returned from the restroom, Tommy was loading the last of the boxes from our car into his truck. Mom supervised with one hand on her narrow waist and her chin tucked to watch Tommy over her sunglasses. She was smiling. When she saw me, she clapped her hands together. "Isn't this great? Tommy closed down the station to drive us to the motel."

"Shouldn't he be looking for a transmission?"

"María . . . Amelia . . . Casimiro . . . Monteiro. You ungrateful—"

"You promised we'd go straight to California."

"What? Do you think I broke the transmission on purpose?" She cradled my face in her hands. I hardened my glare. She pulled me into an embrace. "*Fofa,* honey, this is a minor detour. We'll be back on the road in no time. You worry too much. I promise you won't be late for the first day of classes."

No more Dramamine for me. I needed to stay alert. And no more hiding on the floor of the car. Thousands of people traveled mountain roads daily. The vast majority of them arrived at their destinations without plummeting over the side.

"Tommy," Mom said, "I hope the Pontiac can stay inside. The sun will damage the finish. This is the original paint, you know."

"Of course, Francie. That's no problem. I have the other service bay."

Mom's body softened beside me. "Thank you, Tommy."

I climbed into Tommy's truck, pressed against the door beside Mom, holding the velvet box with the tiara inside. Driving down the full length of Cordial's business district, two whole blocks, I recited over and over to myself: *He makes my feet like hinds' feet. He makes my feet like hinds' feet.*

WHILE MOM REGISTERED for our stay at the Lazy J Motel, I studied the map of Colorado on the wall. With my finger I traced the route we had taken from the Nebraska-Colorado border to Denver and up through mountain towns like Idaho Springs, Dillon, and Eagle, about where I fell into a drugged stupor and slept. From there, Mom should have driven on to Glenwood Springs, Rifle, and then Orchard City, just a few miles from Utah. No town named Cordial appeared along the route. I asked the motel clerk, Bonnie, a round-faced woman with honeyed eyes. "I was sleeping when we got to Cordial. How far are we from Orchard City?"

"Well, little missy, if you can avoid driving behind a hay wagon or some flatlander camper, the drive won't take you more than a couple hours."

"Two hours?"

Mom kept her head down, giving all of her attention to the registration card.

"So anyone coming to Cordial would have to get off the highway and travel . . . ?"

"South on Highway 50 until they got to Clearwater," Bonnie said. "Then they'd have to turn east on—"

"East? That's interesting," I said. "East is the exact opposite direction of California."

Either Bonnie didn't notice the sarcasm in my voice, or she thought I'd failed geography in a big way. "That's right, missy, you and your mom came east on Highway 92 to Highway 133, and then you followed the signs and—*ta-dah!*—you landed yourselves in Cordial."

I softened my tone in light of Bonnie's sincerity. "I don't suppose too many people just happen upon Cordial."

Mom crossed the *t* and dotted the *i* of her last name with sharp jabs. "That's enough, Amy." I slumped in the only chair of the tiny reception area. Mom asked Bonnie what being single was like in Cordial.

"Well, I'll tell ya. Cordial is known for its fruit. Before very long, they'll be picking cherries as big as golf balls from the orchards. They grow in huge clusters. All you have to do is reach up and grab what you want. Since the Raven Mesa Coal Mine reopened, men in town have been just as plentiful. They're lonely and their pockets are bulging with dough. You can take your pick."

More than anything, I wanted to sit with Mom to watch Bobby and Cissy dance the mambo on *The Lawrence Welk Show.* I was that desperate to stop Bonnie's unwitting threat to my journey westward. "Shouldn't we get to our room, Mom?"

If anyone heard me, they didn't let on.

Bonnie leaned in. "Why, we've had more weddings than funerals this spring, and that's saying something." Bonnie and Mom agreed to try their luck at the Lost Mine Saloon that night. There was no sense reminding Mom of her pinkie pledge. She wore the very look I'd seen on Robbie Coleman's face outside Baumgartner's Bakery.

Mom stepped into the motel room in front of me, and I drew a breath. She threw up her hands. "Don't start with me, Amy. I'm tired. I've driven all day. You have no idea how scary it was driving those last thirty miles in low gear. Big trucks passing us on double-yellow lines. Rough-looking guys in pickups honking their horns and shaking their fists at me. I'm going out for one drink with a nice lady. That's all."

"Just tell me why you left the highway."

"No reason," she said, turning on the bathroom light. She pulled back the plastic curtain to inspect the bathtub and broke the label proclaiming the toilet sanitized. I followed her to the kitchenette. "Cordial sounded like a lovely place to—"

"We're in the middle of nowhere."

"What's done is done," she said, opening and closing all of the drawers and dragging her finger across the dresser and smiling. "Let's make the best of it, shall we? Bonnie gets off in an hour. The two of us are going out."

"How much is this room costing us?"

"You're such a worry wart, *querida.* Relax. Bonnie gave us the weekday rate. Make a nest for yourself on the bed and read one of your old books. Watch some television. Isn't *The Rockford Files* on tonight?" Mom opened her suitcase. Her robe, the one I'd made in advanced sewing, lay in a flattened wad on the top of her clothes. She shook out the wrinkles and disappeared into the bathroom. The lock clicked into place.

Surrounded by a forest of pine paneling, my pulse quickened. How long had my mother planned on coming to Cordial? Staring at the varnished bathroom door, I yelled, "We are not staying here one minute longer than absolutely necessary! And don't forget your promise. No men! I mean it, Mom. I'm going to California with or without you. I'll hitchhike if I have to." While studying a knot in the door's grain, a brilliant plan came to me. "Mom, are you listening?"

"Amy, I'm getting in the shower now," she said through the door.

"Wait! Open the door. I have a plan."

The door opened. Only the widow's peak of her black hair showed under her terry cloth turban. She pushed past me. "I forgot my razor."

I stood between her and the bathroom door.

"Okay, Amy, what's your plan?"

"We should sell the car and—"

My mother had only struck me twice that I could remember. Once for bringing a swear word home from school and once for mimicking the Pope during an Easter blessing on television. Now she slapped me for defaming a car with a failed transmission. "You have no idea what you're talking about," she said.

And I didn't. My mother's devotion to the Pontiac defied reason. More than once I'd envied the attention she lavished on the leather seats. She polished them religiously. Her passion for the car was but one more snag in Mom's fabric that kept her enigmatic even to me. Yes, she loved flamboyant clothing and window-shopping for things she couldn't afford, but if someone complimented what she wore—a scarf, a pair of sunglasses, one of hundreds of hoop earrings she owned—she would say, "Here, take it. It's yours." I once watched her wiggle out of a skirt in a restaurant bathroom. A woman had dropped soup in her lap and was only too happy to accept Mom's skirt in exchange for her sodden skirt.

What's with that stupid car, anyway?

Truthfully, I didn't ask that question out loud for many years, long after the sting of her slap had faded in my memory. That day,

I covered my face with my hands and turned my back on her. Nothing would hurt her more. To increase the drama, I threw myself across the bed, which smelled of cigarettes and hair spray.

Blecch!

"Ah, *gatihno,* I'm so sorry," she cooed, lying beside me. "Oh, baby, I can be so stupid. I'm so, so sorry. Are you okay?" I didn't want my face in the bedspread one more second. I sat up. Mom embraced me with Herculean strength. We cried on each other's shoulders. I'd acted like a brat. I could be so ugly, so condescending. She was doing her best, I supposed, and I hadn't appreciated her efforts.

She only acted crazy when she was scared. I should have remembered. Moving to California meant she would live alone for the first time in her life. She was traveling thousands of miles with no definite plans but many, many questions. Where would she live? Where would she work? Could she earn enough to pay her rent and buy all the lovely treasures California had to offer? Her real worry was that I would sift through her fingers like sand and blow away with the first off-shore breeze.

"I'm sorry, Mom. I shouldn't have—"

"I don't know what came over me. Maybe tension. I drove for a long time not knowing if we'd reach civilization. Not one tree grew in that stinking desert. God was looking out for us."

How could I argue with that?

"And, Amy, don't play your guitar in the motel room. Bonnie promises a peaceful night's sleep, or she returns her patrons' money. I don't want her to lose money over us."

After Mom left with Bonnie, I knelt beside the bed to say the Lord's Prayer and added, "Help Mom remember her pinkie pledge about men." The prayer stuck in my throat. I started again, "Lord, watch over Mom tonight. Don't let any drunk guys throw up on her.

Let her have a good time but not too good of a time. In Jesus' name, amen."

Playing my guitar was like a warm glass of milk. At home, I'd close my bedroom door to play praise songs from youth group or my favorite Carole King or Linda Ronstadt songs. I loved "Desperado." If Mom didn't have a man to keep her distracted, she'd request down-and-out country songs, usually something by Patsy Cline, the patron saint of broken hearts. There had been nights I sang "Crazy" until my voice had fatigued from an alto to a baritone, and then Mom would ask me to sing a Charley Pride song. Anticipating the day when I would no longer serenade Mom lifted my spirits. I read *Pride and Prejudice* until the words blurred on the page. I turned off the light just before midnight.

IN MY DREAM, Lauren cowered in a jail cell. No matter how much I coaxed her, she wouldn't follow me down the hole I'd dug to break her out. She crawled to the edge just as another train horn shocked me awake. The lumbering cars shook the floor and bounced a framed sampler against the wall. Long after the caboose had passed my hands rested on my pounding chest. My mother's pillow lay plump and smooth. By the light of the motel's vacancy sign, I read my watch. 2:12. A key slid into the lock. I hated watching Mom stagger, so I turned to the wall and slowed my breathing.

Mom clicked on the bedside lamp and jumped on the bed. "Wake up, *fofa,* wake up! Oh, my sweet one, this town is magic. You aren't going to believe the good fortune that has come our way."

I feigned a yawn and stretched before turning over to squint in the lamp's light. The odor of beer and cigarette smoke clung to Mom's clothes and hair. I breathed in deeply. Her face wore the sting of cold like a mask. She lifted the covers. "Move over. I'm freezing." The cold from her clothes penetrated my flannel nightgown. She kicked one shoe onto the linoleum floor, then the other.

I drew up my knees. "Don't you dare put your cold feet on me."

"Do I have feet? I don't know. I stopped feeling them an hour ago."

"Where have you been?"

"I can't wait to tell you." She scooted closer.

I slipped off my socks for her. "Put these on first."

She kissed my cheek.

"Your nose is like ice!" I wiped moisture from my cheek with the sheet. "And you got snot on me. *Gross!*"

"Shh, you'll wake our neighbors."

I doubted anyone actually slept in the motel, not with the trains marking off the hours like they did, but Mom was—is—indomitable. Once she snared an idea, her enthusiasm transformed her into a cliché. She was a raging storm, a force of nature, a bull in a china shop. I would listen to the adventure of her night in Cordial or never know peace in my lifetime.

With the socks on her feet, she locked arms with me. We lay on the same pillow, our heads touching. "*Querida,* sweetheart, Bonnie is destined to be the best friend I've ever had. She knows everyone in this town—"

"Does one of them own an extra transmission?"

Mom sniffed. "You can be such a little toad, *fofa.* This is good news. Listen now. She has an aunt, a *great* aunt who's desperate to find a caretaker for her home. She's been looking for months."

Dread squeezed my heart. "Mom, we're not going to be here that long."

"No, but we have to live somewhere until the car is fixed."

"Mom . . ."

"Bonnie took me to see the house. It's a block from Main Street and so charming and big. We can sit on the front porch to drink lemonade, and we won't have to share a bedroom. There are *three* bedrooms. And the trees and lawn are huge. You can read your books in the shade. The house is like the Ponderosa."

"A log cabin?"

"Just like that, only much, much bigger."

I loved *Bonanza*. Lauren and I had watched reruns after school while eating peanut-butter-and-jelly sandwiches. The only fight we'd ever had was over who would marry Little Joe. I imagined Lauren groaning with envy. "Tell me more."

"Bonnie says there's a fireplace in the front parlor. We've never had a fireplace."

We'd never had a parlor. Our rentals had been small, bland, and cold. A fireplace would be nice. "But still, we aren't going to be here that—"

"We'd be doing her aunt a favor. The house has been in Mrs. Clancy's family for three generations. The upkeep overwhelms her, and she worries that someone will break in—"

"And she expects us to protect her?"

Mom laughed. How I envied her ability to shrug off my fears.

"Mrs. Clancy won't be living with us. She built another house near the cemetery—imagine owning two houses."

"Near a cemetery? That's creepy."

"Why? Death is as natural as life, *querida.*"

Hearing this from Mom, who crossed herself every time she walked by the hospital, only deepened my apprehension. What was she willing to do to keep me from attending college without her?

"Don't you see?" she said. "God is taking care of us." Mom only visited church to light a candle when her period was late, but no one spoke of God's benevolence with more authority.

"What happens if Tommy finds a transmission tomorrow and the car is ready by the end of the week?" I asked.

"California, here we come!"

"Really?" A train sounded its whistle a long way off. "We should look inside the house before we agree to anything. Remember the apartment on Oak Street?"

She laughed again and pulled me into her embrace. "You only remember the bad. Bonnie says her aunt is a meticulous housekeeper. Someone like that would never have more than one cat and certainly not more than thirty."

The train's whistle sounded again, only closer.

"We could have broken down in that horrible desert," she said, "but we didn't. This is a nice town. Let's give it a try. Okay?"

Four

Forget the Ponderosa.

The cabin, painted deep brown with startling white chink, was a multi-layered cake of Bavarian chocolate and marshmallow crème. The roof, a topping of raspberry shingles, quickened my pulse. Pines lorded the lush lawn surrounding the cabin—stout, anchored, beckoning. I half expected Lizzy Bennet's Lord Fitzwilliam Darcy to stride out the front door with his hunting rifle. I turned to apologize to Mom for pouting all morning. That's when I saw the sign over the mailbox: *Clancy and Sons Funeral Home, Serving the North Fork Valley since 1920.*

Mrs. Clancy, the owner, led us through the cabin, reading our caretaker duties from a clipboard. I walked as if folded in on myself, afraid to disturb the quietness, reluctant to discover what or who lay behind the closed doors. Mom's platform shoes *tap, tap, tap*ped on the wooden floors behind me. Mrs. Clancy clomped ahead, her broad hips dipping and rising with sluggish indifference. I stifled shushing her by biting my lip.

Mrs. Clancy stopped to swish a feather duster over porcelain figurines. "Death keeps no hours. You never know when clients will call or come knocking at the door." She looked directly at me. "Don't put things off. You don't want to be caught unprepared."

When she turned to continue the tour, I whispered in Mom's ear. "This place smells funny."

Mom shooed my words away with a flip of her wrist. She bent forward to take in Mrs. Clancy's every word, like she would actually do any of the dusting. I knew better. We turned down a hall lined with more closed doors. Mrs. Clancy tucked the feather duster under her arm and hefted her shoulder against the closest door, which turned out to be a bedroom. Mom and I expelled breaths in unison. No one, living or dead, lay on the bed. Mrs. Clancy opened a window, and a playful breeze flicked the curtain's hem. Before she closed the door again, I imagined myself lying across the chenille bedspread, fingering its channels and lobes as I read about Lizzy Bennet's visit to Pembroke.

Mrs. Clancy brought me back to reality by slamming the door shut. "The girl can sleep there."

A brass bed commanded attention in the room assigned to Mom. Breathy with excitement, Mom asked, "Will you be moving this furniture to your new home?"

"Good heavens, no. I've had my fill of old things. Dust traps, that's all they are. I ordered everything new—from the coffee pot to the brocade headboard—out of the Montgomery Ward catalog."

Mom's eyes glistened with tears. I feared she would wrap her arms around Mrs. Clancy's mole-covered neck. "Mom has always wanted a brass bed," I said and nudged Mom away from the room.

"Suit yourself," Mrs. Clancy said, leading us into the kitchen.

"The kitchen door will serve as your main entrance. Only clients use the front door."

The kitchen, painted a fleshy pink, reminded me of every other kitchen of every apartment and house we had ever rented. Cracked linoleum. A gorilla of a refrigerator. Pitted countertops. A match dispenser hanging by the gas stove added a sense of danger to the room. Off the kitchen, a brown sofa and two matching chairs pointed toward a television with a bulging screen and inquisitive rabbit ears. Beyond, an accordion partition served as a wall.

"What's behind the partition?" Mom asked. I dreaded Mrs. Clancy's answer.

"The business end of the cabin—my office, a chapel, the reposing room, and the casket showroom."

Mom brushed past me to follow Mrs. Clancy. "Try to keep up, Amy."

I agreed with Mom. Let's get the tour over and then we could say *Vaya con Dios, señora* with a clear conscience.

Mom stopped abruptly at the doorway of the casket showroom. Caskets hung on the walls and filled the floor space. The hair on my arms popped to attention. Burnished mahogany. Sun-warmed oak. Pine, rough and raw. When Mrs. Clancy flipped a switch, track lighting highlighted a metal casket, yawning open and tipped toward the middle of the room. A ring of finish samples lay among the tucks of satiny upholstery inside the casket. Mrs. Clancy snatched the ring to stash in a desk drawer. More to herself than to us, she said, "Everything in its place. A place for everything."

With her hands clasped behind her back, her buttons struggled to hold the bodice of her blouse together, providing a keyhole view of her purely structural bra. "Besides the reposing room," she said, "this is the most important room in the house. You must keep the caskets shiny bright. Not one speck of dust or a single fingerprint must mar the finishes. You'll need to become familiar with the special cleaners kept in the maintenance closet. We keep the economy caskets in the attic. There's no need to climb up there today. The caskets are wrapped in plastic. Buying the caskets in bulk increases my margin, but the families don't need to know that. In a small market maximizing margin is important."

I shook off the image of a small market for dead people—a storefront with a black wreath on the door and a sales banner taped to the window—and reentered the conversation in time to hear Mom say, "Amy loves to clean."

At times like this I wished I'd been blessed with a tribe of siblings. I would say, "Excuse me, Mother, you're thinking of Jane or Laurie or Debbie or that little miscreant, Danny." I must have groaned because Mom shot me a hard look. This was exactly why I was so determined to get to California.

Mrs. Clancy either missed or ignored our exchange. "To clean the pillow and overlay, I take them outside for a good shake every few days. No one wants to think of their loved ones sleeping with spiders."

At the mention of spiders, I expected Mom to back out of the house spewing apologies, and we would be buying bus tickets by the end of the day. Instead, Mom played the part of a competent funeral home caretaker by taking the bedding from Mrs. Clancy and returning it to the casket.

Mrs. Clancy stepped in front of Mom to smooth the wrinkles out of the pillow and straighten the gathers in the overlay. "Like I said, death doesn't keep a schedule and doesn't mind one iota about upsetting your plans, so you must always be ready. Have your chores done by ten o'clock in the morning seven days a week—earlier, once you get the routine down. I will be here Monday through Friday from 10:00 a.m. to 3:00 p.m. I leave earlier on the days I make a deposit at the bank. At all other times, I expect one of you to be here."

Mom cocked her head as if assessing Mrs. Clancy. "You have such beautiful skin, the kind of skin that wins beauty pageants."

"Well," Mrs. Clancy said, taking a furtive look at her image in a casket's finish, "I was Miss Ranch Days back in 1931."

"I believe you. I was Miss Sleepy Eye the year before Amy was born. I must show you the tiara I wore during my reign."

"Do tell."

"What do you use to keep your skin looking so lovely?"

Mrs. Clancy squared her shoulders and stretched her neck. "My mother forbade me to play in the sun. Freckles are for common girls, she used to say. Mother was born to Pittsburgh society. She ingrained the attributes of ladylike behavior in my sisters and me. I've never had one freckle on my face, not one. This high country sun is harsh. We—my sisters and I—wore bonnets everywhere we went."

Sure enough. Not one freckle polluted Mrs. Clancy's face, but gray whiskers stood out from her chin like porcupine quills.

Mom followed Mrs. Clancy toward the front of the house. Whatever I'd imagined about Mr. Darcy and his hunting rifle evaporated the minute I joined Mom and Mrs. Clancy in the front parlor. Converted into a chapel, the red velvet draperies muffled the outside world. Rows of wooden folding chairs filled the darkened room, except for the space before the fireplace where a small podium served as an altar. On the far wall, a niche held the organ.

I sniffed the air again. Biology lab. Fourth hour. Just before lunch. "Is that formaldehyde I smell?"

Mrs. Clancy closed her eyes and drew in a breath. "I don't smell anything."

"Mom, do you smell—?"

"Please excuse my daughter. She knows better than to discuss odors." Mom looked at me with pleading eyes. "Amy, listen to Mrs. Clancy. We want to do a good job for her, so she won't have a worry in her head."

Mrs. Clancy's eyebrows arched over the rims of her glasses. "In the course of your daily living, the chapel is completely off limits—excepting, of course, when you're attending to chores or hosting viewings. Do I make myself clear?"

"Hosting viewings? Us?" Mom asked.

"Yes, I'm done with all of that," said Mrs. Clancy, and her shoulders sagged. "I've done everything myself for years. Too many of my friends are coming through here now. It's terribly difficult." A shadow darkened her eyes and then quickly lifted. "But someone has to be here to stand with the family, manage the guest book, and set up the flowers. That will be you. There's a list of your duties by the back door. The families are as lost as kittens in their grief." With a hanky from her belt, Mrs. Clancy buffed her fingerprints out of the organ's lacquered finish.

She looked Mom up and down. Dressed in fuchsia slacks, a broad white belt, and a polka-dot blouse, Mom dressed as if auditioning for a chewing-gum commercial. I relaxed. No one in their right minds would hire Mom to host anything as solemn as a viewing. Entertaining for Mom meant shaking martinis and pouring peanuts into a bowl.

Mrs. Clancy said, "You will wear a black dress hemmed below your knees during viewings out of respect for the deceased and the living. It's traditional. People expect it. I won't tolerate anything else."

The blood drained from Mom's olive skin. Wearing black was

bad luck. At that moment, considering the spiders and the wearing of black, the deal was doomed. I turned toward the door.

"Amy looks beautiful in black," Mom said.

I stopped, pivoted.

"Anyone greeting grievers will be expected to dress appropriately," Mrs. Clancy said, lowering her glasses to meet Mom's gaze with leaden eyes.

"Of course, Mrs. Clancy, I understand, and you mustn't worry a bit that we won't follow your instructions to the smallest detail."

"Here's the bottom line," Mrs. Clancy said. "If you do a good job keeping the place clean and working with the families, I'll be happy and you'll have free rent. The minute I'm not happy is the minute you pack your bags. It's up to you."

"Perfect! We'll do it." Mom grasped her hand. Mrs. Clancy's chin folded like an accordion as she leaned away from Mom.

"There's something else." Mrs. Clancy hefted two large suitcases. "There's a pad by the kitchen phone. If I leave to run errands, and let's see, during my lunch break, and, of course, any time I'm not here, you'll be taking the death calls."

Mom's mouth dropped open.

"Especially at night. I'm an old woman. I need my sleep. Get the name of the deceased and who will take financial responsibility for preparing the body. And for goodness' sake, don't forget to ask for their address and phone number. Then call the mortician before you call my nephew, H. He'll pick up the body and get the deceased to the preparation room in the basement. Don't call me until the next morning, not one minute earlier than eight."

Mrs. Clancy pushed the screen door open with her foot. "Making ends meet must be difficult as a single woman raising a daughter. I pay H twenty-five dollars to pick up a body. If you want to earn that twenty-five dollars for yourself, you're free to use the hearse. H won't mind. He's an industrious boy. He reminds me of my own William. If there's work to be done, H will find it. And you don't have to worry about loading the body into the hearse. There's always someone—a spouse or a neighbor—who'll help you. We're all friends in Cordial. Between the two of you, I imagine you can wheel the body to the preparation room without any difficulties. I won't concern myself with who brings the bodies in. Unless I hear differently, I'll expect H is doing the job."

Mrs. Clancy held a set of keys in front of Mom's face. She enumerated the purpose of each key before handing them over. She took a few steps before turning and setting her suitcases down again. "On days I'm meeting with families to make funeral arrangements or when memorial services are held in the chapel, there will be no cooking of any kind and no listening to the radio. Whispers only. No one should know you're here."

Mrs. Clancy grunted when she picked up her suitcases.

Mom darted after her, catching her by a doughy arm. "How many . . . um, dead—"

"Terminology is everything in this business. You can be 'dead tired' or a 'dead ringer for a movie star.' You might drop an oar to be 'dead in the water.' Sometimes life seems as senseless as 'beating a dead horse.' There are dead ducks, dead weights, the dead of night, and Errol Flynn was drop-dead handsome. But the people brought here are 'deceased,' 'beloved,' or 'dearly departed,' most certainly not *dead*."

"Okay," Mom said, perfectly cowed by Mrs. Clancy's speech. Mom called after her. "Wait a minute. How many dearly departeds come through here in, say, a week?"

Mrs. Clancy's shoulders fell under the weight of the question.

"As many as there will be, which usually means one, but we've had as many as five."

"Cordial is a small town. I wouldn't expect that many."

"We service the whole North Fork Valley. Buckley, Cedarton, Hanford. Sometimes Clearwater. Numbers vary." Mrs. Clancy closed the trunk. "I expect I'll see you in church on Sunday," she said with a tilt of her head toward the church across the street.

Mom held Mrs. Clancy's gaze. "Amy's the churchgoer of the family."

Mrs. Clancy looked from Mom to me and back to Mom. "Families are more comfortable bringing their deceased to pious people."

"Then they should be perfectly fine bringing their dearly departeds here. Amy reads her Bible every day, rain or shine."

Mrs. Clancy looked like she had bitten into a pithy apple. To hire Mom and me meant living closer to the edge than she liked. Mrs. Clancy closed her eyes. Whatever her imagination played out for her helped her overlook Mom's lack of church attendance. "Okay," she said, getting into her car, "as long as the girl attends church services every Sunday."

"She definitely will."

"Do either one of you sing? We haven't had a good vocalist for in-house memorial services since Maude Hinckley passed on."

Mom hooked her arm around my waist. "Amy sings like a meadowlark."

"There's a twenty-dollar honorarium to split with the organist, if you're a hymn singer."

Mom squeezed me tighter. "Oh my goodness, that's all she sings around the house. Her favorite is 'Rock of Ages Clapped for Me.'"

Mrs. Clancy frowned at Mom.

"I play the guitar too," I offered, hoping to divert Mrs. Clancy's attention from Mom's near-blasphemy.

The lines around Mrs. Clancy's mouth hardened, and her words jabbed at my chest. "There won't be any of that hippie music in the Clancy and Sons Funeral Home, not while I'm alive there won't. Hymns are what the Good Book tells us to sing, and that's all you'll sing. Guitars and tambourines have no place in church, so there's no place for them at Clancy and Sons. We must be cognizant of Satan's work. Guitars and the like draw us away from traditions of the faith and bring obscene rhythms into houses of worship. The last youth worker they sent to Spruce Street Church taught the kids those songs. I can assure you he didn't last long."

I inched backward. Mom's grip tightened around my waist. Mrs. Clancy looked out the windshield, blinking and breathing as if she'd run up a long hill. When she spoke again, her voice flowed like a deep river. "When people are hurting, they lean on what they know, what's familiar. Traditions take us back to happier times when our voices melded with those we loved. Without traditions, we're adrift on an endless ocean."

This wasn't the time to lecture Mrs. Clancy on the recent acceptance of the hymns she held so dear. Besides, I grew up singing hymns. "I love the hymns too," I said. "I can play and sing anything in the hymnal. I was just offering in case the organist got sick or something."

Mrs. Clancy pumped the accelerator before starting her long black Lincoln. The car roared to life. Mom made me wave until Mrs. Clancy turned toward her new home.

I'm not proud of what happened next. I was young, scared, and stuck in a lifeless burg. I spun out of Mom's grip to hurl accusations at her like a tennis ball machine. I accused her of planning the ill-fated detour to Cordial. "You won't be happy until I'm a waitress at the nearest truck stop, will you?" I pushed through the chain-link gate. "I'm not you. I don't want to be you. And I am most certainly not going back into that cabin! Do what you like. I'm out of here."

Mom leaned against a porch timber with her face buried in her hands and her shoulders heaving with sobs, a common occurrence in our lives.

She did things, impulsive things, things that seemed foolish from the outside, but underneath it all was love and a crazy kind of insatiable curiosity. I wrapped my arms around her shoulders.

"There is something I have to tell you," she said, sniffing. "We left that drafty old house in Gilbertsville better than the day we moved in. We painted the whole house, made the curtains, and polished the floors. And yet, last winter, we almost froze to death because Mr. Cochran was so stingy with the coal. Fofa, I had no intention of paying him that rent money, but then he showed up. The pittance he returned to me is already spent."

"Mom, what are you telling me?"

She blew her nose on the hanky she kept in her bra. "I have seven dollars and change in my wallet. And I still owe Bonnie for a night at the motel. That's all we have for food and shelter." She crossed herself. "God forbid that one of us should get sick. Being caretakers for that old bag is the only way to keep a roof over our heads."

I'd hidden over two hundred dollars among the pages of *Emma* to buy a bus ticket to California in this kind of emergency. But I hadn't planned on being forced to use the funds so early. The dorms didn't reopen until September. I hadn't saved enough for transportation and three months of rent. I was stuck in Cordial for the summer. That didn't mean I intended to be pleasant about my destiny.

"What about a black dress?" I asked.

"I'll make one. Bonnie's cousin owns the mercantile on Main. She gets a twenty-five percent family discount. We should be able to buy what we need."

TWO DAYS LATER, I had my dress. Straight sleeves to my wrists. Collarless. Fitted with buttons up the back. Hemmed below my knee. Polyester double-knit. I'd had the dress on for five minutes, and my body already felt damp under the fabric. With the pair of black-patent shoes we'd found at St. John's thrift store, my viewing outfit was complete. Mom smoothed the fabric over my hips and tugged at a sleeve.

"I'm the one who looks dead," I said, and yes, I was pouting.

That was the third time that day I'd caused Mom to cross herself. "Please, Amy, don't say such things. It's bad luck." Our eyes met in the mirror. Hers were glossy with tears. "You look beautiful, very chic," she said and pulled my hair into a ponytail, twisting and tucking the ends into place until she held a lumpy chignon in place. "You can wear the pearls Hank gave me." She spat out the bad taste of his name. "The clean lines flatter your figure. You're just not used to seeing yourself as a woman."

She was right about that. My silhouette surprised me. When had my boobs and hips swollen? "The dress is hot. I want to take it off."

Five

I'd known plenty of guys like H Van Hoorn. They were my lab partners in biology and chemistry, whose loud greetings in the hall I answered with lukewarm smiles, who ate lunch with me and Lauren, although we'd kept our backs slightly turned to avoid a stigmatizing association. They had names like Henry, Edward, and Roger. Dependable names. Boy Scouts. Audio-visual aides. Adoring. More than likely H stood for a name he didn't want anyone to know.

He proved how wrong I was when he presented his driver's license. "My name is H. Just H." The youngest of eight children and the sixth boy, H's mom and dad had run out of names they liked starting with *H*. I learned all this and more when he knocked at the door to ask for a drink of water. The mower idled in the middle of the lawn.

"Could I bother you for another glass of water?" he asked.

He removed his John Deere cap to swipe sweat from his forehead with the hem of his T-shirt. That was when I saw his soft, dimpled belly cantilevered over his belt. *Eew. Not good.* Under his hat, his scalp showed through his blond crew cut, and the sweat that stuck to his arm hairs made him sparkle in the sunlight. Even so, I envied him—his nose. It was straight and perfectly proportioned to his face.

"When I turn eighteen, I'm going to a lawyer to change my name to Hawk." He said this without a bit of self-consciousness, like he was telling me he'd been accepted at Harvard, which I seriously doubted would ever happen for H.

"Sharp-shinned hawks migrate through here in the fall," he said. "They're stealth fighters. They fly low to the ground, using their tails as rudders, to surprise small birds. *Accipiter straiatus,* that's the scientific name. *Accipiter* is Greek for 'swift wing.' *Straiatus* comes from the Latin and refers to the striped wing of the juveniles. There's a neat place to observe them not too far from here."

Just what I need, encyclopedic knowledge about hawks.

If Lauren had been there, she would have known just what to say, something cutting enough to get the door closed but oblique enough to leave H stunned silent. Despite my general loathing, I felt sorry for him. No one deserved a name starting with *H.* Think of one name that doesn't make you imagine old men spitting tobacco. Howard. Hamish. Harry. Harvey. Herman and Hector. Homer. Men with *H* names were born with yellow teeth and wispy gray hair. *Poor H.* I poured vanilla wafers on a plate and joined him on the porch, ignoring Lauren's admonishments against encouraging guys like H with too much attention.

He filled me in on his brothers and sisters. Some were already married with children, which made him Uncle H. How weird was that? The sister just a year older worked summers for their dad while she went to college in Alamosa, the coldest place in the U.S. of A., according to H. She wanted to be a teacher.

"My dad owns the ranch supply store on the highway," he said, talking around the cookie he'd popped in his mouth. "He started with livestock fencing when we moved here three years ago. He did so well, he added the ranch wear. Van Hoorn's Ranch and Wear is the only place between here and Clearwater to buy a good pair of working boots, and that's thirty miles west. Maybe you've seen the store. It isn't much to look at from the outside, but we completely paneled the inside walls."

H was conversational fly paper. He had a story about whatever happened to come up. There was no shaking him once he made a connection between my *uh-huhs* and his vast catalog of experiences.

"I could drive you out there sometime," he said.

Not on your life. "I have to stay here in case someone calls."

H looked at my feet. "You should wear shoes with better arch support."

The place between my toes had finally toughened enough to wear my rubber flip-flops, the official footwear of summer. "I do fine in these."

"You pick the shoe to fit your job. Look at mine." He stretched out his long legs and turned his boot to show off the topstitching and riveted seams. "And this is a Vibram sole. You won't see me falling on wet surfaces. The most important part of the shoe is what you can't see, like the steel in the toe that protects me from those whirling mower blades, and then there's the arch support. I can wear these babies from sunup to sundown. My feet never hurt. And they're waterproof."

It was clear H had spent plenty of time listening to his father sell boots. "Do you work for your dad too?"

"Only the girls do. Dad says the guys have to get used to surviving on our own. I irrigate fields for a rancher and do yard work most days."

In Cordial, you felt the softening of the day before the sun slid toward Bridger Mesa. The coolness lit on my bare shoulders like a silk scarf. I shivered with anticipation. H kept talking. He listed the brands of sensible shoes I should wear for domestic work. I yawned, looked at my watch, and ate the last three cookies on the plate.

I rose to go inside. "I have to get dinner ready."

"You're real pretty, Amy."

My face warmed, and I wondered what possessed the Boy Scout type. Did they feel honor bound to rescue homely girls from their poor self-esteem? Lauren, never one to soften her words, had told me I was homely enough to be cute but definitely not pretty. In a popped-pimple sort of way, having the truth out in the open had been a relief.

"You don't have to blush," he said. "It's true. You look like one of those peasant girls in the old paintings Mr. Doorenbos hangs in World History, especially now with the sun shining through your hair."

I stepped inside the screen door. "Mom hates dinner to be late."

H put his face to the screen. "I'm going to kiss you before the end of summer."

I slammed the kitchen door in his face, thought of opening it again to apologize, but quickly reconsidered when he rapped on the window. "I'll grow on you. I grow on everybody," he shouted through the closed window.

Six

The telephone rang, and I nearly jumped out of my skin. I'd lived and worked in the funeral home for four whole days, waiting for that telephone to ring, my skin itching with anticipation. Honestly, I would have preferred a trip to the dentist. My heart beat so hard in my chest, I coughed just as Mrs. Clancy appeared at the casket room door. "This is why we must be ready at all times. Put the rag down and follow me."

"Where?" I asked, but she was already gone.

Mrs. Clancy stood at the phone desk in the kitchen, resting her hand on the receiver. "Where's your mother?"

"Hanging the laundry." *How convenient.*

The phone rang again.

Mrs. Clancy turned the telephone to face me. "Answer the telephone. The sooner you know your job, the sooner I'll be able to come and go as I please."

She handed me the receiver.

"What do I say?"

"Hello?" a male voice said on the other end of the line.

Mrs. Clancy's dentures clacked as she whispered in my ear. "Clancy and Sons Funeral Home, serving the North Fork Valley since 1920."

"Georgia, is that you?" the man asked.

"No, this is Amy. Would you like to talk to Mrs. Clancy?"

Mrs. Clancy shook her head sharply and pushed a notepad and pen across the desk.

I repeated Mrs. Clancy's prompt and added, "How may I help you?"

"There's not much to be done now," the man said, "but to bury her."

My breakfast burned the back of my throat. "Oh."

"Who's calling?" Mrs. Clancy asked.

"May I ask who's calling?"

Once Henry T. Bigelow hit his conversational stride, no detail seemed too mundane or intimate to exclude about his sister's death. "We found her just after we'd come back from moving the irrigation pipes up t' the mesa, you know. She was feeling poorly most of last week, complained about feeling tired, spent a lot of time in the outhouse, she did. Other than that, whatever was bothering her didn't seem to slow her down none. Bert says she was stronger than most men though she weren't much taller than my belt buckle. But she was getting old, that's for sure."

Mrs. Clancy put her cheek to mine to listen in. She smelled sour like she hadn't taken a bath in a few days. Old people and twelve-year-old boys couldn't smell themselves coming or going. I breathed through my mouth.

The man continued his reverie. "We knowed something was wrong when we didn't smell no bacon from the kitchen. It wasn't like her, though, to leave good meat on the counter where the flies could get to it. Bert swore up and down, but he wrapped the bacon up neatlike 'cause that's how Mildred always done it. Then he goes stomping off 'cause he says we'll be needing some more ice here pretty quick. Bringing the ice up from the ice house, that was Mildred's job. She done got the cows milked and the cream skimmed before she lay down in her daffodil bed to die."

Mrs. Clancy took the phone. "Henry T. Bigelow, you old coot." She shook her finger at the receiver. "Don't be rattling off a bunch of nonsense. The sooner we get Mildred in here, the better she'll look come viewing day."

Whatever Henry T. Bigelow said made Mrs. Clancy roll her eyes. "Suit yourself, Henry, but you wrap her up nice. I won't be picking manure out of her hair. And make sure she doesn't roll around that trailer. Do you hear me, you old fool?"

THE DOORBELL RANG. Mom and I huddled behind her bedroom door.

Mrs. Clancy bellowed, "What are you doing? Not through the kitchen. For heaven's sake, we have a ramp out back."

"The trapdoor's in the hall, ain't it, Georgie?" asked a male voice I recognized as Mr. Bigelow.

"Henry, people stopped calling me Georgie fifty years ago."

"I think it's been more like sixty, don't you, Bert?"

"Bring her in then, you old fool."

Men shuffled and grunted in the hall, and the floor groaned under their weight. One uttered an epitaph no one would dare chisel into a headstone. Mrs. Clancy called for me, but Mom held me tightly.

"Not yet, *fofa*. Not yet. Stay here."

"Are you happy, Henry?" asked Mrs. Clancy.

"I'd heard about the chute, but I never believed it. Thanks, Georgie, that settles my mind a bit."

"Now get out of here. I've got work to do."

Outside, sparrows chirped and bicycle tires clattered over gravel. "Mom, I'll be okay. They have her in the basement. I don't want to make Mrs. Clancy mad."

Mom crossed herself and glanced toward heaven. "I must be crazy. Blessed Mary, what was I thinking? A funeral home? Dead people in the basement? I never should have brought you here, *fofa.*" She pulled her suitcase off the closet shelf and threw it open. With a shove, she pushed me toward the door. "Amy, go pack. We can't stay here." She scooped handfuls of satin and lace out of the dresser drawer. "Why are you standing there? Go tell that woman we're moving out."

I took the wad of lingerie from Mom's hands. "Mom, really, we've been in tough places before. This isn't any different—"

"Oh, *fofa,* you don't know. Nothing good can come of this."

"We could pray."

"Don't start with me, Amy."

I returned her lingerie to her pleading hands. "Fine, where exactly do you propose we go? And how will we get there? Perhaps Prince Charming will pick us up."

"Yes, that's what we need." Mom rifled through her purse. "I wouldn't call him Prince Charming, but he seemed friendly enough, and he has a big truck." Mom dumped her fat wallet and several tubes of lipstick onto the bed. "He wrote his name and phone number on a napkin." Out came the embroidered hanky I'd made for her in Blue Birds and a bundle of coupons. "I wasn't going to tell you. He bought me a drink, just one. I think his name is Bruce. He offered his help, said to call if we needed anything." She held up a cocktail napkin. "Here's the number. I'll call while you talk to Mrs. Clancy."

I blocked the path to the door.

"Amy, please, I can't stay here."

I ignored Mom's violation of her pinkie pledge about men and softened my voice like you would to coax a kitten out of a tree. "Living here is ideal. You were right about that. We don't pay rent. It's so nice to have a washing machine and clothesline right here. The flower garden is pretty, the prettiest we've ever had. And that boy H will keep the lawn nice. We only have to treat the families with kindness and keep the place tidy. We can do that. You're the kindest person I know."

"There is a dead person in this house at this very moment."

"I know. It's hard. Think of something else. Think of how brave you were after Daddy died. You searched and searched for the perfect place to raise me, and you found Gilbertsville. And remember how we ate popcorn on the porch and waited for the first call of the loons on a summer night? Remember baking lavadores for the carnival? I love those cookies. Even old Mrs. Prinzki wanted the recipe. And Mom, think of the night of the Sleepy Eye pageant, how beautiful you felt on the runway with every eye in the auditorium watching just you."

Mom stood taller. "Yes. You're right. We have to be strong." She leaned into the mirror to check her reflection. "Hand me a tissue." Once she'd cleared her face of mascara, she knotted her blouse at her waist. "Look out the window. Make sure those terrible men are gone."

I assured her they were. That wasn't good enough. Mom insisted I confirm that Miss Bigelow had been safely deposited in the basement workroom. I stood outside the bedroom door for a long time, waiting for my heart to settle behind my sternum. I slipped off my shoes to walk from room to room. In the kitchen the drippy faucet filled my cereal bowl. A fan stirred the dust mites in the reposing room. A moth flitted around a lamp in the chapel. Ordinary things continued on as if Miss Bigelow was still there to see and hear them. At the closed basement door, I stopped to wonder who, besides her brothers (and that was debatable), would notice she was no longer there to tighten a dripping faucet or to turn off a fan or to shoo a moth out the door? Could someone leave so light a footprint on this earth that her passing was forgotten by the next rainfall?

That night, I lay in bed like a plank, trying but failing to think of anything but the dead body that lay in the basement. Surely Mrs. Clancy had covered Miss Bigelow with a blanket. Did she still wear her house dress? Her shoes? Her watch? Would the mortician check to see if she wore clean underwear? To settle my brain, I prayed for everyone I knew from *A* to *Z*. First, Annette, the only person I'd ever known with hair coarser than mine. She'd come new to my school in the middle of third grade, wearing her hair parted down the middle and held flat to her head by two barrettes the size of tongue depressors. Now that she was headed for the University of Illinois in Chicago, I prayed that she had cut her hair into one of those short curly-top dos that had become popular. I prayed for Bobby Kennedy's eleven children, although technically they weren't anyone I knew. They all paid so dearly for having a dad too noble for this world. I drew a breath. Maybe the same had been true of my father.

Carlos came to mind when I thought of names that began with *C*. He'd fled Cuba with his mother and sister when his father had been jailed for disagreeing with Castro. Carlos barely spoke English when he arrived at my elementary school, but he told me he loved me every day. I prayed for his father to join him in America. *D* is for dad. I know. It was useless to pray for someone who had already died, but reason never seemed to matter when I thought of seeing my dad in heaven someday. When I'd been saved, I drove Mom to madness asking about Dad's standing with God. Mom finally assured me that he'd been a faithful member of the Beautiful Savior Lutheran Church.

"But he was Portuguese," I said.

"It was a mixed marriage. His mother was a Lutheran."

I figured the Lutherans preached a good come-to-Jesus sermon. They had churches in every city I'd ever visited, so I prayed for my dad, that he was enjoying the fine mansion Jesus had built for him and that he thought of me, even while basking in the glory of God's presence. I possessed a surety that he was there waiting for me.

Thank you, Lord.

By the time I got to the *V*s, Vinita Mae Lundquist popped into my head. She was Gilbertsville's old maid. She never opened her shades. *Lord, be her light.* I lay there listening to the clock ticking and the cricket's chirrup, and because I couldn't help myself, I wondered if Miss Bigelow had ever counted a cricket's chirrups to determine the temperature.

The latch of my bedroom door clicked and the whine of the hinges slid to a higher octave as the door opened. My mother trotted on tiptoe to my bed and lifted the covers to join me. There was no sense pretending to be asleep, so I scooted close to drape my arm over her stomach. At my touch, her belly softened with a sigh.

"There's something I have to tell you," she said.

"You don't have to whisper."

"I got a job at the hardware store."

"But—"

"We need cash to pay for the car repairs and for living expenses in California."

"We were going to do this funeral thing together."

"You and I both know I won't answer any death calls or drive a hearse."

"You can't leave me here alone."

"In a couple months, you'll be living alone in Santa Barbara. This is good training for you. If you can manage a funeral home, you'll do fine in the big city." She turned away from me. "I have to be there by seven o'clock. Farmers like to shop early."

"How . . . when did you get a job?"

She yawned. "Last night at the Stop-and-Chomp when Bonnie and me—"

"Bonnie and *I*."

"Bonnie and *me* stopped there for coffee and pie. I was just about to ask the waitress for an application when the Gartleys walked in. They own the hardware store on Main Street. Bonnie went to high school with Russell. They joined us and showed great interest in my story. The wife, I can't remember her name, wants to see my tiara. When I told them about the Pontiac, Russell offered me a job—Kno application, no nothing. The wife . . ." Mom yawned again. "I wish I could remember her name. She's nice too."

Uh-oh.

"They have the cutest chicks at the store. You should come to see them when you're done cleaning."

"I have to feed the mortician, remember?"

"Make sure Mrs. Clancy pays for the ingredients."

Seven

I scraped at the meatloaf's blackened glaze. The telephone rang. Not one of those friendly Princess-phone rings, but an irascible alarm. I ran to the chapel window to see if Mrs. Clancy was still within shouting distance. The postman waved from the mailbox. I dropped the drape and returned to the kitchen just in time to be startled by the ringing telephone again.

The mortician had returned to the basement to prepare Miss Bigelow by doing things my imagination constructed without consent. The last thing I needed was another death call. Hot tears rolled down my cheeks. Through my teeth, I said, "I hate my mother." The telephone rang again. Yet another reason to envy Lizzy Bennet. True, she endures interminable teas in the company of Lady Catherine de Bourgh, but she is never startled at the sound of a telephone announcing a dearly departed.

Briiing!

"Aren't you going to answer that?" A young girl with a pointed chin and a pouf of lemonade hair stood with her nose to the screen door. A wire basket full of eggs sat by her bare feet. The girl was young, maybe ten, no older than twelve.

I wiped the tears from my face. "It's impolite to answer a phone too soon," I said. "You should always let it ring at least three times."

The telephone trilled again.

The girl opened the door and carried her egg basket to the counter beside the refrigerator. A smudge of dirt from the screen darkened the tip of her nose. "Says who?"

I wavered between shooing her outside and demonstrating my superior knowledge of the world. "All the magazines," I said, and the phone rang for what seemed like the zillionth time. Though the snot in my nose distorted my words, I said with more confidence that I owned, "There, I can answer the phone now."

Under the girl's watchful gaze, I forgot the Clancy and Sons official greeting. "Hello?"

On the other end of the phone line, a woman coughed to clear her throat. Still, she spoke haltingly with a voice rubbed raw from crying. "Is–is Georgia there?"

"Who is it?" asked the pixie-faced girl.

I held the handset to my chest. "She wants to talk to Georgia."

"She means Mrs. Clancy."

"I know that," I said, but I'd forgotten. *Who called adults by their first names?*

The girl said, "Tell her Georgia will call her as soon as you gather the needed information."

I obeyed the girl.

"My Arthur, he's gone," said the woman on the phone. "I need someone to come pick him up. He passed in his sleep, the dear man. I've never slept alone, not in the whole sixty-two years we've been married."

The girl, who only came to my shoulder, pressed the list of questions I was supposed to ask into my hands. She stood on tiptoe and leaned in, putting her ear next to mine at the receiver. Her hair smelled of rosemary. I laid the list on the counter and scribbled the answers. "Where do you live, ma'am? I'll send someone right out."

She gave me her address and said, "Thank you for your kindness."

The dial tone hummed in my ear.

The girl said, "You better call Georgia."

"No, I think I'll call H first."

The girl opened the refrigerator. She picked our eggs out of the egg tray and tossed them in the trash.

"Hey!" I said, tethered to the telephone.

"The first dozen are free," she said, loading eggs the color of sand and moss into the refrigerator. "I collected these fresh this morning. If you don't think they're the finest eggs you ever ate, I'll bring you a dozen store-bought eggs to replace them tomorrow." She looked up from her work and smiled. "I've promised that to lots of people, but I've never had to replace one egg."

The girl wore a peasant blouse cinched tightly at the neck and wrists, but still the blouse hung to her knees over a pair of baggy pants hemmed with a chain of embroidered daisies. A hippie girl? The last thing I needed was a know-it-all hippie feeding me bad information and filling the refrigerator with rotten eggs. As the telephone at H's house rang, I hit my forehead with the palm of my hand. "I didn't ask the lady's name."

"That was Leoti Masterson," the girl said. "She's been tending her sick husband for as long as I can remember. Cancer of some kind."

I scowled at the girl, aggravated by her composure, and because she knew the lady's name. How dumb was that?

The girl shrugged and turned for the door. "I listen is all."

I put my hand over the mouthpiece. "What's your name?"

"Feather."

"Is that an Indian name?"

"Huh?"

"You know, like Black Kettle or Crazy Horse, something like that."

"Oh that. I have a birth certificate name same as you, but I keep that name secret. It has nothing to do with who I am. Once my parents saw how good I was with the hens, they named me Feather. My annoying twin brothers are Mule and Frog, and you can probably guess why once you meet them. Sometimes I think their names should be Good-bye and Long-Gone. The baby just has his birth certificate name—so far."

H STOPPED THE hearse in front of a two-story house with a swooning front porch and weathered siding. White geraniums planted in a rusted bucket sat by the front door. From around the side of the house, a dog as big as a pony charged the frail fence with bared teeth. I stepped behind H who offered his hand to the dog.

"Barlow, don't make me look bad in front of the lady." At the sound of H's voice, Barlow rolled onto his back. H leaned over the fence to rub the dog's spotted belly. "He's blind and dumber than a post, but he won't let strangers inside the fence." He patted the dog's belly. "Good boy."

H offered a dog biscuit to Barlow as he opened the gate. "It pays to be prepared."

"You got another one of those biscuits?"

"It'll cost you," he said, winking.

I pushed past H to the front door. From inside, a woman as

tenuous as a newly hatched chick pushed open the screen. She spoke to H. "I called Will and George to help you carry Arthur out, dear. Do you think I should call anyone else?"

H extended his hand to Mrs. Masterson, and she stepped into his embrace.

"I'm already lost without him."

H patted her shoulder. "There, there now Mrs. Masterson."

She backed out of his embrace to blot her tears with a hankie. She looked down and flinched with surprise. "Look at me. I can't even decide what to wear." She clutched her robe to her neck and combed her hair with her fingers. She said, "Arthur and I met at a dance. He paid every boy on my dance card two bits so he could dance with me all night. I fell in love with him long before the last waltz."

I would have too. "I'm so sorry—"

"Do you know the time?" she asked, looking from me to H.

H popped his pocket watch open. "It's 2:30, ma'am."

Mrs. Masterson sighed. "Oh dear, it's almost time for tea." Her eyes had gone sleepy. H and I exchanged glances.

"Mrs. Masterson?" H prodded.

She blinked and that seemed to restart her motor.

"Can you take us to Dr. Masterson?" he asked.

"Yes, come on in. He's still in bed."

H pulled back the many blankets covering Mr. Masterson one by one as if peeling an onion. When he lifted the sheet, I swallowed down a gasp.

H said, "Ma'am, you can call Willie and George. I can handle this myself." H sent me to the hearse for a sheet and told me to leave the gurney by the tailgate. "I can carry him down."

By the time I returned to the couple's bedroom, H had buttoned Dr. Masterson's pajamas and run a comb through his hair. The oxygen mask had left a red mark that cut deep into Dr. Masterson's nose and circled his chin. "Would you like some time with him before I carry him downstairs?" H asked.

Mrs. Masterson studied her husband's face. "That would be lovely."

H and I stepped into the hall. Photographs of babies and wedding couples and graduates hung all along the wall. In a sepia photograph, a stoic couple stood like mannequins before a painted backdrop, the groom sitting in a carved wooden chair, the bride standing slightly behind him with her hand on his shoulder. His head was blurred as if he couldn't resist taking a peek at his bride. Although the bride's face was solemn, the corners of her eyes smiled in response. I motioned for H to look at the photograph. He raised his eyebrows to indicate he had no idea why I would draw his attention to such a thing. To be fair, not many males would connect the photograph to the Mastersons. The apple-faced couple in the photograph sat erect. Now Mrs. Masterson's skin hung from her bent frame, and Dr. Masterson, well, his disheveled pajamas had revealed legs as narrow as my wrist. But if I were Mrs. Masterson, I would have hung my wedding photo in the very same place, just outside the bedroom where I could look at it and remember what I'd once been and to remember my husband in better days.

From the bedroom, Mrs. Masterson expelled a sob. "Oh, Arthur, what am I to do?"

H raised his hand to stop me from returning to the bedroom. He whispered, "Give her a minute. She'll be okay."

I leaned against the wall and closed my eyes, my way of giving the Mastersons the privacy they deserved. When Mrs. Masterson spoke again, her voice was breathy with wonderment. I can't explain what happened next. I never asked her about what I heard. It was a one-sided conversation, like I was listening to someone talk on the phone. What Mrs. Masterson heard, I couldn't say.

"Oh my," she said. "Oh my, you're here.

"Why not?

"You've seen the Master?

"Arthur, how about our Abigail? Have you seen her?

"She did? That's wonderful, just wonderful.

"What kinds of things are you learning, dear?"

H and I exchanged looks. I felt awkward listening in on such an intimate conversation. To busy my mind, I imagined the groom in the photograph carrying his bride over the threshold, the walls freshly painted, the floors polished to a sheen, and the smell of lilacs rather than mildew welcoming the newlyweds. And I imagined cherub-fat babies fingering dandelions in the grass while Mrs. Masterson hung the laundry. Those babies would now be in their sixties. Had they heard about their father's death? I squeezed my eyes tight to hold the tears, but that proved futile. Before wiping them away, I looked at H. Tears streamed down his cheeks too. He dug in his pocket for a hankie for me and wiped his own tears on his sleeve.

"Arthur," Mrs. Masterson said, sounding alarmed yet pleased, "have you come for me?

"Why not, darling? Why not? You look wonderful, and here I am still in my nightgown.

"But I'm so old, dear. Oh, please, take me with you.

"Don't tease me, Arthur.

"Yes, yes, I know. You're right. I will serve Him. I promise. Yes." The bedsprings complained under her weight. "Good-bye, my darling. Good-bye."

I mouthed to H, *Now?*

He shook his head.

Mrs. Masterson stepped into the hallway. "I'm ready for you to take him now."

H wrapped Mr. Masterson in the white sheet, tenderly rolling him to his side to straighten his pajamas and crossing his arms over his chest. H left the man's face exposed until the last. He looked to Mrs. Masterson who nodded her approval before he closed the flaps over her husband's face.

"He's not in there anymore," she said.

Mrs. Masterson stood on the porch while H loaded Dr. Masterson into the hearse. H returned to her to say something I couldn't hear. We drove in silence until we left the pastures and farmland behind.

"What happened back there?" I asked.

"I have no idea, but whatever she saw or heard, the conversation was only for her. We should keep this to ourselves, don't you think?"

I agreed, but I knew I would tell Lauren, but not on a postcard like I usually wrote to save pennies. I didn't want Myron, the postal clerk, spreading Mrs. Masterson's story to all of his customers.

Two dimples pocked H's cheeks as he talked about lifting weights in the Mastersons' shed and how he ran to the top of Ragged Mountain Road to prepare for football try-outs in August. Somehow, the vision of H huffing and puffing and sweating sullied the mystery of what we had just witnessed.

"Not now, H. Okay?"

CHARLES MOBERLY, THE mortician, slathered Miracle Whip on each bite of his meatloaf sandwich.

"Would you care for some more milk?" I asked.

He swallowed a bite of sandwich and dabbed his mouth with the napkin he kept in his lap. "Thank you. Yes, that would be nice."

Charles looked like the kind of man you would want for a substitute teacher, soft and gullible. By the end of the hour, not one student would be left in class. His eyes were small gray marbles behind large wire-rimmed glasses, a surprising fashion-conscious choice for a man who wore white shirts with, quite honestly, the ugliest tie ever made. He had already insisted I call him Charles, a true softy.

"Are you sure your sandwich isn't too dry?" I asked. "I could use less oatmeal next time."

He worked his tongue over his teeth, and his Adam's apple bounced as he downed the glass of milk. "Nope, I like my meatloaf on the dry side." When I poured him a third glass of milk, he invited me to join him at the table. If I'd known he was going to yammer about mortuary stuff, I would have told him the oven needed cleaning. For my lack of forethought, Charles rewarded me with a blow by blow of the improvements he'd made to Clancy and Sons.

"Before Mrs. Clancy agreed to build a ramp that allowed bodies to be wheeled directly into the basement preparation area, three men were required, four if the deceased was a large man, to heft the body through the trapdoor in the hallway. Once the body was on the ramp, it slid to a bumper-like stop I fashioned from a one-by-ten board and a piano hinge. That sure made my end of the job a bit easier."

Adults can be quite enamored with their cleverness. They can't help telling the whole world about their achievements, whether the world, meaning me, wanted to know about them or not.

He continued. "Now, if I could just convince Mrs. Clancy to add steps directly out the front door. The narrow porch makes that right-angle turn quite difficult with a heavy casket. I've seen more than one casket dropped." He sighed. "As you can imagine, the families are upset when that happens."

Hoping to shift the conversation away from bodies moving hither and yon, I asked, "How long have you been a mortician?"

Charles told me all about his family who had owned a funeral home in Lexington, Kentucky. His father taught him the family business, but Charles wanted to go out on his own. From how he described his father, he had been a tough act to follow. I sure understood that. Charles had answered an ad placed in the Clearwater County Herald for an itinerate mortician. "Every day is different," he said, folding his napkin. "I'm rarely in the same town two days in a row. I'd be happy to show you how I prepare a body for burial. It's quite fascinating. Do you have plans after lunch?"

These types of situations made me happy I'd been a member of the debate team. I could think on my feet. "Sorry, I have to clean the oven."

Eight

The post office closed before Mom came home in the evening, so on the days when Mrs. Clancy went to the Stop-and-Chomp for lunch, I pleaded with Mom to eat her lunches at the funeral home. That way I could keep my promise to write Lauren every day. After Mom and I ate our bologna sandwiches, she sat behind the garage drinking coffee and smoking cigarettes while I went to the post office. Mom said she could hear the phone from where she sat, but she never took one death call that whole summer.

Myron the postal clerk knew my name by the end of our first week in Cordial, and he asked about Mom regularly, the kinds of questions I'd answered for men since I could talk. No, she's a widow. Yes, she likes movies. No, she's not much of a bowler. And the answer I hated most of all—yes, people do confuse us as sisters.

Jane Austen would have described Myron as an affable man with an alabaster dome with no regard for physical exertion, a rare contrast to the great majority of Cordial's ruddy citizenry. Since

I wasn't sure if Myron read the postcards I dropped into the mailbox, I told Lauren that Myron was nice enough to ask after Mom's well-being. Lauren would know what I meant.

A woman with hips broader than her shoulders and a teeny-tiny waist stepped up to the counter. Myron slid a sheet of stamps toward her. "Here ya go, Clarice."

Stamps in hand, Clarice leaned against the counter. "You might want to stop by the house around eight or so. Oscar was out pickin' strawberries as soon as the sun came up this morning, and he sent me to buy cream and rock salt." She patted Myron's hand. "You can bring Sheila, if you've a mind to."

Myron glanced at me and blushed. He busied himself brushing invisible bits of dust off the counter. "I'll have to see about that."

Clarice tucked her stamps into her purse, and the next customer, a woman I placed as a rancher's wife with her jeans and mud-crusted boots, took her place at Myron's counter.

Myron called after Clarice. "Tell Oscar I'll take a turn at the churn for some of his ice cream."

Clarice returned to the counter, nudging away the rancher's wife who rolled her eyes for the people waiting in line. Behind me, a man cleared his throat. The shoulders of the man in front of me sagged. Clarice whispered loud enough for all of us to hear. "You'll get an earful, Myron. He's all perturbed about what's going on up on the mesas. Won't shut up about it." Clarice glanced at the man in front of me. He wore his hair pulled into a shaggy ponytail that reached the middle of his back. I'd already moved as close to him as I dared to get a good whiff. He smelled like a musty barn where the straw hadn't been freshened in a long time, but he didn't smell as bad as Lauren's brother after wrestling practice.

Clarice stood on tiptoe to put her face close to Myron's. "He heard they don't wear no clothes up there."

The long-haired man shifted his weight and expelled a sharp breath.

Myron shot the man a glance. "You can't believe everything you hear, Clarice."

"Tell that to Oscar," she said, pivoting toward the door. With a wave over her shoulder she was gone.

Myron gave his attention to the woman with the crusty boots.

"I need a money order, Myron," she said, setting her feet in a broad stance.

While Myron issued the money order and received an update on Macon and Karen's upcoming wedding, I read the postcard I'd written to Lauren the night before. I'd made tiny circles instead of periods or dots just as we'd done since we started passing notes in Sunday school.

> *Hi Lauren! I miss you soooooo much! I'm still in Cordial. As I'm writing this, there are TWO dead people in the basement. Help! The viewing for the woman is this afternoon. Still haven't heard a thing about the transmission. Grrr. Found the library. It's small, but they have Jane's S&S. WRITE SOON! PLEASE!!!!! Going crazy, Amy*

There was just enough room under my signature to add,

> *P.S. Hippies don't smell as bad as we feared.*

Myron took the hippie's package and placed it on the scales. "Parcel post?" he asked without looking up.

"That's cool."

"Insurance?"

"No, thank you."

"Anything else?

"This will be all, thanks."

"Next."

The hippie pushed the glass door hard enough that it swung to bang the side of the building. He trotted across the street, shaking his head.

"Amy? Can I help you?"

I hesitated before I took my place at the counter. Myron grinned broadly. My stomach churned. "The usual?" he asked, sliding a post-card across the counter. "How's your mother?"

I dropped a nickel and two pennies into his glistening palm. "Fine."

"How's she getting by at Gartley's Hardware?"

"Fine."

"Does she like strawberry ice cream?"

"The last time she looked at strawberry ice cream, she went into anaphylactic shock. She would have died if a doctor hadn't been nearby."

Myron coughed into his hand. "Give her my regards."

Mom had no idea that Myron the postal clerk existed, and I planned on keeping it that way. "Sure."

"Next."

I TURNED TOWARD the funeral home and stopped. What was the hurry? Mom said she would answer the phone. The Gartleys gave her a half hour for lunch. That left me ten minutes to do some exploring.

I walked down Main Street. Erase every romantic notion ever held about small-town Main Streets. They didn't apply to Cordial.

I passed a realtor and a barber and the First National Bank, which possessed all of the conventions of longevity and security—stone, brass, and gold lettering on the window—but I walked past the building in only eight paces. I half expected a resident of Lilliput to stumble over the threshold. When I came to Gartley's Hardware Store, I crossed the street, even though the sign in the window reminded me of the chicks inside. Main Street ended at Second Street where a steep rise of earth and the railroad tracks marked the end of the shopping district, such as it was. I followed Second Street past a lumber yard, a feed co-op, and a plumbing outfit with a giant faucet hanging over its door, the only attempt at charm I'd seen in Cordial. The town wore working clothes of blistered paint and rust, not at all like my hometown, Gilbertsville. As a resort town, Gilbertsville bulged with souvenir shops like the Whirligig and a dress shop called The Girl from Ipanema and my personal favorite, Get 'Em While They're Hot, a cookie shop near the marina.

A flash of color caught my eye down a residential street, so I turned to investigate. A row of identical houses about the size of boxcars lined the street, each one painted a rainbow color. Babies slept in the shade on dandelion lawns, and their naked brothers and sisters ran squealing through sprinklers. The mothers, all with long hair and wearing homemade skirts with peasant blouses, sipped tea from mason jars. Between two trees, gauzy hankies the colors of crayons rose and fell with the breeze.

A mother holding a sleeping infant called out to me. "Hey, what's happening?"

"Oh, I'm new in town. Just passing through, really. Thought I'd walk around to get my bearings."

She left her perch on the steps to walk toward me, her baby undisturbed by her movement. "Would you like some tea?"

The mothers on the porch returned my smile. "I don't have much time."

She handed over her sleeping child. The weight of him surprised me but not as much as the joy that bubbled in my gut at his touch.

"It won't take me a minute," she said and disappeared into the lavender house. By the time she returned, I'd taken her seat on the step and rested my cheek on the baby's damp forehead. His white hair rose to tickle my nose with each shift of the breeze. I wasn't thirsty anymore.

"It's chamomile tea," his mother said. "I grew the herbs and dried the leaves myself. I traded some babysitting for the honey." She introduced herself as Sasha and her friends as Mildred and Tana. She smiled open-faced, like a sunflower on a cloudless day. She bent to kiss her infant's head. "And this sweet little babe is Zachary, a carbon copy of his old man, Jackson." She pointed over her shoulder with her thumb towards the front door. "He's there, on the couch, doing what he does best."

We talked as newly acquainted people do to find the commonalities that linked us. I doubted Sasha and I would find that ground. I told her about Gilbertsville, how the population swelled each summer and receded each fall. "I'm only in Cordial because Mom insists on driving a really old car and the transmission finally died."

"It's your karma," she said, lifting the babe from my arms. "Make of it what you will."

Oh boy. Baptists did not talk about karma. Baptists talked about praising God in the midst of their trials. Being stuck in Cordial to answer death calls and bake meatloaf for a mortician definitely qualified as a trial in my book. But truthfully, I wasn't singing hallelujahs. I ignored the karma remark and chose to wow the mothers with my scholarly pursuits. "I'm headed to California to attend college."

"Cool. What will you study?" asked Sasha.

"Mom wants me to study nursing or become a teacher. You know, something that will get me a good job."

"What do you want?"

"I love Jane Austen. In fact, I prefer the earliest novels, and by that I mean the eighteenth century. England."

"You're going to study English literature then?"

"Yeah, which means I'll probably end up as a high school English teacher anyway." I pictured Miss Benedict in her orthopedic shoes. She never smiled, not even when we read about the Yahoos attacking the Houyhnhnms in *Gulliver's Travels.* I must have shuddered because Sasha touched my arm.

"Just because you have a degree in English lit, doesn't mean you have to do something you hate."

"It's real important that I support myself."

"There's lots of ways to do that." The baby stirred, fussed. Sasha lifted her blouse to expose her breast. Zachary attached himself greedily. My face got hot and I stood.

"I have an M.A. in English literature," she said.

"You do?"

Her smiled disappeared. "From Harvard."

"I'm sorry. It's just—"

"No, it's cool. I'm used to it."

"Are you teaching?"

She laughed. "In Cordial? They'd never . . ."

"Then what are you doing here?"

"My old man and I were working on our doctorates when we found out I was pregnant with Christina—the mischievous one there, chasing poor Alex with the hose. She's named after Christina Rossetti, poet, nineteenth century. You're familiar with her, of course."

I wasn't.

"Anyway, living in the city was getting us down. The whole adversarial process of getting a doctorate wasn't our bag. Nothing Gregory wrote or said pleased his dissertation committee, so we called a friend who owns an organic farm here. We packed up the car the next day. He's in Texas now—or Florida." Sasha raised Zachary to her shoulder to pat a burp out of him. "You can know a lot of stuff without knowing how to live, Amy. Life is a journey."

One of the churches in town let out a single bong from its bell tower to mark the half hour. "I have to go."

AT THE FUNERAL home, Mom paced the front porch. "Amy, where have you been?"

"There was a long line at the post office."

"I'm ten minutes late." She sat on the bench by the door to tie her tennis shoes.

"I'm really sorry. I stopped to talk to some ladies drinking tea, and they offered me some. I lost track of time."

She sucked a long drag off her cigarette. "Were they hippies?"

"How am I supposed to know?"

"Were they wearing shoes?"

I pictured Sasha's long toes curled over the edge of the step. "I don't remember."

"Walk with me," she said, shouldering her purse. "Listen, I want you to stay away from the hippies. Do you hear me? You should read the newspaper. The hippies aren't exactly loved around here. Things go missing from the store whenever they come in. Their children are wild. Russell says most of them believe the world owes them a living." She snuffed out her cigarette under the toe of her shoe and handed it to me. "Flush this for me, will you? I left some hamburgers thawing on the counter. Put them in the frig in an hour or so."

Mom walked toward the corner. She made her work uniform—Wranglers and a chambray shirt—look fashionable. She had tied the shirt at her waist and rolled the sleeves to her elbows, but no amount of bleach would whiten her tennis shoes again.

"Be home on time," I called after her. "There's a viewing tonight for Miss Bigelow."

Mom skidded to a stop on the gravel and turned. "Oh rats, Amy, I've already made plans with Bonnie."

"I was hoping you'd help me."

She blew me a kiss. "I will, *fofa*. I promise. Another time."

The hamburger hit the back of the freezer with a thud. "No hamburgers for us," I said, slamming the freezer door. Because of the viewing, we would have peanut butter and jelly sandwiches for dinner.

I knelt by my bed and prayed. "Lord, you have to save my mother. She's driving me crazy. Amen."

Nine

When I was in second grade, Santa Claus arrived at my school with a bagful of books wrapped in red and green tissue paper. As I climbed onto Santa's knee, he said, "You're Amy, aren't you? I've been watching you, and you've been very, very good. I see you reading at the library and in school and at home. Is there a book you would like for Christmas?"

"Do I have to share it with anyone?"

"Not if you don't want to."

"Let me think about this." I slid down from his lap, so the other students could have their book wishes fulfilled by Santa. The boys asked for books about baseball and rockets. At least the girls knew the titles of books, like *The Adventures of Peter Rabbit* and *Goldilocks and the Three Bears.* Still, their childish choices embarrassed me. Did they want Santa to think they were stupid? For me, I agonized over asking for one of the new books I'd fingered in the library or for a tried-and-true classic.

I tugged on Santa's sleeve. "I've made my decision: *Little Women* by Louisa May Alcott."

Santa cleared his throat. "That's an awfully big book for a little girl like you. Couldn't I interest you in *Madeline's Christmas* or *Kitty's Big Day*? They have lots of pretty pictures. You like kitties, don't you?"

The man behind the white beard couldn't be Santa Claus. Someone who knew me as well as Santa would never offer me a picture book about an annoying little girl. And what would make a big day for a cat? A day without a hairball?

Santa scratched his beard. All around me, my classmates ripped wrapping from their books and pushed them aside for one of Mrs. Ferguson's cupcakes with red and green sprinkles. I took pity on the poor man whom the teacher had pressed into playing Santa. He'd done an okay job. He knew to *ho-ho-ho* and pat his belly. I took *Madeline's Christmas* home, still wrapped, and placed it under our Christmas tree.

Sitting on the bathtub, I watched Mom apply her makeup for her night out with Bonnie. True, Mom wasn't Santa Claus, but I faced a similar dilemma with her. I'd adored Mom like I'd adored Santa Claus. I had considered her a super mom, always prettier and more fashionable than the moms of my friends, always game for a party, and always a source of intrigue. But the gig was up, her cover blown. Honestly, she was barely tolerable. I wasn't sure when the change had started, but even money was on our recent pilgrimage through Nebraska. No other landscape provided more time to enumerate her flaws, even while reading *People* magazine. Easier to pinpoint was the culmination of the process—the moment she'd handed over her crushed cigarette butt.

Now that Mom was a mere mortal, what was I going to do with her? For leaving me alone to face Miss Bigelow's mourners, I would loathe her until I went to bed. After all, I wanted to be spiteful, not tumble from God's grace.

Do I have to love her?

I'd memorized a boatload of verses about love in Sunday school. "You shall love the Lord your God with all your heart, and with all your soul, and with all your mind." "Love one another." "You shall love your neighbor as yourself." "Love your enemies and pray for those who persecute you." And, oh yeah, "Honor your father and mother." Never had my inclinations and God's admonitions been at greater odds. Only he could fix her.

Mom loved to be considered more friend than mother, so I said to her, "Please come with me to church on Sunday. Don't make me sit alone with Mrs. Clancy."

She turned from her reflection, sheathing her mascara wand and frowning. "I thought we made a pinkie pledge, Amy. No come-to-Jesus sermons until my death bed."

"Oh no, that's not what I agreed to. Besides, I saw you and some guy out my window last night. I figure the pinkie pledges are null and void after all."

Mom's face flushed. "You saw that?" She shook the tube of mascara at me. "Listen to me, little lady. I won't have you spying on me or pestering me every other minute to accept Jesus as my personal Lord and whatever. Do you hear me?"

"But he loves you. He died for you."

She turned back to the mirror to coat her lashes with mascara. "That's just dandy, but I need a man with skin on. This is a tough old world, and I could use some help."

"Jesus will help you."

"This conversation is over, Amelia."

Mom only called me Amelia when she neared the verge of blowing like Mount Vesuvius. That didn't stop me, because I did love her. Picturing her wading through a lake of fire started me crying. "I don't want you to go to hell!"

"Amy, I'm warning you. I don't want to talk about this." She shrugged. "Sure, I'll spend some time in purgatory, but I've been a good person, better than most who go to church every week. Save your tears for them."

"Mom, Jesus already suffered for your sins. What's the point of purgatory?"

"Amelia, don't say another word. Go read one of your books or watch television. I'm in no mood to hear one of your sermons."

I left to prepare for Miss Bigelow's viewing, feeling worse for having tried to share Christ's love with Mom than if I'd continued loathing her.

FIVE WOMEN AS gnarled as driftwood shuffled into the chapel, some with walkers, others walking with such caution that I moved closer in case they fell. They smelled of mentholated lozenges and joint ointment with a generous dousing of rose water. Each woman signed her name in the guest book, taking roughly the time it took Thomas Jefferson to pen the entire Declaration of Independence. The fifth lady struggled to return the pen to its stand, so I asked to see it.

"I'm so sorry," I said. "This is the wrong pen."

She smiled and toddled off to the reposing room to join the other ladies, shaking their heads and *tsk-tsk*ing over Miss Bigelow. One of the women came out after a cursory look at Miss Bigelow. She used her cane like a third leg, jutting it out before her and shuffling to catch up, not unlike an inchworm moving along a branch. I moved my foot to avoid being jabbed by her cane.

"Where's the coffee and cookies?" she asked, looking around the chapel before meeting my gaze with her verdigris eyes. "There's always coffee and cookies at a proper viewing."

I scanned the viewing checklist. "I'm sorry. Cookies aren't on my list. Are you hungry? I could make you a peanut butter and jelly sandwich."

"No coffee? No cookies? The *idea*." She returned to the reposing room, dragging the cane behind her. "There aren't any refreshments, girls. Let's go."

As if Custer had sounded the retreat, the women left the funeral home to shuffle toward the Alpenglow Rest Home van parked at the end of the sidewalk. Once the van was out of sight, I sat with my back to the opened double doors of the reposing room, reading *Pride and Prejudice* for the second time that week. The only light in the room, as per Mrs. Clancy's instructions, was the light of the podium lamp, where visitors signed in, and a lamp shining down on Miss Bigelow's face. A truck stopped at the end of the sidewalk, and I laid the book face down inside the organ stool. The truck revved and made a U-turn. I retrieved the book. After an hour, more or less, of tucking the book away every time a vehicle drove by—mostly trucks with mud-spattered fenders and radios blaring country-western music—I kicked off my shoes and moved to where I could see at a glance if vehicles actually parked in front of the funeral home. Viewings lasted from five o'clock to eight o'clock.

Two hours to go.

When my Snoopy watch—another "gift" from Lauren—read eight, or as near to eight as I could determine when reading paws rather than hands, I stepped with reticence out of Lizzy Bennet's orchestrated life and back into mine. It was time to close down shop on Miss Bigelow's viewing. Her brothers hadn't bothered to attend. I couldn't tell you if I was relieved or angry about that.

I wiped my hands on my dress and ran a finger down the checklist Mrs. Clancy had typed for me. I clutched the clipboard to my chest and prayed, "Father, forgive me for hating my mother just now and for calling the Bigelow brothers something unkind, even though I didn't say it out loud. And please, oh please, give me courage to face what I'm about to do. Amen."

Lock the door.

Check.

Turn off the porch light.

Check.

Set the guest book and pen on Mrs. Clancy's desk.

Check.

Close the casket.

Oh boy.

I stood at the threshold of the reposing room to observe Miss Bigelow from a distance. Her face hung like a tablecloth over her features, making nothing but a fold of her mouth that extended to the flap of her ear. No wonder the ladies of Alpenglow Rest Home had stayed for such a short time. Keeping my eyes on her rumpled eyelids, I walked noiselessly over the deep-pile rug toward Miss Bigelow. Something more amazing than lifeless eyelids popping open happened as I stood over her: My curiosity outpaced my fear.

Miss Bigelow lay among tucks of white satin in the pine casket the brothers had chosen for her. I supposed they had chosen the threadbare cotton dress she wore too. Typical. A brown amoeba of a stain soiled the shelf of her motionless bosom.

"Jesus will dress you in white," I whispered.

I tugged the bodice of her dress in place to cover her bra strap. I leaned closer. "If heaven is the heaven I think it is, you won't have to wear a bra either." I pulled at the elastic band of my own bra.

Miss Bigelow's hands sheltered her heart. She wore no rings. No fingernail polish. Her yellowed nails were cut to the quick. In death, the skin of her hands looked like gloves that were much too large. Calluses. Scars. Scratches. The heavy powder Bonnie had used to enliven her skin tone clung to her body hair, making her seem out of focus. I'd planned on closing the casket while turning off the light, only to bolt to my bedroom. Instead, I used a tissue to blot the excess rouge from Miss Bigelow's checks and straightened the bows of her shoelaces.

From the bottom drawer of my dresser, I retrieved the padded envelope that held Lauren's gifts and spilled the contents onto the bed. Five pairs of hoop earrings. A tube of Elizabeth Arden lipstick. A pair of owl-eye sunglasses. A rhinestone-and-pearl brooch. *Perfect.* Pinned onto Miss Bigelow's dress, the brooch covered the stain completely.

"Jesus will clothe you in his righteousness, better than any wedding dress you could have worn here on earth. He'll throw you a wedding feast. You won't have to cook, and if your dress gets dirty he'll give you a new one."

I closed the casket and switched off the light. In my bedroom I read *P & P.* I found myself impatient with Lizzy. *Come on, Lizzy, Mr. Darcy is crazy about you. He bailed your sister out of trouble and betrayed his own conscience to do so. Get off your high horse. Take it all back. Kiss him, already.*

I LOCKED THE bedroom door, pulled the shade, and stood in front of the bureau's mirror in Mom's lacy black slip, the closest thing to an evening gown in the house. The fabric puckered where Mom's breasts strained the fabric. The lacy hem hovered six inches above my knees, the shapeliest part of my legs. Mom's tiara slid on my head every time I moved.

I counted the tracks of the LP and set the needle down on "My Man" from the *Funny Girl* soundtrack. With the first note out of Barbra Streisand's mouth, I raised the hairbrush microphone, and I was Miss Streisand's understudy performing on opening night. The entire student body from Gilbertsville High School sat in the audience, drop-jawed and envious. The thunderous applause of the audience assured me that my performance as Fanny Brice had disappointed no one. But in reality, in my dream reality at least, I sang for one man and one man only—Cliff Taylor. Captain of the varsity basketball team. Lead of the senior play. President of my youth group. Tall. Broad-shouldered yet slim. A curve of mahogany hair fell across his forehead. Sure, he had been Dixie's boyfriend since ninth grade, and yes, he gave her a promise ring at prom, which, of course, I didn't attend. What did his past devotion to Dixie mean that night? Absolutely nothing. He smiled approvingly as I belted out the ballad.

I fell across the bed. "How pathetic can I be?"

I inventoried the very short list of boys I'd known whom I'd had half a chance of kissing. There was Ronnie, a really nice guy, polite and attentive. His father owned the bakery in Gilbertsville. Ronnie ate most of the stale donuts himself. He huffed and puffed his way through the school halls. The girls stepped aside, making faces like they had swallowed a bug. Ronnie saw them, I was sure, so I'd agreed to be his lab partner in biology. Even though he had skinned the frog for me, kissing him was out of the question. Doug was the most athletic of the bunch, but clusters of hot pimples covered his face and he constantly played with the coins in his pocket. One night, Jerry, a senior when I was only a sophomore, asked to walk me home from youth group. He had memorized whole chapters of Scripture and wanted to be a missionary along the Amazon in Brazil. As our footsteps tapped on the sidewalk, I tried to picture myself living where people picked lice from each other's hair. Who would have the patience to blaze a trail through my dense locks? Worrying had turned out to be a waste of time. As we sat on the curb in front of my house he said, "I've been thinking about you a lot, and I was really considering liking you as more than a friend, but God told me you weren't the one for me."

I said my prayers on my knees that night, but still, I'd never been kissed.

The record player's needle *scritch, scritch, scritch*ed against the label. I lifted the record from the turntable to read the label. "I'd Rather be Blue"? Faulty logic. "People"? *Oh, please.* "Don't Rain on My Parade"? Too triumphant. Too singular.

A familiar ache roosted under my heart. I hugged a pillow to my chest.

"Lord, will anyone ever love me?"

Ten

I peeked through the velvet draperies of the chapel to watch for Mrs. Clancy. She had insisted I accompany her on my first Sunday at Spruce Street Church. The church itself intrigued me. Constructed of tan stone, the building evoked images of King Arthur with its round turret crowned by a stone parapet. To emphasize the church's identity crisis, a brass ball topped the party-hat roof rather than a cross. The stained-glass windows bore none of the themes you would expect, say the Good Shepherd or Jesus praying in the Garden of Gethsemane. Varying shades of green glass patched the windows on the south side, only to taint the glory of the remaining windows.

Old women with Easter-egg hair walked up the steps of the church, most leaning heavily on the railing to steady themselves in the wind that plastered skirts around arthritic knees and cushioned bottoms. I returned to the bathroom for one more dousing of White Rain. My bun felt like a Brillo pad.

On the way back to the chapel, I stopped to check on Mom. Even her snores were delicate, melodious. I blinked away the tears to grab my purse, Bible, and a notebook. I met Mrs. Clancy at the kitchen door.

"You won't need that," said Mrs. Clancy. She stepped inside, straining her neck to look from the kitchen to the small sitting room. She tugged at her bodice. "The church has Bibles in every pew."

If she had told me to leave my dress at home, I couldn't have been more surprised. I'd won a galaxy of gold stars for bringing my Bible to Sunday school. I stood there dumbly, vacillating between my ache to belong, if only for a few months, and wanting to please Mrs. Clancy because I believed many had tried and failed. I was competitive that way.

"Never mind," she said, walking down the stairs. Her hind end tipped precariously with each step. "Bring your Bible if doing so will keep your jaw from slacking like a dolt. The service starts in five minutes." She looked at her watch and held up three fingers. "Three minutes."

A brood of women stopped their clucking the moment Mrs. Clancy entered the narthex, but their eyes were on me. They nodded, cooed, touched my arms with their cool hands. One patted my cheek and welcomed me to Spruce Street Church. The churn of my stomach slowed. I was a chick safely returned to the henhouse after a misadventure in the coyote-infested hinterlands. I learned from a woman with three chins that the young people came for the Sunday school hour in the basement at eleven and left the moment the clock chimed noon.

"I don't know what they do down there," she said, wringing her hands. "How are they expecting to be part of the church if they don't attend services? I fear for the future of the church."

"It's so nice to see a young person interested in the heart of the church," another woman offered. She looked me up and down. "You don't seem like other folks new to Cordial. You're sensible and modest. Lovely, just lovely, and you have a sweet face."

I'd chosen what I wore carefully, a gingham and eyelet dress with a flounce that covered my ankles. "Thanks."

"Last year's summer intern was a bit too progressive, I think," added a woman doused with rose water and powdered like a donut. "Without asking, he up and painted the youth room a ghastly blue. Terribly gaudy, I don't mind telling you. Some families stopped attending altogether." And as surprising as a garter snake, her anger flared. "We sent the intern back where he came from, we did."

I must have jumped because she leaned toward me. "Oh, we have a very nice youth director now. I was on the selection committee."

Mrs. Clancy tugged my arm, and I followed her to the second row. I pushed a needlepoint pillow over to clear a spot before sitting. A woman as flighty as a finch grabbed the pillow with a huff and off she went, shaking her head.

Above me, the plastered walls arched toward each other on wooden beams as graceful as whale bones. And I'd been wrong about the stained-glass windows. An opened Bible topped each trio of windows.

Good.

A tall man in a black robe that barely cleared his knees entered from a door behind the pulpit and sat in a throne of a chair. I jumped when the organist pounced on the hymn's first chord. I'd never sung a hymn with six verses before. I shared a hymnal with Mrs. Clancy, and when the high notes pinched her throat, she spat on my hand. By the time we sang amen, the bubble of sputum had slid into my palm. *Yuck!* Rather than embarrass Mrs. Clancy, I waited until we sat down to smooth the folds of my dress. No more spit. She tugged on my arm to stand for the doxology, so I paid closer attention to the bulletin. An asterisk beside a hymn or a congregational prayer meant to stand, but there was no corresponding signal to sit down. Instead, I listened for the grunts and sighs of the women around me. Those proved signal enough.

As the ushers gathered the offering, the Reverend Dr. Theodore Maxwell, whom Mrs. Clancy referred to as Pastor Ted, thrummed his fingers on a black notebook. He watched his congregation with round black eyes as two creases deepened between them. He removed his glasses to rub the folds, but the creases persisted. His eyes appeared even smaller with his glasses resting in his lap. He wasn't a bad-looking man, in a scholarly-pallor and soft-hands sort of way. He looked to be older than Mom but much younger than Mrs. Clancy. What a disappointing time that must be for adults, when all that is fresh and new has passed and heaven is all they have to look forward to. The absence of a wedding ring kept speculations flying through my head until he returned his glasses to his face to bless the offering.

Pastor Ted stepped behind the pulpit, opened the black notebook with deliberation, licking his finger to find his place among the many pages. I would crochet him a bookmark so he could find his place faster. I dated the first blank page of my notebook. He cast a wary eye over the congregation and cleared his throat. "Please turn with me to the Gospel of Luke, chapter one, verse five, page 948 in the pew Bibles."

He read the Scripture like a lullaby. Every word enunciated. No hesitation. As he described the significance of Zechariah's priestly service, his voice grew stronger. He described the inner and outer chambers of the temple—the sights, the sounds, the smells. He spoke with great tenderness of Elizabeth's disappointment and piety, and as he did, his mouth curled into a slight smile. At first, I thought he was looking at me, but when a woman with wrought-iron posture in front of me squirmed under his gaze, I knew his attention had landed on her.

Interesting.

As Pastor Ted gave the benediction from the back of the church, I wrote a note in the margin of my Bible that Zechariah's lack of faith hadn't thwarted God's purposes. Mrs. Clancy looked at me, my Bible, and shook her head.

After the service, I sidled free of the worshipers to read a calendar of events I'd noticed earlier in the narthex. No mid-week Bible study for college students or Bible study of any kind, really, only mission circles and bingo.

Mrs. Clancy caught me by the arm. "They're waiting for you downstairs."

"For me? Who?"

"Your Sunday school class. Our new youth director teaches the class. He certainly has a way with the young people."

I didn't want to hang out with a bunch of squirrelly high school students. "Someone might call the funeral home." I said and leaned into her. "You know, a death call."

"There won't be anyone calling until two o'clock. It's understood that I go to church and out to lunch with the ladies every Sunday. You have plenty of time for Sunday school."

In the basement, I sat on a wooden chair that pinched my left cheek when I shifted to straighten my skirt. I slid over a chair, felt guilty about subjecting someone else to the bottom-pinching chair, and slid back. Since I sat alone, I rehearsed a speech for the youth director, suggesting that a college-bound person might intimidate the high school participants. Having settled on my approach, I took in my surroundings.

Whoever had attempted to cover the electric-blue walls had failed. Blue bled through the roller strokes, and a fringe of blue remained near the ceiling. The photographic posters with inspirational sayings curled away from the tape holding them to the wall. Overhead, pipes gurgled and groaned. The large circle of chairs demonstrated ambitious hopes of attracting the major portion of the teenagers who lived in Cordial. I'd read about their commencement in the newspaper. Less than thirty seniors had graduated from the high school that year. When someone overhead finally rang a bell to announce the start of Sunday school, only H and I sat with the freshly scrubbed intern, John.

"Okay," he said, rubbing his hands together, "this is great. H, our class has doubled in size in just two weeks. You must be out there talking Sunday school up. That's real good. Okay now, let's, well, pray. H, would you lead us?"

H looked at me and then the boy-wonder youth director. "Lord, uh, well, thank Thee for the food we are about to—"

John cleared his throat. A rush of water rumbled the pipes. H rubbed his hands on his pants. "Yeah, well, thanks for all the good stuff you give us. Amen."

John handed H and I each a copy of *How to Be Your Own Best Friend.* "Because you haven't had a chance to read the book, I'll read an essay I wrote for my ministerial chaplaincy class to serve as an introduction."

I'd been going to Sunday school since we had moved in the second grade. I met Lauren at my new school. Her folks didn't want their daughter hanging out with a heathen, so they drove me to church every Sunday. We memorized Scripture verses, listened to Bible stories acted out on flannel boards, and sang songs with hand motions. Crafts meant glue and glitter. Once Lauren and I graduated into the high-school Sunday school class, we read and discussed books like *The Late Great Planet Earth,* which frankly had done more for my prayer life than just about any other book. I prayed earnestly for Jesus to stall his second coming long enough for me to get married and have babies, which started me praying for a boyfriend. I was still waiting for the answer to that prayer. My sophomore year, Mrs. Hinck made the girls read and discuss *The Richest Lady in Town.* For me, the book's enduring message had been to keep my toenails clean on the thin chance of meeting the author, Joyce Landorf.

While John read his essay, I looked over the book. First of all, it was skinny. That was good. And the type was large with many expanded paragraph separations. Even better. A smiling couple, the authors, sat close together for the back cover photograph. *Nice.* I flipped the pages. No Scripture verses quoted. No capitalized masculine pronouns. This wasn't a Sunday school type of book.

John rolled up the essay, *A+* side out, and used it to drum his knee. "So what do you think?"

I held up the photograph of the authors. "Are these people Christians?"

"Truth isn't limited to the Bible, Amy. Just because these folks don't write in the language of Christianese, don't discount the wisdom they've captured in the pages of the book."

"But Jesus is *the* way, *the* truth, and *the* life. This smacks of humanism." That last bit came straight out of the lips of my youth director in Gilbertsville when Garrett Walker admitted reading *I'm Okay—You're Okay.*

"Jesus said loving your neighbor as yourself is one of the two commandments we must keep," John countered. "You can't love others without loving yourself."

I fought to keep my voice even. "You can't truly love yourself if you don't understand the scope of God's love and sacrifice."

"Jesus wasn't the only Jew to die on a Roman cross, Amy. Did you know that?"

H rolled his eyes and stretched. The sleeves of his suit jacket rose to his elbows.

"You know what? I don't belong in this class," I said, standing. "I'm a college student. I only came as a favor to Mrs. Clancy. I don't want to dominate the discussion."

H stood up too. "I have enough credits to graduate early." He directed me toward the door. "Let's go."

THE AIR, COOLED by the rush of the river, settled on me like a sheet fresh from the clothesline. Along the shore a tumble of boulders provided stadium seating to watch the North Fork River cut a languid S across the valley floor. The water was Coke-bottle green where it rippled and foamed over pale stones and deepened to jade over shadowed depths. Beyond the treetops, the mountains lay like slumbering elephants.

H loosened his tie and draped his jacket over a boulder. "You owe me your life."

I lifted my face to the sun. My eyelids went red in the brightness. "You'd be back there becoming your own best friend if I hadn't said something." The sound of shifting rocks piqued my curiosity.

"I was about to fake a fainting spell," he said, hunting for something among the rocks.

I shielded my eyes to watch him. "Will you get in trouble?"

"Definitely." He lofted a stone the size of a volleyball into the river. "My dad will make me apologize to Johnny boy, and he'll dream up a job for me to do. Last time, he made me remove about twenty junipers from the backyard. I itched for a week."

"Thanks, then."

H muscled a rock out of the bank and tossed it into the middle of the river.

"Do you *have* to do that?" The stones of the river clacked like castanets as they tumbled under the rush of water. "The river is singing a song."

H hefted another melon-sized rock into the river. "What song?"

So listening to the music of nature wasn't H's thing. Maybe geography with a bit of speculation would stop his salvos. "Do you ever wonder how far the river will push a stone before it finds that one place where it fits and stays forever?"

Although H stood squinting against the bright sunshine, the question darkened his face. "There's no place like that, not for rocks and certainly not for humans."

My heart plunked like a rock because I knew what he'd said was true. Since receiving my acceptance letter from Westmont, I'd painted a picture of California as my refuge from Hurricane Mom. Her decision to move to California with me had already splattered that notion. What else lay between me and independence? It was a smart, forward-thinking question, but I didn't want to know the answer.

H flung his jacket over his shoulder. "Come on, I want to show you something."

I looked at my watch. "I should get back. Mrs. Clancy will wonder where I am."

"She thinks you're in Sunday school."

True enough. I lifted my skirt to climb up the bank. "Does this something have legs?"

His grin broadened. "You're just going to have to trust me, aren't you?"

Trust him? He'd just torpedoed my dream. "You're not wanted in more than three states are you?"

H laughed and shook his head, "Only two . . . that I know of."

Mom would be glad I asked.

WE SKIRTED A park and followed a two-lane road up a hill. The day was warming, and I regretted agreeing to the walk. Whenever I shook a stone out of my dress sandals, H reminded me of the importance of sturdy shoes. The land leveled at the top of the grade into hay fields dotted with freshly cut bales and a smattering of houses down gravel driveways, all with corrals for livestock—cattle, horses, goats, sheep. Left unpainted, the outbuildings stood gray and frail, something the Germanic farmers in Gilbertsville would have considered an abomination. And the farms seemed cobbled together from bits and pieces gleaned from other farms that had fallen on bad times. We turned up a narrow gravel lane lined with barbed-wire fences. A herd of goats munched on grass with their kids. All the while, H chattered on, updating me on the people who lived in the houses and farmed the land.

I stopped to shake yet another stone out of my sandals. "I should turn back. It's almost noon. My mother—"

"We're almost there."

"Mom won't like me getting home late."

"Let me carry those." H took my Bible and notebook. "Only fifty more yards to go."

We turned up a lane lined with tall hedges. Where the hedges stopped, a sign made of honed branches arched over the road, spelling out the word *cemetery.*

I groaned. "Honestly, H, I get plenty of exposure to death."

"You can see the whole valley from here. I thought you'd like to get the lay of the land."

The cemetery covered a wide slope. The upper slope, terraced by a maze of concrete retaining walls, lay brown and lifeless save for a few gnarled trees. A lush carpet of green peppered with dandelions covered the lower slope. H offered a pragmatic explanation of the disparity. "When they first started burying people up here, there wasn't irrigation water up this high. To a bunch of farmers, it probably seemed like a waste of water, seeing as they weren't growing nothing to take to market."

There was no more irresistible and dissatisfying read than a tombstone. My creative writing teacher back in Gilbertsville had walked us through the cemetery to collect a character for a short story. I chose a girl, not much older than me at the time of her death, with the romantic name of Virginia Mae Ratliff. I made her a brilliant yet homely girl born at the turn of the twentieth century. She died rescuing her mother of questionable moral fortitude from a burning saloon. My teacher had been kind enough not to point out the obvious autobiographical nature of the story.

In Cordial's community cemetery, the tombstone of Barbara Louise McCulloh caught my eye. The infant daughter of Gavin and Aileen McCulloh had been born February 26, 1943, and died on April 17 of the same year. Someone had pressed multicolored stones into the concrete curbing that bordered the family plot before the cement had hardened. The stones, misshapened as arthritic fingers, reached out of their encasement. No embellishment spoke more eloquently of loss. A cluster of irises with tight buds grew out of the dry earth just where the tiny body of Barbara Louise lay. A soup can, now rusted, had also been pressed into the cement. It served as a vase for a wildflower bouquet. The flowers could have been a gift from one of Barbara Louise's siblings, now a parent of school-aged children, or from her aging mother, still perplexed by the brevity of her baby's life.

H scratched at the dry earth with his incredibly sensible shoes. "The view is this way."

More weeds than grass grew in the lush section, but at the town founder's grave, peonies bloomed as big as pom-poms. H pointed out the grave of a recent graduate of Cordial High School who had been killed in Vietnam. A bouquet of red, white, and blue plastic carnations decorated his grave.

"His folks sold their place and moved to Florida. Mom says they wanted to be as far away from their hurt as possible." H tugged on my arm. "This is depressing. Let's go."

Below us, orchards like dark green corduroy padded the valley floor. Pastures and fields faded from springtime green to golden amber.

"That thick line of trees below us there, that's the river." H moved in close so I could follow the line of his arm. "See the railroad tracks there? Follow that up valley and you'll find Raven Mesa Coal Mine. Every train that comes out of there is 101 cars long, and do you know why? It's because the law says trains can only be one mile long. One hundred and one cars equals one mile. There's the high school. Under that scar on Logan Mountain is a hippie commune. What a bunch of nut cases. They grow pot and do as they please. They give each other stupid names, like Arrow and Sunshine and Rainbow. Can you imagine naming a poor kid Rainbow? Geez. Some of them even tried to homestead on Arnie Spengler's land. They put a teepee right over his spring. He said the hippies smelled worse than his granddaddy's pig farm, and there's nothing worse than a hog farm in the summer. Have you ever—"

"I lived in Illinois all of my life."

"Oh. I guess you have then. Straight across," H said, pointing to a mountain, "where you see the cut of a road, follow that up a bit, past where the road disappears through the rise, and that's where the woodsies are held."

I knew about woodsies in theory only. Being a good churchgoing girl like I was, I'd never received an invitation. Not that I would go if anyone had asked me, but I couldn't deny that Lauren and I had lingered after a basketball game or school play, waiting for an invitation to join every other senior down by the river where a bonfire blazed and the beer flowed. More than once Lauren and I'd eaten our way to the bottom of the ice-cream carton, lamenting our notoriety as the only senior girls watching *The Odd Couple* on a Friday night.

"Do you go?" I asked.

H toed the gravel. "Popular kids go."

"It's no great loss. You'd spend the whole next day barfing and wishing you could die. At least, that's what I hear."

From his wistful gaze, my consolation meant nothing to him. "Did they have woodsies where you came from?"

"Sure, but I didn't want to go."

"I'd do anything to be in the popular group."

"Anything?"

"Nothing stupid, but I'm tired of living on the edge of life. Since the first summer we lived here, I've been on the outside looking in. I had no way of knowing what siccing my dog on Jim Warner would cost me. Worse than that, I've been the object of every conceivable prank and joke since my freshman year. My name has become synonymous for *lame*."

"Whatever you did—"

"My dad says the guys were bored, that what they needed was a job to tire them out. Maybe then they wouldn't deface private property.

I got pretty sick and tired of repainting the sign for the store, so I waited for them out behind the store for three nights with my dog, Buster. On that third night, I watched a truck pull into the parking lot with the headlights off. The guys fell over each other, laughing and shaking their spray-paint cans. I figured they'd been drinking up their courage. Hearing them laugh like that made my blood boil. I sent Buster after them. He ripped Jim's back pocket off. Jim screamed like a girl.

"Jim and them would have thought it was my dad, but I couldn't help myself. I ran behind the truck, shaking my fist in triumph. Now I can't turn my back on anyone. They won't stop at anything."

"And you want those jerks for friends?" Irrational thought required desperate measures. I pulled out the speech I'd recited to myself a million times before. "Why? They're cruel, heartless, stupid, and a cliché. Someday, they'll come to you, begging for a job or to cure their glaucoma or treat their incontinence. They'll get fat and lose their hair, just like the rest of the world; only they'll wear ratty toupees and gold medallions, thinking they look cool."

"I'll tell *you* what. I'm getting on the football team this year."

I checked my watch and turned to leave, knowing H would follow. "You're not listening," I said over my shoulder. "A year from now you'll be heading off for college, and they'll be dreaming of the day they'll get a job at the coal mine so they can feed their wife and snot-nosed kids."

"The whole town comes out to watch the games. Even the theater closes down."

"And then the team drinks their brains out?"

"It's not just that. They do everything together. They go to the drive-in and hang out at Burger 'n' Shake. Camping. Fishing. Hunting. Everything." He sighed. "Cool."

"Think barf, H, lots and lots of it—chunky, burning barf."

"Jesus made wine. He probably drank it too."

"Wine was the safest thing to drink. The fermentation process killed parasites in the water."

"If Jesus was so concerned about their health, why didn't he make clean water?"

I didn't have an answer for him, and from the self-satisfied look on his face, H was enjoying himself. That didn't mean I was ready to surrender the point. "Alcohol lowers your inhibitions, messes with your coordination, and takes money away from more important things." I knew all of this better than I wanted to admit.

"It's a moot point. Nobody in this town is inviting me to a woodsy. They'd rather contract dengue fever or kiss their sister or—"

I heard my mother screaming from a block and a half away. From what little I knew of Portuguese, I was no longer a sweetheart.

H stopped to listen. "Boy, somebody's pretty upset about something. You'd think they'd close the windows."

My mother opened the windows when she ranted. An audience was an audience. I lifted my skirt to run home. "G'bye!"

Bonnie met me at the front gate. "I got a call from your neighbor. She said your mom was acting strange."

"Have you talked to her?"

"Your mother?" Bonnie shook her head.

"Have you heard her say my name?"

"Lots of times."

"I'm late getting home. I'm sorry. I'll take care of her. Go on home, Bonnie. When she gets like this, she needs time to settle down."

"She sounds so . . ."

Wild? Mournful? Psychotic? Like a spoiled brat? "I'm used to it."

"Is she, you know, all right?"

"She lets her imagination get the better of her. She'll be okay when she sees me."

"María Amelia Casimiro Monteiro, get your—" Mom yelled.

"I better go."

I started apologizing once I stepped through the kitchen door. "Mom, I'm so sorry. I was very thoughtless. It was such a pretty day."

"Change your clothes!"

I closed the kitchen window. "The funeral home opens in ten minutes. I don't think I should go anywhere."

She followed me into the chapel. "Change your clothes!" she screamed. I closed the window. H stood at the edge of the lawn, his face creased with concern.

"Mom, keep your voice down." I shook my head at H and mouthed that I would be okay. When he didn't move, I waved him off and turned to Mom. My words were a smooth lake on a windless day. "The car isn't getting dirty in the garage. We can wait until next—"

"Never! How can you be so thoughtless? I ask so little of you."

Really?

"You know what that car means to me. You're being hateful. You'd rather be with your boyfriend."

"All right!" I threw up my arms and headed for my room. "Me, a brat? You're the one throwing a temper tantrum because your car isn't going to be washed one week. Just one stupid week."

Mom grabbed my hair, and she nearly pulled me off my feet. "Don't you ever talk to me like that. Go change your clothes, Amelia."

I spoke from a new place, a fiery place that made me feel stronger. "Let go of my hair."

That stopped her in her tracks. "Oh, *fofa,* I'm so—"

I shook off her embrace to pull my dress over my head. "We don't have time. Get the cleaning stuff together. There's a bucket under the sink. And call Tommy."

TOMMY OPENED THE service bay doors and pushed the Pontiac out into the sunshine. "Need any help, Francie?" he asked.

In unison, I said no and Mom said yes.

Tommy looked from Mom to me and back to Mom. "I'll pull the hose around for you." Before he left, Mom talked him out of his spare key for the garage door, and he promised to return in an hour to push the car into the garage.

I told Tommy we would be done in twenty minutes. "You can come back whenever it's convenient for you."

WE FOUND MRS. Clancy sipping coffee at the kitchen table when we returned from washing the car. "Please join me," she said. It was more of a command than an invitation. I felt Mom's gaze on me, but I didn't look at her. Neither one of us took the time to pour a drink, even though my throat stung from the effort of washing the car in Cordial's dry air.

Mrs. Clancy fingered a large paperclip. "I thought I'd been very clear with you. Clancy and Sons has a long and prestigious reputation for excellence. We're trusted to treat the dearly departed with respect and reverence. Never in our fifty-five years of meeting the needs of our community has anyone ever complained about a ruckus coming from this home. I had my doubts about you, but I gave you a chance—"

Mom smoothed her hair. "I'm very sorry, Mrs. Clancy. Nothing like this will ever happen again. Isn't that right, Amy?"

"Sure."

Mrs. Clancy's eyes stormed. "Mr. Peterson passed away this morning. Poor Luann has been waiting since six this morning to call. By the time she finally got a hold of me, she was hysterical, said if I hadn't answered she was going to call Garrison's down in Clearwater. She wants one of the newer stainless-steel caskets with the leak-proof liner. I can't afford to lose a sale like that, and who knows how many more."

"It's my fault," I said. "I went for a walk on the mesa. It was such a beautiful day. I lost track of time."

"*And* you walked out of Sunday school with H," she said with her arms crossed over her bosom.

Mom frowned, but she didn't know I held the ace in my hand. Mrs. Clancy couldn't know about the inappropriate material being taught in Sunday school. "The teacher read from an essay he'd written for a class. The essay didn't even mention Jesus."

Mrs. Clancy blinked. "You can be sure I'll talk to Pastor Ted first thing in the morning." She circled the rim of her coffee cup with her fingertip. "H and his parents don't see eye to eye about church and Sunday school attendance. Most Sundays, they arrive at church looking like they battled every inch of the way. H hasn't worn his suit in over a year. I don't think this being your first Sunday with us was a coincidence, Amy. He's had a terrible time adjusting to Cordial. As another newcomer, you may be just what he needs to acclimate to our way of life."

I was about to tell her how tender H had been with Mrs. Masterson when she looked at me with the intensity of a she-lion protecting her cubs. "I won't have you breaking his heart."

Blecch! "Mrs. Clancy, I can assure—"

"H is older than you. He'll be eighteen in a week. His father caught him drinking by himself. Tore Herbert up, I can tell you. All I ask of you is to use your influence over H for good."

Mrs. Clancy looked to Mom who sat opening and closing a matchbook before she turned back to me with a look of pity. "Amy, I'm not an unreasonable woman," Mrs. Clancy said. "You're still a young girl. You need time for walks and friends and time on your own, especially with the hours your mother works. If you need extra time, please let me know in advance so we can avoid these kinds of problems in the future."

I would never make such a request, but I expressed gratitude for her thoughtfulness.

Mrs. Clancy pushed her cup to the center of the table. She spoke only to me. "I've been meaning to talk to you about an article I read in the *National Funeral Directors and Morticians Journal.* There's a new trend toward pre-need arrangements. I think it's a good idea. I've seen spouses, children, and parents crumble under the weight of the decisions they must make after the passing of a loved one. More times than I can count, they've looked to me with pleading eyes and begged me to take care of the decisions for them. Of course, I'm happy to do so, but then some of those people have insinuated that I took advantage of a difficult situation. Nothing could be further from the truth. The answer, then, is just as the article says—make those difficult decisions long before they're needed, when calmer minds prevail and without the pressure of time. Tell me, Amy, have you done any painting?"

Mom's head shot up. "Amy helped me paint the whole house last year—inside and out."

Mrs. Clancy ignored Mom's comments.

Mom stood. "Excuse me. I have many things to do before work tomorrow." That was the first and last time anyone had been able to ignore Mom's presence in a room. I was both awestruck and angry. Who did Mrs. Clancy think she was, anyway?

"The article suggested meeting with clients in a bright, sunny room, decorated like a living room rather than an office. If the big desk is moved from my office and the writing table from your bedroom is moved in, there should be plenty of room for two upholstered chairs and a coffee table." Mrs. Clancy held my gaze. "Whatever happened here today cannot happen again. Can I count on you, Amy?"

"I'll apologize to the youth director too."

"I expect you to keep the place clean and remain current on all of your other duties whether I'm here or not." Mrs. Clancy pushed her chair away from the table and stood, tugging her dress into place. "Now, go fix your hair and put on a clean dress. Mrs. Peterson will be here shortly to choose the finish for the casket. And Mr. Moberly will want his meatloaf sandwich."

Eleven

The outside of Lauren's package read, *"DO NOT OPEN THE PRESENT UNTIL YOU READ THE LETTER . . . OR ELSE!!!"*

Amy!!!!

I have so much to tell you. Life in Gilbertsville has gotten much more interesting, *but first, the boring stuff.*

Well, its official. I enrolled in classes at the Majestic School of Beauty. Mom wanted to drive me but I insisted on taking the bus to St. Louis by myself. I didn't want to be the only girl with her mommie at registration like I can't fill out my name and address. Honestly! Already I'm wondering if St. Louis was a good choice. You will understand why very soon. Keep reading!!!!

I quit my job at the Bait & Bite to work at a darling shop near the marina called La Chica Feista (Fiesta?) which means the party girl in spanish. My eye for fashion makes me a perfect sales girl and I don't smell like greasy fish anymore. Yeah!!!

STOP TO OPEN GIFT NOW.

What a choice. Either forge ahead to read the juicy news or open a gift that was sure to be something Lauren had shoplifted. Since Lauren exaggerated more than most, I pulled the yellow ribbon off and tore through the red tissue paper to find two Mexican blouses, one with royal-blue cross-stitches and puffed sleeves, the other sleeveless with pink stitching. I hugged the blouses to my chest as I read the rest of Lauren's letter.

Do you love them? Of coarse you do! Every one is wearing them. You can wear the blouses to spy on the hippys to see if everything people say is true. My father says they live like pigs and hate the United States but will happily live off welfare checks. Josie and Debbie (these two amazing college girls who are in Gilbertsville for the summer) say it is nothing for hippys to sleep (and you now what I mean) around. You can be like Harriet the spy. Remember? I sent our spy note book and a pen from the insurance office across the street. Please find out if the hippy girls shave their legs and under arms. I heard they don't. Gross! Without hygene we're no better than monkeys. That's what my dad says and for once I agree with him its a miracle!

NOW FOR THE BIG NEWS! I didn't tell you this first because I didn't want you to think I was braging or any thing but I'm DATING Andy Babcock. We were so wrong about him he is smart. He works at his dads motorcycle and lawn mower dealership. Its the one on the highway near the Husky station. Anyway thats why his finger nails are always dirty.

This is exactly what happened on our first date. We went to the movies to see the Strongest Man In The World. I hope Kurt Russell walks into my Soigné Salon (This is my new name for the salon its french because Andy took french until level 4! Soigné means polished and refined). I'm so sorry I took german. Anyway

Andy HELD MY HAND ALL THE WAY THREW THE MOVIE!!! Our hands got sweaty and still he didn't let go and he took me home in his dads boat and we sat on our dock until 1 in the MORNING talking about every thing accept for things just you and me talk about like cramps or hair. Ha! And here is the biggest news yet . . . He KISSED me. His lips were warm and soft but then he stuck his tounge in my mouth. YUCK! Don't believe a word about kissible lip stick. Nothing could survive a slime bath like that and if this is what kissing is all about I have to say I'm a little disappointed.

Your probably wondering why in the world did she go out with Andy in the first place? Well he delivered my fathers lawn mower after giving it a tune-up and he was very diffrent than what I remembered from school . . . only 3 weeks ago. He jumped in and out of the delivery truck like it was nothing and he smiled a lot. Did you know he has dimples? Now its your turn to find a boyfriend but H sounds like a nerd. Maybe you should wait until you get to California.

I miss you soooooooooo much it hurts.

Love,

Lauren

P.S. It kind of bummed me out that you gave the brooch to someone else. I'm not mad or anything. Is she nice? Is she your new best friend? That would kill me for sure.

Twelve

I recognized the fence of Underhill Manor homestead immediately. Made of cast-off windows, doors, and a collection of picket boards—some pointed, some blunt, all of them uneven—the fence mimicked a crazy quilt with doorknob charms and an ivy vine for the fancy stitches. Over the gate, a bundle of branches created a sort of arbor. A hand-painted sign with a border of white daisies leaned against the mailbox. "Feather's Fresh Eggs Sold Here." It was the friendliness of the sign that bolstered my courage to go inside unannounced, a sin anyplace east of the Mississippi River.

I stood behind a tangle of trumpet vine before approaching the log cabin. Weather had stripped the barn of color, except where someone had patched holes with salvaged lumber. The barn's hayloft gaped open over the double doors. Goats grazed in a paddock that had been reinforced with rope. No one would accuse Feather's log cabin of being anything but function with four walls. There were several mismatched windows and a door made of thick plywood. This wasn't the Ponderosa, that was for sure. Sitting on the door's threshold, a woman with flaxen hair breast-fed her baby as she sang, *"Hush little baby, don't say a word, Mama's going to buy you a mockingbird."* The woman had Feather's angled features, only softer. I knew immediately she was Feather's mother, although Feather called her by her adopted name, Butter.

A toddler leaned against Butter, watching his older brothers, twins from their bookend appearance, struggling to carry a split log. Had Feather not lamented being the only girl among four younger brothers, I might have puzzled over each child's sex. But not the twins. Even though they wore their hair cut as blunt as brooms below their collars, they swaggered with the importance of their task as only males can. The toddler's downy-white curls had yet to meet the scissors. Somewhere out of sight, the thwack of an axe against a wedge provided the beat for the humming bees around the lilacs and the chitter of birds in a lopsided tree.

I stepped into the sunlight. "Excuse me, is Feather home?" I held up the egg basket. "She left her basket at my house."

Butter waved me closer. "She'll be glad to see you. I'm charging her rent to use my basket."

"Butter," demanded one of the twins, "tell Frog to walk faster."

"Boys," she said, "I'd hate to see you miss lunch because the wood isn't stacked, and I mean for you to stack the wood neatly."

One boy dropped his end. His tongue thrust through the space where his front teeth used to be as he talked. "That's gonna take forever."

"It's up to you and Frog how long it takes, but Straw will be in for lunch soon. There's stew on the stove, and the bread's about ready to come out of the oven."

"Come on, Mule, I'm hungry," complained Frog. Mule picked up his end and the boys trotted around the corner of the cabin.

I set the basket at Butter's feet. "Please tell Feather that Amy stopped by."

She laughed. "The only time I get to sit down from sun up to sundown is when I'm feeding the baby and not always then. You're the only adult I've seen since breakfast. Don't make me beg you to sit in the shade and make pleasant conversation." She patted the stoop. "It's not a fancy seat, but it's the coolest one in the house."

Butter asked me questions about my family, how old I was, and how I liked Cordial. I told her about moving to California and the problems with the car.

"It sounds like your mom isn't all that excited about moving to California."

"I'll be living in the dorms." I said. "Mom's never lived alone before." I resisted the urge to tell Butter about my mother's obsession with our Pontiac, because even with all of the craziness that hovers around Mom, I have always felt loved—and smothered and exploited—and lately, resentful.

"Be glad your mother loves you enough to care." Butter bent to kiss the infant's head. "My husband's mother tells her friends that he died in a horrible car accident. She made a bonfire of his stuff on the driveway." Butter swallowed hard. "Straw doesn't have one picture of his old man."

I could have upstaged her with my dad story, but the light had left her face. "I'm sorry."

"Here," she said, handing over the infant. "I just learned a new braid. Let me try it out on you. Feather's hair is way too fine."

Butter disappeared into the cabin. I held the baby at arms' length, his feet dangling over my lap. He didn't have a neck and his eyes crossed. He burped a stream of milk that dribbled off his chin and onto his bib.

"Great."

The toddler leaned against me, just as he had with Butter. "Anybody will do?" I asked him, but he just continued sucking his thumb. From the cabin, Butter yelled, "The baby is Vernon. The toddler is Lamb."

"Neckless Vernon and yet another name that will be difficult to explain on the schoolyard. I'd complain to the management, if I were you guys." Before Vernon could spit up again, I laid him down the length of my thighs. He held my thumbs and pressed his pudgy feet into my stomach. "You better be careful, little man, you might end up with a name like Spit-Up or Fountain." I hummed the melody of "Jesus Loves Me." A fly landed on Vernon's forehead, and I blew it off.

Butter loosened my bun. "You have hair just like my sister. She absolutely hates it. She spent most of high school and college sleeping with her hair wrapped around orange juice cans. I envied her wild hair. Mine is so fine you can see my scalp." Butter bent to show me her scalp under her wispy hair. "Oh well, Sis is married to a nice banker, so she can afford to have her hair done every week before her bridge game. And here I am, the wild one, baking bread and making babies. Life is funny." Butter pulled the brush through my hair with deep, confident strokes. "Let me know if I hurt you."

Once she was satisfied that every knot in my hair had been loosened, she stood up to part and pull strands from the top of my head into tight braids. She worked toward my neck, gathering strands of hair as she went. Vernon arched his back and stretched with his fists knotted, his toes splayed. He mewed a complaint.

"What should I do?"

"Bounce your knees, but don't move your head."

"I don't know much about babies."

"Hold this," she said, guiding my hand to a clump of hair at my neck. "Now, I'll do the other side."

Butter explained how she made cash for her family by braiding hair at summer Renaissance and craft fairs where Straw sold leather purses and belts. "We trade for most of what we need within our co-op, but we still need bread for the mortgage and taxes, and I'm hoping to get Feather back to the doctor to adjust her meds. They don't seem to be working as well as they had before." She secured a braid with a rubber band. "Has she told you about her seizures?"

Sometimes Feather's eyes, nose, and mouth gathered as if they'd been lassoed with a rope and pulled tight. "When her face puckers?" I asked.

Butter laughed the way you do when something isn't funny at all. "Those are petit mal seizures. Feather puts on a brave face, but she cries when she thinks no one is around. It breaks my heart. They make fun of her at school, call her 'prune face.' That bothers her a lot, but what she really hates is being in special-ed classes. I fought putting her in the self-contained classroom for a while, but she can hardly read, which makes sense since she's, like, tripping out all of the time. Doc Marty told us half of the kids with petit mals outgrow them. The rest go on to have grand mal seizures." Butter's hands rested on the top of my head. "I don't know what we'll do if that happens."

This part of being an adult made my skin itch. Butter had peeled back the layers of her heart to reveal its most tender landscape, and I had nothing to say, no salve or Band-Aid to offer. Vernon's eyes grew heavy. I slowed the bouncing, and his body went soft. "Are the drugs expensive?" I asked.

"Very." She took Vernon from my lap and laid him in a cradle lined with white fur. "Come to the mirror to have a look at your hair."

I held a hand mirror and turned my back to the mirror over an enameled bowl that served as the kitchen sink.

"Do you see the heart?" she asked. "This is my best one yet. You look beautiful."

I avoided mirrors. No matter how hard I concentrated on Butter's handiwork, my eyes only saw what I hated most about me, my nose. Long. Full-bodied. Definitely not a Gidget nose. Mom harped after me to leave my hair down to soften my features. "You don't think the braid is too severe?" I asked.

"Your bun makes your head seem odd, you know, misshapen. You're an exotic beauty, Amy, with those green eyes and full lips." She took the mirror and returned it to a nail. Vernon sucked on his fist. "It looks like the little man is still hungry."

Butter settled into a rocking chair and pulled up her blouse.

"Do you want me to go outside," I asked.

"No way. Feather will be up from the henhouse soon to help with lunch. Why don't you help yourself to the cookies in the jar by the stove?"

Open shelves of jars, large and small, lined the kitchen walls. Some held things I recognized, like brown rice and brown sugar, but the dried leaves could have been anything.

"The big jar on the second shelf," she prompted.

"Your kitchen, it's so . . ." *Primitive? Rustic? In the middle of your bedroom and bathroom and dining room?*

"Rough, isn't it? Two summers ago, Feather, the twins, Lamb, and I stayed in Kansas City until our house sold. But Straw couldn't wait to build the cabin. That was the longest summer of my life. Take it from me: Never sell a house with twin boy toddlers running around. You'll shorten your lifespan by a decade."

The one-room cabin wasn't worth a decade of anyone's life. A plank counter served as the kitchen, and a picnic table of sorts was the dining table. No two chairs matched in style or color. Crocks held cooking utensils. Beyond the counter, the space shifted toward bathroom functions. A camping toilet hung from a hook on the wall—I didn't want to know anything about that—and a galvanized metal bathtub leaned against the wall. On the opposite end of the cabin, a bed and two homemade bunk beds were separated from one another with curtains hung from the ceiling. In the middle of the room, a braided rug covered the floor in front of the wood-burning stove. Several chairs, recently rescued from someone's trash, no doubt, sat around a keg serving as an end table.

"Our neighbors helped Straw with the cabin when they could, but it was a mad dash to get the roof on and the wood-burning stove installed before winter set in. We expected to add things, like walls and doors, and a bathroom would be heavenly. It's been harder to get to the luxuries than we'd thought. I shouldn't complain. Most of our friends have to go outside for their water. Straw sold his car to drill a well before we built the house. He read every issue of *Mother Earth News* before we left Missouri. Some of the information saved our lives. Other things made me wonder if the article was meant to be short fiction." Butter squinted down on a memory. "I can still remember the first time I saw the cabin. Straw was so proud of himself."

"Why don't you call him Woody?"

She smiled. "You'll know the answer when you see his beard."

Butter excused herself to put Vernon down for a nap. Lamb followed his mother behind a fabric drape, gripping her skirt and glancing over his shoulder. I waved and his face disappeared into the folds of her skirt. Butter spoke through the curtain. "I'm going to lay with Vernon for a while to get him to sleep. I'll be out in a minute."

"No problem."

I walked around the kitchen area with my hands behind my back, like I was in a store where the items were too expensive to buy. Only the open door and the windows allowed light to enter the cabin, so I instinctively looked for a light switch. There wasn't one. Instead, kerosene lanterns hung from the ceiling and sat on the dining table. No refrigerator, toaster, or television. I scanned the counters and shelves to see if I'd missed a radio, a music box, anything to fill the silence. I hummed the melody of "Softly and Tenderly, Jesus Is Calling."

Straw's woodworking reminded me of the function and simplicity—not necessarily the craftsmanship—of the Amish farm museum I'd visited in elementary school. Straw relied on plywood and two-by-fours, not the solid hardwoods of the northern forests. Finger holes worked as pulls for cabinets that opened on iron hinges. Butter kept food items in large jars. Some of the contents looked familiar but were definitely homemade—fruit leather, jerky, pickles, and cherry pie filling—while other jars held dried leaves. I screwed the lid off of one. The smell was familiar. *Oregano.* I shook my head. What was I expecting? Eye of newt? Marijuana?

When my stomach grumbled, I looked at my watch. 11:30. Six mismatched chairs stood around the table. I set a ceramic plate at each place and glasses cut from amber, brown, and green bottles. Flies buzzed in and out of the opened door, landing on the plates and glasses. *Eew.* I startled at the sound of boots on the front steps.

Unlike the other hippies I'd seen around Cordial, this man wore long sideburns tinged with red, but his face was clean-shaven. Sawdust clung to the hairs of his arms and his forehead. He stood bare-chested with his flannel shirt in his hand. His jeans rode low on his hips to reveal the gathers of his boxer shorts. I considered looking away, but I couldn't. His blond hair pulled into a ponytail made him look more typically male to me, more like someone who could step out of an Austen novel—earthy yet regal, definitely not a hillbilly wannabe.

"You're not Straw, are you?" I asked, my voice breathy.

"Nope, I'm hungry," he said and strode toward the sink.

I wanted to hear his voice again. "Is Butter expecting you?"

He laughed. "I'm helping her out today. A better question might be, is Butter expecting *you*?"

Butter said from behind the curtain, "He's okay, Amy."

The man worked the pump until a surge of water gushed into the bowl. He bent over to splash water on his face. The hard muscles of his back and shoulders reminded me of the farm boys back in Gilbertsville. Of course, the boys back home wore buzz cuts all summer, and I'd never seen any of them lather their faces, chests, and arms. I clamped my mouth closed when a fly buzzed too close. The twins appeared in the doorway. "Falcon's got a girlfriend," said one, and the brother joined in the sing-song taunt.

Falcon? Is this a zoo or a farm?

He spun from the basin, arms stretched high, his fingers arched into claws, his face masked by suds. He chased the boys with a throaty growl out into the yard. "And don't come back until the wood has been stacked, or I'll eat you for lunch, I will."

Butter padded into the room with Lamb on her hip and buried a kiss deep into his chubby cheek as she sat him on the floor. She tipped a basket of wooden blocks before him. "Make something pretty for me."

Falcon told Butter, "The twins will sleep well tonight. There's more than a cord of wood down there."

Butter thanked me for setting the table and invited me for lunch. I declined, saying I was expected at the funeral home. Honestly, my instinct was to run, and I would have done just that if Butter hadn't intervened. "You can't leave without seeing Feather. She'd never forgive me." Flour billowed when Butter spilled a heap of soft dough out of a ceramic bowl. "Falcon, you know how Feather gets. She's likely to be with her hens all day. Would you take Amy down to the henhouse?"

With a clean shirt and face, Falcon could have been a young Eric the Conqueror, he was that Nordic. North Sea eyes. Straight nose. Lots of white teeth. His arms swung loosely with his long stride. Not one hint of self-consciousness sullied the grace of his gait. I smoothed the front of the Mexican blouse Lauren had sent me, only to trip over an exposed root and stumble. Falcon caught me with a hand under my elbow. We walked past the barn and a vast vegetable garden. Falcon turned me away from the garden. "Let's go this way. It's easier." We swung wide of the barn and walked down a hill of tall grass dotted with purple flowers. To settle my pulse, I asked, "So how did you end up with a name like Falcon?"

"How did you end up with a name like Amy?"

"It's short for Amelia. And Falcon?"

"The twins came up with the name."

"So you're a predator?"

"It depends on whom you ask," he said and winked.

The wink was nice, playful, but he had used whom correctly. Doing so raised the tempo of my pulse and made my armpits sticky. An alarm went off in my head. This guy was a hippie. Who knew what kind of craziness he'd dabbled in.

"Listen, I hate to bother you," I said. "Just point the way to the henhouse. I'm sure I can find it. All that clucking, you know."

"It's no bother," he said and smiled.

I nearly whimpered. We walked toward a stand of trees. "Back home," I said, talking around my pounding heart, "the henhouses are closer to the barn."

"Straw got tired of the roosters waking the twins up at four in the morning."

Our eyes met. Falcon was smiling. His eyes squeezed down on an idea.

"What?" I asked, looking at my feet.

"You are a timeless beauty, Miss Amelia."

I covered my nose with my hands. Falcon stopped and pulled them away. "The people on Madison Avenue try to lay a trip on anyone who doesn't fit their definition of beauty. You have nothing to be ashamed of, Amelia. Your nose is perfect. Don't let anyone tell you differently. Your long neck. Those bedroom—How old are you, anyway?"

The place where he held my arm tingled. To make seventeen seem more mature, I told him I was going to be a freshman at Westmont College that fall. He wasn't impressed. In fact, his voice got hard.

"That's a Christian college, right?"

"You know it?"

"My dad offered to pay my tuition to any Christian college in America, so I could follow in the family business of saving souls." He lengthened his stride. I trotted every few steps to keep up with him. "So we have a nice Christian girl among us, do we? A virgin, no doubt. You *are* a virgin, aren't you?"

"I don't see how that's any of your business."

"So you *are* a virgin." He stopped. "Why? Why would a loving God who made you a sexual being deny you a source of great pleasure?

Does that make sense to you? If you're headed for college, if you want to be a scholar, Amelia, you can't be afraid to ask the hard questions." He continued toward the henhouse.

"You don't even know me," I said. "I *have* asked the hard questions, and it comes down to this: I trust God to know what's best for me, and I don't want to settle for anything else."

"My, my, that gives you a lofty seat from whence to judge. Have you come as a missionary to us poor, misguided hippies? Have you come to save us? Or maybe you're like the twelve spies sent into the Promised Land. What will you report back to the church ladies? Is the gossip true? I'd be careful, if I were you. You could lose your soul standing this close to a real hippie."

Part of what he said was true. I'd come with more than a bit of curiosity. After all, I wore the Mexican blouse and carried Lauren's notebook in my pocket. "I came to return Feather's basket. I met her mother and four brothers. It's been a pleasant afternoon, thank you. Now, which way to the henhouse?"

Falcon pointed down a trail through the trees. "Watch out for the rooster. His name is Spartacus, and he lives up to his gladiator name."

INSIDE THE CHICKEN yard, a large turkey greeted me with a puffy display of rust-and-white tail feathers. As handsome as his feathers were, his lumpy red-and-blue wattle gave him a face a mother would find difficult to love. I'd seen plenty of the white turkeys raised for the Thanksgiving table, but they lived in large buildings with attached yards. This turkey drew ever nearer until I chanced a touch of his feathery ruff. He nudged closer. I backed off. "You're not a rooster in disguise are you?" He shimmied his feathers to laugh off the idea. "Good, because I hear the rooster isn't so nice."

A clutch of hens as varied as stones in a stream, scurried around the corner of the henhouse. White. Black with white speckles. Tweedy hens of rust and black. The rooster strutted behind them, cocking his head in my direction.

"Feather?" I called.

The rooster scratched in the dirt and puffed his feathers.

Uh-oh. "Feather?"

Feather stepped out of the henhouse stroking a ginger-colored hen she held under her arm. Bits of straw stubble and feathers clung to her hair. "Don't worry. Pick will take care of Spartacus."

"Pick?"

"The turkey."

Spartacus stretched his neck to crow at the sky and sound the charge. Pick stepped in front of me, lowered his head, and countered the rooster's attack. It was clear these two had sparred before. Spartacus relinquished the fight to hightail it toward the outer reaches of the yard. Pick followed, all but scooping Spartacus along with his wings. When Spartacus made a move to dart away, Pick anticipated his move to block his escape, effectively holding the rooster in place.

"Pick loves girls. He'd protect you to the death. But let one of my rotten brothers come in here, Pick leaves them to Spartacus. All those scabs on Frog's legs? That was Spartacus."

Feather invited me into the henhouse. Rows of laying boxes filled with fresh hay lined one wall, and a roost like bleachers at a football stadium occupied another.

"Do you have to train the chickens to lay their eggs in the boxes?" I asked.

Feather laughed. "Nobody tells a chicken what to do. If they want to lay their eggs in the boxes, that's what they'll do. Usually, I have to hunt around the yard for their eggs. It helps that the hens are so prideful. They cluck and strut each time they lay an egg. The other hens join in. Everybody's happy when a new egg arrives."

Feather transferred the eggs from Butter's basket to hers. "You saved me a quarter for today's rent." She hung the basket over a nail and paused. She turned her inquisitive eyes on me. "Could we make a trade? When I delivered the eggs the other day, I noticed you sure have a lot of books. Are you any good at it, reading I mean?"

Reading was like breathing for me. "I'm okay."

"Do you think you could teach me?"

"Feather—"

"Don't say no yet. Think about it. I'll come to you so you won't have to walk to the farm."

I thought about Mrs. Clancy's reaction to Feather's last visit. "That wouldn't work. Besides, I enjoyed the walk."

"So you'll do it?" She nestled her cheek into the hen's feathery back. "It's just that some kids make fun of me. Not being able to read . . ." Feather's head came up. Her face contorted into a grimace, and her eyes drained of light.

"Feather?" And again I said, *"Feather?"*

Her eyes focused on me. "So you'll do it?"

I agreed to read with her two days a week until I left for California. She threw her arms around my waist and held me tight. I returned her hug. Her boney shoulders shook under my arms.

"Feather?"

"I'm going to love you forever."

"YOU BOUGHT A dress? Why would you do such a thing? The transmission could come from Denver any day."

"You can be such a *sapa*."

"Calling me a toad isn't going to put the money back in your purse. You have to take the dress back. You kept the tags, right?"

Mom lifted the skirt of the dress, admiring its fullness and the snug fit of the bodice. "It's too bad they don't wear petticoats anymore."

"You're not listening to me."

"That's because I didn't buy the dress."

Uh-oh. "Mom, you promised, you pinkie promised you wouldn't get mixed up with a man until we got to California."

"You said our pinkie pledges were null and void." She twirled in front of the mirror. "Besides, I'm not mixed up with anybody. Bruce is good to me. He knows how to treat me nice. He makes tons of money."

This was how her relationships started. The guy bought her a gift, and if the gift was nice, meaning something she could never afford to buy for herself, he was a winner. Without exception, the guy turned out to be a Trojan horse of trouble. Who knew what would spew out of Bruce?

"Bruce and me were walking down Main Street—"

"So everyone in Cordial knows about this guy but me?"

"He isn't like any other man I've known."

"They never are." I flopped on the bed.

"He talks about taking me places, exotic places, places I've never heard of. He's been to Hawaii and Mexico and that little island off the coast of California, the one they sing the song about."

"Catalina?"

"Doesn't that sound romantic?" She purred the island's name. "Catalina."

We'd been in Cordial less than four weeks, a new record for

Mom. The rest of her speech could have been cut and pasted from a dozen previous scripts. No one had met as many Prince Charmings as Mom, until, without fail, they'd all turned into wart-faced Rumpelstiltskins.

The doorbell rang.

"That's him." Mom smoothed the broad white collar of the dress. She bent forward and shimmied. When she rose, the swell of her breasts filled the neckline. "Fofa, go answer the door." She spritzed her neck, wrists, and the back of her knees with Tabu and shooed me toward the door. "And be nice."

I paused before closing the bedroom door. I glanced toward the tiara's velvet box on the dresser. "You're not thinking of wearing the tiara tonight, are you?"

"Bruce hasn't seen it yet."

"Then take a scepter, too, in case he gets fresh," I said and slammed the door closed.

Something menacing but not lethal hit the door behind me, probably a shoe.

Bruce stood beyond the glass of the kitchen door. I would have known him anywhere. Mom attracted his type like flies to buttermilk. With his chiseled-chin good looks and deep dimples, he couldn't see past his ego to picture his future as minced meat. Contrary to my instincts, I let him in. My eyes burned from his aftershave. Brut, what else?

With my back to the sink, I leaned against the cabinet and recited my script with words as flat as Kansas. "She wants to look nice for you, so she needs a couple more minutes. Would you like a drink of water?"

He shook his head, smiled uneasily. "This here's a real home, just like Francie said." He scratched the back of his head, popped all of his knuckles, and widened his stance, hands on hips, only to stand gape-jawed for lack of anything to say.

I took pity on him. "Run while you can."

He crossed his considerable triceps over his chest. "Say what?"

"The dress is only the beginning. I've seen it a million times. She'll take you for all your worth."

"The dress was my idea.'"

"Was it you or her who stopped to look in the window?"

Bruce studied the ceiling, rubbing his chin. He wasn't making this easy.

I said, "Look, as soon as a new transmission comes from Denver, we're out of here. It could be here tomorrow. I just don't want to see you hurt, that's all."

Mom turned off the radio in the bedroom, my signal to excuse myself and call her out. Before I left Bruce, I gave him one more thing to think about. "Keep an eye on your wallet."

His hand went straight to his back pocket.

Thirteen

The shed creaked as H did his chin-ups on the bar across the door. "Must do hundred," he said and lowered himself, only to heft himself into another chin-up. "Forty-one," he said through his teeth. "Count for me."

"I came to visit Mrs. Masterson."

"Forty-two. Helps me . . . forty-three . . . save energy. Forty-five."

"You skipped forty-four."

He groaned but pulled his chin to the bar again.

"Forty-five. Why are you doing this?" I asked.

"Football," he said through a grunt.

"Forty-six." Light shone through the slats of the shed. An odd array of equipment filled the small space. There were dumbbells made of broom handles and coffee cans filled with concrete, a row of tires, and a burlap sack hanging from the rafters filled with who-knew-what. "Forty-seven."

H's arms quivered with the effort of pulling his bulk toward the bar.

"Forty . . . eight."

H fell to the ground outside the shed's door and splayed on his back across the path. His spongy middle lay flat under his T-shirt. "Oh man, I did fifty yesterday."

I sat on a stack of tires by the door. "How long have you been doing this?"

"I emptied the shed for the Mastersons early this spring. We trade. I mow the lawn; she lets me use the shed."

"Do you talk to her?"

"She never comes out, if that's what you mean."

"You could knock on the door."

H seemed to consider that for a while. "I figured she wanted to be alone."

I'd figured the same thing too until Pastor Ted's sermon the day before. I'd never been fond of the book of James. Considering trials pure joy. Celebrating humble circumstances. Persevering through trials. James's writing reminded me too much of my P.E. teacher, Miss Gustafson. "Girls, your body is a machine. Put bad food in, you can expect poor performance. I can tell by the way you run that most of you didn't have a well-balanced breakfast this morning." During this part of her speech, she had frowned at Lauren and me until her caterpillar eyebrows touched in the middle. "I mean protein, carbohydrates, dairy, and fresh fruit. It's for you to decide right now. *Will my machine be finely tuned and strong, or will I wear queen-sized panty hose the rest of my life?* Now get up and run your hearts out."

When Pastor Ted read from James, Mrs. Masterson's face came to mind. Seeing as she was the most recent widow of Spruce Street church, I figured everyone from church had already beaten me to the front door.

H stood and brushed the dirt from his clothes. "Hand me that Thermos." He shook the plaid container vigorously and chugged the contents. He swiped his mouth with the back of his hand and swallowed hard. Tears welled in his eyes.

"Do I want to know what you just drank?"

He swallowed again. "Raw eggs and Tabasco. Protein."

I shivered. "Gross."

He struck a John Wayne pose, hands on hips, head cocked. "Yup, gross all right."

I ignored his swagger. "What did you think of Pastor Ted's sermon yesterday, what he said about widows and all?" Part of me wanted to make him feel bad for being so self-absorbed he'd forgotten to visit Mrs. Masterson. The other part hoped H had already discovered a biblical loophole he'd be willing to share.

"I don't know."

"Don't you think we should visit Mrs. Masterson in her time of distress?"

He tossed a football up and down, up and down. "I . . . uh . . . I . . ." Was this the same guy who had opened his arms to Mrs. Masterson and wrapped Dr. Masterson in a shroud?

"Never mind. You stay out here and toss your football. I'll check on her." I skidded to a stop on the gravel driveway. All I had to offer her were some Junior Mints that had been in my purse since the night before, a gift from Mom's lover boy, Bruce. "Help me pick some of these flowers."

H smiled and obeyed. By the time I stood at Mrs. Masterson's door, H was setting up an obstacle course of tires. The bouquet of dandelions wilted in my hand. *Pathetic.* The doorknob clicked. I tossed the bouquet over the porch railing.

"Hello, Mrs. Masterson, I thought I'd stop by to say hello, but if you're too busy . . ."

"Amy, isn't it? Come in, come in."

I HELD MY breath as Mrs. Masterson set the tray on the parlor table with trembling hands, laden as it was with a teapot, cups, and saucers. A smear of lipstick colored her front teeth. "Oh dear, I didn't bring the sugar bowl. Do you take sugar, my dear?"

This was my first hot tea. "No, I like it brown."

A breeze tickled the leaves of the trees outside and creaked the rafters, but the windows of the parlor remained closed. My forehead dampened and my blouse stuck to my chest. Mrs. Masterson wore a sweater draped over her shoulders. Hot tea sounded awful. The cup jostled on its saucer as Mrs. Masterson poured the tea. I crossed my legs at my ankles and tucked them under the chair just as my home economics teacher had taught us. I regretted wearing my flip-flops and shorts.

All the typical accoutrements occupied the parlor. Doilies. Marble-topped tables with knobby legs. Deceptively uncomfortable velvet chairs. What I hadn't expected were cobwebs in every corner and the dust that dulled the sheen of the furniture. On the mantel, candles slumped like sleeping sentries on either side of a crystal bowl dulled by dust. This was a new awareness—this dust-free expectation—that working for Mrs. Clancy had created. When I got to know Mrs. Masterson better, I would offer to bring a duster and some of Mrs. Clancy's furniture polish.

"Next time you come," she said, "I'll have cookies."

"I should have called first."

"Don't be silly. Your kindness to Arthur and me makes you a welcomed guest at any time." She sipped her tea and I copied her. Every book I'd ever read about the English made tea the cure-all to every human dilemma. Rain soaked? *Drink a cup of tea.* The house burned to the ground? *Won't you have some tea?* Your cat died? *Oh, let me put the kettle on.* What the English drank could not have resembled what Mrs. Masterson served that day. The bitter brew stripped the enamel clean off my teeth.

"Is the tea too strong? That's how Arthur liked it. I guess I've gotten used to it."

I appreciated how Mrs. Masterson spoke her deceased husband's name without sniffing and grabbing for a tissue. I touched the tea to my upper lip without sipping.

"You're very young, but you'll discover soon enough how a woman gets used to so many things when she has lived with a man as long as I lived with Arthur. Men have their ways, but women do too." She shifted as if to rise. "Let me get the sugar." Mrs. Masterson teetered.

"Oh no, please don't. The tea is perfect." I figured ten tablespoons of tea remained in the cup. I remembered H chugging the raw eggs. "What's the sense in drinking tea if it isn't robust?"

Mrs. Masterson laughed. "You sound just like my Arthur." She lowered her eyes. "It's a terrible thing to confess . . . I loved Arthur as much as a woman can love a man. I believe he was God's sweetest gift to me in this lifetime." She raised her eyes to meet my gaze. "But it's a relief, really, that he's gone. I can sleep through the night and not wake with a start, wondering if he is still here or not." She set her cup in its saucer. "During the night, I would touch his chest. When it rattled under my hand, I knew he was alive, and I would dose off again."

I gulped a mouthful of tea.

"And then that night, the night Arthur finally left me, I was so tired. I'd climbed up and down the stairs for anything he needed. He wouldn't eat, so I prepared all of his favorite things. He showed no interest at all. Finally, I dipped my finger in honey and spread it over his lower lip. That he sucked off, so I felt a bit better. Before I turned the light off, I told him if he needed anything, anything at all, I would get it for him. He said, 'Just hold my hand.' I slept through the whole night, didn't wake once. In the morning, he was gone. I should have sat up, I suppose, and kept the light on to stay awake."

She spoke the words as a statement, but she meant them as a question. "I hope I have someone like you to take care of me when I'm sick," I said.

Mrs. Masterson sighed and gazed out the window. What she saw made her smile, so I turned to see H catch his foot on the rim of a tire and hit the ground hard. He looked over his shoulder. I turned back to Mrs. Masterson. Her hand covered her smile. "I don't think he can see us." She winced, "Oh no, there he goes again."

Like a goose flapping its wings to take off, H hopped with waving arms through the tires.

"Males are a determined lot, aren't they?" asked Mrs. Masterson, blotting her mouth with her napkin. "But then they have to be, what with taking chances to make things better for their families. Whatever poor H is working toward, no doubt he will achieve it. My Arthur was like that. If anyone, and it was usually me, told him a dream was impossible, he kept at it until he proved me wrong."

With Mrs. Masterson occupied watching H out the window, I tilted my head back to empty the cup of tea, something Lizzy Bennet never would have done. That was when I noticed the yellow stains on my hands from picking the dandelions. "Do you like to read, Mrs. Masterson?"

Her eyes lit from within. "Follow me." We paused at double oak doors. "Arthur saw his patients in this room until he retired. That was more than twenty years ago. He treated every last one of Cordial's residents, but he held a special place in his heart for the coal miners and their families. The men came to him broken from accidents or with their lungs clogged with coal dust. Arthur worked and worked to improve ventilation in the mines. Testified before Congress, he did. It's quite ironic that he died of lung cancer. He'd never smoked a day in his life." She pushed open the doors. "Now this is my reading room. I didn't spend much time in here during Arthur's illness. Before that I read at the end of every day. Now I read in the morning when the light is strong and my eyes are at their freshest."

Books crammed the shelves of one entire wall, and books that couldn't fit in vertically were piled atop the rows. Beside an overstuffed chair, stacks of books completely covered a tabletop near the window. My heart beat excitedly. I recognized many of the titles from literature courses. Others were intriguing strangers.

I took *Sense and Sensibility* out of my bag and held it out to Mrs. Masterson. "Would you like to read this? I love Jane Austen's books. Even though I know she's making fun of the gentry, I crave the kind of civility she lived."

She took the book. "Even when her characters are being complete scoundrels, they use such pretty words." We shared a laugh. She flipped through the pages of the book. "You've read this many times."

I admitted to buying the book used but also that I'd read it at least a dozen times.

"How sweet of you to lend such a dear book. I promise to take good care of it. My copy disappeared years ago. I may have loaned it to a friend or one of Arthur's patients. But now I must share one of my favorites with you." She ran a finger along the spines of the books. The skin of her hands was transparent like waxed paper, and a dark bruise as big as a plum marked her wrist. "Something more recent. A story you will carry with you always.

"This was my mother's copy of *Sister Carrie*," she said, tilting the book and biting her lip in concentration. "My father made her throw the book away. I dug through the trash heap until I found it. A significant book to be sure, but not what I'd recommend for summer reading." She slid *Sister Carrie* back into place and continued to finger the spines of the books. "Yes, this is it, *My Àntonia* by Willa Cather. Have you read it?"

Had I? "I don't think so."

"Perfect. I was born in Nebraska, and I can tell you Willa Cather gets it right. You'll be transported back to a simpler time where women had to be as strong as men . . . and they still do," she said and winked.

"I'll start the book tonight." I checked my watch. "I need to leave soon, but I have time to help you with the dishes, Mrs. Masterson."

"Now that we're exchanging favorite books, you must call me Leoti, and then I'll let you help me."

Stacks of pastel casseroles covered the kitchen table and vases of perishing flowers filled the countertop. "Oh my, I should have brought you something for dinner," I said.

"You should have done no such thing. My friends have been wonderful, even the ones I've tangled with on the elder board. I'll never eat all the food they've brought, and some of it I wouldn't want to." She smiled and filled the sink with water. I started to relax. She was stronger than she looked. "The book and visit are the best gifts you could have brought. Folks are comfortable dropping by a meal, and I must admit, I'd done the same when others have lost dear ones, but it's difficult for friends to sit and chat. Everything we think to say seems terribly trite. And I know they loved Arthur too. I suppose in time . . ."

Leoti's hands stilled in the water. "Only you and Pastor Ted have truly come to visit. H hasn't been in the house. Poor boy, I see him staring at the house, his eyes watery with tears, and I start to go out to him, but then I think of my boys. They hated being caught expressing any kind of emotion. Do you suppose men believe they'll melt if they shed a tear or two?" Caught in a memory, she shook her head.

"Leoti?"

She leaned heavily against the sink.

"Please rest while I finish washing the dishes." I said. "It's the least I can do."

Fourteen

"That's exactly what August feels like." Feather lifted the book from my lap where I'd let it settle to absorb the author's true words. "Keep reading," she said.

"I'm here to help *you* read. That's what I promised Butter, so you have to try."

"I will," she said, burying her face into the ginger-colored feathers of a hen.

Clearly, Feather had no intentions of reading in front of me, but that suited me fine. I loved to read and she loved to listen. I'd declared the henhouse too hot for reading or thinking, so we sat along Terry Creek, nothing but a trickle, really, that watered the stand of trees and provided drinks for the deer that roamed the mesa at dawn and dusk. Feather had propped two faded sofa cushions against a cottonwood.

Honestly, I didn't have a clue how to teach anyone to read, so I held Feather's finger to follow under the words as I read. If I felt her hand tense, I stopped until she relaxed and the seizure passed. This happened less and less the longer I read.

To get dibs on new books at the library, I'd volunteered to shelve books after the summer reading program. Each week elementary-aged children returned a hundred or so books, only to check out a hundred more. The children flitted from shelf to shelf, like honeybees hunting nectar. When they found a new book by Maurice Sendak or Madeleine L'Engle or Richard Scarry, they hugged the books to their chests and buzzed about for another treasure.

The children reflected the divergent population of Cordial. The ranch boys came with snowy-white foreheads from wearing their cowboy hats. The ranch girls dressed in Wranglers and boots, just like the boys. The coal miners' children wore striped T-shirts with cut-offs, while the townies wore coordinating outfits—the girls in Good & Plenty colors, the boys in blue and brown. The hippie children dressed in secondhand T-shirts and pants that seldom matched. Boxes of shoes were kept under the check-out counter for the children who showed up barefooted.

One urchin noticed me looking at her patched jeans. She said, "It's foolish to pay full price for clothes. The markup is obscene." Her tie-dyed T-shirt made her a colorful parrot of her parents' ideology. Even so, I squirmed in my matching Woolworth's shorts and T-shirt.

It didn't matter what they wore or what they said. None of the children returned all of the books they'd borrowed, and all of them read with sticky fingers. Dealing with self-righteous nine-year-olds and rough-and-tumble boys was a small price to pay for reading *Tuck Everlasting* with Feather.

I closed the book.

"You can't stop there," she said. "How can a woman look the same for eighty-seven years? And her husband is so unhappy. Do you think there's magic in that spring?"

I dropped the book in my bag. "You'll know in a couple days."

"I won't know until Monday. You're stuck at that stupid funeral home." Feather clasped her hands to plead. "Please, one more chapter. They're awfully short."

I flipped through the pages of chapter three. "Okay, but this is the last one." When I finished reading, Feather said, "I've thought of running away like Winnie."

"Where would you go?"

"Somewhere without brothers."

I laughed, but I'd settled on my own plans to run away from Cordial. Mom's new boyfriend, Bruce, hadn't taken my warning. He came for Mom most nights. They went dancing in Clearwater or played cards with Bonnie and her boyfriend, Louie, at her place, never at the funeral home. I called Bonnie's boyfriend Louie the lobster because his eyes were small and black and his claws explored her constantly.

I'd begun to worry a new transmission would never arrive for the Pontiac, and truthfully, I wasn't sure Mom would drive away from Cordial if it did, so I'd made a call to the Greyhound Bus Depot in Clearwater. My plan included H driving me to Clearwater for a two-day trip to Santa Barbara, California. If that required me to kiss H, I would. Getting to Westmont from the bus station was the problem. I supposed a large place like Santa Barbara would have buses, but that meant managing my luggage on my own—one suitcase, a book bag, and a guitar.

A man in overalls jumped from behind the tree with a ferocious growl. Feather and I shrilled. He tilted his head back, hands on hips, and laughed. His sun-bleached beard and hair fanned out from his face like an unkempt mane. Butter had been right. There was no better name for him than Straw.

Feather jumped up to scold him. "You almost scared us to death."

"I'm so very sorry," he said, crossing his fingers.

"You're not one bit sorry, or you'd stop doing it."

"Like I've promised you, daughter of mine, I'll stop scaring you when you stop squawking like your chickens. Until then, it's too much fun."

Feather stomped her foot. "My chickens don't squawk."

"Really?"

"You know they don't."

Although I'd never seen Straw and Feather together, this surely was a common exchange between the father and daughter. The glint each held in their eyes gave them away.

"You better introduce me to your friend."

"You know who she is."

I introduced myself anyway. His hand smothered mine.

He said to Feather, "Butter sent me down here to get you. The laundry's about ready to be hung on the line. The sooner you show up, the sweeter her disposition will be. You know how your mother loves laundry day." And having heard Butter curse over the grease-stained and mud-encrusted overalls Straw usually wore, I feared her disposition would only sink further.

"Don't forget where we left off," she said, running toward the cabin.

Straw eyed the cushions. "I don't think Butter's going to appreciate her cushions being down here."

I jumped up. "Let me brush them off."

Straw laughed again. "I've never seen those cushions before. Feather probably traded eggs for what somebody was going to toss out. She's quite a wheeler-dealer."

I promised myself to be more skeptical around Straw.

"So, Amy, I hear you're headed for college." He shook his head at a memory as we walked toward the cabin. "You're headed for the adventure of a lifetime, but I wish somebody had told me to be careful who you listen to. There's a lot of wackos out there who'd love to sell you a bill of goods."

Was this the stove calling the kettle black? "How so?"

"You head off to school thinking, *I'm going to show my old man and my old lady how to live.* You picture yourself in a big ol' brick house overlooking the river and a fancy-dancy car in the driveway. Then you graduate and get that job that's going to pay for all this luxury, only it's bone-crushing boredom from sunup to sundown. You go home, check out what the neighbor has parked in his driveway, you kiss your kids goodnight, and then you get up to do it all again the next day, just so some fat cat at the top of the heap can jet off to his villa somewhere.

"Butter and I looked down a long road to our future and asked, *Do we want to be sitting at a desk all of our lives, worried about keepin' up with the neighbors, and attending Christmas parties year after year with people we don't like because we owe a monstrous mortgage on a house we can't really afford?*

"The minute we stepped away from our jobs, the freedom bell started tolling. We're no longer slaves to fourteen-percent inflation and waiting in line for gas. Out here, it's man—and beautiful woman—against nature. That's pure, real pure. No phone. No television. No radio. And we aren't missing a thing. The world can go to hell in a handbasket, and we'd never know it. We have our own little piece of heaven right here at Underhill Manor. I see my kids all through the day, and they're learning to cooperate and help out the family."

We crested the hill to find Butter and Feather shaking a sheet so hard it snapped before hanging it on the clothesline. Straw stopped to admire the scene. "And I like the spontaneity of living on the land. No one has phones, so our friends drop by when they want to borrow something or need help. That's friendship based on meeting needs, not on competition. When it came to setting the purlins for the roof of the cabin, I rounded up six men to help me, right on the spot, no questions asked. I couldn't get anyone to help load up the moving trailer back in Kansas City."

Butter scooped a squalling Vernon off a blanket to hand to Straw. "If you're going to make the biggest mess of your clothes," she said, "the least you can do is change the baby."

Fifteen

With her glasses perched on the end of her nose, Mrs. Clancy inspected my work. "I didn't expect you'd finish so quickly." She scratched at a dot of paint on the woodwork. "You'll have to remove this spot with mineral spirits. Is there any left?"

"Almost the whole can."

"That's excellent. You've been frugal with your supplies. The room looks very nice, Amy. I've ordered some of those open-weave draperies and two crushed-velvet swivel rockers from Penney's. My sister-in-law, who fancies herself an interior decorator, insists they're what everyone's buying these days. I'm sick to death of avocado green, so I ordered the harvest gold. Everything will be in by the end of next week. Then the room will be ready for clients."

I filled my arms with drop cloths and rollers to store in the garage, but Mrs. Clancy kept talking. "The Founder's Day celebration is taking place in the park today. I met the gals there for breakfast this morning. The Optimists served up pancakes, ham, and eggs." Mrs. Clancy looked like she'd eaten a worm. "Since

Hector Langston took over the Founder's Day committee, they've been using those powdered eggs, and I can tell. I have an extremely delicate palate."

"I read about Founder's Day in the paper," I said, but I'd known about the craft fair for several weeks. Feather's family considered Founder's Day the kickoff to their craft season, and a good craft season meant mortgage payments through the long winter.

"It's mostly stuff the hippies make," she said, not bothering to hide her disdain, "but a few ladies from church are selling crocheted work for their mission circles."

Typical. Something festive was happening in Cordial, and I was a prisoner of the dead. I would have to remember to write that down in my journal. *Prisoner of the Dead* would make a great title for a book.

"I suppose your mother has plans for the day," said Mrs. Clancy.

"She's gone to Orchard City with Bonnie to the drag races." Actually, it was a double date with Bruce and some burly guy Bonnie mooned over like a teenager, but Mrs. Clancy didn't have to know that. At least Mom didn't seem to think so.

"I'm not surprised one bit that your mother has paired up with Bonnie Luptovic, that silly girl. Her mother died of a broken heart, I'm sure of it."

Adults were sure of everything. Mrs. Clancy opened her wallet. "They have food booths at the park." She pulled out a five, changed her mind, and took out three crisp one-dollar bills. And then she did the last thing on earth I expected of her. She handed the money to me.

"Do you need something at the store?" I asked.

"No, this is for you. A treat, you know, for doing a good job. You never can tell. You might find something nice for your dorm room and help missions."

I was all for African children learning about Jesus, but I'd seen a preview of the mission circle's crocheted poodles. No thanks. "I have to stay—"

"Fiddlesticks. You've finished your work for the day. I have some paperwork to do, orders for Charles, things like that. Clean yourself up. Spend an hour . . . or two at the park. Being out in the fresh air will do you good." She lowered her voice and put her hands on her hips. I hadn't known Mrs. Clancy all that long, but I knew this stance. It meant, *This may sound like a friendly suggestion, but it's meant to be the eleventh commandment.* "I wouldn't have anything to do with the arts and crafts fair. A group of hippies started that whole affair a few years back. They should call it Sodom and Gomorrah for all the free this-and-that and the contempt they have for the law. You might as well walk through a pigpen on a hot summer day."

She thought I was hesitating, but I was measuring the cost of telling her what I'd learned of the so-called hippies and their hospitality. From the set of her bristly chin, nothing I could say would change her mind. Mrs. Clancy stepped around the paint cans and ladder. She stopped at the door. "I fancy the pink poodle toilet paper covers Alice Frank crochets."

BACK IN GILBERTSVILLE, I had played guitar with the Basement Beacons, a folk-bluegrass-gospel group. Don't go picturing me on *Hee Haw* or the *Grand Ole Opry* playing frenetic renditions of hymns and singing with a vinegar voice. I sang as an alto, thank you very much. We were invited to perform at all kinds of events in Gilbert County. We opened the Walleye Weekend and entertained folks before the fireworks on the Fourth of July. When my church held a baptism at the river, I sang "Nothing but the Blood of Jesus" until every sinner got dunked. I was the youngest member until Bud, the fiddle player, invited Lauren to play the tambourine.

Betty Jane Cope, an ant of a woman with the intensity of a bulldog, was our dulcimer player. Although the instrument looked like a stretched peanut, the dulcimer sounded like a harp and a banjo with a bit of mandolin thrown in and served as the true voice of our group. While the rest of us chimed in on our guitars, fiddles, and basses, Betty Jane sang lead on her dulcimer with her strong, swift fingers.

I followed the song of a dulcimer at the Founder's Day celebration to a booth where a man with a black tumble of hair played "Amazing Grace." When he finished, he stroked the dulcimer like a sleeping cat while he answered questions from the gathered crowd. To explain how he'd come to be a dulcimer maker, he said, "I found me some used books from the 1900s, so these little darlin's are the real thing. I use walnut and cherry mostly, and I guarantee this will be the loudest instrument at the party or your money back."

"Now I'm not saying I'm ready to buy one today," said a man with his arms folded over his chest and his chin tucked in like he was looking to haggle for the man's prized heifer, not buy a piece of art that sang like an angel, "but just supposing I ordered one of your instruments today. How long would it be until I held one in my hands?"

"I'm a one-horse operation. During the summer, I'm on the road a lot, selling and playing, going to these little backwater shows. That's where I find my customers. Anywho, you could expect your dulcimer by the first of September or there 'bouts."

The husband exchanged a look with a woman I assumed was his wife.

The dulcimer man sat with his instrument across his lap. "Let me play fer ya a little more while you make up your mind." He picked and strummed "Just a Closer Walk with Thee." I almost swooned.

All he needed was the strum of my guitar to lay a thick blanket of harmony beneath his melody. My fingers itched to play. Before the man finished his song, I left the booth. If the couple decided against the dulcimer, I would be embarrassed for the maker for missing a sale and embarrassed for the couple for not knowing real quality when they heard it.

The broad canopy of trees mottled the jumble of booths in John Kretlow Park. Canvas awnings heaved a sigh with every gust of the breeze. Craftspeople competed for the attention of shoppers strolling between the booths with free samples of fragrant oils and fresh-baked breads. Incense sweetened the air along with cotton candy and the hot dogs grilled by the Rotarians. I admired the needlework of a young woman until I recognized the marijuana leaves sewn onto everything from scarves to bandanas to baby bibs. I refused a flier she offered about legalizing pot and moved on. Leather and suede—purses, belts, hair clips, and hats—clogged every other booth, which reminded me to look for Feather and her family.

As usual, Feather found me. "Where have you been? I've been looking for you all day. Come see our booth."

She dragged me past a smoothie booth with whirring blenders and the ambrosial scent of strawberries and bananas. I promised myself to return with the money Mrs. Clancy had given me. Straw and Butter sat under a pitched tent of orange, green, blue, and purple. On one side, belly dancers gyrated for money tossed into a hat. On the other side, women bent over a velvet-covered table full of handmade jewelry. Their husbands stood several paces back, shifting their weight from one leg to the other. I thanked Jesus that Lauren wasn't there. All those trinkets would have been way too tempting for her.

"Let me braid your hair," offered Butter after she had hugged me to her bosom. "Customers are bolder if they see me working on someone else." She gestured to a board covered with photographs of braided hair. "Choose the style you like." She charged five dollars.

"I only have three dollars."

"Silly girl, there's no charge for friends and family."

My chest warmed. I pointed to the picture I liked, small braids that began at the hairline and attached like hands over a flow of loose hair down the back. She told Feather, "Go find the twins. They're probably terrorizing the toymaker from Telluride."

Feather turned to run off.

Butter called after her. "Wait! Pick some of those purple flowers we saw by Carolyn's booth for Amy's hair."

Butter's brush stopped mid-stroke. Her breath warmed my ear. "I don't know what you're doing with Feather, but she won't leave me alone about going to the library every other day. She reads to her chickens and swears they lay more eggs."

A woman stopped to watch Butter work my hair. "Oh my, your hands just fly through her hair. My mother braided my hair every morning before school. We sat in front of the stove in the kitchen. It was the warmest place in the house."

"I could braid your hair," said Butter.

"Really?" The woman touched her head. "It's not too short?"

"I can braid hair of any length."

"I'll be right back. I just have to tell my friend where I am."

Butter patted my shoulder. "See what I mean?"

I STOOD IN line for a smoothie, trying to decide on mango, which I'd never tasted, or sticking with my all-time favorite, pineapple. A tap on my shoulder made me jump.

"I owe you an apology," Falcon said.

"You do?"

"I wasn't very nice to you the other day. I made some assumptions about you. Anyway, I hear you've been helping Feather."

The smoothie woman bent over the counter of her booth. Her hair was almost as unruly as mine. A hairnet would have been nice. I regretted choosing a smoothie over a falafel pita. The guy cooking falafels was bald.

"Definitely go with the mango," Falcon said.

The woman peeled the mango with easy strokes of her knife and added a banana and apple cider she declared *organic* and *unfiltered*, both terms I'd heard repeatedly since landing in Cordial but didn't have a clue to their meaning. I could have asked, but I figured once I escaped Hippieville, as Mom had come to call Cordial, I would never hear the words again.

Although I kept my eyes on the woman making my smoothie, Falcon's presence made my skin hum. I liked the way he looked at me, approving and welcoming. He touched my shoulder and spoke in my ear to be heard over the whirling blades of the blender. "I need to get back to my booth. I have an extra chair if you'd like to sit in the shade while you drink your smoothie," he said and left.

When I'd been left alone while Mom had worked or gone out with one of her zillion boyfriends, I had entertained myself blowing out the pilot light on the stovetop and relighting it with various flammable objects, starting with matches and moving on to rolled-up papers and shish-kabob skewers. From numerous visits by firemen to my classrooms, I had known the game to be dangerous, but I couldn't—and I still can't—explain the trill of excitement that pulsed just below my heart when the flame *whumphed* to life. And now there was this invitation from Falcon. The same trill resounded within me. Red flags waved. Whistles blew. Bells sounded alarms. But I followed him anyway.

To display his wares, Falcon had hinged glassless French doors together. A stained-glass sun catcher hung inside each mullion. Their beveled frames split the sun's light into prisms that swept over the crowd of people sauntering by. A purple columbine. A cabin in the woods. Snowy mountain peaks. My art class attempt at stained glass had resulted in blobby mounds of solder and an amoeba-like sun. So precise were the joints of Falcon's stained glass that the lead cames disappeared, leaving only the movement of the watery glass.

"They're beautiful. Just beautiful," I gushed, and my face warmed.

"It would seem from the surprise in your voice that you've been making some assumptions yourself."

"I . . . uh . . ."

He waved my response away. "Don't worry about it."

Falcon helped a woman looking for a hostess gift. When a couple wearing his-and-hers navy windbreakers with white jeans came to his booth, he asked me to help them. They stood opposite me behind a wall of Falcon's sun catchers, puzzling over which one to purchase for each of their children left for a week at Grandma's house. They wanted something that represented Colorado and the things they had seen on their second honeymoon.

"Do both of you make the sun catchers," the woman asked.

I shook my head, because my mouth went dry at the idea of being associated with Falcon. For all the couple knew, I was his girlfriend—or his wife.

I worked up enough spit in my mouth to ask: "Are you buying for girls or boys?"

"One girl, thirteen, and two boys, eleven and nine."

I pointed out the columbine for the girl, a rainbow trout for the older boy, and the brown bear for the youngest. With their purchases wrapped in newspaper for safe travel back to Ohio, the couple left the booth satisfied with their purchases.

Falcon kissed my cheek. "Thanks."

While he helped a middle-aged woman decide between a dragonfly and a bumblebee, the place where his lips touched my cheek tingled. I feared that touching the spot would douse the heat of his kiss. I went deaf, dumb, and blind. The warmth swirled in my stomach and ignited a new and surprising place.

A woman dressed as an awning in green and white stripes picked that unfortunate moment to purchase a sun catcher. "Miss?"

My reply curdled in my mouth. "What?"

The woman froze with her hand in her purse.

I smiled an apology. "This is my favorite. What a great choice."

She opened her wallet. I glanced at Falcon, but he was talking with an eager-faced couple about living in Cordial. Falcon told them he was just passing through. My chest caved in. My customer pressed the money into my hand and leaned closer. "Honey, you better take it easy with the pot."

Pot?

I'd just experienced my first kiss, albeit a peck on the cheek, and the ecstasy of being *with* someone, and a woman dressed as a window covering thought I'd been smoking too much pot? I took the money for the sun catcher and handed it to Falcon.

"The cash box is under the table," he said over his shoulder and smiled.

I sat in the chair to drink the smoothie. The banana had turned bitter. Falcon stood with one foot on the seat of a chair. He talked and laughed with a couple from Connecticut who lived near the town where Falcon had grown up. "Is old man Kinsley still the county sheriff there?" he asked.

"He won re-election last fall," said the man.

Falcon threw his head back and laughed. "Oh man, I'll give you a ten-percent discount if you promise to keep mum about my whereabouts."

The couple laughed with him, but the woman looked over her shoulder, looking for Sheriff Kinsley, no doubt. "It's a deal," said the husband.

Falcon greeted fairgoers as they passed his booth. Most couldn't resist coming closer to get a better look at his wares. A couple wearing crease-pressed slacks and polo shirts admired a larger work displayed in front of a light box. Falcon had created the piece from the perspective of an inquisitive child who had dipped below the surface of a cool, green pond to watch the watery dance of a koi pair. Looking up through the water, a shimmer of sky and a blooming water lily awaited the diver. Did the boy squirm in the mud and catch a bulbous root in his toes? Of course he did. So enchanting was the piece that I held my breath, waiting to surface.

"How much?" asked the man.

When Falcon named his price, the man rocked back on his heals. The woman leaned into him as if to say, *Come on, you spend that much playing a round of golf with your buddies.*

"Is that firm?"

"I get where you're coming from, man," Falcon said. "The sun catchers are my bread-and-butter. They're cute. Most people come to these fairs looking for a souvenir to take home to their dog sitter. I know that. That's why I make them. I like to eat and drive my van around." Falcon spoke evenly. His eyes remained cloudless, playful. "The difference between the sun catchers and the koi piece is similar to the difference between a LTD Brougham and a Pinto. Both cars are made by Ford, but they are very different vehicles."

The man's head bobbled with understanding.

"The koi are a work of artistic passion. I researched my subject, sketched maybe twenty preliminary ideas. I searched five states to find the glass for the water with the right balance of translucence and depth, a shade of green that evokes the freshness of a pond on a hot summer day and the organic richness of underwater life. I finally met a glassmaker who worked with me until all those elements came together, and then I started looking for the sky glass. If you prefer a piece that looks like a coloring book, there's a real nice guy around the corner who'll sell you one of his pieces for half my price."

The woman kept her eyes on the koi as she tilted her head toward the man. "It's like you always say, Marvin—"

"Yes, yes, Joan, I know. You get what you pay for. We'll take it."

After the couple left with their package, Falcon rubbed his face. "Oh man, Marvin and Joan were not who I had in mind when I designed that piece. I pictured someone like you, Amelia, someone with a heart and a soul who would dream of being a water sprite among the tangle of water lily stems." He groaned. "That woman will hang the koi like a trophy in her front window where her neighbors will stop to gawk." He mimicked the couple's nasal accent. "Oh, Gladys, look what Joan's got in her window. Are those fish? What's with that? She goes out west and she brings back fish? She never had any sense."

"I'm sorry."

"I doubled the price, hoping he wouldn't buy it." His shoulders slumped. "I'm bummed."

"Maybe you're all wrong about Marvin and Joan. Maybe he paints seascapes and burns incense. Or better yet, Marvin is an architect. While designing a skyscraper for a toy manufacturer in Tokyo, he fell in love with the simplicity of traditional Japanese architecture.

The floors of their home are covered by *tatami* mats, and the rooms are separated by *fusuma*, those sliding doors made of wood and rice paper. The koi will be hung in the place of greatest honor, the *tokonoma*, in a Japanese home."

"You're full of surprises."

"I read a lot."

"You have a beautiful mind, little sister."

Little? Sister?

Sixteen

It happened like this every morning of the summer I lived in Cordial. A chill woke me by settling on my arms around four in the morning. I welcomed the interruption of my sleep and dreams. That may seem crazy, but waking to find that I had three more hours of sleep somehow made pulling the bedspread up to my neck and turning away from the clock decadent. Later, when I surrendered my dream world for the waking world of polishing and dusting, I left the bed without regrets. I had beaten the system.

That morning I woke up ravenously hungry. My heart sank. I pulled the covers over my head. The scent of sweet lemons seeped under the door of my room. Mom was baking lavadores, and that could only mean one thing: An outing with Bruce was imminent. Mom believed cookies bridged the distance between me and her boyfriends. I'd never given her a reason to continue believing this myth, but about some things Mom was a hopeless optimist.

I dressed in cleaning clothes and shuffled into the kitchen. Mom rifled through the refrigerator, filling her arms with plastic containers of fried chicken, potato salad, and *bagna cauda,* an Italian dipping sauce that tasted like rancid envelope paste.

Over the weeks she'd been dating Bruce, I had watched her transform herself into a coal miner's gal. She wore Wrangler jeans and pearl-snapped blouses with the first four snaps left undone. Her name was tooled on the back of her belt. We had argued over her frivolous spending for things she'd only wear to Halloween parties once we left Cordial. In the end, she cried that I never gave her boyfriends a chance, which I didn't. The promise of long life being tied to the honor we give our parents never failed to pop into my head during these arguments. I promised to give Bruce a chance. That didn't mean a get-to-know-you picnic sweetened my attitude.

My opening argument: "You'll go off alone with Bruce to—"

"I wouldn't."

"You *always* do, and I'll be left sitting on a log with nothing to do. I'd rather stay home, please."

Mom held my hands. "This time is different. Bruce is different. I want you to get to know him. That's been hard with him commuting between two work sites and our responsibilities at the funeral home."

Our responsibilities? "Mrs. Clancy will have a cow if we leave for the day."

"I've already talked to her, *fofa.* She says we deserve a day off." Mom looked at her watch. "She'll be here in a half hour, and Bruce will be here soon after."

"Why so early?"

"Bruce is working the swing shift."

"Mom, pl*eee*ase."

"This is an important day for me. Everything has come together to make it special. Bruce told his father he wanted to stay in Cordial to spend time with us this weekend. And you know how cranky Mrs. Clancy can be. Please, *fofa,* for me?"

THE TRUCK CLIMBED steadily on a narrow gravel road out of the lush North Fork Valley to wind through miner's huts no bigger than shoeboxes among mountains of coal and mammoth concrete silos. I groaned inwardly at each squiggly-arrow sign that warned Bruce to slow to 20 mph. He did not. On the north-facing slope, the forest deepened, but I took no delight in the scenery. Beyond the itty-bitty shoulder, the mountainside plummeted. I leaned toward Mom to gain a millimeter of safety. Mom's hand massaged Bruce's thigh, which seemed like an especially bad idea, considering the concentration required to drive a serpentine track of road.

"Mom," I said, hoping to distract her, "have you talked to Tommy about the transmission?"

"Let's not talk about our troubles. It's too beautiful. Look at that view. I feel like I'm flying."

When Mom warned Bruce about my queasy stomach, he insisted I roll down the window. "Fresh air helps, and keep your eyes on the road," he said. This bit of information turned out to be the gold nugget I took from Mom's relationship with Bruce.

We entered a forest of conifers and trees with round, dancing leaves. The curves softened, and I sighed. We passed beaver ponds and welcoming roads that led off into a Christmas-tree forest. This could have been Lake Kaskaskia, only much, much higher.

"This here is McClure Pass," Bruce said. "It's all downhill from here."

The force of each turn either pressed me against the door or into Mom. I glanced at Bruce before the curves to make sure his eyes stayed on the road, which they did, but both hands did not stay on the wheel. His arm remained around Mom's shoulders. At each curve, he held his cigarette with his teeth to shift with his left hand as he steered with his knee. He grabbed the steering wheel just in time to navigate the turn. I whimpered at the bottom of a long, downward slope when a sign warned of a right-angle turn.

"She always been this nervous?" Bruce asked.

"Only on windy roads."

Only on curves taken at the speed of light.

Once we reached the V-shaped valley, Bruce turned the truck toward Marble and stopped at a campground called Bogan Flats. Mom selected a picnic table in a stand of pine trees as holy as a cathedral. Bruce and Mom insisted on pre-lunch cigarettes, so I excused myself to walk toward the hiss of the river. From the dimple of skin between Mom's eyes, I knew she wasn't happy with me for wandering off, but Bruce offered the use of the binoculars he kept in the truck. "You might see an eagle or a red fox. A fella at the mine has seen bears roaming around heres somewhere."

Mom's dimple deepened. "Bears?"

"Don't worry, Mom. If I see any bears, I'll come right back."

Sitting on a cushion of moss by the river, I enumerated all the ways my life would improve once I lived on my own. Number one: No more suicidal drives on mountainous roads. Number two: No more picnics with men who used bad grammar. Number three: Absolutely and positively no more get-to-know-you picnics. With that settled, I closed my eyes to enjoy the slosh and glug of the river's song.

A throaty thrum startled my eyes open but not soon enough. Whatever had come to visit left only a blur of movement for me to wonder about. A giant bee? A dragonfly? A flying bear?

Don't be stupid.

Soon a hummingbird hovered within a foot of my nose. I sat breathless, completely cowed by his boldness and awed by his aerobatics. "I guess your mom didn't tell you about personal space." He squeaked as if to say I'd taken his seat. The bird lost interest in me and revved his throttle to fly away. I sat as still as a stone. Within minutes another hummingbird hovered before my face. Curious? Hungry? "Do I look like a flower you once knew?" I laughed and our relationship shattered. I sat there for some time, watching, waiting, even holding my finger out for a roost. Not one hummingbird accepted my hospitality.

MOM AND BRUCE snuggled on the opposite side of the picnic table.

"Sing a song for Bruce," she said.

"You told me to leave my guitar at home."

"You sing all the time without your guitar." She leaned into Bruce. "She sings like an angel, and not one of those high-pitched angels like you hear at Christmas. Amy sings like a velvet angel."

"I refuse to sing Elvis songs."

Bruce squirmed. "She don't have to sing if she don't want to."

Mom stood. "Let me just clean up this mess, and I'll get the cookies out. Bruce, I brought coffee. Would you like some?"

I rose to help her.

"No, no," she said, pushing me back on the bench. "You talk with Bruce. I'll only be a minute." She gave me one of those pleading looks meant to make me feel guilty. I didn't. This was not my first picnic with men like Bruce. I'd sung "I'm a Little Teapot" and "He's Got the Whole World in His Hands" over potato salad since I was three. In Mom's eyes each boyfriend had arrived to love her and provide for her in a manner befitting a queen. My unenviable job was to keep her grounded in reality, but that didn't mean I had to be pleasant if I didn't want to.

"So, Bruce, how long have you lived in Cordial?"

"I don't know. Six weeks, maybe."

This could mean a fresh beginning or trouble keeping a job.

"Do you like living there?" I asked.

"I guess. I ain't thought about it much. It's a nice enough town. Housing ain't too bad. The grub's okay."

So if children came from this union, we wouldn't be expecting rocket scientists, now would we?

"Do you like being a coal miner?"

"It's a living."

Uh-oh, this guy lacked ambition. The future meant more waitress jobs for Mom and yet another break-up. This was getting depressing.

"Do you know Jesus as your personal Lord and Savior?" I asked.

"Amelia!"

"I'm trying to get to know him. Isn't that what you wanted?"

Bruce squirmed and looked at everything but me.

"For goodness' sake, religion is a personal issue. Talk about the weather. Tell him about Westmont."

I had a better idea. "I think we should take the coffee and cookies on a hike to the marble mine. What do you say to that?"

"Sounds good to me," Bruce said, standing up. "But it ain't far, is it?"

I read from the pamphlet Bonnie had given Mom. "'The hike to the base of the mine is an easy walk along a tributary of the Crystal River.'"

"That's a beautiful name for a river," Mom gushed.

"'Along the trail you'll see wildflowers like Indian paintbrush and fireweed. A waterfall and a dramatic slope of marble awaits you at the end of the trail. To view the quarry, follow the signs through the massive marble blocks to the trailhead. This portion of the hike is steeper and should only be attempted by healthy individuals acclimated to the elevation.'"

"We're all accumulated, aren't we?" Mom asked.

Bruce looked sideways at Mom.

"Let's go," she said.

WE HIKED ALONG a chiseled wall of granite. The valley below us was no wider than a country road. A stream rushed over stony steps, like someone had forgotten the water running in the bathtub upstairs. Where a slab of granite had sloughed away from the wall, a niche of gunmetal gray had been created. Instead of a statue of a perpetually pious Mary, the niche housed a choir of purple flowers with leaves as slender as fingers. Mom and Bruce walked right by the spectacle until I asked Mom if I could use the camera. Then she wanted a photograph of her and Bruce kneeling next to the flowers. Mom reapplied her lipstick, wiping away the excess at the corners of her mouth. Bruce knelt on the pebbled path and Mom sat on his knee. Chest up. Shoulders back. Smile dazzling.

"Smile," I said, but Bruce only cocked his head.

When Mom and Bruce walked ahead, I took a picture of the flowers to send to Lauren, knowing she would put them in her to-paint-someday box she kept under her bed. Lauren was about the worst artist I'd ever seen, but that didn't stop her from being one. I hoped she remembered her promise to take art lessons in St. Louis. Then she could paint the purple flowers and give the painting to me for a birthday present. I couldn't imagine Lauren being happy tinting little old ladies' hair all day. I fingered the cross necklace she'd stolen for me. Thinking about Lauren made my heart ache, but it was difficult maintaining a worthwhile funk in the narrow canyon that cupped its walls like hands to project the stream's aria.

Farther up the trail the stream cut a smooth trough through solid marble where we rounded a curve, and the three of us stood slack-jawed at what we saw. A landslide of marble, like sugar cubes the size of Volkswagens, some bugs and some vans, covered the mountainside.

"Oh my," Mom said. "Now why do you suppose they left all that beautiful marble lying there like that?"

Her question was my cue to read from the brochure. "'The Italian and Austrian—'"

"Not Portuguese, *fofa*?"

Mom's Portuguese pride confounded me. Her family had left Portugal before World War II, and she hadn't even been born yet. Even so, Portuguese was her first language. How she'd found a nice Portuguese boy to marry in America was a piece of wonderment and statistical improbability meant for more developed intellects than mine. As proud as she was of her heritage, she never spoke of her parents unless I asked. She had answered me with, "They didn't understand me, and then they died. End of story."

I looked up from the brochure. "None that they mention, no." I continued reading. "'The Italian and Austrian stonecutters left the area in 1917 to fight in World War I. All of the marble for the Lincoln Memorial had been shipped in five hundred train cars by the end of 1918.'"

"Ah, that's it," she said. "The Portuguese stonecutters stayed in Washington to finish the work of the Italians and Austrians. That wasn't the first time."

I ignored her. "'In 1926, a flawless block of Yule Marble was sent to Washington D.C. for the Tomb of the Unknown Soldier.'"

"I seen that when I was a boy."

Arrows painted on the marble blocks directed us to the trail that led up the mountainside to the quarry entrance. Bruce leaned against a block of startling, white marble with an unlit cigarette hanging from his mouth as he fished around his shirt pocket for matches. "If it's all the same to you, I'll sit here for a smoke. You girls go ahead."

Mom and I exchanged glances. "You don't have to sit here alone," she said. "We'll wait. I wouldn't mind a cigarette myself."

"I think I'll start up," I said.

Mom started to protest, but Bruce was already tapping a cigarette out of a pack for her. He nodded toward the trailhead. "Be careful."

You're not much of a Marlboro Man, cowboy.

The grade steepened. Within a few yards my heart pounded in my chest. Mrs. Clancy had warned me about the effects of high altitude. I stopped to gulp water from the canteen she'd loaned me and waited for my heart to settle down. I resumed the climb through the forest at a slower pace, stopping to take pictures down the trail I'd climbed. Lauren would be impressed. Cresting the trail, I stood at eye level with the surrounding mountains. Not one tree grew on their peaks. The air, light and congenial, made me giddy. I wished H was there to tell me about the bare mountaintops. That was how magnanimous the scenery had made me.

I sang "Rocky Mountain High" as I strode toward the gaping hole of the quarry. I stopped several feet away from a rusted chain that served as a safety rail. Whereas the marble blocks left in the sunshine had made my eyes ache with their brilliance, gray smudged the walls of the quarry that settled into black pools on the bottom. Very disappointing. Empty. A great gaping hole. Dead. I backed away. As a tourist attraction, the abandoned quarry proved the journey made the destination inconsequential. I turned to follow the trail back to where Bruce and Mom smoked their cigarettes.

Nuts to that.

I sat on a low boulder beyond the mine's gapping entrance, a front-row seat to take in the bold landscape. Jutting mountains. Singing rivers. Angel-hair clouds stretched across a jubilant sky. Insects hummed and jays called. I hugged my knees to my chest. Only a thousand miles and a range of mountains separated me from California. My chest ached. A breeze as welcomed as a kiss lifted my hair.

The story of David came to mind. Mountains had separated him from his destiny when he asked, "I will lift my eyes to the mountains; from whence shall my help come?" David made it to the throne of Israel despite the machinations of Saul, treachery and arrows, betrayal and spears. All that menaced me was my hopelessly lovesick and easily sidetracked mother.

My help comes from the Lord, who made heaven and earth.

"Lord, you made heaven and earth. Please make a transmission for a 1958 Pontiac Bonneville Sport Coupe Jubilee Edition show up in Cordial. I'd be much obliged."

Feeling fortified, I tromped down the trail to find Mom and Bruce making out.

"I'll wait by the truck," I said.

Seventeen

I emptied gewgaws, mortuary science books, journals, and ledgers from a bookcase in Mrs. Clancy's office to spray the shelves with lemon-fresh Pledge. She answered the telephone. "Clancy and Sons Funeral Home serving the North Fork Valley sin—"

I turned to listen, like I could see who dared to interrupt Mrs. Clancy's greeting. She hummed her agreement to the person on the other end of the telephone. With a flip of her wrist, she shooed me back to work.

"Yes, they brought your mother here yesterday," she said. "We can certainly take care of all that for . . ."

I stole a peek at Mrs. Clancy. Her eyebrows came together as she wrapped the phone cord around her finger.

"As you like, yes, that's all included."

I spread the polish over the wood in apathetic circles.

Mrs. Clancy flipped through a stenographer's pad until she found a clean page. "You'll want an obituary at least. Let me—

"Are you sure, dear?

"How long has your mother lived in this area?

"Really?

"No, I can't say I ever had the pleasure."

Mrs. Clancy swiveled her chair to look out the window. I held the dust rag in my lap. Her voice took on a quality I'd never heard from her. "Funerals aren't for the . . . they're for the living. Your mother may have had friends you know nothing about. Not having a service is like coming to the end of a good book and finding the last chapter has been ripped out—it's terribly unsatisfying. A funeral would give her friends a chance to say their good-byes.

"I see. Yes, I see." She turned back to her desk to massage a temple as she listened. "Please don't take what I'm about to say as prying. I'm an old woman, my dear. I've been providing funeral services most of my life. My father and grandfather were morticians, and I grew up in this very house with my two brothers. In fact, my ties to this place and my profession are so strong, I reverted to the family name when my husband passed away. So you can see, I've seen every imaginable scenario, more than one like what you're describing." She sighed heavily. "Please understand that I will not make one cent more than what I've quoted you for basic funeral services, but I think you and your sisters may want to reconsider a service for your mother. In fact, you should consider the service a gift you give each other. It sounds like you girls have a lot to talk about, and more than a mother to bury to get on with your lives. If you change your mind, call back by Friday. That will give us plenty of time to make arrangements."

Mrs. Clancy thrummed her fingers on the desk. I replaced the books and gewgaws.

"Hello?" Mrs. Clancy asked. "Are you still there?

"That's a good plan. I'll be waiting to hear from you."

Mrs. Clancy leaned back in her chair, cradling the receiver to her chest. I let the figurines clank together to remind her I was in the room. She pulled a hanky out of her belt to blow her nose and dab her eyes. "Amy, do I smell Mr. Moberly's meatloaf burning?"

I'd put the meatloaf in the oven twenty minutes earlier. "I better go check."

Mrs. Clancy called me back. "Would you sing a hymn for this woman's service? I don't expect too many people to attend, and Pearl can be so heavy-handed with the organ. The strumming of a guitar would be quite nice."

Eighteen

"Everyone eats a hot dog at the drive-in," H said.

"Do you know what they put in those things?"

"Okay, okay. One small popcorn and one small Coke." H turned toward the concession stand.

"Wait!" I called to him.

"What is it now?"

I tilted my purse and shook loose change into my hand. "You're not paying for the refreshments. You already paid for the admission."

H rested his arms on the truck's door and heaved a sigh. "You can pay for everything next time. Does that make you happy?" Clearly, H wasn't. I'd taken the whole we're-just-friends thing too far, and now he was hurt. I knew this would happen.

"I'm sorry," I said.

He shrugged off my apology. "Are you sure you don't want a hot dog? How about some ice cream?"

"Just some popcorn and—"

"I know, a Coke." And he was gone.

Over the speaker hooked on H's window, the Beach Boys sang about California girls. *Oh brother.* H had convinced me that the Big Chief drive-in was Cordial's hottest cultural event, that summer wasn't complete without at least one night at the drive-in. To be there, I banked on the consistency of Mom's schedule—out at six, back by midnight—which meant skipping the second movie, *Herbie Rides Again!* I wasn't one bit sorry to miss it. But I was also playing the odds. Two people had required the services of the funeral home that week—a rest home resident with no near relatives and a woman who had come home to be buried by her husband and infant son. Based on the seven weeks I'd been in Cordial, my chances were better than even that no one would die that weekend.

Gravel popped and pinged as drivers doused their headlights to stalk the aisles for the perfect parking spot. As twilight slid into night, kids played on the swings and slide under the screen.

A family—dad, mom, and two small daughters—sat in their station wagon next to H's truck. The younger sister, dressed in her pajamas, climbed over the seat to be with her parents, then returned to the backseat to annoy her sister. "Ruthie, wherever you are when the movie starts, that's where you're sitting." Her father's warning started the game in earnest. Where would Ruthie be when the movie started? Ruthie wiggled over the seat head first, her feet kicking the air beside her dad's head.

"I can stand on my head, Daddy."

The mother turned toward the passenger window to stifle a laugh. The dad flipped Ruthie upright and drew her into the crook of his arm. I watched Ruthie's silky curls out of the corner of my eye, waiting for her to restart her game of seat hopping. Ruthie nestled into her dad's chest and stayed put. The scene warmed and pierced me.

From the back of the drive-in, girls screamed and boys yelled, "Fight! A fight!" Dust floated in the beams of headlights, and a crowd gathered. I ran toward the concession stand, stooping under the speaker wires as I ran up and down the parking humps. Inside the cinder-block building, wide-eyed customers turned toward the growing commotion but stayed in line. No H in sight.

Outside, I stood with my back to the concession stand. Two men with flashlights hurried toward a cluster of onlookers and pushed their way into the circle. "That's enough! Go back to your cars!" The onlookers fell away. Three boys plowed punches into a boy on the ground. My heart sank when H's sensible boots flailed to make contact with his attackers. Their taunts continued.

"Boo-hoo, little baby. Did you leave your doggie at home?"

"Go back to fairyland, fag boy!"

The boys stopped mid-punch when the flashlights lit their faces.

"You heard what I said," the man in a blue vest shouted. "Get back to your cars, Tom! Mark! You don't want me calling your dad, do you, Jim?" The last boy standing over H hesitated, looked down at him and tapped H's shoulder with his fist.

Counting coup?

The thick-necked goon strutted toward the back of the parking area where a welcoming crowd high-fived him into the darkness. The man in the vest offered H a hand up, but H stood on his own. Empty cups and spilled popcorn lay at his feet. When H started to pick up the containers, the man said, "Leave it. I'll get you some more, on the house."

The lights on the concession stand winked and darkened as the projector rattled from its room on top of the building. From a hundred speakers, the Looney Tunes theme played. H strode toward the exit. I ran to catch him.

"Are you all right?" I asked, trotting to keep up with him. "Who were those guys?"

He walked faster, his head down and turned slightly away.

"Your elbow's bleeding. H, stop and talk to me. Shouldn't we get your truck?"

We walked past the twin box offices. A few stragglers waited as a boy in a cap and T-shirt opened the trunk of his car for the box office attendant. "Well, look what we've got here. That'll be another $1.50, young man."

As we reached the street, the toe plug of my flip-flops popped loose. "H, can you slow down? I have a shoe problem here."

He stopped. "This was a really bad idea." He swiped at his eyes with the sleeves of his T-shirt.

I kept my head down, like putting a flip-flop together required the same concentration as brain surgery. I didn't want to make H feel any worse, but I sure didn't want him bullied by those creeps either. "Those are the guys you want for friends?"

He continued walking. "You don't get it."

"You've got that right," I yelled after him. I slid my foot in the flip-flop and quick stepped to catch up with him. "My friends don't throw me to the ground—"

"I was tripped."

Lauren had lied and stolen for me, but she had never tripped me. "Friends don't trip each other, either."

H threw his arms up and kept walking.

"H!"

"What?"

"You deserve better."

"Talking doesn't help."

That couldn't be true. I'd been the captain of the debate team for two years. All I needed was one counterexample to disprove the fallacy that silence solved problems. Let's see, although the Gettysburg Address expressed the urgency and divine necessity of a strong union, battle weariness and the collapse of the Southern war machine ended the Civil War at Appomattox. The negotiators at the Paris Peace Talks took months to agree on the shape of the conference table and another five years to end American involvement in the war. And just a couple months earlier, I'd debated for continued American involvement in Vietnam the very week Saigon fell. I lost. My heart wasn't in it.

H and I walked in silence along Main Street and turned on Second Street toward the funeral home. A car shot out of the alley to straddle the sidewalk just feet in front of us. The driver was the thick-necked goon from the drive-in.

H swore.

"Hey, dork face," the driver called, flicking cigarette ash on H's shoes. "You left before the cartoon. Did Porky Pig scare you?"

I pulled on H's arm. "Come on, H. Let's go."

H stood his ground.

The power of the boy's car engine rumbled against my chest. His chunky bicep rested on the opened window. It was bigger than my thigh. Too bad. I was the voice of reason in this otherwise Neanderthal match of wits. I took a tentative step toward the car. "Excuse me."

H held the crook of my elbow. "Amy . . . don't."

"It's okay. I can handle this," I said. "You're Jim, right?"

His passenger, a girl, with smooth blonde hair parted as straight as the Nebraska highway, leaned around the hunk of a boy with mild curiosity. Two tiny barrettes held her hair in place. "His name is Jim, all right," she said.

"Okay, Jim, you owe my friend an apology."

The driver's door flew open, and Jim the giant stood glaring down at me. His finger hit my sternum. "Look, bi—"

H pushed against Jim's shoulder and landed a punch to the side of his nose. Jim collapsed to his knees. The girl screamed. Blood oozed between Jim's fingers.

H grabbed my hand. "Run!"

We ran down the hill and cut across a lawn, up a driveway, past a garage, and into another alley. We leaned against the back of a garage. "Where are we going?" I asked.

"As far away as possible."

My hand ached in H's grip. "You can let go of my hand now." I kneaded the blood back into my fingers. "What a—"

H stopped me with a raised hand. "Listen," he whispered. The engine of Jim's car throbbed nearby. "Let's go." We ran between two houses and crossed a road. H held the strands of a barbed-wire fence as I squeezed through the opening into a field of waist-high hay. We hadn't run very far when an engine revved nearby.

H pushed me to the ground. "Don't move."

"My feet are killing me," I whispered.

"Shh."

We lay there, listening to Jim's car trolling for us down the streets and alleys of Cordial. Lightning flashed over Logan Mountain, but over us the sky was polished ebony, sparkling with stars.

"Do you know how many galaxies there are?" H asked.

"Shouldn't we be quiet?"

"From the sound of the engine, Jim is on Ninth Street. He can't hear us, but I'm impressed that he thinks I can run that far."

"You're hopeless."

"No I'm not. I'm full of hope. I hope to travel among those stars someday, probably driving a huge telescope on top of a mountain instead of a rocket, but I'm cool with that."

"So you've settled on being an astronomer?"

"I've settled on being anything that will take me away from here."

"But you're determined to be on the football team just to fit in. That doesn't make sense."

"It's a man thing. I'm sure you wouldn't understand."

He was right about that. I didn't understand. We lay in silence for a long while. The stars seemed to multiply as the night deepened. I shivered.

"Are you cold?" he asked.

"No, just remembering a movie I saw about the universe in eighth grade. We weren't even studying space at the time."

"Maybe your teacher had papers to grade. My American Lit teacher did that all the time. He made us watch *A Raisin in the Sun* and write a paper about it, which I never got back."

"Nah, I think Mr. Anderson just needed fifty minutes of peace. A group of boys in class made life difficult for him, and he really was a nice man. Probably too nice to teach junior high. For whatever reason he showed the movie, it scared me to death." I turned toward H. "At the beginning of the movie, the camera is focused on a man's pupil, and then it pulls back to show the man lying on a beach. The beach became a cove, and the cove became Florida, and Florida was nothing but a finger of land on Earth, and then the earth was a blue button hanging in space. I felt like I was being pulled from Earth as the camera flew past the moon and Mars and Jupiter. And then, the solar system became points of light indiscernible from the stars. Other galaxies, like purple and fuchsia cotton candy churned as I whizzed by. Seeing how small I was in the infinite blackness made my heart pound in my chest. I was never so glad to hear the passing bell ring."

"That sounds cool," H said with awe in his voice.

"I sneaked out of the house that night to look at the sky. Even from my backyard, despite the stars and a fingernail moon, the universe seemed empty. It scared me to death. I've never told anyone."

"You think too much."

"Maybe. Do *you* believe God made it all, made you and me, that on the edge of this sea of matter there is a loving God who gives a hoot?"

"Sure."

"Why?"

"Because he said he did. God's no liar."

We lay there a long time. A shooting star—which H quickly pointed out wasn't a star at all but a meteorite flaming out as it traveled through the atmosphere—flashed across the sky. So much for that romantic notion. A shadowy pair of hawks glided over us.

"Night hawks," H said. "They mostly eat bugs, so don't look like a moth, whatever you do." He snorted a laugh at his own joke.

I smiled to myself, and the connection with H warmed me. If he asked me for a kiss, I think I would have given him one. Faster than the idea had come to me, I repressed it. Kiss H? *I don't think so.* Instead, I asked him, "So how's Sunday school going? Has John cleaned up his act?"

H groaned. "Just when I thought we had us a romantic moment, you have to bring up Sunday school."

"Let me set you straight on this one. Hiding from a sadistic football player isn't romantic."

"What? You've got the stars and the sound of rustling hay. What else could you possibly want?"

I thought of Falcon, but I didn't want to hear H cry. It was better to steer the conversation to something neutral, something not related to romance. For neutrality, you couldn't beat a conversation about Sunday school. "Come on, tell me what's going on in Sunday school."

"If you must know—first of all, it's just me and John. And, you know, he's an okay guy once you get to know him. He's feeling his way around. I think it was his parents who wanted him to be a youth pastor."

"Which means?"

"We're reading *Jonathan Livingston Seagull.*"

Who hadn't? "So you're studying talking seagulls during the Sunday school hour?"

"Hey, there's some pretty deep stuff in there."

"Like?"

H spoke with an English accent. "'The gull sees farthest who flies highest,'" and he snorted again.

"That's deep, all right," I said, but rewarded H by laughing.

"There isn't one new idea in that stupid book," he said, "but because a seagull is doing all the talking, the book is selling like hot cakes."

"Maybe you could write a book about a crime-fighting dog."

"Let's talk about something else."

And so we did. H pointed out star constellations. I told him how close the Gilbertsville debate team had come to winning the Illinois state championship. We talked about our most embarrassing moments and how scary the world had become.

"Wait until you get to California. That's a scary place."

"How would you know?"

"We visited my aunt and uncle in Pasadena a couple years ago. They live above the Los Angeles basin in the San Gabriel Mountains.

In the week we stayed there, the smog was so thick, you couldn't see anything in the valley. It was like flying above the clouds. They'll be wearing gas masks before long."

The girls with straight, blonde hair would figure out a way to look cute with their hair plastered down by gas mask straps. For me, it would be *Bozo Rides Again,* chapter three thousand. "That's depressing."

"Disneyland was neat, and despite third-degree burns on my shoulders, I liked the beach. Maybe I could visit you and teach you how to body surf."

"I'm not that good in the water, remember?"

We discussed the Equal Rights Amendment, the Cold War, and Earth Shoes.

"Do you have a theme song?" he asked. "Mine's 'One Tin Soldier.'"

"I didn't know I needed one."

"It's a cool song. It's about people who are only interested in the material value of things. They don't get what really matters. The heroes will be the people who stand up to protect the spiritual things, the things that can't be bought and sold."

"You sound like a hippie."

"No way. They're the ones destroying all that's sacred. They say they've found a better way, but all they're doing is making excuses for bad behavior."

I yawned. "They're not all like that, H. You can't make generalizations."

"Why not? They do."

"If you believe that, then you'll need a new theme song."

H eased himself up to one knee. "The coast is clear. Let's go."

H AND I squatted in the lilac hedge behind the funeral home. "You have to go straight home," I said.

"I'm walking you to the door."

"That's too dangerous. I'm going through the basement. Jim won't be able to see me from the street." I fished the key ring out of my purse. I gripped the padlock key with one hand and touched H's arm with the other. "You're ten times the man he is."

"Only ten times?"

"Don't press your luck."

"I deserve a kiss for saving your life, don't I?"

"You almost crushed my hand." I left H and sprinted across the lawn. The closer I got to the basement door, the faster my heart pounded. This would be my first visit to the preparation room where Charles worked with the bodies. That was how badly I didn't want to see any more of Jim that night. I waved H off and stepped into the darkness of the basement.

I waited for my eyes to adjust to the dark. The stairs to the kitchen couldn't be far off, but I wasn't interested in feeling my way to a light switch. The streetlight's beam barely bled through the narrow windows. Before long the form of a table took shape along with an assortment of bottles hanging from poles and rubbery hoses.

Enough!

I oriented myself. The stairs to the kitchen should be just a few paces to the right. *Right . . . okay . . . just a few steps and I'm home free.*

"Oh Lord, get H home safely and help me find the stairs."

A passing car's headlights scanned the room through the window and stopped to illuminate the wooden stair railing. "Thanks, Lord."

Nineteen

Mrs. Clancy tugged at the lapels of her funeral suit, a polyester jacket that no longer closed over a white blouse and a skirt that pulled tightly over her bottom. She nodded at Pastor Ted who surprised us all by setting two chairs in front of the casket to face the three daughters of Vilda Hardin, the deceased. He patted the seat next to him. "Amy, why don't you join us?"

I turned to offer Mrs. Clancy my seat, but she had already left the room.

Mrs. Clancy had run Mrs. Hardin's obituary in the newspapers of three neighboring towns. Only the daughters appeared to pay their last respects. None of them looked happy about being there, but even if people weren't particularly broken up about someone's demise, they usually maintained a somber countenance. The daughters looked more disgusted than mournful.

The most outspoken daughter wore motorcycle leathers—jacket emblazoned with skulls, fringed chaps over skin-tight jeans, and boots Paul Bunyan would have rejected as too cumbersome. Since she didn't sign the guest book or introduce herself, I dubbed her Motorcycle Mama. Next to her sat a mouse of a woman. Her gray hair lay down her back in a spindly ponytail. She busied her hands straightening her collar, smoothing her perfectly obedient hair, and snapping the clasp of her purse open and closed, open and closed. Her eyes scanned the room as if judging the shortest distance to an exit. Of the three daughters, the next woman—Jane, from the introduction she'd made as the first to arrive—was the kind of woman who worked at a bank or sold real estate: confident, comfortable, and collected. Her navy suit followed the curves of her body, and her hair bent into a smooth bob with winged bangs. If she'd been in Home Economics with Lauren and me, we would have dosed her brownies with Feen-a-Mint when she wasn't looking. That kind of perfection couldn't go unchallenged.

Pastor Ted checked his watch. "I guess it's time to get started. Since this is an intimate gathering, I think we'll all be more comfortable sitting together."

The mouse sister redoubled her search for an exit.

"Let me say a little prayer to get us started, and then Amy will perform the song she prepared for today." He bowed his head and clasped his hands. I paused long enough to see the sisters exchange looks. I felt three pairs of eyes boring holes into my scalp as I waited for Pastor Ted to pray.

"Dear Father in heaven, you understand the pain of separation these sisters are feeling today. Comfort them. Be near as they say good-bye to their dear mother."

I cringed at Pastor Ted's prayer. Obviously, Mrs. Clancy hadn't briefed him on the broken relationship between the deceased and her daughters.

"We ask you for grace to remember the good times and the mercy to release the bad. In Jesus' name, Amen."

Pastor Ted nodded at me, and I strummed the introduction to "Great Is Thy Faithfulness." When singing for a crowd, I sang over their heads to the people standing near doorways, the ones ready to flee if the program proved disappointing. I appreciated their honest and immediate feedback. The circle of chairs felt claustrophobic. I closed my eyes.

"Is this absolutely necessary?" asked Jane.

I stopped singing.

Motorcycle Mama and the mouse stared Jane down.

"One verse will be sufficient," Jane conceded.

Pastor Ted patted my knee, a signal meant to start me playing. I sat frozen.

Motorcycle Mama said, "Do you know 'The Old Rugged Cross'? That was Mama's favorite."

Jane leaned forward to speak around Mouse. "And just how do you know that?"

"You'd be surprised what I know about Mama." Motorcycle Mama turned to me. "Sing all of the verses, won't you?"

"Sure." I played a short introduction and sang a bit up-tempo for a funeral to speed things along. When I sang, "Then He'll call me someday to my home far away," Motorcycle Mama sniffed, Mouse sighed, and Jane groaned. I plucked faster to hurry through the chorus one last time. The chair scraped against the floor as I stood to leave.

"That was lovely," said Pastor Ted with a hint of surprise in his voice. "But don't go away. We would love to hear you sing again. I had no idea you were so talented."

I scanned the faces of the sisters. Motorcycle Mama smiled to reveal a golden front tooth. I sat down, but I held my guitar like a shield.

Pastor Ted leaned back in his chair. "Let me be perfectly honest with you ladies. I didn't have the pleasure of knowing your mother. I did some calling around to see if I could talk to a few of her friends, learn a bit about her for my message, but your mother treaded lightly on this earth. I didn't find one soul who knew her."

"Treaded lightly? That's because she used us as her stepping stones," Jane said. "I could have saved you a lot of trouble, Reverend."

"It wasn't any trouble at all." He cocked his head as I'd seen boys do when they wanted to soften a girl's heart. "Perhaps you can help me."

"I can help you, all right." Jane crossed her legs. "Our mother wasn't happy unless everyone around her was miserable. I can hold my own in a roomful of businessmen without breaking a sweat, but every time I saw her—and I made a point of coming to Colorado four times a year—she pushed and pushed until I cried. Nothing I did satisfied her. If I brought her a yellow nightgown, she wanted a blue one. If I extended my stay as she wished, I should have stayed longer. She ruined every event she attended." Jane leaned back in her chair and crossed her arms. "After I'd been awarded a scholarship to any school in Michigan, she bragged about a friend's daughter who had won a Duncan Scholarship to Harvard." Jane's eyes became slits and she sneered as she mimicked her mother. "'Why didn't you do something I could be proud of? Going to Harvard, now that's something.'"

Mouse played with the hem of her jacket. "She wasn't always like that."

"How would you know, Monica?" Jane countered. "I can't remember you speaking to her, let alone incurring her wrath. Did you enjoy watching me take all the hits?"

Motorcycle Mama scooted her chair to look at Jane. "We all know Mama would never win Mother of the Year, but she didn't have the greatest teacher either."

Jane wagged her finger at Motorcycle Mama. "You've always made excuses for her."

Pastor Ted raised his hand. "Now, girls—"

Jane scooted to the edge of her chair. "You didn't look over your shoulder when you left."

"You had a way of getting under her skin."

"A mother's love should be unconditional."

"Interesting. You're an expert on mothering, are you? That would explain why you haven't spoken to your son in six months."

Jane slid back in her chair. "You don't know anything about me or my son. I haven't seen you in—" She glanced at Pastor Ted. "It's been several years."

"It's been eight years this August." Motorcycle Mama tucked her chin. "Your son calls me every Sunday."

Jane deflated as if someone had poked her with a pin. Outside, yet another truck thundered by, and children riding by on bicycles called to each other. Pastor Ted sat motionless. Surely the man had something magical to say to lighten the mood.

Instead, Monica asked him, "Why are you even here? There's not one solitary thing you can do for her. Our mother is in hell."

"Is she?" he asked.

Monica blinked at the question. "Of course she is. She never went to church . . . and she used the Lord's name in vain constantly. *And* she smoked tobacco."

"We did too go to church. At least we did when I was little," Motorcycle Mama said. "Just Mama and me, and Monica. Jane joined us when she was born. We went every Sunday. I remember because Mama wouldn't let me wear my cowboy hat into the church. I put up an awful stink about that, and she still made me go."

Pastor Ted rested his elbows on his knees to talk to Monica.

"Anyone who claims to know where your Mama is right now would only be guessing or wishing. She has only one judge, and he has a welcoming heart for sinners. He keeps knocking at our heart's door until we respond—or not. In fact, Jesus granted the thief on the cross entrance into Paradise. That wretch of a man had never attended a church in his whole life, made his living preying on the hardworking and guileless, and yet he walks with the Savior today." Pastor Ted straightened. His voice cradled me. I felt safe. "I'm not here to judge your mother or to pray her into heaven. You and me, we have the same job, to love God and those around us and to tell the story of God's love to anyone who will listen."

"So you're telling us there's room in heaven for women who treat their daughters like dirt?" Jane asked.

Motorcycle Mama's chair fell backward when she stood. "Do you remember the last time I got sick of listening to your sarcasm, Janey dear?"

Jane made a tent of her hands over her nose.

"Okay, okay, okay," Pastor Ted said. "Let's all take a deep breath, take a moment to collect ourselves." He righted Motorcycle Mama's chair. "Have a seat, Raylinia."

Raylinia?

"It's Ray."

Jane cradled her head in her hands. Monica crossed and uncrossed her legs. Ray flexed her neck until it popped.

"Your mother left a painful legacy of disappointment for you girls, but that doesn't matter to us today." All heads popped up, including mine. Pastor Ted took on the vigor of a coach whose team had given away home-field advantage. It was halftime. The dispirited team members needed reminding of their objective. "Your mother had her life and her chance to make of it what she would. Now it's your turn.

God has given you a sphere of influence. You have family—certainly two sisters each—maybe a husband and children, I don't know. You have friends, coworkers, neighbors, a postal carrier who brings your mail, and clerks where you shop, or a trusted mechanic.

"What legacy will *you* leave behind? It's up to you. Your mother's gone. She won't be looking over your shoulder to pass judgment on what you do or don't do. You're free to be the people God created you to be. Will you choose to be happy? Will you choose to be generous with your approval and kind to people who disappoint you? Will you be an understanding ear for someone who has experienced crushing shame?"

Jane started to speak, but Pastor Ted held his hand like a stop sign. "I wouldn't try to answer these questions today. There's too much swimming around in your heads. I'm going to pray for you, and Amy will sing something of her choosing. Is that all right with you, Amy?"

The first song that came to mind was "She'll Be Coming Around the Mountain," a song the Basement Beacons performed to rouse a quiet audience. *Keep thinking.* Something spiritual. Something comforting. I plucked an introduction for a chorus I'd learned for Vacation Bible School.

Have you seen Jesus my Lord?

He's here in plain view.

After the service, I peeked through the drapes to watch the sisters linger in the shade of a tornado tree, taking turns looking at their feet and sharing a hankie for their tears. Ray opened her arms to Jane who fiercely gripped her sister. Monica inched closer to join the knot of sisters.

"Close that drape," ordered Mrs. Clancy, her purse and ledger book in hand. "This isn't a circus. People deserve their privacy." And she left.

I moved to the kitchen door, feeling the need to hug Mom and to cook something special for dinner. Maybe she would stay home that night and play Monopoly. She usually sat in the shade of the garage during services, smoking and reading magazines. That day wasn't any different, except she wasn't alone. Through the screen door, I watched Charles bend to light Mom's cigarette. She turned her head to blow the first puff of smoke away from him. He leaned against the garage. Mom laughed at something he said and closed the magazine in her lap. She had never closed a magazine for me.

Charles crouched against the garage. Mom sat a car's length away. The image of a man coaxing a feral dog to take a bone from his hand came to mind. I shook the image away. He was probably telling her about his dream to own a mortuary with a state-of-the-art preparation room and a room equipped with lighting to eliminate postmortem makeup. No wonder Mom had stopped laughing. Besides, Charles was old, thirty-eight he'd told me, and not much to look at with his meatloaf belly and bland features.

Twenty

I refused the cup of tea Leoti poured for me. "I'll have a cup when I've finished dusting the parlor."

"You must tell me what you thought of *My Àntonia,"* she said but continued to speak excitedly about *Sense and Sensibility.* She stirred her tea absentmindedly as she spoke. "Of course, you know I loved reading Miss Austen's book. Edward is certainly sweet and affable, but it's Colonel Brandon I fall in love with at each reading. His quiet strength and his honorable devotion to the ladies of Barton Cottage reminds me of Arthur and how he behaved so graciously toward my parents and siblings. He came from a world of culture and possibilities. My parents were tenant farmers, you see, happy but poor as church mice." She set her spoon on the tray. "Are you sure you won't have some tea? I can't see the dust, so it doesn't bother me one bit."

I swept at the cobwebs beside the window. "I enjoy cleaning." I prayed that God would forgive me for that small lie.

"I haven't given you a chance to talk about *My Àntonia.* Did you like it? I so hope you did."

The book held commonalities between Àntonia and me. Both of us were fatherless and poor with younger, at least in school years, boys pining after us. But the comparison stopped there. I would never go off to meet a scoundrel with lofty promises, only to come back with an illegitimate child. *Never.* And if I married and had ten children, I would run away from home long before any of the children thought about doing so.

There were similarities between the people of Cordial and Black Hawk, Nebraska too. The boy who loved Àntonia longed for the Nebraska of his youth—expansive and naïve. These were the very sentiments I'd heard from life-long residents of Cordial. Resentment for the hippies ran deep. Weekly columns in the *Cordial Chronicle* condemned skinny-dipping in the irrigation canals, the strain on the county welfare system, and the poor management of farms in the area. H added stories from the ranchers and farmers who loitered at his father's store. Àntonia and Jim could never hope to marry because of the prejudice toward new immigrants from Northern Europe. That same prejudice thrived in Cordial, but not just from the locals. The hippies rejected all that was conventional about life in America. They flaunted their Ivy League educations, were self-righteous, really, about the purity of their lifestyles, their harmonious existence with nature. Anything, even a shave and a haircut, represented the arbitrariness of our patriarchal society. All in all, reading *My Àntonia* demonstrated there was nothing new under the sun.

"It's sad that Jim and Àntonia don't end up together," I said. "He loved her. Remember, at the end he told her sons so, but she laughed at him. I think she was protecting herself from rejection. And I'm not even sure what he felt for Àntonia could be considered love. He idolized her as a symbol, not as a woman. She was a bookmark that held a special place in his life. If he dared to love her as a woman, he would lose what he loved most about the land. That's what I resent most about him."

"Yes, I think you're right, but lucky for you, the world has changed. In my hometown, a little speck of a burg in Nebraska, migrant farm workers came to help with the sugar beet harvest. The year I was ten, or was I eleven?—it doesn't matter—my cousin Ruth visited from Omaha to help my mother with the twins. She was a beautiful girl, just sixteen, although she seemed much older to me at the time. Her auburn hair hung down her back, and her green eyes were like nothing I'd ever seen before. One of the workers from Mexico was quite a charmer. What was his name?" Leoti searched among the cobwebs for his name. "With his dark eyes and white teeth, all the girls thought he was the most exotic thing to happen upon Ellsworth. But what was his name? Oh dear, I've gone and forgotten . . . Lorenzo! His name was Lorenzo. His mother and father had come north to flee the Mexican Revolution. He had no business working in the beet fields. He was well educated. He spoke perfect English. Of course, Mother didn't know we had even talked with him. We took water to the fields in the afternoon. He loved to tell us about his home in Mexico and the cruelty of General Diaz.

"One day, I went looking for a kitten to dress up. There were always plenty to choose from in the barn. That day I caught Ruth and Lorenzo spooning in the hayloft. They made me swear to never tell a soul, and because they both looked so frightened, I never did, until now. She eventually married an engineer for the railroad. Lorenzo left with his family to work in California. I often wondered what would have happened if they had been allowed to marry and raise a family in Ellsworth. The children would have been stunningly handsome and brilliant. That is what prejudice can do."

I brushed dust off a lamp shade and sneezed.

"Bless you," she said and disappeared into her thoughts. I swiped dust out of the carved legs of a chair and the grandfather clock near the front door.

"Did you leave a beau behind in Illinois, Amy?"

"Me? No." I didn't want to admit, even to Leoti, that I'd never gone out on a date. No need to worry. She had already leapfrogged to another memory.

"We had the most wonderful dances back home." Leoti caught a stray curl in a bobby pin. Her self-conscious primping provided a glimpse of the young Leoti. "We cleared all the desks out of the schoolhouse. The schoolmarm played the piano, even though it was terribly off key. Her brother played the fiddle. The girls brought pies, and the boys all got haircuts." Leoti closed her eyes. A smile deepened the creases of her mouth.

"Do you like living in Cordial, Amy?"

"Not so much."

"Is it the mountains? I felt like a caged animal when we first arrived. My apprehension didn't last very long. Not really. I got caught up in the daily drama of the mountains—the way the sunrise seems to magnify their size and the rosy glow of light at twilight reflects off the snowy crevices, and how the clouds glow like embers when the sun dips below the horizon. Even the way the shadows of the clouds blotch the mountains thrills me. I love it all.

"I knew I'd made the transition from being a plains girl to a mountain girl when Arthur and I traveled by train to visit my parents one Christmas. Coming back to Colorado, I watched the mountains grow on the horizon until they lorded over the sky. Oh, my heart fluttered in my chest. After that, I could never stay away from the mountains for very long.

"Listen to me prattle on like an old woman." She caught herself, laughed. "I am an old woman, a foolish old woman who spends too much time thinking about the past." Leoti's face grew serious. "You seem like a very sensible young woman. May I share a dream with you?"

I pushed the dust cloth into my apron pocket.

"No doubt you've noticed the mismatched windows at the Spruce Street Church. Before Johnston Avenue was paved, the windows on the west side were constantly being broken by rocks thrown up by passing automobiles. The elder board never considered the repair of the windows a high priority. I wouldn't have either, if the choice was between heating the church in the winter and having replacement windows made. I spoke to Pastor Ted when he first came last fall. Bless him, he found someone in the east who specializes in repairing stained-glass windows. The artist wanted a ridiculous amount of money for each sash—ten thousand dollars, I think it was. You've seen how many broken windows there are."

While Mrs. Bergman had sung a solo for the offertory during my first visit to Spruce Street church, I'd focused on the six solid-green panes. A wattle of her skin had shimmied with each high note. Looking at the windows had kept me from laughing.

"I know my days are numbered," she continued, "but I haven't given up the dream of seeing those windows restored. It was Arthur and I who had commissioned the original windows, and what a fuss we caused. We sat and talked right here. Arthur had just come back from calling on a young family with the measles. I made us tea, and he shared how he wanted to give the church stained-glass windows. I was shocked. I'd never heard him say a word about the windows, but he had already spoken to an artist. We agreed that the windows should not bear any images of the Christ. No man knows what he looked like anyway, and does it matter? We didn't think so. Instead, we selected a pleasing style that emphasized the Word of God. We certainly didn't want anything gaudy, like what the Methodists had done in Clearwater. We thought we had chosen the most logical design. Half of the church up and left over those windows. Can you think of anything more ludicrous than that? Maylene Elberfeld still crosses the street when she sees me coming."

When it was time to leave, I apologized to Leoti for not completing the dusting.

"I guess you'll just have to come back again," she said and winked playfully. "The tea kettle is always on, and there's always another book to read."

I left with Leoti's all-time favorite, *The Good Earth.*

"Pearl S. Buck, how I love to say her name," she said. "She's the only woman to win both the Pulitzer and Nobel prizes for literature."

H STEPPED OUT of the shed. I hadn't seen him since the night of the drive-in almost three weeks earlier. He greeted me with large rings of sweat darkening his tank top and breathing hard. But there was something new about him, a bulge of muscle in his shoulders and arms. He seemed older. Taller? His work had paid off, but I wasn't about to say anything. Guys like H overvalued any compliment. But it was good to see that the cut on his chin had healed.

He gulped air. "You were with Mrs. Masterson a long time."

"We were talking about books. Leoti . . . Mrs. Masterson loves to read. She has a room with books to the ceiling. She gave me *The Good Earth* to read."

"Never heard of it."

H motioned me inside the shed and threw punches at the stuffed burlap bag hanging from the rafters. I was supposed to be impressed, I know, but sweat and grunts grossed me out.

"She's doing okay. Mrs. Masterson is, I mean." The dust flying out of the bag made me sneeze. "You should visit her."

H looked at me like I'd suggested he kiss one of his sisters.

"She's very upbeat," I assured him. "She'll bake you cookies if she knows you're coming."

"Have you ever asked her about what we heard? You know, how she talked to Dr. Masterson?"

"You could ask her about it."

"My dad says people hallucinate under stress."

I supposed his dad knew that from reading farm-implement catalogs.

"Dad said the devil can appear as an angel of light," H said.

"Would the devil encourage her to serve the Master?"

H spat at the ground, the male equivalent of *Heck if I know.*

"I think God sent Dr. Masterson as a special gift to Mrs. Masterson," I said, "so she could wait for her time in peace, knowing her husband was okay."

H stilled the punching bag. "Can we talk about something else?"

"Did you tell the police what happened at the drive-in?"

"Nah, that would only make things worse," he said, and attacked the punching bag with a salvo of punches. "Guys like Jim only understand one way of talking."

"What about your parents? Didn't they notice your cuts and bruises?"

"Mom told me to stay away from troublemakers. Dad told me to stay and fight like a man."

Obviously, H's dad held more weight in the advice department of the Van Hoorn family. A sheepish grin deepened H's dimples. "If you're so worried about me, you better give me that kiss you owe me now."

"H, as a friend, I think you should know that girls don't find sweating men all that appealing."

"*Men*, huh?"

"Don't miss my point."

"Got it. You don't like sweating men." H punched the bag off center and set it spinning. "You see me as a man, do you? That's great."

Oh brother.

Twenty-One

Clear the end table, *querida*. We're yanking this place into the twentieth century." I cradled Mrs. Clancy's milk-glass lamp and doily in my arms. Mom set a new lamp in its place—crushed-velvet shade with amber crystals hanging from the base. She snapped on the light and stood back to admire its warm glow. Bruce sauntered in from the kitchen where he'd filled the counters with shopping bags. Mom said, "I told you the lamp was perfect, sweetie. Isn't it beautiful?"

"Why are you buying stuff for a place we'll be leaving soon?" I asked.

"We'll need a pretty lamp and a nice clock in California too."

Bruce stood in the doorway with a hammer. "Where's that there clock you wanted hung?"

"It's here with the candleholders." Mom kissed my cheek. "Just because we live with dead people doesn't mean we have to decorate like old fogeys. Wait until you see the material I bought to make you a peasant blouse like all the girls are wearing."

Bruce held a clock with a daisy face and stem. "Where do you want this, doll?"

I grabbed *The Good Earth.* "I'm going outside."

"Don't go too far. Bruce is grilling steaks."

"We don't have a—"

"But we do. Those cute little hibachis were on sale at the hardware store."

AFTER DINNER, MOM and Bruce went to the Lost Mine saloon. I tried to read, but the house felt claustrophobic. Each knickknack and paddywack Mom bought for the house added another link to the chain that held me to Cordial. More and more I believed Mom never intended to reach California.

Fine, I'll go alone.

The phone rang. It was Mrs. Clancy. "Put the coffee pot on. Some crazy Mexican drank himself stupid and got killed walking on the highway. We're the closest funeral home, so the body is on its way. We have a long night ahead of us. You might as well start a meatloaf too. Mr. Moberly has to put the body back together."

I wiped my face on the hem of my T-shirt.

"Are you there? Amy? I can't have you falling to pieces on me. I'll be there as soon as I can." The dial tone hummed in my ear.

Lord?

Someone pounded on the kitchen door. "Mrs. Clancy?" a male voice called.

Flipping light switches as I went, I opened the door for a man with a shining star and bold stripes down each leg. He held his cowboy hat with one hand and blotted his nose with a hankie. A rash rimmed his eyes.

"Mrs. Clancy is on the way," I said.

"Coffee?" he pleaded. "I just came from the . . . where the Mexican was hit."

"I was just going to make some."

The sheriff drank his coffee by the mailbox, waiting for the body and reinforcements to arrive. Mrs. Clancy stopped briefly to talk to him before parking in front of the garage and hefting her weight up the steps to the kitchen.

"Is your mother here?" she asked.

"She's—"

"It's just as well. Have you started the meatloaf?"

I motioned to a brick of meat on the counter. "The hamburger's frozen."

"Put the meat back in the freezer. We'll figure something out later."

A crush of tires on the gravel driveway announced the arrival of the body. Two state patrol officers sat with the sheriff in the living room, drinking coffee and filling out reports. "Ain't it just like one of those spics to get drunk and wander into traffic?"

Mom's new daisy clock read 3:00 a.m., long past the Lost Mine's closing time. I scowled at the clock. *What do I care?* Mrs. Clancy had woken the grocery store manager to get the meatloaf ingredients delivered, plus sandwich makings and a variety of sweets to set out as a buffet for the officials who came and went. I made twenty pots of coffee that night and refilled the sugar bowl three times.

Every so often one of the officers would open the basement door about an inch and ask Charles if he'd come across any identifying marks on the body. Charles yelled back, "You'll be the first to know."

A hand shook me out of sleep. "Amy, there's no reason for you to be up. Go to bed."

"I have to make coffee."

Charles offered a hand to pull me out of the chair. "If they want coffee, they can go down to the Stop-and-Chomp."

"It's closed."

"It just opened."

On the way to my bedroom, I tapped on Mom's bedroom door and peeked in. She sat on her bed, shivering and hugging a pillow. The predawn air raised goose bumps on my arms and legs. I closed the window and pulled back the covers. She still wore the slack outfit she'd worn to go out with Bruce.

"They're almost done," I said. "I'll stay with you until they leave. Lay down with me, Mom."

She obeyed and I lay next to her, sharing a pillow and wrapping my arm around her trembling shoulders.

"Shh," I cooed. "Don't cry. It's no one you know. It's a Mexican. He wasn't carrying identification. He walked into traffic on the highway and someone hit him."

Her body softened. "Is that why the police are here, because of someone who died?"

"Why else would they be here?" I didn't tell her how shaken they had all been under their matter-of-fact collection of facts for their voluminous reports, how they had all huddled around the buffet, shuffling their feet and coughing into their hands as the firemen wheeled the body into the basement.

Soon Mom's snores filled the room. I didn't leave her right away. The night's events had pushed me into a black place where all I could hear was my own breathing. I started a prayer, but the words wouldn't come. I called out silently for Lauren. If she had been there, we would have made fun of the sheriffs, whose bellies hid their belt buckles, eating donuts and trembling like campers listening to ghost stories around a campfire. Lauren told the best ghost stories, but now she had a boyfriend with no time to write to a friend who was a thousand miles away.

A thousand miles?

I let Mom's head slide down my arm to her pillow and straightened her legs before pulling the blankets to her chin. I stood frozen, waiting for her snores to resume. When they did, I tiptoed to my room to write a letter to Lauren. At least I had something to tell her.

Twenty-Two

In the weeks I'd attended the Spruce Street Church, I had become a trophy of sorts for the congregation. "Cordial would be much better off if all newcomers were like you," a gray-haired pew hen would coo. "You wear such pretty dresses, and your face glows with health." Translation: *You're just like us. You wear old-fashioned clothes, and you take a bath every day. Welcome!*

I took little pride in their approval. I winced at their snide references to the rigid Lutherans and the idolatrous Catholics, but I never so much as *tsk-tsk*ed their self-righteous judgments. Confronting the biddies was up to Pastor Ted, but I'd never seen a more patient man. He faithfully presented the Word of God like a gentleman offering a hand to a lady: *Will you receive the Father's love today?*

This Sunday was different. Feathers—pardon the pun—would fly.

I carried my guitar case in one hand and led Feather with the other. She scooted behind me toward the church, wearing my flip-flops since she had shown up barefooted. For the hundredth time, she tripped. Undaunted, Feather wiggled the elastic waistband of her skirt to her armpits, and still her feet remained hidden. Dust coated her feet, so hidden feet were preferred. Butter had tucked red clover in Feather's braids. From the neck up, Feather was ready for church. Good enough for me. As we walked into the sanctuary, the murmur of voices inquiring about visiting grandchildren and the latest doctor's visit fell silent, but only until we sat down. Their whispers and the disapproval that fueled them reached us loud and clear.

"A hippie girl?"

"We'll never get the smell out."

"Did you see that skirt she was wearing?"

"Is nothing sacred?"

Feather pulled on my shoulder. Her breath warmed my ear. "You're hurting my hand."

I released it. "Sorry."

She slipped her hand back in mine.

"We can leave if you want to," I said.

"Don't worry. I've heard it all before. I just ignore them." She squeezed my hand. "I want to hear you sing."

Feather jumped when the organist pounded on the first chord of "Give of Your Best to the Master." We stood to sing along. Feather took in the baptistery, the stained-glass windows, and the wide, arched ceilings. At the end of the hymn, Pastor Ted climbed the steps of the chancel and raised his arms to pray for the congregation.

Feather found his attire amusing. "He's wearing a dress," she said loud enough for everyone to hear. I shushed her, saying I'd explain his vestments later.

"I like his tie," she said.

"That's his stole. Now shush."

Pastor Ted welcomed Feather with a smile.

Besides Feather saying "Oh brother" every time we stood up just to sit down again, she seemed genuinely taken with the ceremony of worship. I wanted Feather to fall in love with Jesus from listening to one of Pastor Ted's sermons. Unfortunately, it was stewardship Sunday, which in Gilbertsville always happened in the fall, and the pastor always started the sermon with an apology to visitors. "Close your ears," he said. "This message is for members only." To my surprise, Pastor Ted riveted us with a story from the prophet Malachi about the forgetful and stingy children of Israel. They had robbed God by withholding their tithes and offerings. The way Pastor Ted told the story, we managed God's money to benefit the kingdom. My face warmed when I thought about the money stashed away in *Emma*. At least twenty of those dollars belonged to the Lord. A collective sigh sounded once Pastor Ted told us the tithe was no longer twenty percent.

He read from Malachi, "'Prove me now herewith, saith the Lord of hosts, if I will not open you the windows of heaven, and pour you out a blessing, that there shall not be room enough to receive it.'"

Feather blurted, "Why's he talking so funny?"

The congregation hummed like a swarm of bees. I pressed a finger to my lips in hopes of silencing her. Pastor Ted sucked in his lips to stifle a laugh. "In other words," he said to Feather, "the Lord gives us permission to test him. Happily return to him the first fruits of your wages, and he'll bless your socks off."

"But I sell eggs," she said.

"Every good gift and every perfect gift—and that includes eggs—is from above." He closed the black notebook and his Bible. "And now, Elder Ryland Burns from the stewardship committee will say a few words."

Feather, I learned that day, didn't know how to whisper. "When are you going to sing?" she asked as Elder Burns shuffled his lecture notes.

I pointed to my name in the bulletin. "I'm next."

Elder Burns gripped the lectern and cast a wary eye at Feather. His broad, smooth forehead reflected a spot of light. As far as I could tell, he had no lips. "We're family here at Spruce Street Church, and a family needs a place to come together to worship like we're used to." His voice dropped an octave. "Unless we see a significant increase in giving, we may lose that privilege."

Over my shoulder the congregation sat less than astonished. Something told me they'd heard this speech, or something like it, many times before. Their indifference only fueled the elder's vigor. He pounded the lectern.

"We got us some urgent needs in this facility. The boiler was installed before the Second World War. Don Jacobson, and he's a straight up Christian man, from Triple-A Heating and Plumbing says the boiler is so full of silt that we're burning four times the coal we should just to keep the pipes from freezing. That's why you ladies have to bring your lap robes in the winter. It might be hard to remember how cold the sanctuary gets while sitting here on a hot Sunday in July, but this here's the Lord's house, and it's our job to take care of it. And that ain't all."

The women of the church huffed at the elder's use of *ain't*.

"The benevolent fund is stone dry. I look around here, and I see lots of you who have benefited when a crop's failed or an illness meant a big doctor bill. That's what the fund is for. But I can also look around the room, and as the elder over the stewardship committee, I know what you're giving toward the Lord's work, and it—"

The congregation gasped in anticipation of his *ain't*.

"And it *isn't* ten percent." He scanned the congregation, making eye contact with the congregants. "Will the ushers come forward, please? It's time for us to make a promise we'll keep. And one more thing: Some of you can give more than ten percent and you wouldn't even notice the money missing from your checking account."

Pastor Ted sat with his head in his hands, either praying for a mighty wind to open wallets or for a lightning bolt to strike Elder Burns. My money was on the lightning. Just after the offertory, we stood to sing the doxology. Feather flipped through the hymnal and pulled on my shoulder yet again. "Where's the words?"

"Never mind. The song will be over soon."

The *amen* was a sigh of relief for the congregation.

Pastor Ted set a microphone in the middle of the chancel. He stooped to test it with a tap and to introduce me. "We have a special treat today. I heard Amy sing at a funeral service last week, and it was a true blessing. I asked her to sing the same song for us today. Prepare to be blessed. Amy?"

Heads nearly touched as I strapped on my guitar and plucked each string to be sure it was still tuned. I adjusted the E string. I heard words like *inappropriate, heathen*, and *hippie*. My eyes burned with tears and my throat tightened. I closed my eyes. *This is for you, Jesus.*

Have you ever looked at the sunset

With the sky mellowing red,

And the clouds suspended like feathers?

Then I say you've seen Jesus my Lord.

Halfway through the second verse, I felt a tug at my dress. Feather motioned with her head toward the back of the church where a pew hen had risen and was walking out. As if she were the Pied Piper of Hamelin, others got up and followed her, shaking their heads. I looked to Pastor Ted. He smiled and mouthed, *Keep going.* I scanned the congregation for receptive faces. There was H, beaming like a birthday cake, and Leoti nodding encouragingly. And there were others, too, more than I'd expected, including the Gartleys and Myron from the post office with a lady who covered her mouth when she smiled. *That must be Sheila.* Mrs. Clancy's face sagged with disapproval. I looked back to Leoti, smiled, and closed my eyes to finish the song.

Have you ever stood with the family
with the Lord there in your midst,
and the face of Christ on your brother?
Then I say you've seen Jesus my Lord.

Feather and I waited our turn to shake hands with Pastor Ted in the narthex. While kicking off the flip-flops and pulling off her skirt to reveal grungy pink shorts, she told Pastor Ted how nice he looked in his dress. The congregants gasped behind us. "I liked the story you told too."

Pastor Ted's large hands covered hers. "I hope you come again, Feather."

"You put on one crazy show, that's for sure."

I pulled Feather down the steps.

"That was weird," she said, hugging the wadded skirt to her chest. "Butter told me different, but I had this idea about church people, that they got themselves fixed somehow, and that they were as nice as could be once they walked inside those doors. So much for that. Why, they smelled like roses, all right, but their manners stunk like chicken poop."

I didn't know what to say. Sure, inviting Feather to church had been risky, but she came. She had stepped inside the double doors to dip her toes into the believer's world. I wanted her to be welcomed at Spruce Street Church as if she'd walked into Jesus' very own dining room. He would have pulled out a chair for Feather and offered her a plate of brownies with walnuts, and then he would have asked her questions about her family and her chickens and what she liked best about the world he'd made for her. She would have fallen in love with him for all the attention he paid her and how earnest he was about getting to know her. Every question she thought of, from how many stars are in the galaxy to which came first—the chicken or the egg?—he would answer. And because suffering fills him with compassion, he'd brush the hair from her forehead and she would never have another seizure.

I guess I'd experienced plenty of disappointment in my life with my daddy dying before he sang me a Portuguese lullaby. And instead of being pretty, I was smart. And not one boy had even considered inviting me to the senior prom. There was Watergate. Dippity-Do only made my hair sticky. Sea Monkeys. X-ray glasses. And becoming a woman meant monthly cramps that made me turn green. But Feather's visit to the Spruce Street Church topped them all.

"You don't have to feel bad," she said, taking my hand. "It all happened the way Butter said it would, but I'm glad I got to hear you sing."

Arrgh!

Twenty-Three

The day after Feather had attended church with me, I paced from the chapel window to the kitchen door, rehearsing my speech for Pastor Ted. Through a narrow slit of the drapes, I watched him mow his lawn, pull weeds along the driveway, and claw at the earth around the roses. I hated to interrupt a man doing his yard work, mostly because I knew church staff never felt bad about asking anyone for help. But I pitied the poor man. He was about to be assaulted with the righteous indignation of a teenager—and on his day off too.

When he wheeled his lawn mower into the garage, I jogged across the street to meet him. He stood in the doorway, shielding his eyes from the sun. His shirt was translucent with sweat, and grass stains covered his tennis shoes, just like a regular person. The strain of physical labor deepened the furrows of his brow and the slump of his shoulders. I couldn't let his vulnerability sway me. His congregants had walked out on my song because it wasn't a hymn. Sure, their exits had hurt and angered me, but that wasn't enough to confront Pastor Ted. The pew hens' world was changing. I got that. What I didn't, couldn't, accept was their treatment of Feather. Hadn't the congregants of Spruce Street Church read their Bibles? Jesus preferred the company of sinners to the religious hypocrites. Now I knew why. Butter did her best to keep her family clean. She pumped water from the well for each load of laundry and heated it in a cauldron on the wood burning stove. I bet those sinners Jesus dined with didn't smell like roses either, and maybe Jesus didn't smell so good after a long day of walking and teaching and healing those lepers who wore mantels of rotting flesh. Would the pew hens welcome Jesus into their stupid church?

Pastor Ted squinted when he stepped into the sunlight. "Amy, how nice to see you."

I stood there like a nitwit.

"Is something wrong?"

"I . . . I guess I wanted to talk to you."

"How about a cool drink? Do you like iced tea?"

It only seemed fair to warn him. "This isn't a pleasure visit."

"Oh, I see." He beckoned me toward the shade of the patio and a small table with two chairs. "I'm still thirsty, and the offer still stands."

He wasn't going to make this easy. "Sure. Okay. I guess that would be good."

We sat under the aluminum awning. He drank his first glass of tea straight down and poured himself another. I waited for him to ask me what the problem was. He talked about his garden instead.

"I didn't know if the new lawn would make it through the winter, but it greened up real nice. I put my back out twice installing the sprinkler system. My father was the very first groundskeeper at the Wilshire Country Club in 1920. I think I was ten years old when he started. That's where I developed a fondness for green lawns, I guess. Every morning, I climbed onto a mower just as the sky was lightening in the east. Mom cooked a farmer's breakfast. I could smell bacon frying from the sixteenth fairway. Dad joined us for breakfast, but he returned to the links until all the greens and tee boxes were perfectly trimmed.

"He supervised over twenty men. Most of them came from Mexico. When I got older, I worked with them leveling out the greens and repairing the tee boxes. They shared their tamales with me at lunchtime. I developed an appetite for fresh tortillas those years that has yet to be quenched.

"Keeping a pretty lawn is a tribute to my dad. And then I moved to Cordial. I'd never seen a place so taken to weeds or congested with rocks." Pastor Ted paused to admire the emerald green of his lawn. "Some members of the church happened by when I was installing the new sprinkler system to ask where I'd gotten the money and to ask who had given me permission to dig up the lawn. They told me that every pastor before me had been satisfied to pull a hose and sprinkler around the yard."

If what he'd told me were examples of the challenges he'd faced as pastor of the Spruce Street Church, I was no better than the folks who had "happened" by to question the way he took care of his lawn. On the other hand, maybe the story had been a way to ease us into a weighty conversation. Adults were maddening that way. Before he started reminiscing about his first week of junior high, I blurted, "The congregation was horrible to Feather."

Pastor Ted sighed and nodded. "Yes, they were."

"Aren't you going to do something, say something to them?"

"You're a smart and passionate young lady. I admire that in you. Those qualities endeared me to the pastoral search committee upon my graduation from seminary. Still, I troubled over my first sermon. I wrote and rewrote my twenty-minute epic until I just plain ran out of time. Otherwise, I would still be working on it." He snickered. "I added observations in the margins while the choir sang. I'll never forget the text. It came from the second chapter of Philippians. I considered the passage foundational to the fresh start God had given the church and me. As his people we were to imitate the humility of Christ in our dealings with one another, the community, and the world.

"Monday morning I went to my tiny office convinced I'd hit a home run with that sermon. There had been generous back slapping and hearty handshakes from the congregants afterward. I wasn't a bit surprised to see a dozen or so envelopes lying on my desk the next morning. I expected notes of congratulations. I slit the first note open and read. The contents will be forever engraved on my memory. There was no salutation. It read: 'Too much talk of Jesus, not enough funny stories. I have a book of stories you can borrow until you find one for your library.' The next note questioned my credentials. One woman included twenty-five cents for a haircut. And dear Mrs. Grossman, she hoped I would take control of the choir. She felt they sang far too many hymns of lamentation. I understood her complaint after several Sundays." Pastor Ted raised his face to the breeze that rustled the leaves of an old poplar.

I asked, "Why didn't those people stay home if they didn't want to hear about Jesus?"

"I wondered that myself, so I wrote a seminary professor who had mentored me through a mighty tough hermeneutics class, asking what I should do with a congregation who didn't want to hear about Jesus. I'm not too proud to tell you that I'd hoped he would tell me to knock the dust off my shoes and pack my bags. Months passed before I heard from him. All he wrote was the Scripture reference for the parable of the tares. I wadded the paper up and tossed it into the waste basket."

"You did?"

"Amy, it will take your whole life to learn and relearn what you think you know about the Scriptures. The Christ will be both an enigma and a friend. The older I get the more wondrous and mysterious he becomes, and the more needful I am of his mercy." Pastor Ted wiped his forehead on his sleeve. "Jesus teaches his disciples that the kingdom of heaven is like a man who planted good seeds in his field. His enemy comes under the cover of night to sow weeds called tares, a very insidious plant. Are you much of a gardener?"

I watered houseplants and mowed the lawn in Gilbertsville. "Not really."

"Weeds compete with crops for nutrients in the soil and can rob the plants of the sunshine and water they need to mature—not a healthy situation for a garden."

"That's why people pick weeds."

"That's right, but tares look just like wheat until harvest time. How would the field hands know which to pull and which to leave? The master of the field in Jesus' story feared the wheat would be pulled out with the tares. So, Amy, even before the first group of believers thought to meet together, Jesus the vinedresser knew tares would take shelter in his church."

"That's nuts. Why do they bother coming? If I didn't want to hear about Jesus, I'd sleep in on Sunday mornings, read the funny papers in my pajamas, and make pancakes and fry bacon. I wouldn't bother going to church. It's . . . it's early."

Pastor Ted tipped his chair back. "People come for many reasons, most out of a sense of tradition and continuity. Perhaps they're crazy about potlucks, or they carry a horrible burden of guilt they hope to assuage by attending services or more potlucks. Honestly, I don't know why some people come, but in the time I've been shepherding flocks much like this one, I've seen some of those tares become what they are not. They become wheat. That's redemption, a real miracle."

"So we can't rip the tares out of the fields?"

"The Father's perfect love is very patient."

"But in the meantime, their behavior repels people from God."

Pastor Ted rubbed his eyes with the heels of his hands and sighed. "Yes, I'm afraid that is so."

THE DELIVERY VAN stopped in front of the funeral home. Glen, the driver, shorter than me by a head with muscled legs and a basketball belly, delivered caskets to Mrs. Clancy regularly. The caskets came C.O.D., and Mrs. Clancy had already gone home for the day. I met Glen at the back of his truck. "Mrs. Clancy isn't here to accept a delivery. She wasn't expecting you until tomorrow."

"This package is for you. It's pretty heavy." He snapped his suspenders against his chest. "I think I should carry it inside."

Glen hefted a long cylinder wrapped in brown paper that bent where he carried it on his shoulder. That pretty much ruled out a transmission, so I figured the package must be from Lauren. I led Glen to the kitchen door, considered having him leave the package in the living room but thought better of it. "Would you mind carrying the package to my room?"

With the hefty package on my bedroom floor, I walked Glen to the kitchen door. I asked him if he delivered car parts to Tommy's.

"All the time," he said, snapping his suspenders again.

"Anything as big as a transmission?"

"I've delivered whole engines."

"Anything lately? He's waiting for a transmission for our Pontiac."

"Let's see." He ran his thumbs under his suspenders. "A couple weeks ago, I delivered something to Tommy. That sucker was heavy." Glen scratched the day's growth on his chin. "Tommy seemed mighty glad to see that part. He may have said something about a transmission, but . . . maybe you'd better ask him."

I agonized between opening Lauren's package and running straight to Tommy's to ask about the Pontiac. Lauren's package won.

Clancy and Sons was at the end of Glen's delivery route. He liked to gossip about the valley with Mrs. Clancy until she tired of his stories and told him she needed to make a bank deposit. Since I had no such excuse, Glen blathered on about the nervous flatlanders driving the winding roads, how you couldn't go anywhere in Clearwater County without smelling a hippy, and how some people didn't know anything about the delivery business but were always willing to offer advice. I shifted from one foot to the other, muttered "uh-huh" with scant enthusiasm, and still he asked for a drink of water. Some people can't take a hint.

After he'd finally driven off, I opened one end of Lauren's package and slid a rug onto the floor. The beauty of the rug caught my breath, but the size of it made me groan. "Lauren, what have you done?" This was no ordinary rug. On a field of the ripest apricot imaginable, royal-blue flourishes and red poppies splashed about, all contained within a sky-blue border. I bent to trace a green vine with my finger. The pile buried my fingernail. I sat in the middle of the rug Indian-style to read her letter.

Dear Amy,

This is turning out to be the worst summer of my life. First you move away and then Andy broke up with me for no good reason. The pain is like the worst cramps you've ever had only higher and nothing makes you feel better and do not beleive what those nuts tell you about time heeling all wounds. Its been five days and I still cant eat.

Amy this is the worst of it. I did what I swore I wood never do. Do you remember snow camp last winter? Do you remember what they asked us to promise? I broke that promise. Are you shocked? Do you hate me? Even if you do don't stop reading now althouogh I would understand if you did. I want you to know it was nothing like that book I found in my mothers underwear drawer. Its not worth the worry and how dirty you feel. Please beleive me when I say we didn't plan on what happened it just did. That's whats so weird and sad. Now that I think about it maybe you should take those pills your mother gave you. You don't want to go threw this. I'm counting the days (if you know what I mean) and I'm scared to death. I wish you were here. My parents will kill me. Maybe I will come to California with you. I'm soooo scared.

Are we still friends? Please, please, please say yes. Write me today or I'll die.

Love forever and ever,

Lauren

P.S. They fired me from La Chica Fiesta but won't tell me why.

P.S.S. My parents are leaving on a trip to Chicago. If I don't have a new job by the time they get back there will be no beauty school for me. This is so unfair!!! Theres a help wanted sign at the Bait & Bite. I know I swore I'd never work around fried food again. Say goodby to clear skin.

P.S.S.S. I hope you like the rug. You can bet it was expensive. Lets just say that Andy's mother has learned to keep her front door locked.

I rolled up the rug and wrestled it back into the paper wrapping before cramming it under the bed. I tore Lauren's letter up into tiny pieces and buried them in the funeral home's dumpster. Then I threw up.

That night, Mom babbled all through dinner. She and Bonnie were going shopping in Orchard City on Saturday.

"Do you want to go?" she asked. "Bruce says they have a used bookstore there."

When I said no, she seemed relieved. I welcomed the time alone. My head buzzed with questions for Lauren. Calling her on a party line was definitely out of the question. But what would I say to her? She'd forgotten all about reciting John 3:16 if a boy got fresh. From the date on the postmark, it had been over a week. By now she definitely knew if she was pregnant or not. Without trying, I pictured her and Andy together. *Eew.* How could she possibly—? *Don't think about it!*

And what about the rug? I couldn't plop a fifty pound rug into an envelope to hide under my underwear. How did she expect me to explain a Persian rug to Mom? I knew exactly where the Babcocks lived—across town, of course, in the historic district. Grecian columns and a deep porch. It was Scarlett O'Hara's Tara all over again. A constant stream of traffic flowed by the house. Did Lauren watch the house for a time when everyone, including the dog, was out? Did she carry the rug home, or did she bring her brother's wagon? And most importantly, why hadn't she chosen something lighter and cheaper to ship back? A flare of resentment warmed my face.

By sending the rug to me, she made me an accessory to a crime. Anyone who watched *Perry Mason* knew that.

"I'M MEETING BRUCE at the Lost Mine in an hour." Mom examined her fingernails. "My nails are a mess. Amy, run the tub for me while I remove my nail polish. I smell like fertilizer and chicken feed. Put some Skin So Soft in the water."

After Mom left with Bruce, I sat down to write Lauren a letter. First, I printed out Scriptures on index cards for her to memorize. Then I demanded an apology and a refund for having to ship the rug back to Gilbertsville. I stifled an impulse to send the Mexican blouses back to Lauren with the rug. Those I liked. Shipping the rug meant dipping into my travel money, so I let her questions about friendship go unanswered. I rolled up the letter and pushed it down the center of the rug. I taped the wrapping paper shut and made a new label to send the rug back to Lauren. For my next trick, I would get the package out of the house without Mrs. Clancy or Mom seeing it.

"Thanks a lot, Lauren."

Twenty-Four

Each evening that week at four o'clock, Mexican families began lining the sidewalk in front of the funeral home. Somber and silent, they stood in tight familial groups. The women dressed in black with their heads veiled in lace. The children leaned into their mothers' skirts, watchful with eyes of bittersweet chocolate. The boys wore crisp white shirts. The girls wore starched dresses that billowed out from their waists. Sometimes the children gazed up at their mothers, pleading with their eyes to retreat to the shade, only to have their mothers rebuke their requests with a sharp shake of the head. The men wore dark suits with their hair slicked into place. Some had pencil-thin mustaches. They smelled of aftershave. No one spoke. I only made eye contact with several of the children who then quickly looked away.

A few minutes before five, I opened the casket, careful not to look at the man's face. I'd overheard the sheriff telling a deputy that Charles had spent most of that first night and all the next day putting the man's face together. I wasn't all that anxious to see how well he'd accomplished his task. I snapped the lamp on.

By the time the first family stepped onto the porch, their faces glistened with sweat. They entered, one family at a time, walking past the guest book. The mother and the children stopped inside the door with their gazes to the floor. The father stepped up to the casket. I held my breath.

Is this the man's family?

With a sigh, the father's shoulders relaxed. Only then did the wife raise her gaze to meet his. He shook his head, crossed himself. The room exhaled.

And another family took their place.

When I locked the door at eight, no one complained. They stepped off the porch and walked hand in hand back to their vehicles parked up and down both sides of the street. On the fifth night, I kept the doors open until everyone in line had a chance to view the body that lay as it had all week, broken and singular. Somewhere a mother or young wife wondered where her son or husband had gone or why the check had not arrived from America. She would never know. I cried for her as I closed the casket for the last time and turned off the lamp. I slipped the guest book back in its box and placed it on Mrs. Clancy's desk along with the forms I'd been instructed to fill out for the family.

I fell on the bed and the tears flowed. "I hate this place. I hate Mrs. Clancy. I hate my mother." The words burned my throat. "I hate death and the business of death. And I hate Cordial. I hate that somewhere a child doesn't know where his daddy is. I hate that most of all." I ranted until my eyes felt like cotton and my rage was spent.

Twenty-Five

The shade snapped open. I turned away from the window, wrapping my head in a pillow. Mom bent over me. The scents of Tabu, White Rain hair spray, and Lily of the Valley lotion spilled over me but didn't camouflage her first cigarettes of the day. These were the scents of Mom. My throat tightened.

"*Fofa,* you slept in your dress? You'll have to launder it today."

I'd drifted in and out of sleep since seven, my usual wake-up time.

"I'm late for work," she said. "And Mrs. Clancy will expect the funeral home to be spotless by the time she gets here."

I spoke into the pillow. "I'm tired."

"Are you sick?"

"I'm tired."

"I'll come home at lunch to check on you." Her shoes tapped out her retreat. She stopped at the door. "Don't lie in bed too long. I think the old biddy is still upset about your song. We can't chance making her mad again." And she was gone.

After she left, I rolled onto my back. The full force of the sun's optimism stung my eyes. That wouldn't do. Down came the shade, and I stepped out of the dress and pulled a nightgown over my head. The sheets had barely chilled. Before I fell asleep again, I considered reading the final chapters of *The Good Earth.* Wang Lung was a miserable little man. *Forget him.* My guitar leaned in the corner. Straw had loaned me a John Denver songbook. Maybe a little "Rocky Mountain High"? My arms felt leaden. Lauren had written to say she wasn't pregnant and to ask why she hadn't heard from me. I would write her later. I turned to the wall and disappeared into sleep.

The squeal of the kitchen door's hinges woke me. "Amy? Are you here?" It was Mrs. Clancy. I kept my eyes closed and slowed my breathing. The bedroom door opened and closed. The kitchen floor groaned under her footsteps as she clicked light switches and made coffee before clomping toward her office. The quiet settled on me, and I dreamed of swimming in a sparkling blue lake.

"Wake up!" Feather said, shaking my shoulder. "We're kidnapping you."

"I'm tired."

Another voice. Male. "Are your eyes always that puffy in the morning?"

H? I covered my head with the sheet. "Get out of here, both of you."

"Go wait for her on the porch," Mrs. Clancy said. She sat on the bed. Either I rolled into the valley she created in the mattress, or I sat up.

"They're gone," she said. "You can come out now."

I sat up and pushed hair from my face.

With her hands in her lap, she cocked her head to smile. "It's been a tough week for you. You could use a little fun, so H and Feather are taking you floating down the canal. It's what I used to do as a girl when life got too burdensome. My brothers took me. It'll be good for you." She patted my leg. "Come on, get out of bed. You don't want to miss this day." At the door she turned and threw a garden hat onto the bed. "You'll want to wear this—freckles, you know."

H BENT OVER an inner tube that lay half in the water. "I'll hold the tube while you sit in it, and then I'll push you into the current. It's easy."

"But how will I get out?" I asked.

"I'll let you know when—"

"How?"

"I won't be that far behind you. You'll be able to hear me. And I can jump out and help you."

"Water makes me nervous," I whispered only for H to hear.

"I know. If it wasn't safe, I wouldn't let you do it."

"I'll go first, H," Feather offered.

"Do you think that's wise?" I asked H.

"We'll only be a few feet apart. I can be out of the water in a second if there's a problem."

"Promise?"

"I promise."

Every spring, back in Gilbertsville, bulbs sprouted like green noses out of the black earth along Market Street. I walked past the planters twice a day on my way to school and back home again. After the initial shock of seeing anything green after a long, colorless winter, the tulips grew their sword-like leaves and meaty stems without much notice from me. But when their blood-red flower cups exploded, Lauren and I celebrated by eating warm donuts and drinking hot chocolate in Baumgartner's Bakery. We sat at tiny café tables, breathing in the scents of butter and yeast and chocolate. We gossiped about classmates and admired each other's chocolate mustaches. Sadly, horticultural miracles had held our attention for only three nanoseconds. But I remembered that shock of color and the hope it birthed in me. That's how I felt being with H just then. The change in him was that noticeable. One day he had been an oaf full of false bravado. That day, with his new strength, he surprised and reassured me.

Feather set her inner tube on the canal bank and climbed in. "Push me," she demanded of H.

H shoved her off and the current pulled her away. She squealed. I pulled Mrs. Clancy's garden hat to my eyebrows and scooted my inner tube closer to the bank. H all but lifted me into the water. The inner tube bounced below the water's surface, dunking me up to my chest. The cold water shocked a gasp right out of me.

"Look at H!" Feather shouted over her shoulder.

H cannonballed into the canal, holding the inner tube over his fanny. He disappeared under the water and bobbed to the surface. "Oh, baby, that feels good."

Feather used her hand like a rudder to face me. "This is fun." Seeing that she possessed some control in the water helped me relax. I leaned back and lifted my face to the sun. Freckles didn't scare me.

"That's more like it," H called.

I smiled to myself. I could be such a worry wart.

Feather called out, "Check out the adorable goats."

A trio of goats munched stubbles of hay in the field. The goats reminded me of the Hubbard sisters with their identical bobbed hairdos and a preference for Mr. Baumgartner's sticky buns.

"Goats are not adorable," H muttered.

"Where's your sense of wonder?" I asked him.

"I have plenty of wonder. I just happen to save it for things worth wondering about."

"Like?"

"Like how many touchdowns I'll make my first year on the football team." And yet, H remained H.

"Oh yes, football, the beginning place for all wonderment, like black holes, the northern lights, and a baby's first step. H, you need to dream bigger. Build a taller skyscraper. Discover a vaccine for chicken pox. Develop the safest working boot in history."

A spray of water drenched my hat. I caught the current with my hand to face my attacker. Before I could retaliate, I was spitting canal water, the home of ducks and fishes and too many unknown things that emptied their bowels into the water. I covered my face. "Uncle!"

The canal wound along the base of Logan Mountain, bouncing us gently off the grassy banks and spinning us at will. We passed cattle too busy grazing to notice us. In an apple orchard, young trees bent under the load of green fruit on their branches. The sky was a herd of disorganized clouds in a forget-me-not sky.

"This is where Falcon lives," Feather called out.

My head snapped up. Men and women in overalls and broad hats harvested squash and tomatoes with a twist and a pull. Row upon row of beans, carrots, and marijuana—lots and lots of marijuana grew in arrow-straight rows.

"I'm not supposed to go there," Feather said. "Butter says they're different."

How they were different was obvious. Butter didn't even allow alcohol on their farm. But knowing that Falcon lived there made me curious. "How are they different?"

Feather shrugged.

H hooked my inner tube with his feet and back-paddled to widen the distance between us and Feather. "I can tell you how they're different," H whispered. "They're a bunch of dopers, for one. They let their kids run around naked. And they aren't too discreet about . . . I mean, it's not unusual to . . ."

"H, what are you trying to say?"

"You've heard of free love, haven't you? Well, they invented it right there."

H released my inner tube, and I paddled to catch up to Feather. When I did, I turned to look back at what H had called New Morning farm. Besides a weathered farmhouse and barn, there was a school bus with a stove pipe and mismatched curtains and a smattering of outbuildings no bigger than garages, cobbled together with odd lengths of timbers and boards. A stand of teepees filled a paddock.

That shouldn't be too hard to find again.

We floated by another farmhouse with a bright-red barn. The owner had draped a rope to give his barn a smile to go along with two windows that served as eyes and a hayloft nose. After that, pastures of grazing cattle and horses stretched below us. I closed my eyes, only to see the faces of the Mexican women waiting to see their son or brother or husband.

H ran by me on the bank. "Amy, get out! Feather's having a seizure!"

Feather arched her back, her mouth agape, and flipped out of her tube. H grabbed her shirt and pulled her out of the canal. The current pulled me past them as I clawed at the grass to heft myself out of the water. By the time I ran back to H and Feather, H held her head in his lap. Her arms and legs jerked rhythmically.

Jesus! "Shouldn't we put something in her mouth?" I asked.

"Run back to the house we just passed. Ask them to call for help."

I hesitated, feeling responsible for Feather.

"Go," demanded H. "We'll follow when she stops."

I worried I had run past the house when I recognized the roof in the trees. I bent to ease my way through a barbed-wire fence, but a barb caught my T-shirt, ripping a hole and cutting my arm from my shoulder to my elbow. I ignored the pain to run through a pasture. Cattle moseyed out of my path without looking up. When I got within shouting distance of the house, I yelled for help. Only a few chickens pecking at the lawn acknowledged me. I pushed through the gate and pounded on the back door. I moved to a window, pounding and yelling, "Is anyone here? I need help! My friend needs help!" I ran to the front door. No one answered. I looked up and down the road. No houses. I rang the doorbell. "Please help me. *Please!*"

I rested my forehead on the door. "Lord, please, let Feather be okay. Bring help."

I turned the doorknob, and the door opened. I walked in. "Hello? I'm not a burglar," I said, scanning the room for a telephone. "I'm here to call an ambulance." I walked through the silent living room to the kitchen where I opened and closed drawers looking for a telephone book. Inside a wall cabinet over the telephone, a list of phone numbers had been taped to the door.

I dialed the ambulance.

FEATHER LAY ON the clinic bed in a tight ball. "My head is killing me."

"Do you want me to rub your back?" I asked.

"Would you?"

I sat on the bed. Feather's shoulders relaxed under my touch. I couldn't say anything to ease her physical pain, but I was more disappointed that I couldn't think of one solitary thing to offer her hope. "I'm so sorry, Feather."

Feather wiped tears from her eyes. "I know."

I tilted my head back to let my tears run down my cheeks to my neck where they collected on the collar of my blouse. I ran my hands up the sides of her spine and circled the bony hills of her shoulder blades.

"Are you crying?" she asked.

"A little."

"There's tissue on the nightstand."

"Do you want one?"

"Sure." Feather sat up to wipe her face and blow her nose. "Butter's real upset. She called her mother. I'm not supposed to know, but Mule told me. I can't remember the last time Butter called her." Feather threw her arms around me, and I pulled her onto my lap. Her tears soaked my shoulder. I sniffed to keep my snot out of her hair. The clock on the wall *tick, tick, tick*ed. Butter looked in on us, gave me a weak smile, and closed the door.

"I knew you'd be my best-ever friend the moment I saw you," Feather said.

I deeply regretted not being a world-class brain doctor or rich enough to employ one. Her hair tickled my nose, so I patted it down. "Feather, when I'm scared, I say a prayer."

"I don't know any prayers."

"I can pray for you."

"Will it help?"

"It will, but I don't know how. We'll have to watch and see."

Feather searched my face with sea-glass eyes. "I get it. Prayer is like a vitamin."

A vitamin? Oh boy, I didn't know if prayer was anything like a vitamin or not. "Prayer is talking to God and asking for his help."

"And he helps?"

"Yes, but he's more like a parent than a Santa Claus. He listens to our requests and then does what's best for us anyway."

Feather laid her head on the pillow. "Maybe later, then."

MOM ADDED A casserole of *pudim de fiambre* to the picnic basket, a sort of ham bread pudding that Lauren always asked for when she spent the night. "The ham is not so good as Uncle Eusebio brought your *avós.*" She crossed herself. "May the Lord have mercy on their souls." She looked me up and down. "You're filthy. Go wash up and put a cool cloth on your eyes. They're puffy. And change your clothes, *fofa.* We're going to a softball game. It will do you a world of good. You can't sit around here worrying about Feather."

Of course, I can. "Mom, really, a softball game? I'm not in the mood. My arm hurts."

Mom embraced me, stroking my hair. "You are a good friend to the girl, but only her mama and papa can help her now. She will be better soon, and then the two of you can read your books together. The softball game will take your mind off your troubles. The coal miners are playing the hippies."

"So Bruce is playing?" *And Falcon?*

"Maybe."

"Mom?"

"Okay, yes, he's playing on the coal miners' team."

I peeked inside the picnic basket. "You baked a cake? So what are you feeling guilty about?"

"What? I can't bake a cake for the man I love without having a reason?"

"It's just that—"

"I'll show you how much you know about me. This is a just-in-case cake."

I raised my eyebrows.

"Just in case Bruce gets angry that we go to the game."

I threw up my hands and groaned.

"All right, you little *sapa,* I'll tell you." She slapped the picnic basket closed. "I've already been to a couple of these games. Does that surprise you? Nothing interesting happens. The hippies always win, but no one seems upset about that. We share food. We laugh at the men tripping over the bags."

"The bases?"

"Yes, the bases. There are rumors about the game tonight. That nasty little man who writes the articles in the paper called for the locals to come to the game with sheep dip for the hippies. Bruce is concerned about my safety . . . and yours—"

"Even though I'm a toad?"

"Bruce thinks you're nice for a *sapa,* most of the time, and so do I. I may tell him the truth about you tonight since you keep interrupting me like an old woman who can't hear." Mom busied herself wiping the counters. "He asked me not to come. None of the women or children are going. He didn't want to worry about our safety."

"Maybe he's right. Maybe we should stay home."

"I hear these old men talking tough in the store every day. They're like sailboats without wind. They're bluffing, I tell you. Nothing will come of it, and then the men will be hungry after all of their playing."

"I don't know . . ."

"Amy, they are a bunch of old, fat men who have nothing better to do than make idle threats. They won't stop me from enjoying a fine summer evening like this." She turned me by the shoulders toward the bedroom and patted my bottom. "Now, go do as I told you. I need your help carrying the basket. It weighs a ton."

A gray quilt of clouds held the day's heat to the valley floor. I regretted not taking the time to pull my hair into a bun. Mom dabbed her face with a hankie, careful not to undo all the makeup she'd applied. On the three-block walk to the softball field, Mom and I sat the basket down every fifty yards or so and switched sides. The wooden handles dug into our hands. Before we made the turn up Sawyer Street, we stopped in front of Cordell's Gun Shop. A hand-printed sign in the window asked, *Where have gun laws reduced crime?*

"Are you sure we're doing the right thing?" I asked.

"Keep complaining, my little *sapa,* and I'll give your slice of *bolo da iha* to a stinky hippie." The anticipation of her chocolate cake laced with cinnamon and honey made my mouth water.

When we arrived at the softball field, Mom stopped abruptly to set down the basket. With hands on hips she scanned the scene. Spectators, mostly women with children, filled the bleachers. Other women sat on blankets in the grass with their infants.

Mom frowned at the crowd. "I think Bruce got his nights mixed up." We spread our blanket near the coal miners' bench.

A chain-link backstop and fence protected the crowd and the players' benches from errant balls, and that was the extent of the facilities. Period. No grass. No concession stand. No pitcher's mound. A rambling stripe of flour marked the foul lines, and mismatched pillows filled in for bases.

Bruce stood behind a pink velveteen pillow, presumably second base. He pounded his glove with his fist and shifted his weight from one foot to the other as the batter dug into the dust to set his stance. Mom waved wildly to catch Bruce's attention. He nodded curtly and scanned the bleachers. I followed his gaze. No fat men with malice on their minds sat among the wives, children, and parents.

Who are you looking at?

Mom patted my knee. "He sees us."

The hippies wore athletic shorts that revealed their roped muscles. Their hair bushed out from their baseball caps. *Hmm, Bozo plays baseball.* Just looking at them made me hot. I twisted my hair off my neck and secured it with a pencil from my purse. When Falcon came up to bat, he made the center fielder chase after a home run. My heart pounded wildly as he ran around the bases. The hippies scored six runs before the coal miners finally managed a turn at bat, but the hippies sent them right back to the outfield with two strikeouts and an underhanded toss to first base. Really, the coal miners played like a bunch of girls.

A line of pick-up trucks drove slowly past the field—first one way and then the other, some taunting the hippies with hog calls and worse. The spectators booed, but the players remained engaged with the game.

The hippies took the field after a failed bunt. Another player took Falcon's place in the field, so he sat alone on the bench. If I was going to ask him about repairing the church windows for Leoti, this was the time.

"Mom, I need to talk to someone. I'll be right back."

Bruce trotted toward the coal miners' bench and stopped. The fear in his eyes made me hesitate. He looked over his shoulder toward the bleachers, turned and trotted to a woman who kissed him smack on the lips. A young girl with pigtails jumped into his embrace, and when he sat down, a towheaded boy climbed onto his shoulders. A family. Bruce was married.

Mom stiffened. I sat back down.

"Do you want to leave?" I asked.

"Not yet. Soon."

We sat through two of the longest innings ever played. Mom smiled as she filled a plate with ham pudding and sliced tomatoes. Eating was like trying to swallow a tennis ball. The hippies scored run after run. Mom set aside her dinner and used her fork to gouge a bite out of the cake. With chocolate on her teeth, she told me a story about a little girl who had returned a rooster to the store that morning, complaining that it didn't lay eggs. I couldn't laugh, but I offered her an understanding smile that probably looked more like a grimace.

The trucks I'd watched drive back and forth now idled behind us. I recognized Jim Warner as one of the passengers. Although the cool mountain air flowed through the valley to clear the clouds and tame the heat, my palms dampened with sweat. The drivers exchanged glances and stopped their engines. A stock tank, perfect for dipping sheep or hippies, filled the back of one truck. The men left the cabs of the trucks to lean against the truck hoods. They spat in the dirt and covered their broad chests with forearms the size of pineapples.

"Mom, I think we should go home now. The mosquitoes are biting."

Mom followed my gaze to the men behind us. "I'm ready."

We walked home in silence. Mom hoisted the picnic basket onto the kitchen counter. "Would you mind, Amy? I'm very tired." She closed the bedroom door. I listened to her muffled sobs as I stored our leftovers and read toward the final chapters of *The Good Earth*. Truthfully, I'd lost interest in the story since O-lan had died. I read of Wang's plan to buy opium for his lecherous uncle and his wife while Mom's cries ebbed and flowed. I prayed for her.

Father, bring someone to love Mom with a pure heart who isn't married or cruel or exploitative or a jerk.

And I prayed for Feather to be comforted in her disappointment.

Before long, Mom's sobs subsided, and I tiptoed into the room to remove her sandals and cover her with a sheet. Even in sleep, her breaths snagged on her heartbreak. I slumped to the floor to lean against her bed, waiting for sirens or angry shouts from the softball field. Crickets chirruped. Dogs barked greetings. A train blew its warning blasts as it entered the town's northern limits. The chatter of the sparrows that roosted in the spruce trees crescendoed and faded until the little flock slept.

A trill of hopefulness brightened my mood when I realized Mom would be willing to leave Cordial now that she knew about Bruce. And just as quickly my hope turned to shame, based as it was on Mom's heartache.

I'm so selfish, Lord.

I considered visiting Feather at the clinic, but visiting hours had long since passed. Leoti, too, would be in bed by this hour. I rose to leave Mom to her dreams and to see if Wang Lung would actually fool his uncle into using the opium.

Phooey with that.

I made my way to the softball field, curious about what had happened after we left and, more truthfully, hoping Falcon was still there. By the time I reached the field, I'd fully convinced myself that I only wanted to talk with him about repairing the church's windows.

A group of men sat on the lawn behind the back stop, passing a cigarette around the circle. The moment the sickly sweet smoke reached me, I stepped back, hoping my presence would go unnoticed. I turned to leave.

"Hey! Amelia, is that you?" Falcon asked, rising and walking toward me.

"I couldn't sleep. I thought if I walked for awhile . . . I didn't mean to interrupt anything."

"You shouldn't be out alone. I'll walk you home." He waved to the circle of men. "Catch you later." He put his arm around my shoulders. "I just need some steadying, little sister." He smelled of old sweat and dust and marijuana. Then why did my stomach flip at his touch? I should have been calling the sheriff to report drug use, but honestly, Falcon's touch undid me. The farther we walked the more I relaxed into him. When he pulled my arm around his waist, I didn't resist.

"You left early," he said. "You missed my grand slammer."

You noticed? "My mom wasn't feeling well. And those men . . . they made us nervous. Did they give you any trouble?"

"Did they dip us like sheep? Nah. The coal miners stood shoulder to shoulder so the families could leave without being hassled. When the locals saw how outnumbered they were, they took off."

"And you stayed behind?"

"Somebody had to thank those guys."

The sun had stored its warmth in the sidewalk, and now it bled through my flip-flops. Lightning flashed over Logan Mountain.

Don't rain. Don't rain.

"You had a big scare with Feather," he said with rubbery lips. "I guess you saved the day."

"I ran for help is all. H carried her to a house to meet the ambulance."

"Straw and Butter are trippin' over this epilepsy thing."

"They're worried. They want to do what's best for her. The tests, the meds. Everything is so expensive."

"Still, you showed a lot of courage, Amelia."

I enumerated all of the reasons that being with Falcon and enjoying his touch was a very bad idea. For one, there was the whole unequally yoked thing. But, come on, I wasn't going to marry him or anything. For two, he was a lot older than me. But didn't that make him more mature and responsible? It showed in how he cared about Feather and her family. Besides, he had a Masters degree in sociology. That meant he had a deep appreciation for human struggles. Sure, he smoked marijuana, but what was marijuana but hippie moonshine? Smoking marijuana would probably be legal before the end of the year. Instead of wine cellars, people would have greenhouses for their hybrid marijuana plants. No big deal. Really, what was the difference between my mother swilling beer and Falcon puffing on a joint? Then I remembered Falcon's contempt for all things Christian. That meant something, but did it mean I couldn't have his arm around me, that he couldn't kiss me? I really wanted him to kiss me, so I chanted in my thoughts, *Kiss me, kiss me, kiss me.* Only a kiss, a real kiss, would satisfy the ache yawning under my heart.

He belched. "Excuse me," he said, covering his mouth, but it was too late. The full force of his breath awakened my reason. *Get down to business, girl.*

"Falcon, I need your help with something." I told him about my friendship with Leoti and how Arthur had helped the coal miners. "Arthur and Leoti commissioned the original stained-glass windows at Spruce Street Church. Three of the windows were broken before they paved Johnston Avenue."

Falcon stopped. "Wow, that's a coincidence. I noticed those windows the very first day I got here," he said, walking again. His arm remained around my shoulders. Could he feel my heart racing? "The craftsmanship is amazing. In fact, a bro from the farm helped me copy the pattern. It took me a while to gather the glass to match, but I eventually duplicated one of the sashes. Honestly, you couldn't tell the old from the new. I showed the new sash to the pastor—some dude named Ed."

"You showed your work to Pastor Ted?"

"Ted, yeah, that was his name. He was impressed with the work, but the elder board needed to appropriate funds. I figured they'd refuse, and I was right. But the pastor was cool. He found out where I was crashing to return the sash. I told him to keep it. He gave me thirty dollars, said it was all he had on him, which was kind of a trip because that was how much I was going to charge him anyway."

"Thirty dollars? Is that how much you'd charge now?"

"I should charge more, but I'm a sucker for restoration work. That's how I started with stained glass."

We stopped at the front gate of the funeral home. We stood face to face. "Falcon, I need a straight answer. Will you or won't you make the remaining five sashes for thirty dollars apiece?"

Falcon rested his hand on my cheek. "Lovely Amelia, I'm leaving soon. If this lady has to convince a committee to take the project to the elder board, I'll be long gone."

A lump tightened my throat. "When are you leaving?"

"Before the nights get cold. Besides, September is best for surfing in California."

"If we didn't have to worry about approval from the elder board, and Leoti agrees to the price, could you start right away?"

"Can you help me? The curved pieces need grinding to smooth the edges after they're cut. You could do the grinding while I solder the joints. If you're willing, we can get 'em done before I leave."

"You're sure?"

"Absolutely."

"Will you even remember what you promised tonight?"

He kissed my forehead. "I'll remember."

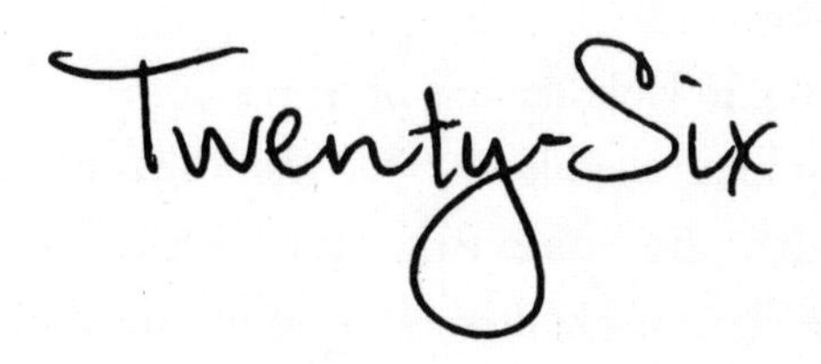

H pulled onto the highway, shifting fiercely through the gears. Out the truck's rear window, I watched the window sashes slide across the truck bed. Pastor Ted had helped me wrap each sash with a blanket and secure them with twine. The sashes weighed a ton, which was only a modest exaggeration. "Watch how you take the corners, H. The sashes are sliding." H remained mute, scowling at the road ahead of us.

"We'll be turning at DeCrane Road," I said.

"I thought this artsy guy lived near Clearwater."

"The artist lives on the *way* to Clearwater." I twisted my hair off my neck.

"He doesn't live at that New Morning place, does he?"

"You saw his work. You couldn't tell which sash was the original. That kind of skill is a gift from God." How was that for justification?

H downshifted and skidded to a stop on the shoulder. "I'm not moving another inch until I know exactly where we're going."

"What are you so worked up about?"

"Why's your hair down? You always wear it tied back or something."

I let my hair fall over my shoulders. "What does my hair have to do with anything?"

"You're trying to look like one of them."

"*Them?* You mean the hippies? You think I'm trying to look like a hippie?" Of course, that was exactly what I was trying to do, but that wasn't his business. "Are you driving me to the artist's studio or not? If not, then take me back to Cordial, so I can have Pastor Ted drive me."

"He wouldn't drive you to New Morning."

"A lot you know. Pastor Ted has met the artist *and* been to his studio."

H sat staring out the windshield, his jaw twitching.

"Can we go now?" I asked.

It took H several attempts to get the truck into first gear, but we finally pulled onto the highway. By the time he was in third gear, we turned onto DeCrane Road.

"Head for the teepees," I told him.

H stopped the truck at the New Morning gate. He barely moved his lips as he spoke. "They do crazy things here. You saw the marijuana they grow. It's not for ornamental purposes, you know. And I've heard things at school. You're libel to come across almost anything. They're like rabbits." He left the cab and lowered the tailgate.

H unloaded two sashes at a time and leaned them against the fence. I could only carry one at a time. I sidled up to him. "You're getting as bad as the old men who hang out at Gartley's, talking about stuff they know nothing about."

H motioned over his shoulder to a group of children splashing in a stock tank near a barn. Naked children jumped in and out of the tank. A bearded man prowled the water, grabbing at ankles. The children squealed with delight. "Look at that," H said. "What's a grown man doing in a kid's swimming pool?" H turned away from the scene. "And what are those kids doing running around without clothes on? That might be cute for toddlers, but I bet those boys are in the fourth grade. That's not right. And the man? When he stands up, you're in for a big surprise."

H hefted the last pair of sashes from the truck.

"Aren't you going to help me carry these in?"

Walking away from me, H mumbled over his shoulder. "Find another way home."

"Fine, H, just fine."

Walking toward me on the other side of the gate, Sasha cocked her head, her smile a question. She really should have been wearing a bra. "Hey, Amy, remember me? Sasha? What brings you to the farm?" She asked this like I was the last person she expected to see that day.

"I'm bringing work to Falcon."

Her surprise stopped her in her tracks. "How do you know Falcon?"

All that had been welcoming and generous about our last chance encounter in town had turned into something I'd only observed from a distance between rival teenage girls. I decided to enjoy the intrigue. "I've known Falcon since we moved here. I think I met him at Straw and Butter's farm. Yes, that's right. He was chopping wood, and I helped him out at the Founder's Day craft sale." I looked around the yard, hoping Falcon would show up. "Could you help me find his studio?"

She shielded her eyes from the sun to study my face. "Sure. I guess. I'll lead the way." I tilted a sash toward me, and she picked up the other end. "So you know Falcon pretty well?" she asked. She said his name like she enjoyed the play of its sound on her tongue.

What did I know of Falcon? He was a gifted artist. He liked to play with kids. He wasn't too keen on Christians but was magnanimous enough to judge us individually. When he touched me, all sense and sensibility drained out of me. "Not really. He's doing some work for the church I attend."

"Is that so? Wow, that's a trip." She sounded incredulous rather than intrigued.

A man stooped to step out of the barn and into the sunlight. He wore overalls but no shirt. Tattoos of shapely women and scaly sea creatures wound their way around his forearms, past his elbow to his biceps and shoulders. The man was an illustrated edition of Dante's *Inferno.* Sasha disappeared between the tired-looking house and a shed. The man squinted over my shoulder to the road before he settled his black eyes on me. "Who are you and what's your business at the farm?"

Clearly, this man had never seen a bottle of Tame crème rinse or used a hair brush. Long hair, I'd learned from Butter, was meant to be a statement but became an issue of economy. With what little cash they earned going toward necessities, a barber and razor blades became expendable. But I still couldn't help wondering what lived inside the man's beard. He asked me the same questions again, only this time I understood he saw me as an intruder. I spilled my life story.

"My name is Amy. I'm delivering stained-glass work to Falcon's studio. In fact, this is one of the windows he'll repair. I could take the blanket off, if you want to see it." I worked at the knotted twine. "I'll just be a minute," I said, hoping he would tell me not to bother, but he didn't.

"How'd you get here?"

I stopped fidgeting with the string. "If this is a bad time—"

He stepped closer, lowering his face to mine. His breath would make a dog whimper. "Don't make me ask you again."

"My friend H drove me," I squeaked.

"Is that the kid who sicced his dog on them boys who was messing with private property?"

"That's H."

"Good kid." The man pulled on his beard. "How long will you be here?"

I turned my attention back to the knots. "Do you have some scissors?"

His frown deepened.

I worked the knots as I talked. "I have to be to work by 3:00 so no later than 2:45, unless I have to walk home, then I'll be leaving earlier, probably by 2:15 because I'll have to shower." The man's face remained unreadable. I told him more. "I work at the funeral home. I keep the place clean and supervise the viewings. The mortician likes meatloaf sandwiches, so I'm in charge of preparing his lunches when he's around. Sometimes, just once, actually, I went on a death call to pick up the deceased. You never want to call the dearly departed *dead* to the survivors. That's a rule morticians have." The blanket fell away from the window, and the sun shone through the glass to color the dirt a sickly green.

"Wait here until Falcon comes to escort you to his studio, and don't you go wandering around alone," the man said.

A woman wearing cutoffs with a man's shirt closed the gate. If not for the windows and my promise to Leoti, I could have hurdled it.

The man's attention shifted from me to scan the jumble of teepees and converted buses and a sandbag hut with a chalet roof, shingles included, that filled a paddock. Beyond the house and barn, more temporary dwellings leaned, billowed, and swayed with the breeze. Up close, none of the structures seemed inhabitable beyond a two-day, one-night camping trip. That was my limit for using an outhouse, although the outhouse was by far the most conventional of the structures. In spite of the domestic behaviors I observed that morning—women hanging laundry, workers bent over gardens, and dogs sleeping in the shade—the ordinary and the extraordinary pooled like oil on water at New Morning farm.

Satisfied that I hadn't disturbed his universe, the man disappeared back into the shadows of the barn. Only then did the weight of his suspicion and the sun's heat threaten to topple me. I squatted to rest my forehead on the sash and closed my eyes to stifle my tears.

Jesus, get me out of here.

Falcon put his arm around me and pulled my head to his shoulder. "It's okay. I should have been here. Frank scares everybody at first. He's a vet. Nam messed him up real bad."

CARRYING THE WINDOW sash between us, Falcon and I followed an orange extension cord that wound its way from the house to his studio. Hay stubble scrunched under our feet, and grasshoppers hopped gracelessly from one toasted hay stalk to another. The studio turned out to be part Volkswagen van, part tent, and part lean-to. Falcon pulled back an orange flap for me to enter. He followed, hefting the sash easily onto a long table made of plywood and sawhorses. I rubbed the indentations the sash had made in my hands.

Falcon noticed. "Would a cool cloth help? I could get some water from the canal."

I held my hands behind my back. "I'll be fine, really. Shouldn't we go get the other sashes?"

"It's cool to leave them where they are. Frank will help me later." Falcon spread his arms in a grand gesture. "Well, Amelia, welcome to my home and studio, such as it is."

"It's . . . it's a little cooler in here."

"Wait until we start soldering."

Sasha entered with an infant on her hip. Looking from Falcon to me, she said, "Good. You found each other." She switched the pudgy baby to her other hip. "Don't let Frank scare you, Amy. He's a pussy cat, really. It's just that we get hassled by the locals. He's very protective. He was a Green Beret or something."

"He was a marine," corrected Falcon.

"I'll try to remember," she said evenly.

Falcon rubbed his palms together. "We better get to work then."

Sasha said, "I'm watching Sunshine's boys this morning so she can get some beading done." She pivoted as sharply as any marching soldier. Falcon watched her walk away with long, purposeful strides.

"I'll be right back," he said, following her.

Left alone in the studio, I felt less conspicuous studying the details of Falcon's life. Constructed of mixed tarps and tent fragments draped over a wooden frame, the studio and home possessed all the permanence of a gypsy wagon. Overhead, a canvas tarp, army surplus from its dill-pickle color, provided deep shade. The side of the van created one wall with its side door left open to reveal a lumpy mattress and an assortment of cotton blankets, those thin panels from India as ubiquitous as the buffalo robes of a hundred years earlier. The opposite wall, the lean-to, held a small crib, and two children's sleeping bags, zipped and smoothed, glowed orange from its nylon covering.

Oh.

This was Sasha and her children's home too. What had happened to Jackson? Disappointment wrung my heart. I sat on a three-legged camping stool. Was Falcon married? Was he living with Sasha? I wanted to run.

How stupid could I be?

Relax. Breathe. Remember why you're here.

And that reason would be?

Leoti's windows, of course. Right?

Right.

Yes. Yes, I was there to help Leoti realize her dream. I wiped my palms on my shorts and continued the self-guided tour, trying to piece together a better picture of Falcon without being too snoopy.

Although temporary, the studio modeled order. A partitioned wooden box held scraps of glass filed by color. So, Falcon preferred some predictability in his life, like knowing where the red or green or purple glass could be found. In the center of the studio, two tables constructed of plywood and sawhorses filled the space. On one, line drawings of the top and bottom sashes had been taped on the surface. On the other table, an appliance I assumed to be the grinder sat beside a pitcher of water. This would be where I worked. I sat in front of the machine and waited.

Falcon returned, breathless. He spoke, but I might as well have been one of the flies that buzzed in and out of the studio. "Everything's cool. Let's get to work." He set a stack of glass pieces with paper patterns taped to them by the grinder. I worked at this table and referred often to what I learned was the master cartoon taped down to the table, comparing the pieces of glass I'd ground and hoping the glass fit just inside the lines. Doing so allowed for the lead came Falcon used to build the sashes. The sashes were assembled and soldered on the base cartoons at the second table where Falcon worked. Had I known working over the table would knot the space between my shoulders, I'm not sure I would have volunteered my help.

Whom am I kidding?

Twenty-Seven

Through the screen door I watched Mom reach across the kitchen table to dab Charles's chin with her napkin. "Miracle Whip," she said. "I hope you don't mind."

He smiled with a bite of sandwich in his cheek. Despite the deep coves of his hairline, he looked twelve years old.

The walk home from the farm had sullied my mood. My arms and legs stung from sunburn. My feet ached from walking on gravel in my flip-flops. And my teeth stuck to my lips. I let the screen door slam behind me to announce my arrival. "Boy, it's hot out there."

"*Fofa,* where have you been? You're as red as a beet." Mom rose from her seat. "Sit here, in front of the fan. I made some iced tea."

I rolled the glass across my forehead. "Did a death call come?" I asked Charles.

"I'm in town to . . . to get a haircut." A rim of white flesh bordered his hairline at the nape of his neck and over his ears. I was surprised that Charles got out in the sun enough to get a tan, even a modest one. But then, he had been spending more and more time behind the garage visiting with mom. He looked at his watch. "I should get going, I guess."

Was he squirming? The man plugged orifices of dead people, and he was definitely squirming under my gaze.

Mom patted his hand. "Nonsense. It takes two minutes to walk to the barber shop from here. You have time to finish your sandwich. Relax."

And what was Mom doing home from work? Before I could ask, she said, "I have too many overtime hours at the hardware store. They gave me the rest of the day off. Isn't that a nice surprise?" What surprised me were her clothes. She wore a blouse with puffy sleeves and a Peter-Pan collar buttoned to her throat with a navy skirt. She looked like my eighth-grade math teacher.

Strange. Very, very strange.

Charles and Mom exchanged glances and then looked at me.

"I think I'll read in my room," I said.

"A shower would cool you down," Mom said.

I looked at Charles. He averted his eyes. Even though I could smell myself, Mom knew I never showered with men in the house. "Maybe later."

"As you wish."

As you wish? Mom had never said *as you wish* my whole life. This was getting creepy.

I PACED MY bedroom, avoiding the spots in the floor that squeaked. Mom, still glowing from her clandestine lunch with Charles, had stopped by to deliver a letter from Lauren. Truth be known, I hadn't written Lauren since she told me about her and Andy, and this was the sixth letter I'd received from her. The other five letters had gone straight into the trash because no matter how hard I tried, I couldn't think of one thing to say that wasn't snippy or mean. And there was the whole rug issue to think about. I leaned against the bed and tore open the envelope.

Dear lost friend Amy,

Since you haven't answered any of my letters, I guess our freindship is over. Just in case its not I'm writing one more time. Maybe your in a body cast from riding a horse like Annie Oakley. If thats what happened I hope you are better soon. Maybe your mom would write me. I know that isn't true because your letters stopped coming after I told you about Andy so I understand what your trying to say without saying it. Do you hate me? Whether you hate me or not I need a friend to talk to and you will know why soon. One of the summer boys who came into the Bait & Bite with his dad over the weekend asked me to go boweling but I don't want to write his name because every time I think of it I almost throw up. At the boweling alley Jeannie, Shelly, Linda B, and Janet L were in the lane next to ours. Yep, the brat-o-ramas!!! Them with no guys and me with a guy who looks like a surfer. (I am not exagerating!) His hands were on me from the minute we left the house. He held my hand and he hugged me after every gutter ball and there were tons of those. I wanted to push him away but then what would the four brat-o-ramas think? Anyway we are driving home and he says you don't want to go home do you. This was NOT a question. He meant I know you don't want to go home. He tells me there is a nice boat house at the end of his parent's dock with a bed in it for extra guests. Here goes the bad part. When I told him I wanted to go home he said he new better because he TALKED TO ANDY!!!!! I screamed bloody murder and demanded that he let me out of his car and we were on the NORTH end of the lake but he didn't stop right away and I went nuts. I pounded on the window begging him to let me out and he gets real concerned and starts talking to me like I'm going to jump off a bridge or something. Its just that I couldn't wait to get away from him. He finally lets me out but he yells that I'm a crazy slut who should know what a guy wants. I wanted to dye. I walked home all the way from the A&W crying like the day you left. A sheriff drove by me real slow so I turned up someone's sidewalk and he drove on. I don't want to go out of the house so I quit my job which made my parents very angry but I do not want to face people because E-V-E-R-Y-B-O-D-Y knows. I'm counting the days until I leave for St. Louis. My parents think I'm going through a stage and they want me to talk to the pastor. What a great idea! I'm trying to act normal so they will let me go to St. Louis. I never want another boy to touch me ever again.

Amy, even if you hate me there are two questions I need answered. I worry about dying all the time. I watch the tv so I won't have to think so much but it doesn't always help me to forget that I will dye someday. So here are the questions. 1. Does God hate me? 2. Am I going to hell? Please, please, please write!!!!!!!

Love ya, (I really really do!!)

Lauren

Lauren deserved an answer. That didn't mean she would like what I had to say. I wrote to her explaining the utter importance of a daily quiet time and regular prayer and told her it was her Christian duty to flee from sexual immorality. Each morning she should put on the full armor of God to "stand firm against the schemes of the devil." I wrote twenty more Scripture verses on index cards, like "For this is the will of God, your sanctification; that is, that you abstain from sexual immorality" and "But do not let immorality or any impurity or greed even be named among you, as is proper among saints."

I prayed for her every day.

Twenty-Eight

Boy, this is a fat one," Myron said, testing the weight of the letter in his hand.

"Does it need extra postage?" I asked.

He dropped the letter on the scale. "Say, is that your green Pontiac Tommy's been driving around town?"

"It couldn't be. The transmission hasn't come in yet."

"Let's see," he said, scratching his chin and looking at the ceiling. The customer behind me pretended to be interested in the Ten-Most-Wanted poster, like a bank robber could hide in Cordial. "The car I saw was mint green with dark-green on the top and along the sides, a real beauty. Brought back many a fond memory for this old man." His eyebrows popped over his glasses. "I suppose you and your mom will be leaving us pretty soon."

There was no sense wondering how Myron knew about the car and our travel plans. Dead men told no tales, and small towns kept no secrets. Just ask Lauren. "Does the letter need another stamp or not?" I smiled so he wouldn't think I was being rude, but I was already rehearsing what I would say to Mom about hiding the repair of the car.

I ran the two blocks to Tommy's garage. Only his shoes stuck out from under a car. In the next bay, the Pontiac occupied its usual place. "Excuse me, Tommy, can we talk?"

"I've got fifteen minutes to get this muffler back in place. You better speak up and get to your point fast."

"Tommy, it's me, Amy. I hate to keep bugging you, but I was wondering about the transmission. Has it come yet?"

Tommy slid out from under the car. He blocked the sun with his arm. "Hey there, Amy. I guess your mom wanted to surprise you. The new transmission's been in since early last week. Runs like a charm. All I need is a check, and you'll be on your way."

"How much?"

"I discounted the labor as much as I could."

"And?"

"Four hundred and seventy-five dollars. That's the lowest I can go."

MY THINNING FLIP-FLOPS barely protected my feet from rocks on the unpaved road, so I walked on the tire tracks where the gravel had been mostly pulverized. I didn't dare spend a dime to replace the shoes since I would need every penny to travel to California, thanks to my irresponsible mother. Every penny she hadn't frittered away on decorating the funeral home, clothes, and gifts for Bruce, and yes, me, she'd spent padding the Lost Mine's till. With only the buzzing insects to hear me, I clenched my fists and screamed until my throat stung. More therapeutic was imagining her shock when she discovered my empty bed—unmade, of course—and my empty closet. I still hadn't decided if I would leave a note. With the sun drilling me from above, informing Mom of my whereabouts seemed an undeserved courtesy.

An irrigation ditch clogged with cattails gurgled beside the road, teasing me with its refreshing lilt. Clouds tethered to the mountains like giant zephyrs withheld their cooling influence. I definitely wouldn't leave a note.

A strap of my flip-flop snapped, and I stepped out of the shoe. I growled like a mongrel and threw the worthless flip-flop into the ditch, only to look down the long road toward New Morning to reconsider my reckless decision. I dropped my purse and hopped back along the ditch bank, trying to catch up to the broken flip-flop. The shoe caught on a cattail, spun, and continued on. I jumped into the ditch. Water covered my knees, and the muddy bottom pulled at my feet with each step.

"Stop! Stop!"

I lunged, but the ditch narrowed and dropped to create a mini waterfall. The force of the water held the flip-flop under the surface while I climbed out of the ditch to lay on the bank. I used my hands as nets to trap the shoe once it escaped. The flip-flop popped out of the waterfall's watery grip several feet past my hands to float into a culvert and disappear under the road. I picked my way through the intersection, avoiding the rocks I could see but finding plenty that my haste rendered invisible. I sat at the opposite end of the culvert with my feet dangling in the water, ready to pounce on the flip-flop when it emerged. While waiting, I planned my escape from Cordial.

I'll talk H into driving me to Clearwater, that's what I'll do. I'll apologize to him, and if I have to, I'll give him a peck on the cheek. That wouldn't be so bad, especially if he has just showered and doused himself with Old Spice. But then again, there might be a DQ in Clearwater.

He wouldn't turn down a butterscotch sundae with whipped cream and nuts, not H.

A terrifying thought occurred to me. I was willing to use H as ruthlessly as my mother had manipulated, say, Mr. Cochran and countless other men before him. My heart raced.

"I'm not my mother!" I yelled at a pasture of grazing llamas. Only one llama looked up, a speckled thing with a clump of grass hanging out of its mouth. His interest proved fleeting as he bent immediately to tear at another clump of grass. "Well, I'm not!"

Mom had purposely deceived me, making me believe she'd saved money to repair the car and get us out of Cordial. And what was up with Charles? He wasn't her type. He was shorter than Mom, even before she ratted her hair or put on heels. Mom liked her men tall, good-looking in a long-time-in-the-saddle sort of way, the kind of guy who kept his eye on the horizon, scouting for hostile Indians. At the first sign of trouble or entanglement, up into the saddle he went, spurring his horse and leaving only dust to let us know he'd ever been there.

She had talked endlessly about finding me a father and someone to take care of her, but I doubted her procedural integrity. You might expect her to flirt with a pharmacist or one of my teachers, which she'd refused to do. "How boring," she'd said. I was undeterred. I pummeled her with suggestions about smartly dressed loan officers, insurance salesmen with large fishing boats, even grocery clerks who belonged to the Optimist Club, all men anchored to society, not casual observers of all things civilized. None of them interested Mom who preferred big-rig truck drivers. She'd served them steak and eggs at the Good Buddy Restaurant on the highway. They drove back and forth between Chicago and the Gulf Coast states, only staying in Gilbertsville overnight and returning on their homeward run. She would drop everything, including me, to dance and drink with them at the tavern. Had it ever dawned on her that her modus operandi wasn't working? A parade of men marched through my memories, from Roger the two-timer to Bruce the unfaithful. The longer I sat there waiting for my flip-flop to appear, the angrier I became.

"This isn't helping."

I squeezed what water I could from my shorts and the hem of the peasant blouse, one of Mom's recovery projects in her quest to get over Bruce, which made me wonder, who was my mother, really? Was she Suzie Homemaker or Madame Bovary? Unlike Madame Bovary's daughter, I wasn't about to end up working in a cotton mill to support myself.

I yelled at the llama, the only available witness. "You can bet money on that, you grass-gnashing sorry excuse for a mammal!"

A flash of pink caught my eye. I snagged the flip-flop with a stick, attached it to my foot with two hair bands, and slumped toward New Morning.

FRANK STEPPED OUT of the barn's shadows to smile and wave as I climbed the gate. "Did you bring any of them cookies with you?" he asked.

I reached into my purse for a handful of lavadores. "You better eat these fast before the kids discover what you have."

He pocketed the cookies. "I learned that, by golly." I hated to think how long it had been since he'd washed his overalls. My nose registered more than a week. More like two weeks. Or more.

A tumble-haired boy with chestnut skin called out my new given name. "Cookie!" Children ran out of teepees and jumped from trees, echoing the boy. Frank receded into the barn. Hands with dirt-caked fingernails reached into the bag I held.

A round-faced boy with winsome eyes looked up at me. "What do you calls these things again?" he asked, pulling a fistful of cookies out of the bag.

"Lavadores. It means 'washboard' in Portuguese." But the boy had already disappeared around the barn with a scarecrow of a girl in chase.

"We have a washboard," said a girl.

"So do we."

"My mom uses a wringer washer. She calls it The Beast."

An earnest boy, wearing a straw cowboy hat and boots with his cutoffs, held out his hand. "Could I have an extra cookie for my little sister, ma'am?"

"Sure enough, little pilgrim," I said, à la John Wayne.

The boy's request reminded the circle of children of their siblings, real or imagined. In a matter of seconds the bag was empty. "I promise, I'll bake more next time," I said to the latecomers. A chorus of thank-you's trailed the lucky ones as they returned to their activities.

Coming to New Morning most weekdays was like sidestepping into another era, not necessarily the past but definitely not a time or place congenial to the present or the future. The residents were archaic in the sense that they lived tribally, avoiding contact with industrialization as much as possible. Electrical service was barely tolerated, and frequently the line was cut by a resident with strict ideological beliefs about abandoning the grid. The plumbing in the house proved less dependable than the outhouse, which confirmed their mistrust of anything linked to the government or large business. For the pragmatists of New Morning, the constant electrical repairs proved incredibly frustrating, so the rules of communal living were constantly revised. Residents called meetings to discuss everything from entrance requirements for newcomers to mandatory farm responsibilities, which translated into arguing over those who considered their cooperation voluntary. Being on the farm was watching a new form of society emerge. Labor and delivery proved painful.

New Morning presented challenges to every facet of my cultural and spiritual beliefs. Talking philosophy and belief systems was the preferred pastime of the residents. They genuinely wanted to know what I believed about everything, depending on their particular bent, which led to intense debates. At first, I took the conservative side of any debate, but I lacked their experience on topics like Vietnam, Watergate, DDT, Wounded Knee, and Kent State. And Christianity? Well, how do you talk about God to people who mistrust the Bible? Feeling freakishly trite after a debate on consumerism and democracy, I became a listener, but doing so didn't make my visits any less vexing. These people practically worshipped the produce they grew. I winced when they praised Gaia, or the Earth Mother, for a bountiful harvest of green beans, or spoke about their transitory relationships with the fathers of their children or the unity of vision they experienced while tripping communally on LSD. Part of me wanted to flee. The other part of me, the part of me that reveled in the questions and passion of New Morning, compelled me to return whenever possible.

Needless to say, my motives for being at New Morning blurred. One minute I was there to fulfill Leoti's dream to replace the broken sashes. In a breath, I morphed into a missionary to the children, gaining their trust with cookies and awaiting that perfect moment to share the love of God. If I was honest, I was there to be with Falcon, which required more farfetched mental, spiritual, and philosophical gymnastics than I cared to justify. He had a hold on me I couldn't express or understand. I tasted the metallic sting of danger, but once

I stepped inside Falcon's studio, the second-guessing and rationalizations stopped. The sounds of children playing and dogs barking normalized New Morning. The acidic smell of solder and the crates of glass made the studio a place of industry and purpose. Nothing made a Midwesterner like me happier. Falcon bent over a work table, scoring the glass or soldering a joint. On this day, he was foiling the edges of green glass with a ribbon of copper.

"I can do that," I said.

Falcon looked up, smiled. "Amelia, I'd given up on you."

I showed him my makeshift flip-flop and told him of its heroic rescue.

"Maybe Sasha has something you can wear home."

I'd rather chew gum off of Stinky Webster's shoe. "The hair bands work great," I said.

One question remained. It shattered any imaginings I tried to construct of a world that included me and Falcon as a couple. Please note that these imaginings were purely academic in nature. I never expected my reality to include us as a couple, but a lonely girl had to dream. No perfect segue had materialized for my question, so I took the Custer approach and charged recklessly ahead. "How long have you and Sasha been married?"

"What makes you think we're married?"

"Well . . ."

Falcon followed my gaze to the rumpled bedding of the van. "Marriage is a piece of paper. People change, Amelia. There's a time to move on, expand your possibilities." He said this like he was telling me to expect afternoon thunderstorms.

"Marriage has been around for a long time," I said, centering a piece of glass on a ribbon of copper.

"So has malaria."

"Yes, but malaria makes people sick, some to the point of death. In areas susceptible to malaria, productivity is reduced, keeping people steeped in poverty. On the other hand, marriage stabilizes society by providing consistent, long-term relationships for adults and children." I was on home turf now.

"You sound like a *National Geographic.*" He gently squeezed the running pliers and a piece of glass fell onto the table. "Marriage is a big fat lie."

I thought of Leoti's tender longing for Arthur. "You're such a skeptic. Believe it or not, there are people in this very valley who are happily married."

"And how would you know that, Amelia? Anyone observing my parents saw love and fidelity. Mom and Dad put on a pretty good show when his congregation was watching, but good ol' Dad couldn't keep his hands off the women he counseled. Eventually, my mom always found out, and we'd move before a month was up. I attended five elementary schools. I think that's where I got my zest for travel." He smiled, but there was no mirth in his eyes. "The whole gruesome charade was resurrected every time an attractive wife of an alcoholic, or gambler, or scoundrel of any ilk came begging Dad for help."

Falcon propped one foot on a stool and leaned on his knee. "Of course, my brother and I were expected to perform perfectly in and out of the house. We knew the Bible better than anyone and memorized chapters of Scripture to recite for dinner guests. We knew how to greet visitors, depending on their age and position. We attended youth group faithfully and became Eagle Scouts before any of our peers. We did not go to movies, listen to modern music, play games of chance, or attend school dances. Above all, we never discussed family secrets."

He pressed the glass cutter along a sweeping curve of marbled glass. As so often happened in the course of our work time, I felt compelled to defend all Christians, especially from generalizations. "I know a few things about misbehaving parents, but I don't project that onto all parents. There are loving and morally upright parents out there, just like there are sincere, practicing Christians."

"There are five pastor's kids living at New Morning. Their stories bear conspicuous similarities with mine."

"Really?"

He laughed. "As long as I'm exposing family secrets, let's demystify my old woman. She drinks vodka straight from a vinegar bottle. Just like the widow's oil in the Elijah story, the vodka never ran dry. It fell to me or Kevin to tell her Bible study ladies that she had a migraine. We asked the ladies to pray for a quick recovery as Mom had prompted us. Nobody prayed harder than me."

"I'm sorry."

"For what? I'm happy. I've started a new journey with a new destination. Hop on board, Amelia."

"Where, exactly, are you going?"

"I'm not going to hell, if that's what's troubling you. Amelia, I hate to be the one to tell you, but all that Bible reading and church attendance is a colossal waste of your precious time on this earth. There's more to life than *thees* and *thous* and rules only meant to be broken. Church is nothing but an antiquated money machine. Your sins won't send you anywhere. You won't be backstroking in a lake of fire for all eternity for having a little fun."

"I believe in grace. There is nothing that can separate me from the love of Christ."

"Oh yes, you've talked about *grace* before, but that's not how you live. You're all tied up in a knot, worried about what people will think of you. You're playing a role. You dress like a Christian, do your good deeds, carry your Bible, say your prayers for all the starving children in India—and might I add that your chief goal in life at the moment is to escape your mother for embarrassing you by her decidedly unchristian behavior? Once in California, you'll lose her in the crowd. *Poof!* No more mother to worry about. That's not very Christian of you, Amelia. What about the fifth commandment? 'Thou shalt honor thy father and thy mother.' I know of no caveats for moms who don't fit their daughters' ideals."

This was a typical conversation for Falcon and me. At first, I'd gotten red-faced and defensive, but then I realized he enjoyed seeing me flustered. That was his goal. He knew Scripture and theology, and he wielded them like twin blades, always able to one-up me with counterexamples from his life or mine. Still, my hypocrisy about my mother cut deeply. To end this round of our ongoing argument, all I had to do was yell "ouch." Satisfied that he'd drawn blood, the conversation would turn to the adventures of his travels. Instead, I said, "Interesting. I don't remember caveats for mothers who drink vodka from vinegar bottles or for philandering fathers, either."

His smile faded, and he bent over his work. "You got me there."

The victory created a harrowing divide between me and Falcon. The air thickened. He worked less than three feet away, but I was alone. I jostled topics of conversation until I found something safe. "Can you even explain the hippie movement to me? Butter and Straw work a million times harder on their homestead that they ever would in an office job."

Falcon met my gaze with grateful eyes. "The movement boils down to two ideas: freedom and making the world a better place. Not all longhairs are alike. We're like schools of fish—we gather with like-minded people. I spent some time in Boston and Chicago. There, the movement's all about politics. During the whole Vietnam fiasco, we concentrated on antiwar demonstrations. I did all that for a while, but the urban groups are too uptight for me, even self-righteous in their take on the world, always ready to slay the next dragon. I won't put myself back into that again. I prefer the country life, but I think I might like the beach life too. California is by far the easiest place to be a freak. For one, the weather makes crashing much easier. The huge number of freaks out there, that's what makes life sweeter. You're never alone, and no one hassles you."

"And New Morning?"

"Max, the head honcho around here, had an experience early on that opened a whole new reality to him."

"The women talk about community trips when I'm working in the kitchen, and I don't think they mean field trips to the zoo."

Falcon stopped smiling. "Amelia, you understand, don't you, that you can't tell anyone what you hear in the kitchen? They trust you. Things are different now. Back when Max first dropped acid, it was legal. A friend of his brought a beaker of the stuff home from the university laboratory. They'd been doing experiments in the psych department. Are you cool with that?"

I squirmed in my chair. "Maybe you shouldn't tell me anymore."

"I want you to know, Amelia, we're not trippin' very often. For one thing, it's too hard to get the pure stuff. And there's a reason behind trippin'. Acid makes everything crystal clear. Your spirit is free to move around and through things." He drew his cutter across amethyst glass. "There's a lot going on in this world that can't be reasoned away."

An edge of glass slid along my index finger.

"Ouch!" I squeezed the finger and a line of blood oozed from yet another cut.

Falcon lay his hands, palms up, on the work table. "Give me your hands." He wrapped his fingers around mine. "You have to get loose to avoid cuts. Close your eyes." His voice was weightless and captivating. "Okay, relax the muscles in your hands . . . in your palms . . . in your wrists . . . in your forearms." He raised my hands to his mouth to kiss the cut. "Now, release all the tension and hold the memory of relaxation. Better?"

"Sure." I picked up a burnishing tool. "I think I'll burnish for awhile."

"Cool. I'll need your help to stretch the lead pretty soon."

Twenty-Nine

I poured the green-brown tea into Leoti's cup. "The tea was a gift. It's chamomile." Sasha had given me a small bagful of the tea, harvested and dried from the New Morning garden. I didn't know how Leoti would feel about drinking hippie tea, but the thought of forcing down her black tea made my stomach burn. I preferred the decidedly straw-like flavor of chamomile.

"My mother gave me chamomile tea whenever I had a stomach ache," Leoti said. "What a treat."

I offered Leoti the sugar bowl.

"No thank you, dear. Sugar was a rarity in the house where I grew up. I think I'll enjoy the tea much more without sweetening it. Besides, peanut-butter cookies are my favorite. I don't want to lose my girlish figure."

Girlish figure? Leoti's breasts covered the belt of her dress. She laughed at my surprise. "Amy, dear, it's okay to laugh. I haven't had a girlish figure since 1906, but I must say the boys liked to watch me walk by. I swayed my hips as much as I dared. When Father caught me, he said he didn't raise me to walk like an overfed heifer. I thought he was terribly unkind with that remark."

A bead of sweat rolled off my forehead, over my cheek, and down my neck.

"But that was years ago. I'm dying to know what you thought of *The Good Earth*?"

How honest could I be with Leoti? "I had some trouble getting into the story."

"But did you like it?"

"I found the characters difficult to like."

"You didn't enjoy the book?"

"No, not much."

"Would you recommend it to one of your friends?"

Never. "It would depend on the friend's interests." Lauren would use the book for a doorstop.

Leoti rested her teacup and saucer in her lap. "The best conversations I've ever experienced are about books I tossed in the trash."

"Really?" I smoothed the napkin on my lap. "I would toss this book."

Leoti leaned forward, and I feared she would fall out of her chair. "Good. Tell me why."

"All the characters worry about is what people think of them. Everything Wang Lung and O-lan do is for appearances' sake. And what good did it do them? O-lan barely stops her work to birth his sons, and still Wang Lung isn't satisfied with her. He buys a concubine to flaunt his wealth, and . . . well, you know, to have someone pretty to love, even though she is completely useless with her bound feet. And their sons are selfish pigs. And the aunt and uncle? What slobs."

"That's more like it. Now, with nary a character to care about, was reading *The Good Earth* a redemptive experience for you, my dear?"

"O-lan strangled her baby."

"Do you think the author supports infanticide?"

"How could she?"

"Were you aware of such desperate acts before reading *The Good Earth*?"

Before reading the book, I thought I was poor.

"I didn't think so." Leoti held out a plate of cookies. "This is the first baking I've done since . . . since I don't know when. I hope you like peanut-butter cookies as much as I do."

Leoti nibbled on a cookie, savoring each bite and washing it down with a sip of tea. She dabbed her mouth with her napkin, refolded it, and laid it on the tray. "Whenever I read a story like *The Good Earth*, where the author has bravely chosen to create characters who are products of their culture and flawed by their natures, I think of the people Jesus chose to associate with. True, he visited the synagogues and met with Nicodemus who came to him under the cover of darkness. Otherwise, the pompous religious leaders of the day were the objects of his scorn. He sought out the broken people. Why, he accepted a tearful tribute from a prostitute and invited himself into the home of a tax collector, a profligate who stole from his own people and flaunted his wealth. Jesus even ate in the company of lepers."

"He delivered Mary Magdalene of seven demons," I added. "And he cured the centurion's daughter, even though the father was an enemy of Israel."

"Yes, and the woman at the well, a Samaritan, a term used by the Jews as a curse word." Leoti broke a cookie in half but laid both pieces on her plate. "I've often wondered what that woman was like. After all, Jesus chose to walk through hostile territory to meet with her, and she'd rid herself of five husbands. Something tells me she didn't graduate from Miss Buckingham's Charm School for Girls.

"When I picture her, she is leathered from the sun with small flitting eyes, always looking to turn things to her advantage. I'm sure she was a crafty one. And contentious? Nothing satisfied her. She deserved better than her husbands provided, and she wasn't afraid to say so. Ambition wasn't a becoming attribute of a woman of the Middle East. It still isn't. You can be sure her behavior set her up as the brunt of gossip and the taunts of the other women of the village. Why else would she collect water in the heat of the day? I'll tell you. She did so to avoid running into the wagging tongues of her tormentors. But Jesus met her there, weary from meeting the needs of hungry and hurting people, and he must have been terribly thirsty." Leoti sighed. "In that way, my Arthur exhibited the Spirit of Christ. I was always after him to stand up straight, but he carried the weight of this community on his shoulders."

Leoti sipped the last of her tea and returned the cup and saucer to the tray. Her eyes were a deep ocean that kept its secrets, and then she blinked. "What I find so compelling about the story of the Samaritan woman is the grace Jesus extends to her when she speaks the truth. She admits her failings to him, a rabbi who had no business talking to any woman in public, let alone a hussy who lived with a man who was not her husband. He could have ordered her stoned for her sins, but Jesus didn't even gasp. He didn't give her a book to read or ask her to explain her past. No, he opened a door considered closed to the Samaritans—forgiveness—and she ran through it without a second thought. No other story in the Bible speaks more eloquently of Jesus' humility and grace."

I sat there, steeping in the wonder of God's grace. And then

I remembered the door of friendship I had slammed in Lauren's face. I stood up. "I have to go."

"THAT LETTER'S THE property of the United States Postal Service," Myron said, arranging his rubber stamps in a straight line.

I leaned over the counter. "But I wrote it. It's mine, and I've made a terrible mistake."

He tidied a stack of forms. "It's no matter. The letter's probably on its way to Denver."

"How long will it take to get to Gilbertsville, Illinois?"

"It depends on the weather. Of course, this being summer helps things move along. You didn't mail it air mail, did you?" He tapped his chin. "That letter will take a week, give or take a day."

If that counter hadn't been there, I would have kissed him. "Thanks, Myron. Thanks a lot."

"HELLO, MRS. BROWN. This is Amy. Is Lauren there?"

"Amy, how are you?"

"I'm fine."

"Lauren's volunteering at vacation Bible school. She'll be home in a couple hours. You can try back then."

I needed to know when Lauren would be in the house alone, so she could talk. "Are you keeping busy this summer, Mrs. Brown?"

"Yes, I took a part-time job to help with Lauren's school expenses. I work in the office of Grant's furniture store, the one near the A&P. I work all day Saturday. Mr. Brown doesn't like that much, but he likes the money I bring home. He's started playing golf again, which is just as well. He isn't so grumpy when he's been out playing with the boys. These are things you girls will discover. Recess is always a man's favorite thing about life no matter how old he gets."

"Working at the furniture store sounds like a fun job. I'd love to hear more about what's going on in Gilbertsville, but I'm using a pay phone, so I don't have much time."

"I'll tell Lauren you called, sweetie. She sure misses you. All she wants to do is mope around the house. That's why I insisted she help out with VBS."

Saturday was the day to call Lauren. Hopefully, the letter wouldn't reach her first.

Thirty

Spartacus turned his head one way and then the other. I guess he didn't like what he saw with either eye, because he lowered his head and charged. Pick was nowhere in sight. I threw *Julie of the Wolves* at Spartacus, but the rooster dodged the book and kept coming. My only other defense was my purse. I gripped the straps and cocked my arm.

"Feather! Help!"

I swung at Spartacus and landed a blow. He stopped, stunned. I kept my eye on him while I fiddled with the latch of the chicken yard.

"Feather, are you in there? Feather!"

Spartacus shook his head, scratched the ground, and crowed at the sky, sounding the charge once more. The gate opened behind me. I slipped out and slammed it shut. Feather leaned against the gate with her forehead.

"They ate Pick for dinner last night," she said.

A stream of tears rolled down her cheeks.

I drew her into an embrace. "I'm so sorry."

Her tears dampened my blouse. "It's the doctor's bills," she said between gasps. "Butter and Straw are fighting all the time. She wants him to get a job." Feather cried harder. "Look what I've done."

"Did you have that seizure on purpose?"

She shook her head.

"Then it's not your fault. It just happened. You wouldn't blame Frog or Mule or Lamb or baby Vernon for getting sick, would you?"

"Yes, I would."

I would have laughed if she didn't sound so miserable. I held her by the shoulders. "When adults don't know the answer right away, they go a little crazy. You're going to have to be patient with them. They'll figure something out."

Feather scanned the chicken yard. The hens pecked at the ground without one worry in this world. "Who will they eat next?"

I CHOSE THE pay phone in front of the Cap-N-Cork liquor store, figuring I wouldn't see too many people I knew there. With five dollars in quarters stacked in one-dollar piles, I dialed the operator.

"How long for three minutes?" I asked.

"$3.75. What number are you calling from?"

I read the number from the center of the dial.

"Please remain by the telephone after you've hung up to remit the charges."

I inverted the egg timer and prayed, "Jesus, please let Lauren answer." And she did. I said, "Don't talk. Just listen. I only have three minutes."

Lauren's voice muffled. "It's Amy, Mom. I've got it."

"Lauren, are you there?"

"Mom's baking a cake for Dad's birthday." Not one spark of interest lit her voice.

Mrs. Brown called out a greeting.

"Okay, so you can't talk," I said.

"That's right."

"You read my letter."

"Yesterday."

"Lauren—"

"I have to wrap dad's present before he gets home."

Mrs. Leane, one of the pew hens from Spruce Street Church stepped out of the liquor store. She flashed a furtive glance around the parking lot. "Amy, what a nice surprise," she said with her hand over her heart. "Are you alone, dear?"

I put my hand over the receiver. "I'm making a long-distance phone call. It's awfully expensive."

"Yes, it is expensive." She patted her purchase, a large bottle in a paper bag. "My stomach has been acting up."

"I hope you're feeling better soon."

She smiled. "Thank you. That's very kind." Finally, she shuffled off around the corner of the building.

"Lauren, are you still there? This old lady—"

"It's almost five here."

"I'm so sorry. Burn the letter and try to forget about it, please. I was wrong, dead wrong about everything. Andy and that other guy are pigs. You can't let them decide who you are. God loves you so much. He loves you like a lion."

The phone went silent.

"Are you there? Lauren?"

"A lion?"

"I'm not saying this very well. I've learned so much since I wrote the letter. A woman named Leoti—" The last of the sand fell to the bottom of the egg timer. "I have to go. Please promise me you'll burn the letter. Okay?"

Silence.

"Lauren?"

"I have to go."

Thirty-One

Falcon looked up from soldering. "It's too hot to work. Let's blow this joint." He pulled me off the stool by the hand. "Help me unhook the tarp from the van."

Not one leaf fluttered in the still air. My T-shirt stuck to my skin. And the studio? I'd baked brownies in cooler ovens.

"I know a place where we can cool off," he said.

We drove in silence. Falcon slowed and turned onto a dirt road. Dust stuck to my skin. Falcon anticipated the ruts and potholes, steering onto the narrow shoulder. He bit his lip in concentration.

"Where does this road go?" I asked.

"To the river. There's a place where someone created a shallow pool with a dam of boulders. People from the farm bring kids down here for baths and a swim."

A chain with a no-trespassing sign blocked the road. Falcon pressed the brake pedal to the floor. I held my breath until the van stopped. "Amelia, would you mind unhooking the chain?"

I hesitated.

"We do it all the time. No one's ever given us grief. It's cool."

"You're sure?"

He smiled. "You're a good girl, Amelia."

I pulled up hard on the door handle. "All right."

Falcon pulled his shirt off and waded into the water still wearing his jeans. I followed, until the water touched my knees. He turned toward me, spread his arms, and fell backwards into the water. Wiping the water from his eyes and shivering, he sat up. "Man, that's refreshment." His eyelashes were stars around his eyes. "Now it's your turn."

"I'm cooler already, really."

"It's only cold for a second."

"I'll get my clothes wet."

"You could take them off."

I scowled at him.

"Then come on."

I waded into deeper water, raised my arms, and paused.

"Blow out your nose when you hit the water," he said.

That was too much to remember, so I pinched my nose and fell. The icy water punched my chest. I came out of the water gasping and stood, tugging at my T-shirt to keep it in place. My hair hung over my face as I waded back to shore. "You are such a liar. Cold for a second? I don't think so."

"You weren't even in the water for a second. You have to get used to it." He smiled that I-know-you-better-than-you-know-yourself smile that laced boots onto the butterflies in my stomach and infuriated me at the same time. "You're not hot anymore, are you?"

"Not in the least."

Falcon extended his hands, and I accepted his invitation to be pulled back into the water. I leaned back into the subdued current that combed my hair away from my face as I sat up.

"Better?" he asked.

My T-shirt ballooned around me. Air glubbed to the surface when I wrapped my arms around my middle. "Yes, better. It feels good."

Holding my face in his hands, Falcon said, "You don't look me in the eye when you talk. It drives me crazy."

"I . . ."

"There you go, looking at the trees instead of me."

Of course I looked at the trees. Trees. Sky. Sunlight winking off the water. Anything was better than the indifference or disappointment I anticipated in his face. "It's a bad habit," I said.

I lowered my head, but Falcon lifted my face to meet his. "That's better."

I looked down.

His long, strong fingers cradled my head. "Look me in the eye, Amelia."

"With one eye or two?"

"Two."

I raised my eyes to meet his.

"That's better." His breath warmed my face. "I predict many a sorry sap will be vanquished by the cool steadiness of your eyes."

I averted my eyes.

"Come back to me, Amelia."

And so I did. I held his gaze, daring myself not to blink. He pulled me closer with an arm around my waist, his other on the back of my head. My heart pounded wildly. I swallowed down a cough. And then his lips were on mine, warm and abstemious, as if he tasted something unknown. A bud of warmth blossomed in my gut. He released me to slip under the water and resurface out of reach.

"We should probably get going," he said. "I'm scheduled to cook at the farm tonight."

Riding in the van, Falcon spoke, eyes on the road. "Where do you want me to drop you off?"

He regretted the kiss.

I didn't.

"*QUERIDA*, YOU'RE NOT eating."

Falcon's kiss had awakened something within me I couldn't name. The taste of his lips soured my stomach for food but made me ravenous for his touch, which terrified me. What was this recklessness? I pushed macaroni and cheese around my plate, dreaming of excuses for appearing at New Morning farm long after the workday had ended. The faces of Sasha and her three cherubic children flashed before me. My face burned with shame.

"You're flushed. Do you have a fever?" Mom asked.

I blotted the sweat from my forehead and lip. "I can't seem to cool down."

"This heat, it will kill us all. Russell opened boxes of fans and set them around the store, but they only pushed the hot air around. He says August is monsoon season, whatever that means."

"The rainy season," I said, slipping macaroni noodles onto the tines of the fork.

"There isn't a cloud in the sky."

"In order for precipitation to occur, cool air must meet—"

"Yes, well, I think you better get in the shower. You smell like a dead fish. I can't believe you swam in the river alone. You could have drowned." Mom pushed away from the table. "Mrs. Clancy says this kind of weather always brings business. I believe it. This heat sucks the life right out of me."

Mom wore her hair curled softly at her shoulders and pulled away from her face with a headband—no teasing of her hair to spectacular heights or scent trail of White Rain in her wake. She wore a red and white gingham blouse tucked into a flared navy skirt with red espadrilles.

"What are you dressed for?" I asked.

"Dressed for?" She smoothed her skirt. "The skirt isn't too short, is it?"

She looked like Schoolteacher Barbie. "It's a new look for you. It's nice. Are you going somewhere?"

"Mr. Moberly and I are going to the movies. He'll be by to pick me up in twenty minutes. I can answer the phone for you, if you get in the shower and don't dilly-dally."

"So are you and Mr. Moberly dating?"

"What? Me and Charles? Absolutely not. He's just a friend. I promised no men until we got to California, and I meant it. Bruce was a huge mistake. Now, go take a shower."

I stood under the spray of water, remembering the way Falcon cradled the back of my head and the strength of his arm around my waist. I touched my fingers to my lips and they parted, just as they had at his insistence. Mom knocked at the door.

"What's taking you so long?"

"I'll be right out," I said, pouring Prell into my hand and working up lather in my hair. "I'm almost done."

My hair was still wet when a call came in. "This is Nurse Laurie Anne from Alpenglow Rest Home. We need a pick-up. Mr. Kiddoo in room three-oh-nine has expired. His family has been notified and his personal affects cataloged and packed. He's ready for you." The line went silent.

"Hello?"

Laurie Anne sniffed into the phone. "I promised myself I wouldn't cry, but I . . . I'm so sorry. It's just that Mr. Kiddoo was a favorite of mine. He wrote poems for my daughter. If I told him a story about Cindy's kitten, he wrote a poem about Fluffy. In fact, he wrote poems about her selling Girl Scout cookies door to door and how she gave the cookies away because people said they couldn't afford them. That was during the strike, you know. Why, he wrote a poem about her new tennis shoes, for goodness' sake, and the first time she jumped into the deep end of the pool." She blew her nose. "Excuse me. This is terribly difficult. I don't know how I'm going to tell Cindy. She loved that old man."

For all of the Scriptures I'd memorized and Bible studies I'd attended, not one word of comfort came to mind. I finally told her how sorry I was and that H would be there in a jiff to pick up Mr. Kiddoo. That seemed to satisfy her.

"Thank you. Thank you for listening. It's just that the other aides haven't been here long enough to know Mr. Kiddoo like I do . . . did."

H was all business when I called. "Sure thing. I'll leave right now." He came to the funeral home and backed the hearse out of the garage without coming to the kitchen door as he usually had. Watching the headlights back down the driveway created an ache under my heart.

You've got to be kidding. You're just a little frazzled is all. Your mother left the house looking like Barbie, and the best-looking guy in Clearwater County just kissed you. Stay calm!

Calm? Me?

The silence of the drive home from the river with Falcon had crushed me. I saw without seeing, reliving the kiss and the suddenness of Falcon's retreat, caught in a swirl of heat and cold that rattled my bones. I needed a diversion, so I counted off the minutes on the clock, trying to estimate when H would return to the funeral home with Mr. Kiddoo. If he stopped to chat with Laurie Anne for just a minute, I had more than enough time to bake a batch of brownies.

H stood at the kitchen door, backlit from the light over the garage door. It had only been two weeks since the day he'd dropped me off at New Morning farm. His shoulders were square and hard, his stomach flat, his waist as narrow as a hornet. He bent over a clipboard, filling in blanks and noting the time he had retrieved Mr. Kiddoo.

"I just took some brownies out of the oven," I said.

H patted his hard stomach and shrugged. "Training. Sorry."

Was his voice deeper? "I could fix you a meatloaf sandwich."

"That would be good, but just the meatloaf. No bread."

H leaned against the kitchen counter while I sliced thick slabs of meatloaf onto a plate. "It would only take a minute to warm this up."

H crossed his arms over his chest. His biceps bulged under his T-shirt and a taunt rope of muscle bulked his forearms. His neck was thicker, his face thinner. Reddish sideburns reached his earlobe.

"Sure," he said.

I arranged the slabs in a frying pan and adjusted the heat. "Would you like a glass of milk?"

"Skim?"

Yuck. "We drink two percent."

"That'll do."

Evidently, building muscle had robbed blood flow from the part of H's brain that formed sentences. There was only one way to test my hypothesis. I sat the plate of meatloaf on the table before him. "Tell me about your training."

He opened his mouth wide for a hunk of meatloaf, chewed briefly, and swallowed. "Feeling good."

Such a simplistic answer did little to soften my desire to run to Falcon, which would be an incredibly stupid thing to do in light of how he had dismissed me, and did I have to mention Sasha? I pressed H for more information. "I saw you running past the Henry Orchard the other day. How far are you running?"

"Five miles in the morning. Five miles at night."

"Wow!" Maybe he would get chatty if I padded his ego. "You look great. I've never seen a more amazing transformation. You must be feeling good about your chances to make the team. Tell me about the try-out process."

H lowered his head and covered his mouth for a belch of appreciation. "That was good."

A full sentence! But anyone could throw together a pronoun and a linking verb. *Come on, H, make an effort.* "I've missed talking to you."

His head snapped up.

"The windows for the church are almost done," I said. "I never thanked you for the ride to New Morning. You were right. It is a different place, but people exaggerate. I've gotten to know some of the women and found out why they came to Cordial. They have the same concerns as we do about pollution and the economy; they just choose to deal with the threats by becoming self-sufficient. They work really hard. Heck, they even make their own soap." And to spark a conversational fire in H, I said, "I admire them."

"Are you one of them?"

"What if I was?"

"You'd be a fool. Why would anyone want to make their own soap? And they're self-sufficient all right. They drive themselves down to social services to pick up their food stamps. Just last week, Dad caught a hippie stealing a cook stove. The guy had it tucked under his arm and walked out the door. Did he think my dad was blind or something? And I'm sick to death of smelling that patch-a-hooly juice, as if that could cover their B.O."

"It's *patchouli* oil."

"That stuff stinks. I know that much." H popped the last hunk of meatloaf into his mouth. "What bugs me most is how they hate America, but where else in this old world would they have the freedom to be such idiots? Wait until they face a winter in their cute little teepees. They'll pack up real fast then."

"Not all the hippies are the same. You know Feather and her family. They—"

"I guess you haven't heard."

"What?"

"Feather's in the Clearwater Hospital. She had another seizure."

"Will you take me?"

"What about Mr. Kiddoo? Shouldn't you call Mr. Moberly or something?"

"I'll leave him a note."

H frowned.

"He's at the movies with my mother."

"No kidding? That's sort of weird."

AT THE HOSPITAL, Butter slept in a plastic chair, leaning against Feather's bed. Vernon slept in an infant seat at her feet, pursing out his little lips as if nursing in his dreams. I was backing out of the room when Butter's eyes popped open. The fluorescent lights of the hall mottled Butter's skin with purple blotches around her eyes. She pulled me to her bosom, squeezing me tight enough to force the air out of my lungs.

"Thank you for coming," she said repeatedly while H gathered three chairs and lined them along the wall outside Feather's room.

"I don't know how long she was lying there," Butter said, pressing her palms against her eyes. "She didn't come up from the henhouse for dinner, so I sent the twins down to get her. They came running back, crying and saying that Feather had fallen asleep, and they couldn't wake her up. I thought the worst. I grabbed Straw's ax and told the boys to stay with Vernon and Lamb, but they'd already left the cabin to run back to Feather. I didn't know where Straw was. I carried Lamb on my back. Thank goodness Vernon was strapped in the sling. He'd been so fussy." She stilled her trembling lips with her fingers. "Amy," she whispered, "I thought she was dead."

"When I got to the henhouse, Frog and Mule were patting her arms and whispering her name, saying 'Wake up, Feather. Wake up.' I can't remember another time in their whole lives that they whispered anything. I checked her pulse right away. It was strong, thank heaven. I think that's when I started breathing again." Butter lowered her voice. "She messed herself. That's when I knew she'd had another seizure, only worse. She could have aspirated that vomit into her lungs, and we would have lost her."

Butter covered her face with her hands. Her breaths tremored. I laid my arm across her shaking shoulders and let my own tears fall. Next to me, H sniffed loudly. Butter used a waded tissue to wipe her tears. "Straw had the car. I sent the boys to Henry's Orchard. They have a phone. I sat with Feather. The chickens clucked softly around us like they knew she was in trouble. Spartacus stood watch at the door. The whole time we waited for the ambulance, I worried about the cost of another visit to the emergency room, and there my daughter, my firstborn, lay in her vomit and urine."

She pushed her hair away from her face. "This isn't what I signed up for. It's one thing for Straw and me to impoverish ourselves to live off the land, but our children deserve medical care, don't they?"

I nodded, but Butter didn't need or want my approval.

She spoke faster. "I called my mother. She asked me what I wanted to do. Did I want money? Did I want to bring the children home to Chapel Hill? She was so good about it, and I hadn't called or written her in over a year.

"I didn't have an answer for her. Asking for help felt like giving up, but really, that doesn't matter as much as it used to. Straw won't like it that I called, but with the hospital bills and the medication and doctor's visits Feather will need, I can't see how we can keep the homestead. We were just barely paying the mortgage as it was. It's crazy. Two people with masters degrees having trouble scraping together a hundred and seventy-five dollars every month." Butter swiped at her tears. "I have to get myself together, make some decisions, do what's best for the kids."

Butter stood, stretched. "My mother did something she's never done before. She prayed for us right over the phone. She asked God to bless us and provide for our every need. I started bawling, told her I'd denied God, that He wouldn't be interested in helping us. She says Paul, or was it Peter? I know his name started with a *P*. Anyway, she says this guy denied Jesus, but God chose him to do amazing things. I don't know. Maybe we should have thought this through better. I've been bone tired since the day we got here. I think I'm too tired to think anymore."

"I'll stay with Feather," I said. "There's a waiting room down the hall. H and I passed it coming in. There's a soft couch in there. I don't think anyone would mind if you rested awhile."

"Amy—"

"We'll come get you the moment she wakes up."

"They said she would sleep for a long time."

"I'll sit inside the room, and H will come to get you. She'll never be alone."

"Okay then." She carried Vernon and pulled Lamb along as he clung to the hem of her skirt. She'd only taken a few steps before she stopped and turned back with her brows pressed into a question.

"She'll never be alone," I said.

Butter smiled weakly. "Thank you." Her words were as heavy as stones.

The flicker of the television lit the curtain between Feather and the other patient in the room. H carried a chair to Feather's bed. I sat and stroked Feather's hair, but my fingers kept getting stuck, so I stopped.

"Do you want me to call your mom?" asked H. "We might be here for a long time."

I checked the clock on the wall. "She's still at the movies."

"How about Mrs. Clancy?"

I'd broken two cardinal rules visiting Feather in the hospital that night: I'd left the phone unattended at the funeral home and hadn't notified Charles about Mr. Kiddoo's demise. She'd understand about Charles being unavailable, but being away from the phone meant missed opportunities to make money.

I started to stand, but H stopped me with a hand to my shoulder. "I'll call."

If that wasn't taking a bullet for a friend, I didn't know what was.

FEATHER'S EYELASHES FLUTTERED, and her irises danced under the pale skin of her eyelids. I held my breath, but her breathing never faltered, and she slid back into tranquil sleep. Feather's roommate shouted at the television when a contestant on *The $10,000 Pyramid* answered too slowly. I wanted to tell the woman to lower her voice, but who knew what I'd find on the other side of that curtain? Instead, I watched Feather sleep.

Lord. Please, please, please heal her.

I knew in that moment what I had to do.

Thirty-Two

Pastor Ted opened his Bible to the fifth chapter of James. "I know this verse well."

I scooted to the edge of the chair. "So you'll call the elders?"

"Let's take a minute to look at the verse more closely."

Uh-oh.

He read to me. "'Is anyone *among* you sick? Let him call for the elders of the church; and let them pray over him, anointing him with oil in the name of the Lord.'"

He took off his glasses and rubbed the red dents on his nose. "You shouldn't be embarrassed, Amy. This is a common error made when reading Scripture out of context. James—and here *James* is the Lord's brother, although some suggest the author is the *apostle* James, but I disagree. James the apostle was martyred in the Year of Our Lord forty-four. James, the brother, actually the half-brother of Jesus, wrote this letter to Jewish believers scattered by intense persecution by the Romans, and this is an important distinction because the author asks 'if any *among* you are sick.' This implies that he is speaking specifically to the church, not the population in general, and certainly not the Romans."

"Feather's not a Roman. She's a little girl who's expecting the elders because I told her they would come."

Pastor Ted closed his Bible and straightened his stapler and tape dispenser to be perfectly parallel. He avoided eye contact by looking at the pipes on the ceiling of his basement office.

"Will you come?" I asked.

He looked at me briefly before his eyes found something less threatening to look at over my shoulder. "Amy, there are things you know nothing about, difficult adult situations that create tough choices."

"Is this about Feather coming to hear me sing?"

"Only partly. The church is tenuous at best. Key people—"

"The people with money?"

"Yes, but they keep the work of God ongoing. Without them—"

"So you won't come?"

"I can't. I'm sorry."

FEATHER JUMPED OUT of the hospital bed to greet me. In her wake a stack of library books hit the floor.

"Keep it down, will ya? My soap's on," her roommate demanded, pressing the volume button of the remote. The mountainous woman ate from a bag of potato chips resting on her stomach, so she missed Feather sticking her tongue out at her.

Feather bent to help me pick up the books. Every last one of them was about chickens. *Is there that much to know?*

Feather climbed back onto the bed. She spoke rapidly, her gestures barely able to keep up with her. "I was afraid you wouldn't get here in time. Butter called her mom. I guess she's my grandma. That's what she wants us to call her, even though her name is Julia. Not only that, but she wants us to move to North Carolina. Butter showed me on a map. The Atlantic Ocean is right there. Butter says there's lots of room to play, but I can't take the hens. And Straw isn't coming with us; he says the homestead just needs more time. I want to stay, but Butter says that's not going to happen. What she means is that I'm the whole reason we're leaving. She just won't say it. She says she's tired of living in poverty, and Straw's as stubborn as an old mule and won't give up. She can't force him to do what he don't want to do, except that's what she's doing to me." Feather's eyes filled with tears. "Sure as anything, Straw will make chicken and dumplings the minute we leave. When will those darn old elders get here?"

I set a grocery bag filled with the oils I'd collected from the house and garage on Feather's bedside tray. "The elders couldn't come today. They're all scheduled up to pray for other people, so they sent me."

Feather's roommate, a woman with the disposition of a wounded badger, dropped her jaw. I drew the curtain between the beds, praying silently, *Father, forgive me for lying. Don't hold my sin against Feather.*

"I wasn't sure what kind of oil to use, so I'm offering you a choice." I set the bottles and cans in front of her. "We've got good ol' vegetable oil, some WD-40—people use it to stop things from squeaking, like doors and stuff."

Feather added, "Straw says a can of WD-40 and a big hammer will fix anything,"

"This is Skin So Soft. Mom puts it in the bathtub when she's getting ready for a date. And these are some bath beads I got for Christmas last year. There's oil in each one. I figure I could cut them open and squeeze the oil out. They smell like lavender."

Feather pushed the blankets to the foot of the bed and lay with her arms to her side like she was at attention for inspection. "I choose the vegetable oil. You've got lots of that."

"You don't have to lie down."

"The nurse on duty this morning is pretty grumpy. I don't want her to get mad about oil on the sheets."

"I'm just going to dab a little bit on your forehead."

"Wouldn't it be better to cover my whole body?" She rose to lean on her elbows. "Maybe I should take this stupid gown off."

"That won't be necessary."

At my church in Gilbertsville, the pastor had carried a tiny vial of oil in his pocket, always at the ready to anoint and pray for anyone in need. He tipped the vial to coat his thumb with oil. As he prayed, he touched the person on the forehead, right above their nose, and smudged the oil upward. Pastor Frank had about as many degrees as one man can achieve, and some people called him "doctor" until they got to know him better. All I had was a high school diploma.

"You're right. Lay down." I pushed up the sleeves of her gown to expose her shoulders and poured the oil into a paper cup I'd taken from a bottled-water dispenser. I dipped my finger into the golden oil. "Okay, close your eyes."

Feather obeyed. The reality of what I was about to do made me pause. If Pastor Ted had been right, I had no business praying for a nonbeliever, Roman or otherwise.

"Feather, do you believe in God?" I asked.

"You do, don't you?"

"Yes, of course I do."

"Then I do too." Feather searched my face, looking for some evidence of faith, no doubt.

"Close your eyes."

Again, Feather complied and still the prayer wouldn't form in my head. "Feather, do you believe Jesus died for your sins?"

"Did he?"

"Yes, he did."

"Then I believe it."

Faith wasn't supposed to be this easy. I remembered a Wednesday night prayer meeting when Gladys Humphrey had faced surgery to remove her gall bladder. Sweat had poured down her face as she'd raised her fists to heaven and yelled, "Give me faith, Lord. Give me faith."

Truly I say to you, whoever does not receive the kingdom of God like a child shall not enter it at all.

"I'm going to pray now." I traced the bony ridges of her shins with an oily finger. "Good Father, my precious friend Feather needs your healing touch."

Feather opened one eye. "Don't you think he already knows that?"

"Close your eyes."

"You forgot my feet."

I dabbed oil on her feet.

"That's better."

I thought of all the reasons why I wanted God to heal Feather—so she wouldn't have to move away from her hens, so she wouldn't be the brunt of jokes at school, so her parents wouldn't have to surrender their dream to provide her with the medicine she needed, and most importantly, so she wouldn't have to worry when the next seizure would hit her. But I couldn't think of one place in the Bible where a leper said to Jesus, "Hey there, my life and the lives of my family would sure improve if you healed me. It's getting harder and harder to find enough rags to cover my open sores, and I'm so lonely. My friends are afraid of me." Jesus never asked a blind man to justify his healing before he spoke the word to restore his sight, and the woman who reached out to touch the hem of his garment, she never uttered a word, not until she was asked. Nope, people asked for healing and Jesus did it.

I painted an oily line down her arms, being careful to cover the backs of her hands, and then I dipped my thumb in the oil and drew it across her forehead, cheeks, and chin. For good measure, I dabbed the tip of her elfin nose. "Jesus, heal Feather just because you can. Amen."

Feather's eyes popped open. "That's it?"

"That's it."

"I didn't feel nothing."

"Most people don't."

"Shouldn't I thank him or something?"

"Yeah, that would be good."

Feather sat up, threw back her head, and raised her arms to heaven. "Thanks a lot, God." She slid out of bed and ran out the door. As she passed the nurse's station, she yelled, "I've been healed! I've been healed!" The nurses laid down charts, hung up telephone receivers without saying good-bye, and followed Feather to the waiting room where Butter rubbed her eyes and Vernon slept.

"We can go home now," Feather announced. "I'm healed by Jesus."

Then I knew why the elders of Spruce Street Church were reluctant to pray for people outside the church: They actually expected their prayers to be answered.

Thirty-Three

I stood outside Falcon's studio, wavering between entering or running. The familiar sound of glass popping along a scored line was all the invitation my heart needed. "Hello? Is anyone here?"

Inside, I heard a hard thump and an expletive. "Amelia? Yeah, I'm here. Come in, come in." The flap flew open. "I'm surprised to see you. I didn't think—I just didn't know . . . I'm glad you're here." But our eyes didn't meet.

My pulse quickened, but it wasn't like I hadn't spent time with Falcon in the days following the kiss. My imagination had completely restructured reality to make loving Falcon possible—and permissible. Each night when I settled into my pillow, the year was 1901. Sasha and her three children hadn't even been born yet. Falcon was a godly man, a man of letters, on his way to America to forge his own destiny. And I was *not* María Amelia Casimiro Monteiro. As I lay between wakefulness and sleep, I was the witty and beautiful Lizzy Bennet on my way to the New World and marriage to a man I'd never met. A storm sank our ship off the coast of America.

Of course, Falcon rescued me. My pillow was his arm, and we were the lone survivors of the shipwreck, rising and falling on the ocean swells as if my bed were a raft. The stars bent to hear our conversation, and social propriety negated issues of premarital anything. *What a relief!* During the day, he was my silent partner while polishing caskets, or walking to Underhill Manor to read with Feather, or shelving books at the library.

What I faced inside the studio was my true reality. I'd accepted the invitation, and although I had promised myself I wouldn't, I looked in the van. Only one pillow lay embossed by a head. The lean-to stood empty. I busied myself gathering the tools to burnish the copper-edged glass. A guarded joy percolated in me.

"I've been spending time with Feather at the hospital," I said to explain why I hadn't been to the studio in almost two weeks.

"That's what I heard . . . from Straw, I mean. I was afraid maybe . . . it doesn't matter. You're here and that's great. It's really good to see you." He rubbed his hands together. "We better get to work."

I turned away to smile, feigning interest in my work.

Falcon lifted a tarp from the work table. "Hey, you have to see what I've gotten done."

Four completed sashes lay side by side. "Only one more sash and you're done?" I asked.

"I've had plenty of time to work." Falcon finally met my gaze. "Listen, Amelia, I shouldn't have . . . well, I shouldn't have kissed you. It's just that—"

"Don't worry about it." I sat in front of the grinder and batted his concern away. More than anything I did *not* want to hear why he'd kissed me. I already considered the kiss a fluke, a handshake, a fleeting moment of insanity on Falcon's part. It happened. "I haven't given it a second thought." That wasn't a lie. I'd skipped the second thought and sped my way through thoughts three to one million. No matter how busy I'd kept my schedule, the memory of his lips popped into my thoughts constantly. That wasn't very Lizzy Bennet-like of me.

I set aside the burnishing tool. "I'll start grinding these pieces, if that's okay with you," I said as matter-of-factly as my pounding heart would allow.

We worked in an awkward silence. Falcon caught me watching him a couple times. I smiled weakly and bent my head to my work. *Knock it off. Keep your mind on your work.* When Falcon left the studio to fetch more water for the grinder, I allowed the tears to flow down my cheeks. He caught me dabbing my eyes on the sleeve of my T-shirt.

"Are you all right?" he asked. "You should be wearing the safety glasses."

"Something must be blooming. My eyes have been watering and itching for a couple days."

My shoulders burned and my fingers ached. Falcon inspected my work. "You definitely have a knack, Amelia. You already grind the glass better than I do."

I stood up and rolled my shoulders. "That's it then. I guess I better be going."

Falcon pushed his goggles onto his head. "Can't you stay?"

I sat back down.

"I guess you noticed Sasha and her kids are gone," he said. "She got tired of waiting for me, so she left with some guy from Missouri over a week ago."

"I'm sorry."

"Yeah, well, we weren't getting along that well. I think she needed an excuse to leave. I'm missing her kids, though. I hope she finds a way to settle down."

"Are you all right?"

"Mostly I'm bummed for the kids." Falcon unrolled the solder. "Let's talk about something else."

"Okay."

"I hear you play the guitar and sing," he said.

"Who'd you hear that from?"

"I have my sources."

"Really. That's interesting. Well, it couldn't have been the lavender-haired ladies at church. They walked out on me."

"Did you sing one of them newfangled choruses?"

"Only at Pastor Ted's request."

"That's who told me. He also told me to treat you like a lady, no funny stuff. And I'm to protect you from any negative influences you might encounter here."

My face warmed.

"He sounded just like my father before my sister went out with an unsuspecting cretin." Falcon touched the solder with the iron and the silver liquid slid into the joint. "There's a full moon celebration next week. Thursday, I think," he said. "Mostly families come. You should bring your guitar. The musicians jam. We had about thirty people here last month. About half of them brought instruments—guitars, fiddles, flutes, dulcimers, and about a dozen tambourines. Greg's the unofficial conductor. He plays a mandolin made out of a gourd. Your mom is more than welcome too. We build a bonfire. Whoever's inclined just shows up."

Mom had never attended any of my performances with the Basement Beacons. "Mom's not into bluegrass." Nobody at New Morning farm wore a watch. Doing so was considered a tie to the false rhythms of a consumer-driven society, but I asked what time they started anyway.

"At twilight."

"I probably wouldn't know any of the songs you play."

"We don't play devil songs, if that's what you're worried about," he said with a rye smile. "Mostly, it's folk songs and a little John Denver. Some Eagles stuff. And believe it or not, a gospel tune or two, especially the spirituals." He snapped a piece of glass with his running pliers. "And nobody drops acid at these things, not with the kids around. So what do you think, Amelia Bo-belia? Do you need a ride?"

Yes! A thousand times, yes! "I'll think about it."

I LAID THE twenty-dollar bills along the edge of the bed. The empty envelope and the copy of *Emma* lay discarded on the floor. I counted the bills once and twice. It was all there, my escape money, but it was enough cash to make a mortgage payment on Underhill Manor, buying Feather's family a month to harvest the apples and sell them to local markets. Giving the money away would strand me in Cordial until I could figure another way out. I could pawn my guitar, but Cordial didn't have a pawn shop. If I baked H a pan of brownies—or would he prefer a protein shake?—he might drive me to Clearwater, but I wasn't sure they had a pawn shop either, and then I'd be stuck in Clearwater with little more than a song. True, Falcon would be leaving for California soon, but honestly, I wasn't so lovesick to discount all the ways traveling with him would be stupid beyond belief. That left my best option—getting a job in Cordial and postponing the start of my college career until winter quarter. Unless, of course, the scholarship had lapsed.

Lord, I want to do the right thing.

In my mind, there was only one thing to do. I slipped the money into my pocket, opened the bedroom window, and removed the screen.

But when you give alms, do not let your left hand know what your right hand is doing. Matthew 6:3.

Charles and Mom played Scrabble in the living room with Frank Sinatra crooning in the background. I cracked open the bedroom door to watch Charles arrange letters on the board.

"Xebic?" Mom pronounced the word *ex-bic.* "What's that, a former ink pen?"

Charles threw back his head and laughed, not a teasing or condescending laugh but appreciative, like Mom had made the best pun imaginable. My chest warmed. They would never miss me.

I sat on the window sill, estimating the distance to the ground. It sure hadn't looked this high from the lawn. I listened and watched. Only the incessant chirrup of crickets disturbed the night. I jumped to the ground and trotted off toward Underhill Manor.

I counted the bills one more time before sliding the stack of money to the back of the Underhill Manor mailbox. My heart thumped a warning beat at the thought of someone, even the mailman, discovering the money before Butter collected the mail the next morning. I slipped the money back into my pocket. What passed for country quiet, a symphony of chirrups and a chorus of toads bleating like sheep with head colds, and the stuttering *who-oo-oo* of an owl, crowded my thoughts. One thing was clear. My perfect plan had crumbled like a stale cookie.

Where would Butter or Straw or Feather find the money and not know where it came from?

The moon hung over the valley like a beacon, and a beacon creates deep shadows. I tiptoed under the cottonwood and hung close to the barn as I worked my way to the henhouse. Once out of sight of the cabin, I found the worn path that wound through the pasture toward the creek. Closer to the creek, I shuffled rather than walked, fearing I would step on a lovesick toad. Grasshoppers startled from their sleep jumped recklessly, hitting my legs, which reminded me of a discussion I'd had with H about night snakes. There really are such things; I saw them in a book at the library. No more tiptoeing. I high-stepped a beeline to the henhouse.

Once inside, I turned on the flashlight I'd taken from the utility closet. The hens froze in the beam of light. "Don't worry girls. I won't hurt you." I slipped the money under Ginger's downy feathers. She tapped my hand with her beak and murmured softly as if to reassure me she would take care of her new charge.

"Good chicken."

I followed the paddock fence to the road below the henhouse at a dead run through knee-high grass, what Lauren and I'd referred to as snake grass in our rare nature outings. In the relative safety of the moonlit road, I paused to catch my breath. Once my heart found its cadence, I walked past dark farm houses and barns, singing to the bejeweled sky, *"Heaven came down and glory filled my soul."* By the time I reached the third verse, a cock's crow stopped me in my tracks. *Spartacus?* I'd completely forgotten about the power of his spurs when I'd entered the chicken yard, which was a good thing, because I would not have gone in if I'd remembered. I took this forgetfulness and Spartacus's timidity as a bit of God's grace for me. I smiled at the moon as if it were God's own face looking down on me like an attentive father.

Thanks.

At home, Mom stood over me, her eyes rimmed with red, her forehead creased with worry. "I want a straight answer from you, and I want it now. Charles is out there looking for you, so don't even think of lying to me." She expelled a hard breath. "Where have you been?"

Her question presented a dilemma for me on many levels. First, Jesus himself taught that your right hand should not know what your left hand is doing. You don't go around talking about, and certainly not bragging about, the good deeds you've done. Also, to tell her I'd given two hundred dollars to Feather's family meant admitting I'd had money she knew nothing about. Mom hated those kinds of secrets. It also meant admitting to a closer relationship to Feather and her family than she would like. Most hurtful to Mom would be realizing how little I had trusted her to get me to California, even though she fully deserved my skepticism. I wouldn't tell her about giving the money to Feather's family. No, I would take my punishment like a woman—days and days of Patsy Cline on the record player.

"You and Charles were playing Scrabble," I said, "so I decided to take a walk." This was mostly true.

"Then why did you jump out of the window like a cat burglar?"

"I didn't want to bother you. You were having such a good time, and I was bored. I didn't want you guys to feel bad."

Mom's eyes narrowed.

"Honestly, would you have let me go walking at night? My room was hot. I wanted to cool off. It's absolutely beautiful out there tonight. The moon is almost full. What's the big deal?"

"Amy, this is a small town, much smaller than Gilbertsville. There are no secrets here. People have seen you riding in an old van with a hippie. They say he is a transient and much older than you. How could you be so stupid?"

"And who have they seen you with, Mother? A married man? Drunken coal miners? A naïve mortician?"

Mom plopped onto the hard cushions of the couch and buried her face in her hands. She followed a well-rehearsed script. When Mom buried her face in her hands, I moved center stage to apologize and beg for forgiveness. This night would be different. I yawned.

Her head snapped up. "Why, you little . . ."

"Tramp? Is that what you think I am? Don't you know me at all?"

"Tell me, are you taking the pills I gave you?"

"I don't need your stupid pills, tonight or any other night. Mother—"

"Stop calling me Mother!" Her nostrils flared. She hadn't done that since I took her blow-up falsies to the swimming pool. "I want to know exactly what you did tonight."

"I would love to tell you. I forfeited my future. There. Satisfied?"

"What are you talking about?"

"It means I'm stuck with dead people in this worthless town for only God knows how long. Are you happy? Isn't this what you wanted? Isn't this why you left the interstate to drive to Cordial? You planned this. I know you did. I'm going to end up just like you."

Her hand flew back to slap me, but she stopped.

"I'm going to bed," I said and turned away from her.

"Don't you dare walk away from me."

I closed the door and turned the lock. "Goodnight, Mother."

I lay on the bed wondering if I dared sneak back into the henhouse and retrieve the money from Ginger's nest. My skin itched to leave Mom, the house, Cordial, and everything about death behind. The sooner the better.

Another image came to mind—Feather walking into a new high school with clothes her grandmother had chosen, her hair lacquered into those wing-a-ding-like bangs everyone but me was wearing. Stiff shoes, knee-highs, and a sweater buttoned to her neck completed the picture.

No way.

In the past, after fighting with Mom, when my soul was raw with disappointment, I prayed with great certainty, knowing God heard my prayers. For the first time I could remember, my disappointment included God. Why would he open a door only to slam it in my face? I had no answers, so I revisited my fantasies of floating on the ocean with Falcon.

Charles came to the front door. Mom told him I had made it home safely, and then I heard the screen door slam and Mom's heels tapping down the steps.

Thirty-Four

I feigned sleep as Mom barked orders over me. "You are to stay in the house the whole day. In fact, you're grounded for a week."

What? Me? Grounded?

"I've talked to Mrs. Clancy. She knows everything, so don't think you can pull the sheep over her eyes." She stamped her foot on the floor and slapped my bottom. "Sit up and look at me when I'm talking to you."

I rolled over and opened one eye. "You're kidding about the grounding, aren't you?"

"Sit up. Show some respect."

Mom had never shown inclinations of being a drill sergeant. Someone had coached her. Mrs. Clancy? Charles? Attila the Hun? I sat up with arms crossed.

"What's gotten into you?" she said, pacing beside the bed. "Look at you. You've changed. Those stinking hippies have brainwashed you." She wagged a finger at me, and I bit my lip not to laugh. "I'll be home for lunch at noon, and I expect you to be here."

I followed her into the kitchen. "This is a joke, right? I'll be eighteen in April. I'm heading for college. You can't ground me."

"You're not in college yet."

When she reached the door, I said flatly, "You get paid today, don't you? I expect you to give Tommy fifty dollars toward the work he's done on the car."

Her jaw flexed.

"He did the work, Mom. It's only fair that he should be paid."

"I'll be home for lunch," she said through her teeth and left.

I prepared for the day with a lightness I'd not known since being plopped in Cordial. Who knew being the brat of the family could be so satisfying? I breezed through my chores. My reflection in a casket smiled back at me. When a death call came just after eight, I answered the phone cheerfully. "Hello, Clancy and Sons Funeral Home, serving the North Fork area since 1920. How may I help you?"

The deceased was yet another resident of the Alpenglow Rest Home, Arly Folks, lately of Hanford. From the director, I learned his remaining family lived in a suburb of Denver and wouldn't be traveling to Cordial for the memorial service due to poor health.

"I'll send H right over," I said. "Are there any special instructions?"

"Mr. Folks wanted to be buried with his cat."

"His cat? Is the cat . . . deceased?"

"We've been storing the cat in the freezer since the first of the year."

"I'll let Mrs. Clancy know."

I measured the oatmeal into Charles's meatloaf and added another two cups for good measure. Then I shook a bit of cayenne into the meat mixture and set the oven to 500 degrees. It was petty of me, I know, but the man had loaded Mom's arsenal with irritating parenting information, like he knew anything about raising children. He reminded me more and more of Lizzy's insufferable Mr. Collins—bombastic yet servile to his keeper, Lady Catherine de Bourgh. In Charles's case, that would be one María Fracisca Monteiro Santos.

Poor sap.

At lunch, Mom ate her bologna sandwich and smoked a cigarette behind the garage. I was still too mad to apologize or talk to her, so I washed the exterior windows, pulling a rickety step stool from one window to the next. She was still eating by the time I finished, so I pulled the weeds from the flower beds, working on the opposite side of the house, so I wouldn't have to look at her.

Of all people, H showed up. "That's my job," he said.

"Do you want me to stop?" I asked as if spitting venom.

"What's up with you?"

I took pity on him and coiled my claws. "I'm grounded, so I'm avoiding my mother."

"By pulling the weeds? You have a lot to learn about retaliation." He squatted and ripped a dandelion out of the dirt. "What'd you do?"

"Nothing." But knowing anything I said would disseminate through Cordial like the flu, I told H everything—about the fight I'd had with Mom, including the parts about the birth control pills and Charles's late-night visit. Once this information hit the gossip machine, people would be lining up to drive us out of town. *¡Adios, Cordial!*

This was war.

"It's nice that your mom and Charles are dating. He's a great guy. He'll treat your mom like a princess."

Leave it to H to see a patch of blue sky on a cloudy day. Of course, I would've agreed with him if Mom and Charles hadn't become the dynamic duo, battling this criminal mastermind in her quest for independence. Charles definitely topped the evolutionary tree of men Mom had dated, but that didn't mean I would encourage their relationship. Someone like Charles would tie Mom to Cordial forever. Besides, he gave out faulty parenting advice.

"Have you finished the windows for the church?" H asked, ripping a mat of fleshy weeds from under the lilac.

What he really wanted to know was whether I would be going to New Morning again. "What's it to you?"

If a hound dog could talk after losing the scent on a coon, that's exactly how H sounded. "Just curious, I guess."

Oh brother.

"I'm sorry, H. I'm mad at Mom, not you."

H sat beside me in the shade, his long legs stretched out before him.

"The windows look great," I said. "Falcon should deliver them to the church this week."

"Football tryouts are tomorrow." He said this so fast, I had to think about what he'd said.

"Are you nervous?"

"A little."

My information was hearsay, but it came from reliable sources: Other castoffs and nerds had gone off to college and returned relaxed and self-assured. "You know, H, whether you make the team or not has nothing to do with the rest of your life. Take it from someone who also suffered through high school. It doesn't last forever. I'm free." *Sort of.* "Before you know it, you'll be surrounded by beautiful coeds who'll appreciate the person you are and what you know. No one will care how far you can throw a football."

"I want to be a defensive lineman."

"I don't even know what that means."

"I won't be throwing a football." He looked at his upturned hands. "I'm not that good with my hands."

"Did you hear what I said about playing football? You have to hang in there for nine more months, graduate, and kiss those jerks good-bye. Figuratively speaking, of course."

Mom came around the corner of the house. "I'm sorry, H. Amy isn't allowed visitors while she's grounded. You'll have to go."

H stood to leave, and I rose to hold him by the arm. "He's helping me."

"Thanks for your help, H. We'll see you next week."

H scooped up the weeds we'd pulled, nodded to Mom, and mumbled an apology. He whistled "One Tin Soldier" as he threw the weeds in the back of his truck and climbed into the cab.

"Good luck," I yelled after him because I understood the pull of belonging. And although I believed everything I'd just told H, I wanted him to enjoy belonging too.

"I'm going back to work," Mom said. "No more smart stuff from you, young lady. I want you inside this house until I come home tonight, and I want dinner on the table. Charles is eating lunch. Why don't you go in and keep him company?"

I hesitated. I had heard Lauren complain about her parents' constant oversight—the questions, the restrictions, and the punishments. I'd never admitted this even to Lauren, but I had longed for such reining in and the structure of an adult in the house. Now I wasn't so sure.

"Amy, you misunderstand me," Mom said, hands on hips. "I'm not making a suggestion. Get in the house."

My heart sank. Without the two hundred dollars, my fallback position only meant more belated parenting. I swallowed hard and stepped into the kitchen.

Charles stood at the sink, filling his glass with water. "Boy," he said, "the meatloaf has a bite to it. I learned to love spicy food when I lived in New Mexico. This is much better than anything I ate there."

"Charles, I want you to know that I was completely alone last night. Climbing out the window seems stupid to me now, but it made sense to me at the time. I didn't want to disturb the fun you and Mom were having."

"I'm glad you told me." He drank the water straight down. "Making the right decision should be easier for you from here out."

Thirty-Five

Gravel pinged the underside of H's truck as it climbed the hill to Leoti's house. I held *The Optimist's Daughter*, slow of plot even by Austen's standards. I hadn't managed to read beyond the first few pages.

We rode in silence until H blurted, "Well, I made the team, in case you were wondering."

"And you're going to play?"

"Are you kidding? The coach said I was starter material."

"What about that creep Jim Williams?"

"Jim *Warner*?" H flashed a cocky grin. "He's cool now that he's seen what I can do on the field."

"Do you take delight in vexing me?"

"Huh?"

Since H hadn't knuckled under with a reproach from *Pride and Prejudice*, I recited Scripture. "'How blessed is the man who does not walk in the counsel of the wicked, nor stand in the path of sinners, nor sit in the seat of scoffers.' Jim is all of those things, H."

When he didn't answer right away, I finally looked at him. He stared straight ahead, frowning. He hadn't shaved that morning, and his whiskers glistened in the sunlight. H glanced over at me. "You just don't get guys."

"I get insolent behavior."

"Huh?"

"Jim's dangerous, H. He uses people. For crying out loud, don't you remember how he treated you at the drive-in, how he chased us in his car?"

"Drop it. I'm playing and that's it."

LEOTI CAME TO the door with a cookie sheet of smoldering black lumps. "I've ruined the cookies." I followed her to the kitchen. The dishwater hissed as she plunged the cookie sheet into the water. "Open the door, won't you, dear? Let's shoo some of this smoke out."

I fanned at the cloud of smoke with a dish towel. "Did you turn off the oven?"

"I guess I'd better do that." Waving dish towels didn't accomplish much, but she seemed to be enjoying herself. "Arthur would have gotten a big kick out of me turning perfectly good sugar and eggs into lumps of coal. He accused me more than once of trying to turn Granny's molasses cookies into diamonds. Married people talk about the silliest things."

"I think we've done the best we can with the smoke," she said, hanging our towels on the oven handle. "If I can get the windows open, the evening breeze will carry the smoke into town. Everyone will know Leoti is baking cookies again." She tugged at the window with arthritic fingers. When she failed to open the window, she tried another one. "The good people of Cordial may declare a holiday and have a parade. Serves me right for getting all caught up in reading *Newsweek*."

I stepped in front of her. "Let me try."

"Oh, you must hear about the article I was reading. President Ford pardoned Robert E. Lee and restored his citizenship. Just this week, mind you."

I tugged at the window again and tried the next.

"That's the difference between us Yankees and those Southerners," Leoti said, her eyes swimming with tears even though the creases of her face deepened from the delight she took in the story. "The war isn't quite over down there. But don't you suppose President Ford has better things to attend to, and here he is pardoning a dead man? Now that General Lee is a citizen again, he'll be sorry he didn't ask to see his tax bill first."

I tried the window over the sink.

"Listen to me," Leoti said, smoothing her apron. "I'm prattling like a schoolgirl before a dance."

"We'll ask H to open the windows when he picks me up," I said.

"Won't he think highly of himself when he pulls those windows open for a couple of weak girls?" The teapot whistled and Leoti poured the boiling water into a gold-rimmed teapot. I prayed she'd used chamomile tea, and I took the tray from her.

"We have a lovely book to discuss," she said.

In her parlor, Leoti poured the black tea into my cup. I stifled a groan.

"So, what new delights did you reap from *The Optimist's Daughter*?"

I stirred cream into my tea until it was beige. "I didn't read it, Leoti. I'm sorry."

"What do you have to be sorry about? Life gets busy. You're a working girl."

"I do have some good news for you," I said. "The artist finished the windows for the church. He'll deliver them this week."

Leoti clapped her hands. "That's wonderful! Simply wonderful, my dear." She leaned forward. "How do they look?"

"Beautiful. And Pastor Ted assured me they would be installed in time for Ranch Days."

"That soon?"

"The deacons volunteered their time."

"This is marvelous. Amy, I don't know how to thank you. This means so much to me and . . . well, it would have made Arthur very happy too. You tell that young man how happy he has made me."

Her reference to Falcon caused my heart to flutter. "I will."

Thirty-Six

I dreamed I couldn't find my biology class at Westmont. All around me students called out to friends and talked about their summer jobs or the people they'd met on missions trips. I stood in the stream of students like a boulder, only a mild inconvenience to their conversations. I dug through my backpack for my class schedule but found only car wax and window cleaner. My throat tightened. Tardiness earned demerits. My legs were leaden when I tried to run back to the dorm for my schedule. The bell tower chimed. I was late. Every eye turned on me when I finally walked into class.

The scent of Mom's Tabu perfume seeped into my dream world. I wept from gratitude over being rescued.

"Amy, *fofa,* you're having a bad dream," Mom spoke softly into my ear. "You must wake up. I'm so sorry." She stroked my hair away from my face. "Something has happened, something horrible. I'm so very, very sorry. Wake up, honey." She clicked the bedside lamp on.

I sat up. "Wha . . . ?"

Mrs. Clancy stood behind Mom. She lifted her glasses to wipe tears from her eyes.

"Has there been a death?" I asked her.

Mom sniffed. A rash mottled her eyes, and watery snot threatened to run over her lip. She dabbed it away with a wad of tissues.

My pulse raced. "What's going on?"

Mom blew her nose.

An icy finger of dread rode the ridges of my spine. "Feather? Is it Feather? Mom? Mrs. Clancy?"

Mrs. Clancy placed her hand on Mom's shoulder. "Francie, do you mind? I'd like to talk to Amy alone for a moment."

I squeezed Mom's hand.

"I think I should stay," she said.

Mrs. Clancy considered this and said, "Time is of the essence, Francie. Unless you want to help us downstairs . . . ?"

Mom looked at me with pleading eyes.

"I'll be okay," I said as convincingly as my stomach allowed.

She embraced me with a ferocity that frightened me and then strode out of the room. Her bedroom door clicked shut.

Mrs. Clancy sat on the bed. "Amy, I need you to be strong. There will be time for mourning when our work is finished here."

"Who . . . ?"

She covered my hand with hers and squeezed. "There's been a terrible . . . incident. Some boys inhaled spray paint up on the mesa. It was meant to be an initiation of sorts. One of the boys—"

I only knew one boy.

Mrs. Clancy clamped a hand over her mouth. Her eyes filled with tears. When she lowered her hand, her words were pinched, breathy. "One of the boys was H."

"Is he . . . okay?"

"Sheriff Thompson anticipated there would be partying tonight, what with football tryouts completed and school starting Monday, so he patrolled the usual gathering spots." She removed her glasses to staunch the flow of tears with a hankie and sucked in a shuddering breath. "The sheriff tried to resuscitate him, but H was already gone."

"But I just saw him. He gave me a ride to Leoti's. He was fine."

"I know. I can hardly believe this has happened, especially to H." Mrs. Clancy pulled me into her chest. My tears answered her sobs. She rocked me, humming in my ear until my tears drenched her blouse. She loosened her embrace. "Amy, Charles is attending a mortician's seminar in Denver. The sheriff will delay H's parents until I call. His death will be hard enough for them. They shouldn't have to see him looking like this."

I nodded.

"Can you help me clean him up? We don't have much time."

I nodded again, only because part of me disbelieved H needed cleaning up at all. Like the Mexican man, there had been a terrible mix-up. Someone else lay in the preparation room.

"Put some clothes on. I'll be in the kitchen making phone calls. There's no time to spare."

Once dressed, I followed Mrs. Clancy down the basement stairs to the preparation room. She stopped midway and turned to speak in her usual punctilious manner. "I must warn you. He's a mess. There's black paint around his mouth and nose and on his hands, and, of course, his shirt. Thank God, the nights are cool. Besides the paint, he looks good."

She looked down at her shoes for a long moment. When she spoke again, my heart nearly burst. "I've known H since the day he was born.

I lived with my sister and her husband for a month after his birth. She'd lost a good amount of blood during delivery. I took care of him, got up in the middle of the night to feed and change him. I loved him like a son, I did. But we have to put our feelings aside to do our job. Remember, the H we knew is gone. Only a shell remains. He's with the Lord. I'm sure of it." She met my eyes. "We'll see him again, and he'll be laughing at us for taking our good time about joining him."

Mrs. Clancy turned sharply and walked toward the preparation table where H lay covered with a sheet. I stared at the peaks that were surely his feet while she peeled the sheet back.

"We'll use mineral spirits to remove the paint. I'll work on his face. You start on his hands."

Mrs. Clancy tied a rubbery apron around me and shoved protective gloves onto my hands. I kept my head down to avoid looking at H's face. "You're not going to hurt him," she said, "so do what you must to remove the paint before his folks get here. We'll have to wash him too. He smells like a paint factory." She opened the door to the ramp. The predawn air heaved a sigh, and I shivered. "We'll be happy to have the fresh air once we start working."

I doused a handful of cotton with the mineral spirits and studied H's hand. The paint had flowed into the lines and folds of his skin and into his cuticles. This hand had wrapped Dr. Masterson in a sheet, and pulled Feather from the canal, and nearly crushed my hand as we ran from Jim Warner.

Mrs. Clancy stopped her work to look at me. "Amy?"

"I've never touched a . . . a . . ."

"The sheriff got him here fast. He isn't stiff yet. The gloves are thick enough. You shouldn't feel any change in temperature." She swallowed hard. "Can you do this?"

Can I? "I think so, yes. Yes, I can."

Mrs. Clancy scrubbed furiously at H's face, grunting and sniffing as she worked.

I picked up H's hand, surprised by its weight. The harder I scrubbed, the angrier I became—angry at Jim Warner, whom I pictured egging H on, and angry at my mother for hijacking me to Cordial in the first place. And angry at H for not listening to me . . . and for being a guy.

How crazy is that?

Curiously, I wanted to call H to tell him about the death call that had woken me in the middle of the night because, more than anyone, he'd understand. And there I was, preparing him for burial. How jagged runs the line between life and death, hope and reality. A verse I'd memorized for a gold star came to mind:

> *Thine eyes have seen my unformed substance;*
>
> *And in Thy book they were all written,*
>
> *The days that were ordained for me,*
>
> *When as yet there was not one of them.*

I'd clung to the affirmation in these lines when I wearied of mothering Mom. God knew how I had toiled and all about the open wound of disappointment I bore. Who more than God knew what he was doing? I would be a stronger person, I'd reasoned, because while other girls attended to frivolous things like dances and boyfriends and how to escape their parents' watchful eyes, I developed usable life skills. I knew when the utility bill was due, and how to tiptoe around someone with a hang-over, and above all else, how to polish a car. But the affirming words turned to platitudes as I swabbed paint from under H's fingernails.

So, God, this was your plan for H, to be snuffed out by an ignoble act? He deserved better. You saw how he treated Leoti. You watched him protect me from Jim. He loved his parents. He was so proud of what his father had accomplished—

"I think you can move to his right hand, Amy," Mrs. Clancy said close to my ear, like she didn't want to disturb H in his sleep.

Mrs. Clancy cut H's T-shirt from the hem to the neckline and down each sleeve. The shirt fell away to reveal his still chest. My heart beat like a drum roll as I lifted my gaze to his face. Pale. One eye partly opened as if he were squinting. I gasped. Mrs. Clancy adjusted his eyelids to look more natural, like he were sleeping, but already his face, pale and fixed, was more mask than flesh. No wry smile played at his lips. The sun would never glint off his eyes again. There would be no more bold requests for a kiss. His face, with its straight nose and strong chin, was as still as stone. My eyes burned to cry.

"Amy, his parents will be here any minute."

I scrubbed at the paint on his right hand, playing with the irrational belief that I could rub life back into him. His hand slipped from my grasp and hit the table with a thud. I stifled a sob.

"I know this is terribly difficult." Mrs. Clancy combed H's hair into place, although she parted it on the wrong side. "You're doing a great kindness for his parents, Amy . . . and for me. Thank you."

A bar of Ivory floated in a tub of warm water. She scrubbed the bar of soap until the washcloth frothed and stopped, listening. "They're here." She dropped the washcloth back into the tub and removed her apron. "You're going to have to finish. Wash his face and hands and cover him with a clean sheet just to his shoulders. When I hear the basement door close, I'll know H is ready. Do you think you can do that?"

No! "Yes."

I washed his hands and arms up to his elbows. His arms were surprisingly heavy. "You had to go and pump up your muscles, didn't you?" I said to his impassive face and thought better of it. "Oh, I didn't mean . . . you look good . . . strong, I mean. I'm sorry I didn't tell you that before." I washed his face and bent close to sniff. He smelled like the night we'd gone to the drive-in. In life and death, H bathed with Ivory.

"There's something else I never told you," I whispered close to his ear. "I wanted you to kiss me, especially when we hid in the hay field. You didn't need to tease about it or ask, just kiss me. I wouldn't have minded." I bent closer. "I owe you this." I touched my lips to his. His lips were cool, not like being outside on a fine fall day, but cool from the inside. I jumped back, ripping the gloves from my hands to scrub at my mouth with the hem of my T-shirt.

The door at the top of the stairs opened. Mrs. Clancy said, "We're coming down, Amy."

I ran up the ramp into the surrendering night. A halo of gold as soft as fleece outlined Logan Mountain. My flip-flops slapped against my feet, too loud for the unraveling day, so I slipped them off and left them on the sidewalk. I must have run down the hill and across Pinion Road, but I didn't remember anything until I lay facedown in the hayfield, making mud of the rich earth. I beat the ground with my fist to enunciate each word of the question that distressed my soul.

"What were you thinking?" I repeated over and over, not giving God a chance to answer because there wasn't an answer I wanted to hear. I rolled onto my back, watching the colorless sky bloom to blue. If God wasn't going to perform per my expectations, I felt justified in making him feel guilty. "You know, H was a good guy. He could be maddening at times, true, but he had a good heart. He was earnest, a regular guy, the salt of the earth. You need guys like that, don't you?"

Maybe God didn't. Maybe God preferred the likes of Jim Warner.

After all, Jesus called Paul, a murderer, to the mission field and impetuous, ever-the-bungler Peter, a party guy for sure, to preach to the Gentiles. In the early days, had Jesus held Peter's head while he vomited from drinking too much wine? Mary Magdalene's soul had housed seven demons. Thomas doubted Jesus' identity after three years of intimate friendship. And Judas—Judas was Jim Warner, someone who had garnered H's trust only to strip him of his dignity and life.

Over the course of the next few days, Mrs. Clancy, Mom, and I performed our duties like repelling magnets, all positively charged with an unspeakable grief. Feather dropped by daily to fill the refrigerator with eggs from her hens and bread that Butter had baked. I thanked her, but my heart was wrapped in cotton. Kindnesses and ill-spoken condolences dropped to the floor noiselessly. Mrs. Clancy asked me to sing at the funeral.

"I know his favorite song," I said.

She hesitated only slightly before she said, "Anything you choose will bc fine."

I sang "One Tin Soldier" to a packed church, but mostly to Feather and her family in the back row and to Leoti because they would understand the song and why H loved it so.

On that bloody morning after

One tin soldier rides away.

When they lowered his casket into the ground, I cried and couldn't stop. Although I know it hurt her, I pushed Mom away and took long walks down country roads, past the sprightly green of irrigated fields and onto the desert mesas. I listed all of the things H would miss, like the cheering crowd at football games and graduating with his class and going to college and falling in love and getting married and having babies.

Grief turned to shame when I realized the sorrow that swaddled me wasn't as much about missing H as it was about me. I felt vulnerable, fragile. I had believed God would protect me. Now I wasn't so sure. My head accepted the idea that I would die someday, when I was old and worthless. Everyone died. H's passing made death my next-door neighbor, hard to ignore and prone to loud parties that kept me awake at night. That may sound funny coming from a girl who lived and worked in a funeral home, but death is very, very different when it takes a friend, a friend whose breath I'd felt on my face.

If God wasn't my protector, who was?

Thirty-Seven

I discovered that summer why people said they'd "lost" a loved one. I turned constantly to share a story with H, or an aggravating tidbit about Mom, even an observation about life in Cordial. And he wasn't there. He would never be there again, but my heart kept forgetting.

When Feather came to tell me she was moving to North Carolina, an abyss threatened to draw me into its darkness. I felt abandoned. Coming to Cordial had withered my dream of college and freedom, and now I was losing yet another friend.

Later, I gathered my Jane Austen books and delivered them to her cabin as a going-away present. She handed me Vernon and packed the books in a Michelob box.

Straw sat on a stump by the door with his head in his hands. Frog and Mule peeked into the cabin, more serious than I'd ever seen them. They saw me watching and disappeared. Inside, I held Vernon while Butter and Feather filled cardboard boxes with clothes. Little Lamb napped on his parents' bed.

"Just take what you need for the trip, no more than three days' worth. We'll buy new things when we get home," said a woman dressed in a sailor-like short outfit with tennis shoes so white they seemed blue. She stooped to sort through the clothes. Some she threw to the ground. "There's absolutely no reason for my grandchildren to dress like ragamuffins, Deborah."

Deborah? Deborahs barked orders and demanded loyalty with a blood sacrifice. Butter was soft and golden.

"Mom," Butter said, and there was a warning in the way she said it.

"I'm sorry. I know I promised. It's just that—"

"Remember, staying with you is only temporary," Butter said. "Once I've gotten a job and saved some money, we'll find a place of our own."

Straw strode into the cabin. He took a pair of scissors from where they hung on the wall. I stepped back. Butter's mom edged away until she bumped into Feather's bed. The twins returned, somber-faced, holding hands. Straw fell to his knees in front of Butter. He grabbed a fistful of his beard, and cut the clump of hair with the scissors.

"What are you doing? Stop!" Butter screamed.

Feather ran to her father, placing her hand on his arm, but he shook it off. He pulled another fistful of hair straight up from his head and cut close to his scalp. Clumps of his yellow hair littered the cabin floor.

Butter dropped to her knees to look Straw in the eye. "Please! Straw! What are you doing? Stop!"

"My name is Steve." His voice was a roar. He worked the scissors through another clump of hair.

Vernon wailed. I patted his back. I should have left the cabin, so the family could work out their problems in private, but I was too curious. Instead, I busied myself appeasing Vernon.

Butter pleaded with Straw. "Why are you doing this?"

"I'd do anything to keep you and the kids with me. I'll get a job off the homestead. Maybe the bank needs a—"

"Not the bank!"

"I'll harvest peaches by day and stock grocery shelves by night. Anything, Butter, I'll do anything."

His scalp bled where he'd nicked himself with the scissors. He looked like one sorry mutt, but Butter looked at him with pliant eyes. Straw dropped the scissors to open his arms to her. They clutched at each other. Butter's mother inched closer.

"Deborah, winter is only a few months off, and you'll be stoking the fire every hour to keep the children from freezing. And you know, dear, Rebecca needs to see a specialist. The university hospital draws the best doctors in the country. Your father has been asking around. There's a neurologist doing research with new drugs. They look very hopeful."

Straw held Butter at arm's length. "They're hiring at the mine. I can make $25.00 an hour, plus benefits."

"That goes against everything we believe in."

"If I don't dig for coal, someone else will. Feather could see a specialist in Denver. And earning that kind of money, we could insulate the cabin and buy a better stove. And maybe we could get an electrical line hung to the house." Straw held Butter's hands to his chest. "Babe, we made the right decision coming here. We're better for it. It's been tough, but we've survived the hardest years together. We can be the people we want to be. The money Feather found paid the mortgage for another month. Will you give me that long? If I don't have a job, and Feather hasn't seen a doctor, I'll drive you to your mother's myself."

We all waited for Butter's answer. She ran her hand over the stubble of hair on Straw's head and chin. "Kids, put your things away."

Straw howled and kissed Butter.

Thirty-Eight

A shaft of light fell across the bed when Mom opened the bedroom door. I rose to one elbow. "Is everything all right?" I asked, trying to sound compliant and cooperative.

"Goodnight, *querida,*" she said, closing the door.

"Mom?"

"Yes?"

Nothing squeaked louder than the hinges of my bedroom door. "It's really hot in here with the window closed. Would you mind leaving the door open? I can hardly breathe."

"Would you like me to bring in the fan?"

"It's too loud. Really, I'm cooler already with the door open."

She walked toward the bed. I fought to keep from groaning. I feared the full-moon jam session would be over before I got to New Morning.

"You seem a little better, *fofa,* not so sad. That's good. I'm proud of you." She hesitated.

"I am better." *Now, please go away.*

"It helps to talk when you're sad."

"I'm tired, mostly. I think a good night's sleep will be the best thing for me right now."

"You're sure?"

Yes! "Could we go window shopping in Clearwater this weekend? A change of scenery would be nice. Maybe Bonnie could drive us."

"I'll ask her tomorrow." She turned and hesitated again, only to return to the bedside. "In light of all that's happened, it's silly for you to be grounded."

"Thanks, Mom."

"I love you."

"I love you too."

To help the time pass faster, I dove under the covers with a book and a flashlight. After reading the same paragraph five times, I listened instead to Mom's nightly ritual, ticking off each step. Removed makeup. Brushed teeth. Gargled. Brushed hair one hundred times. Slathered feet and hands with petroleum jelly and slid into cotton gloves and socks. Mumbled a few Hail Marys. Punched the pillow. Thrashed about. Punched the pillow again. Settled into the pillow and snored.

I dressed with the clothes I'd stashed under the bed and wrapped my guitar case in a blanket. All that day, I'd walked the house, noting where the floor creaked or groaned. I lifted the trapdoor in the hall. Charles's padded bumper gave the guitar a soundless landing. I waited, listened for stirring from Mom's room. I used a rolled towel as a doorstop to keep the trapdoor from slamming shut. I felt my way down the sloping chute with my feet. With my toes pressed against the bumper, I supported the door with one hand while I removed the towel with the other. My arm quivered under the weight of the door. I left the towel and the blanket on the chute where I could find them on my return.

Once outside, I strapped my guitar to my back and jogged the whole way to New Morning. I stopped only once to catch my breath. My shadow walked before me, but I didn't turn my face to welcome the moon's light. I pressed on to the farm.

I FOLLOWED TWO women wrapped in shawls to the pasture beyond the garden. My plan was to stand in the shadows to observe the other musicians before joining the jam session. If they were too good, I'd leave my guitar by the zucchini and meld into the crowd. The musicians tuned their instruments while parents gathered their children. A fire blazed in a ring of stones. Gretel, one of the farm's urchins with cat eyes and a sunny disposition, spotted me. She called out, "Cookie!" and left the warmth of her mother's lap to embrace me. A herd of children with open hands followed close behind.

"I'm so sorry. I didn't bring any cookies," I said, touching their open hands. "I didn't want to spoil your dinners."

"We already ate," they said as a chorus.

Falcon pushed his way through the throng. "Leave the poor lady alone."

Still, they beseeched me with hungry eyes.

"Honest, I don't have any cookies. Not one."

They groaned and skittered away to their families.

Falcon took my hand to lead me toward the circle of musicians and New Morning residents. The campfire flickered in his eyes. "I didn't think you were coming."

The gourd player, a red-headed man with a sparse beard, offered me a seat by another guitar player. "I'm Greg. I try to keep this ragtag group going in the same direction. Just follow ol' Fergus, and you won't get too lost."

The guitar player, Fergus, I presumed, nodded once.

Falcon bent to whisper in my ear. "Have fun."

While I tuned my guitar, mothers swayed to soothe their babies and issued warnings to the older children to stay within the firelight. The ladies I knew from the kitchen welcomed me before they settled onto a blanket or log.

"Are we ready, then?" asked Greg.

The children called out. "'Pigtown Fling!'"

"'Pigtown Fling' it is. Okay, one . . . two . . . one, two, three, four!"

Within a measure, I recognized the folk song as "Hop Along Sally" and strummed along, enjoying the voice of the fiddle and the strong melody of the dulcimer. I relaxed. If I didn't recognize the song by the title called out, I knew it by the melody and another name, such was the colloquial nature of folk music. A man wearing a flannel shirt without cuffs played and sang "The Curragh of Kildare," a melancholy song about a distant love. Greg livened the mood by selecting a toe-tapper, followed by "The Water Is Wide" and "Swing Low, Sweet Chariot."

He hooked his suspenders and talked to the audience. "I read in *Mother* about the meaning of the herbs in 'Scarborough Fair.' Let's see if I can get this straight. Parsley takes away bitterness and aids digestion, so if we sing really bad, or you ate more of my lovely wife's spicy enchiladas than you should have, parsley is for you. Sage symbolizes strength; rosemary stands for faithfulness, love, and remembrance, which seems like an awful lot for one plant to do; and thyme is courage, something every married man needs."

After "Scarborough Fair," we played an Eagles song, "Take It Easy." Our instruments blended easily, and those of us who sang found a niche in the harmonies.

"As is our tradition here at the full-moon jams, guest jammers are expected to play and sing a solo. Amy, you're destined to be a hundred times better than that fella who passed through here last month. We'd tell you not to play the same song, but honestly, we couldn't tell ya what that was. Whenever you're ready."

I looked to Falcon, and he shrugged. He couldn't save me. The people I knew around the fire were seekers who dabbled with meaning like a child played with a toy until it becomes familiar and went seeking something else. A strong gospel song should've come to mind. It didn't. Instead, I looked at Falcon and sang "Desperado," only not like the gentle plodding of an old gray mare. No, I closed my eyes and sang the song as an invitation, not knowing what I was inviting.

You better let somebody love you

Before it's too late.

The crowd hooted and hollered and clapped enthusiastically. Babies cried. Dogs barked. I bowed my head.

Greg yelled above the cheering. "I can't see how any of us are going to top that. Let's take a break, get the kids to bed, and come back for some mellow tunes when you get around to it."

A slow, satisfied grin spread across Falcon's face. "That was amazing." He offered his hand and pulled me to my feet. He unhooked my guitar strap. A swell of warmth filled my belly.

"Come on," he said, taking my hand.

"Where are we going? Should I take my guitar?"

"We'll be back."

I grabbed my purse anyway. We ran down a hill into an apple orchard. The moon through the trees dappled the ground black and silver. Grasses slashed at my shins. Behind us, the laughs of people around the fire softened and floated on an invisible river of mountain air, sluicing the valley with its refreshing wash. The branches laden with fruit swayed on the air's currents. A fiddler serenaded the night with "Annie's Song."

You fill up my senses . . .

Falcon twirled me to a stop. "Shall we dance?"

"I don't know how."

"It's easy." He looked up. The moon hung over us. "The spotlight is on us." He pulled me closer. I rested my hand on his shoulder, and he lifted my other hand to his lips to kiss my palm. "Let's just sway with the music. That's right. Very good."

"We're just like Bobby and Cissy."

He laughed. "I'm going to step forward; you step back."

"Ouch!"

"My fault. I should have told you which foot."

"Maybe we should keep swaying."

The fire's flame that had warmed his eyes now reflected the cool orb of the moon. As we moved to the music, he eased closer and closer until he bent to touch his cheek to mine. His breath warmed my ear. "You've been holding out on me," he said. "You're good, real good. My desperado days are behind me. I would jump off the Great Wall of China for you."

"Can you feel my heart beating?"

He laughed and held me tighter.

I was a plump pigeon punched from the sky by a falcon's coiled talons, panting her last breaths, waiting to be pounced with a delicious inevitability. But Falcon wasn't going to eat me.

"Hold me, Amelia. Hold me."

I obeyed, wrapping my arms around his shoulders and burying my face in his neck. He smelled of metallic heat and hay and bitter sweat. "I'm going to kiss you, Amelia, but I won't apologize, not again, not ever. Is that okay with you?"

John 3:16 . . . For God so . . .

I nodded.

His lips covered mine.

John 3 . . .

His hands ran under my blouse over the bare skin of my back.

I stepped back. Our eyes met.

J . . . ohn . . .

"Amelia? Are you okay with this?"

What was *this* that both satiated and awakened a ravenous hunger, that made light of promises, that focused the attention of the universe on one moment in time and fogged reason with desire? I wanted to know the answers more than I wanted to breathe.

I stepped into his embrace.

I PUT MY blouse on backwards. "I have to go."

"Did I hurt you?"

I let my hair fall around my face and shook my head. "I just have to go." I took a few steps, but Falcon caught me in an embrace. I pushed at his chest. And still he held me. "Let me go. Please, just let me go."

"Amelia, we didn't do anything wrong. Relax. Stay awhile. Let me hold you."

"I want to go," I said, pressing harder against his chest.

"I'll let go of you, but we should talk. Okay? Let me know that you're okay with that. We're going to talk calmly, right?" He dropped his arms to his side. Down the long row of trees lay my escape. "I asked you if you were okay with what we were doing. You said yes. Do you remember that?"

My stomach cramped, bile burned the back of my throat, and my dinner sprayed Falcon's feet. He spewed expletives that revealed his misunderstanding of anything holy. I turned away from him.

"Amelia, I need to know—"

"What?" I asked, my hands balled into fists. "What exactly do you need to know?"

"Lower your voice, Amelia."

"Then ask your question and let me go."

"You're young, maybe too young. What happened here was beautiful and spontaneous. You'll remember what we shared here your whole life."

"But you *know* what I believe."

"I didn't put a gun to your head."

I saw my fingers pulling at his shirt, and a fresh wave of shame washed over me. "If you're worried that I'll tell my mom, forget about it. I'm not telling anyone, ever." I ran through the trees, pushing back branches and side-stepping orchard ladders until I reached the road. When I was sure Falcon hadn't followed me, I slumped to the ground and pounded the grassy ledge of the drainage ditch. Bile burned my throat, and I threw up again. I wiped my mouth on my blouse and backed away, staying low in the ditch, low where I belonged.

"Oh God, I'm so sorry, so very, very sorry." The letter to Lauren came to mind, complete with memory verses about fleeing sexual immorality and a five-point sermon on purity and heavenly reward.

Oh God, I'm so stupid.

Feet crunched on the graveled road, and voices moved into range. I drew myself into the fetal position. As they walked by, they praised a peach pie and made plans to cooperate with the next day's laundry. One girl said, "I look back to my days of lugging the laundry to the Laundromat with longing. May the Sierra Club dance on my grave, but I lust for a washer-dryer combo, avocado green with a heavy-duty cycle and a tub as big as a swimming pool. Is that too much to ask?" The night rang with their laughter. Before another group happened by, I trotted toward DeCrane Road and the long walk home.

Instead, I turned toward the cemetery.

I LEANED AGAINST Barbara Louise's headstone and rifled through my purse for the birth control pills. I pushed them through the foil backing into my hand—about fifteen of them. I worked up a mouthful of spit and popped the pills into my mouth. Swallowing cotton balls would have been easier. I knew taking the pills was futile. It took three months for them to work. Besides, what would an overdose of birth control pills do to me? I'd read the dire warnings when Mom had first given me the pills. Back then, words like *bleeding* and *nausea* and *stroke* had convinced me doubly that taking the pills for no good reason was a crazy idea. I spat out the pills that remained in my mouth. My primed gag reflex released the pills easily with what remained in my stomach.

"I'm sorry, Barbara Louise."

No matter how enticing the breeze or compelling the silvery light, I pressed my face to the hard ground. I wanted to cease to exist like Barbara Louise McCulloh, to fade to a vapor and blow away.

"I'm ruined. Oh, God in heaven, I'm ruined. I didn't mean for this to happen."

But you did.

When I unbuttoned his shirt?

No, long before that.

Oh God, you're right. I practically ran past him into the orchard.

Before that.

I sat up, wiped my eyes. "I loved his flattery. I lied to my mother. I couldn't even look at the moon."

You stopped talking to me.

"All I wanted was to fulfill Leoti's dream."

The night went silent. The toads surrendered to their loneliness. The crickets abandoned their throbbing calls. And all the songs of heaven ceased. I drew up my legs. I wanted to be as invisible as a thought, as forgotten as a dream, as small as a grain of sand.

MORE THAN ANYTHING, I wanted to be clean. I ran toward the river. The moon lit the way. I stepped out of my clothes and into the river until the water hit my thighs, and I fell under the current. The cold water bit at my scalp and my shoulders and cramped the hot muscles of my legs. My lungs burned for air, and for a moment, I imagined myself floating face down in the water, lifeless and still.

Maybe in a heated pool.

I pushed off the rocky bottom and gulped at the air.

Back on the grassy shore, I started to dress but stepped out of my underwear and threw them into the river before pulling on my shorts and blouse. The relief I craved eluded me, but I possessed no more tears to cry. It wasn't until I returned to the basement that my hands seemed empty. I'd left my guitar at New Morning, and at New Morning it could stay.

Thirty-Nine

I showered before Mom woke and worked my wet hair into a bun. I threw the peasant blouse and the Mexican blouses into the alley trashcans before I laid out a bowl, cup, and utensils for Mom's breakfast. Thus began the reconstruction of Amy the good.

Mom shuffled into the kitchen. "Did you make coffee?"

"Instant. There's a memorial service today, so I can't cook anything. Would you like Cheerios or Frosted Flakes?" Avoiding her gaze, I busied myself washing breakfast dishes I hadn't used.

"*Fofa,* you seem much better this morning."

"I've had time to think, put things in perspective. Cordial isn't so bad. In some ways, it reminds me of Gilbertsville. I can stay here for a while." Actually, I planned on staying inside the funeral home until Falcon hit the road to California. Feather could tell me when he left.

Mom sipped at her coffee. Her face blushed pink as the morning ripened over the mesas. "Are you visiting your Mrs. Masterson today?"

"There's a memorial service. I'm singing. I'll have to go tomorrow."

"You're singing? That's wonderful. We could use the money for groceries."

I'd planned on stashing the money in my get-out-of-town fund. "What about your paycheck?"

"I have some bills to pay."

"What bills?" I asked, careful to keep my annoyance in check.

"Those pills I buy you every month are expensive. The pharmacist lets me make payments. And there are some other incidental things that I'm working to whittle down. You don't need to bother your head about them. I'll take care of it."

"What about the car?"

"That's one of the things I'm whittling down."

"Good for you," I said and left the room to dust the chapel.

BEFORE THE SERVICE, Mrs. Clancy read a portion of a letter the dearly departed, Mrs. Dumont, had only written the week before. "'There will be many a lost soul at the memorial service. My prayer is that a good number of my relatives will hear about the saving grace of Jesus. However, most will attend the service believing my legacy will pad their pockets. It most certainly will not. Please note: More than one of my relatives has spent time in the hoosegow. Propriety demands me to warn you of their contempt for the law and all things civil.'"

Mrs. Clancy glanced around the chapel. "Maybe you should collect the porcelain figurines. I don't want to pad their pockets either."

Mrs. Dumont had vastly overestimated the drawing power of her wealth. Two women, generously padded already, sat in the back row of the chapel, fiddling with their handbag latches and looking furtively toward the door. These were Mrs. Dumont's only mourners. Part of me wanted to offer them popcorn for the show.

A chaplain I hadn't met—a man who moved like a chipmunk—spoke on and on about the many contributions Mrs. Dumont had made to his church. "She contributed much more than her considerable wealth. She exhorted and loved the body of Christ with her time and talents." And then he listed the years and the ages of the Sunday school classes she'd taught, beginning in 1915. Who kept track of such things? Mrs. Dumont herself, no doubt.

I started to thank God that Pearl was there to play the organ, so I didn't have to explain, at least yet, how I'd lost my guitar, but the prayer dissipated long before the amen. My eyes burned with tears the moment Pearl lunged on the first chord of "Softly and Tenderly, Jesus Is Calling." By the time I sang the last verse, tears streamed down my cheeks and my voice faltered with emotion, drawing fresh interest from the two ladies in the back. I closed my eyes.

O for the wonderful love he has promised,

promised for you and for me!

Though we have sinned, he has mercy and pardon,

pardon for you and for me.

Mrs. Clancy blew her nose like an old fisherman. The chaplain sniffed, and the women each dabbed their eyes with embroidered hankies. I retreated to my room where fresh tears lamented how cheaply I had treated God's mercy.

Forty

Dawn drew a cool finger along my arm. Because Logan Mountain stalled the coming day, a gossamer curtain of gray dulled the valley. Sparrows—the perpetual optimists of the bird world—raucously celebrated the new day. *Stupid birds.* I stared at the water stain on the ceiling, the one that resembled Popeye's bloated cheeks, and rehearsed the letter I would write Lauren. Maybe I wouldn't write a letter at all but list every Scripture about God's love and forgiveness from Genesis to Revelation.

"Lord? Are you listening?" But the prayer dissolved in my mouth.

Will you be deaf and mute forever?

I turned to the wall and pulled the blankets over my head.

Gravel scrunched in the driveway. It was too early for Mrs. Clancy, unless someone had called her directly about a dearly departed's passing. How fitting that the relentless march of death continued. I welcomed the distraction. I slid out of bed to trade my nightgown for my cleaning clothes. Brushing my hair into a ponytail, my hands stilled at my reflection. A mixture of acceptance and annoyance over my tasks molded my face, a far cry from the terror of my early days at the funeral home.

Is this a good thing?

The doorbell hummed. A kitchen chair scraped the floor, and the door opened. Mom spoke as if spewing soured milk. "What do you want?"

Bruce?

Falcon's voice answered evenly. "This is Amy's guitar."

I laid the brush on the dresser.

"I know that," Mom said. "Did you steal it?"

"Amy left it at the farm."

"What farm? What is this all about?"

"Can I talk to her? I'm leaving town."

"Tell me how you know my daughter, and I'll consider letting you see her."

During the long silence that followed, I tiptoed back to the bed. I pictured Falcon easing back from the kitchen door to avoid being bludgeoned by Mom. Poe's pendulum swung relentlessly over my bed.

Falcon finally answered. "I don't know her well at all, but she helped a family I worked for, and I'd like to thank her."

"You're leaving Cordial today? For good? Give me the guitar."

At the sound of Mom's nearing footsteps, I pulled the blankets over my head. Mom tugged at the blankets. I held tight. "Amy, wake up. There's a stinking hippie out here who wants to thank you for something."

My heart throbbed in my chest. I lowered the blankets just past my eyes and whispered, "I don't want to see him. Tell him . . . tell him I'm sick. I have a fever and the chills. Tell him that I haven't been out of bed for a week. Better yet, tell him it's giardia and I can't leave the bathroom."

Mom sat on the bed.

"Mom, please. I don't want to see him."

"What is this about?"

I covered my face again. "Don't make me go out there. I'd rather die."

"No man, especially not a stinky one, is worth dying for. Believe me. I know this is true." She rose and walked to the kitchen door, her steps drumming the floorboards like a charge. "Amy doesn't want to see you." The door slammed hard, the lock clicked, and the shade rattled closed. Mom called the Gartleys to tell them she would be late.

She closed the bedroom door behind her. "I think we have some talking to do," she said and kicked off her shoes to sit cross-legged at my feet. "Sit up and tell me everything."

I started back on the first day I'd met Falcon. Perhaps easing up to the grand finale would soften its sting. I explained how I'd been attracted to him from the moment I saw him, even though I fought tooth and nail not to like him.

"Men like him are the worst kind," she said. "Did he flatter you with all kinds of questions and hang on your every word?"

"How did you know? He made me feel like I belonged."

"And then he turned on you?"

"Not exactly."

I told her about the craft fair and working with him to make the windows for Leoti. I left out the part about Sasha; the story was condemning enough without her.

"He took advantage of your good heart. Did he take off with your share of the money from making the windows?"

"I volunteered my time."

"You did?"

"Like I said, I wanted to be near him."

Mom tapped her chin with a red fingernail. "I suppose with a haircut and a bath he would be quite good looking."

I told her about swimming at the river and the kiss.

"He kissed you? Did you have your clothes on?"

My face warmed. "Mom," I complained.

"Did you?"

"Of course I had my clothes on."

"How old is he? You're a child. He's a man. It's a good thing he's leaving town."

"There's more."

"Tell me."

So I did. I told her how I'd sneaked out of the house to attend the jam session at the farm. "I'm so, so sorry."

Mom swallowed hard. "What is this farm?"

"They grow organic vegetables and live simply. They don't want to be caught up in the rat race of urban living." I dared not tell her about the acid trips or their experimental relationships.

"Is this the place where they drop acid?"

"I was never there when they did that."

"Is there more?"

"They have a jam session every month. They build a bonfire and sing folk songs."

"I understood that." Mom wiped her hands on her pants. "You better tell me where this is leading."

"Would you mind if I covered my head with the sheet?"

She said my full name through her teeth.

I buried my face in my hands, and through my sobs I told her what had happened in the apple orchard.

"We better get you to confession then." She pulled back the covers. "Put on a dress."

"Confession? Mom, I'm not Catholic."

"Today, for me, you're Catholic. Trust me, you'll feel much better once the priest gives you absolution for your sin."

"Mom, I don't need—"

"Wash your face and wear stockings."

In truth, absolution sounded wonderful. I hoped the confessional turned out to be one big washing machine that would spill away guilt and memories after the rinse cycle.

I SAT IN the confessional, waiting for Mom to wrangle a priest. No more than a wooden closet with a bench seat, the confessional smelled of wood polish and sweat. A small door with a lattice window opened between the priest and me. Garlic wafted into the tiny cubicle.

"My child, your mother says you've come with a contrite heart. How long has it been since your last confession?"

I'd been telling God how sorry I was for six days.

"Well?" he pressed.

"I . . . uh . . ."

Mom whispered through the curtain that separated the confessional from the sanctuary. "Say bless me, father, for I have sinned."

"Is this your first confession, my daughter?" the priest asked.

"I'm not even Catholic."

Mom gasped.

"But I'm a Christian," I said.

"We Catholics consider ourselves Christians as well."

"You do?"

"Yes, but we have as difficult a time living up to the calling as anyone else, so we have that in common." He cleared his throat. "Well, now, lucky for you it is a slow day for sinning Catholics, so I have plenty of time to hear from Protestants." His voice smiled. "Have you sinned?" Before I could answer, he said, "Oh dear, now I've done it."

"Are you okay?"

"Please excuse me, daughter. The cook took a roast out of the oven moments before your mother found me, and she made me the most wonderful sandwich. Now I have mustard down the front of my rabat."

"Should I come back another time?"

"You could, but I promise confession only gets more difficult with the passing of time." There is a crunch of lettuce from the priest's side of the confessional. He speaks around a bite of sandwich. "Do you want to tell me about it?"

"Honestly?"

"That's the best way."

"No."

"Are you familiar with the verse from the Epistle of James, 'Confess your faults one to another, and pray one for another, that ye may be healed'?"

"I'm not sick. I'm—"

"But you are. Your sin has wounded your soul. Are you sleeping well?"

"I read until I'm exhausted, but still I lay awake forever."

"Are you eating?"

Mom spoke through the curtain. "She hardly touches her plate."

The priest slid his curtain aside. "Perhaps, good mother, it would be better for you to wait outside."

I peeked through the curtain. Mom stood looking at her shoes.

"I'll take good care of your daughter. You've done your work. Now it is up to God." Even Mom knew where she stood with God. The priest remained silent until the heavy door opened and shut. He pulled back the curtain of the confessional. "Let's sit where we can look each other in the eye, shall we?"

Father Raymond shuffled toward the pews and offered me a seat. His voice had made him sound old but not ancient. In truth, I believed Father Raymond had outlived sea turtles, and he moved with the same dogged grace. His rounded shoulders jutted his head forward like a hood ornament. Skin hung from his jaw in cushiony folds, but not one liver spot darkened his complexion. I envied the smoothness of his skin. I guess he didn't get out much. His watery eyes were kind and sincere. I was about to melt.

He wiped mustard from the corner of his mouth. "As the verse says, we should confess our sins to one another. I'll go first." He cleared his throat. "While eating my lunch in the park yesterday, I watched a young father pushing the swing for his tiny daughter, and I coveted the joy that lit his face each time she giggled." He nodded. "Will you pray for me?"

"My sin is much, much worse."

"My soul is wounded. Won't you intercede for me?"

I bowed my head, wondering if I shouldn't warn Father Raymond that my prayers had fallen on deaf ears since my night in the orchard. He would know soon enough. "Jesus, forgive Father Raymond for coveting another man's joy. Give him your joy and heal him of his sorrow. In Jesus' name, amen."

"Now, it's your turn."

"He heard me. God actually heard my prayer."

Father Raymond's eyes smiled, but he asked me again, "Are you ready to confess?"

"Like I said, my sin is much, much worse than—"

"They nailed Jesus to a cross for my covetousness. Did he suffer anymore for your sin?"

He had me there. Just when I thought I'd run out of tears, my eyes filled and my face contorted. This wasn't going to be anything like *The Song of Bernadette.*

Father Raymond leaned closer to whisper. "If it's any comfort to you at all, I have listened to confessions for sixty-two years. You can't surprise me, and you certainly can't surprise God."

I picked at a scab from a mosquito bite.

He finished his sandwich and wiped his mouth with a mustard-stained napkin.

"I'm taking up too much of your time," I said, scooting to the edge of the pew.

"Time is all I have."

"Are you sure?"

"If this is going to take a long time, I could fetch two fat pieces of Mrs. Kubek's chocolate cake." Father Raymond sighed. "No one in Clearwater County or beyond makes a better chocolate cake." He patted his stomach. "She brings a cake by every week, not always the chocolate cake, but all of her—"

"I fornicated."

True to his word, surprise never registered on his face. "Is this a habit of yours?"

"No!"

"Are you pregnant?"

"I don't know."

"Are you sorry for your sin?"

"Oh, yes."

"Will you go and sin no more?"

"Yes. I mean, no, I won't do it ever again."

"I wonder if your tears are more than sorrow for your sin. Maybe you are grieving the loss of who you thought you were—a nice Christian girl who harshly judged others? Is this possible?"

I blubbered again. "When will the pain go away?"

"I would not disdain the pain, my daughter, as long as it draws you to Christ." Father Raymond laid his soft hand upon my arm. "I have good news for you. The Father sees you now and forever through the righteousness of the Son. You are his bride, pure and undefiled. Believing this in the face of our sin is what we Christians call faith."

Father Raymond prayed for me, but I didn't hear a word. I cried too hard. Although I'd mocked the Catholics for keeping Christ on the cross in their churches, seeing Jesus' wounds reminded me what my sin had cost him. Finally, I cried from sorrow. Father Raymond shuffled out of the sanctuary and returned with a box of tissues and two pieces of chocolate cake in plastic wrap.

"One for you and one for your mother." When he spoke again, chocolate stained his teeth. "Old men still believe they are eighteen years old."

I stifled a laugh.

"Go ahead and laugh. I laugh whenever I catch my reflection in a mirror. *Who is that old guy wearing my whippersnapper soul?* I ask. So you see, I may understand what it means to struggle against fleshly desires, and I have seen many, many young girls like you come and confess the very same sin. The ones who listened to this piece of advice I'm about to offer only came to my confessional with venial sins. Do you know what this means?"

"I think so."

"I suggest, daughter, that you take a hiatus from men to devote yourself to Christ."

I'd already decided never to touch another man my whole life, but I humored the priest. "For how long?"

"At least a year, maybe two. Be the Lord's bride. Let him satisfy you with his love." Father Raymond used his pinkie to loosen a piece of meat from his teeth. "Anyone worth his salt will wait twice that long for you, and besides, your grades will be better."

I thanked him for his time and rose to leave.

"Daughter, one more thing. There never lived a perfectly good saint, but true saints learn to enjoy the goodness of God because of their imperfections. Let him love you as he made you and lavish you with his grace."

MOM AND CHARLES walked hand in hand down the front walk toward his orange Pinto station wagon. He opened the door for her. *Just friends? I don't think so.* This was the third night in a row they'd gone out. They waved as the car lurched away from the curb and putt-putted around the corner.

With my bedroom door closed, I thumbed through my Bible, using the concordance to find all of the verses that mentioned brides. When I read "You have made my heart beat faster, my sister, my bride" from the Song of Solomon, I lit a candle and knelt beside the bed.

I prayed, "I don't know what this will be like, being your bride and all, but I don't ever want to be in this place again. I'm sick with remorse. It's all I can think about. I ask you again, pl*eee*ase forgive me . . . for . . . you know I hate to say this . . . well, you know . . .

for settling for much, much less when all the while you wanted to be my bridegroom, the Prince of Peace. So here goes."

I held a plastic ring I'd bought out of a gumball machine between my fingers.

"With this ring . . ."

I slid the ring onto my finger.

". . . I thee wed from this day forward, even though you seem to want me to stay in Cordial for a few more months, and even though . . ." A sob rolled from my gut, plowed over my heart, and exploded out of my mouth. It was better than throwing up, so I let the crying fit run its course while I allowed my worst fear to play out in my imagination—me, an unwed mother, just like Mom. "Even though I may be carrying another man's baby."

The crying I'd done up to this point was just a warm-up. When I imagined myself facing the dean of students at Westmont, and collecting welfare checks, and waving any hopes of a husband good-bye, an artesian well of tears opened.

"Are you sure you want me?"

How beautiful is your love, my sister, my bride!

"Then I'm yours."

Forty-One

Sitting at a small table on the porch, I stared at a blank piece of Clancy and Sons letterhead. I dated the letter and wrote, "Dear Mrs. Brown." Then I looked to Logan Mountain, hoping another way to help Lauren came to mind and resenting Lauren for putting me in the position of finking her out. As annoying and flighty as Mrs. Brown could be, she was the only person to entrust with the stuff Lauren had shoplifted, except the brooch that I'd given to Miss Bigelow, of course, and the Mexican blouses I'd thrown away. I put pen to paper.

> *This is the hardest letter I've ever written, but you need to know that Lauren is in deep trouble. I hope it's okay that I'm sending this package to the furniture store. I didn't want Lauren to intercept it. Please forgive me for keeping this secret from you for so long. I love Lauren like a sister, but I sure haven't acted like it.*

I wrote an overview of Lauren's larcenous history and signed the letter. After sealing the envelope, I pried it back open to add the cross necklace. I attached an address label in care of the furniture store to the package.

"I'm sorry, Lauren."

I finished just as Tommy turned into the driveway. His wife and daughter stayed in the truck, wide-eyed yet smiling. "Where's this giant package you want me to take to the bus station?" he asked.

"Thanks for doing this, Tommy."

THE SALESCLERK AT Fabric Depot cleared her throat for the hundredth time. "The store closes in five minutes."

Mom held a length of translucent fabric to my face and turned me toward the mirror. "See, this is perfect. Gold will emphasize your eyes."

"This is a huge mistake," I said, pushing the fabric away. "I'm not pageant material, Mom. Look at me, really look at me. I have a nose that could pass for a dinner roll. I'll only humiliate myself. The other contestants, who, in case you haven't considered, have lived here all their lives, right next door to the judges and have parents who do business with the judges. There's no way I can win."

"You make this sound like a conspiracy. Beauty is an attitude. If you believe you're beautiful, you're beautiful."

The salesclerk cleared her throat again. "That shade is all wrong for your daughter. It bleeds her face of color. Try this one." She draped a shimmery jade fabric over my shoulders.

"Oh," I said, surprised at the effect.

"Finding complementary colors is my specialty," the clerk said, cocking her head to study my reflection.

Mom met my gaze in the mirror. "I can't think of another way to make $250 in one week. It's worth a try. If you win, you could fly to Los Angeles to start classes with your classmates."

I pushed the fabric away and walked out of the store.

"Where are you going?" Mom called, following me onto the sidewalk.

"Why are you doing this?" I asked. "I'm fine with waiting. I have a job and everything."

"Because *I'm* not fine with you waiting. I got you into this mess, and I'm going to get you out. Amy, *fofa*, we're going back into the fabric store to buy that fabric." Mom dug a flyer for the pageant out of her purse. "It says right here: 'The contestants are judged on poise, their ability to answer questions on current events, and an exhibition of their talent." Mom held me at arm's length. "Poise isn't a problem; your height makes you regal. You can talk about anything. You were captain of the debate team two years in a row. Did you think I forgot about that? I was so proud of you. I probably don't tell you nearly enough, but here is your chance to get what you want. And no one has to tell you how beautifully you sing. When you sing, you're true self shines like a beacon."

I sat on the curb. I was beginning to believe I had a chance at winning the pageant. I ached to rid myself of Cordial. The town represented my failure, but what unnerved me was Mom's determination to get rid of me. I didn't care for her enthusiasm one bit.

"Amy, listen, please don't make me say all of the ways that I've been a terrible mother. Let me do this for you. I want to get you to college. It's very important to you, so it's very important to me."

Mom banged on the fabric store door until the salesclerk let us in to buy the jade fabric.

Forty-Two

Mom eased the iron along the length of my hair. "Try to hold still. I don't want to burn you again."

I sat on a step stool with my head tilted toward the ironing board. "I can't sit like this much longer. My neck is killing me."

"We're almost done."

Charles spoke through the bedroom door. "Francie, do both ends of the cans have to be removed?"

"Keep the iron moving, Mom."

She leaned to whisper in my ear. "Can you believe how helpless men are? That's why we must be nice to them, or they'd fray like an old sweater." She yelled toward the door, "Yes, sweetie, that's exactly right."

"Keep the iron moving, Mom."

"Wait till you see how lovely your hair looks. And don't you worry. A little makeup will cover the burn on your forehead." Mom parted my hair and smoothed another strand down the ironing board. "Are you sure you don't want to wear my tiara?"

Never! "That would seem a bit presumptuous on my part, but thanks."

Of all the men Mom had marched in and out of our lives, I'd never asked her about her relationships. I supposed I'd learned that Mom and men collided, dusted themselves off, and went their separate ways. No one like Charles had ever entered our lives. He didn't collide with Mom so much as he slid into place.

"So what's the deal with you and Charles?" I asked.

"Charles? Well, he's nice. He makes me feel safe."

"And?"

"And I think I might love him."

"Is that my hair I smell?"

THE PAGEANT TOOK place in two parts. In the morning, the contestants ate brunch together at the Moose Lodge before being interviewed by the judges. The other contestants, seven of them, huddled together, exchanging nervous giggles. Once I noticed how uniform their hair and dresses were, I looked for similarities between them like an exercise in a *Highlights* magazine. All parted their hair on the side with a single barrette over their left ear. Their flowered dresses with matching short jackets could have been sewn from the same pattern. Every last one of them possessed a tiny ski-jump nose. I wanted to scream.

Someone with a mean streak had prepared a spinach quiche as the main entrée with a broccoli and almond salad on the side. After each bite, I ran my tongue over my teeth, searching out errant pieces of dark-green vegetables. A girl across the table used the blade of her knife to check her teeth. *Very clever.* With know-how like that, this couldn't have been her first pageant. I sat up straighter.

Mom had dressed me for the interview in her green and white dress with the wide collar and plunging neckline. At my insistence, she'd added a snap-in piece of fabric to raise the neckline, giving the dress a sailor-gone-tropical look. To avoid being mistaken for a figure skater, she lowered the hem two inches. My hair? In a word, my hair was *big*—a true navigational hazard to low-flying airplanes. Two cans of White Rain had turned my hair into a flammable helmet of immense proportions. I feared flames like the brainless scarecrow in *The Wizard of Oz*. Nevertheless, I smiled constantly—even while chewing—as my mother had coached me. Knees together. Shoulders back. Pinkie up.

Bring 'em on!

A woman in a broad-brimmed hat and navy suit, tapped on the microphone. "Girls, welcome to the 53rd Annual Ranch Days Pageant. I'm Mrs. O'Dell, chairwoman of the Ranch Days Pageant committee. I can't remember a more qualified or gracious group of girls vying for the title of Miss Ranch Days."

I looked around to see if the other contestants had found her pinched-nose voice entertaining. The woman held the girls' rapt attention. Even though my cheeks ached, I licked my teeth and smiled.

"Any one of you would represent our community with distinction," she said. "Shall we get started?"

She introduced the judges, Miss Hickman, the Cordial High School home economics teacher for forty-two years. Her skin hung on her like part of her was missing. Doubtless, the other contestants had sewn their first aprons in Miss Hickman's sewing class. Okay, so one of three judges probably had a favorite, a teacher's pet. The next judge served as the president of the bank. From the bulk of him, he performed most of his business at the Stop-and-Chomp during breakfast, lunch, and dinner meetings. Odd, but he had the same last name as one of the other contestants, Ebersbacher. Nothing like a little nepotism to spice up a pageant. The third judge evened the playing field a bit. Pastor Ted winked at me when he stood to take a bow.

When the applause faded, Mrs. O'Dell continued. "Girls, I have a special surprise for you this year. Mrs. Tammy Martin, our local Mary Kay representative, will walk you through a complete makeover from a facial to beautiful-new-you makeup. Let's give Mrs. Martin a huge round of applause for being here today." The applause from the contestants was tentative at best. "We'll call you in random order to be interviewed by the judges."

For our makeovers, Mrs. Martin passed around bobby pins to hold our hair away from our faces and draped us with pink fabric to protect our clothes. When she came to me, she said, "My, you have a lot of hair, don't you? Do the best you can. I'll leave you a few extra pins." Hairpins proved unnecessary. My hair mimicked granite.

A brunette in a dress covered with daisy bouquets left the room to talk to the judges. Mrs. Martin gave us tiny paddles to smear makeup remover over our faces. "Gently girls, gently. You're going to have this skin for a long, long time. Keep your skin looking fresh and lively with feather-light fingers."

Forget that.

Mom had smeared my eyelids with limeade eye shadow and painted Cleopatra eyeliner on my upper and lower lids. I'd complained about looking like the creature from the deep until I saw tears had welled in her eyes. I applied the remover to each eyelid—*thank you, Jesus*—and rubbed vigorously.

Mrs. Martin bent to inspect a blonde wearing pink. "Oh, honey girl, you'll never get your makeup off like that. Be indulgent."

Mrs. Martin scooped a generous portion of the makeup remover onto the girl's cheeks.

The brunette returned from the interview room looking self-satisfied. Mrs. O'Dell called for Debbie Bishop. The blonde wiped fiercely at the black smudges of mascara around her eyes before she walked toward the interview room like she was headed for the firing squad.

Mrs. Martin clapped for our attention. "Now that all of that life-sucking drugstore makeup is off your beautiful faces, the next step is a deep-cleaning mask to remove any remaining impurities." Her voice dropped an octave. "Girls, deep cleaning is the key to healthy, blemish-free skin." She delivered more paddles and jars to each contestant. "Cover your faces completely, but leave a good margin around your eyes."

The girls around the table exchanged glances.

"Go ahead. Don't be shy," Mrs. Martin urged. "We leave the mask on for five minutes. Your faces will glow with health when you're done."

We obeyed like sheep, slathering our faces with a green oatmeal-and-mint facial mask, each of us, I was sure, praying that someone else would be called next for their interview. We stared owl-eyed at the clock.

"Are you ready for the unveiling, girls? I have moist towels for you. Now, remember, don't rub. Pat those impurities away."

I used the hand towel to swipe the oatmeal goop off my forehead, cheeks, and chin, folding and refolding the towel.

Mrs. Martin wrung her hands. "Oh dear, I guess I should have brought more towels. I'll be right back. There must be paper towels in the restroom." Once she left the room, the girls started talking.

"I spent an hour putting my makeup on. What is this?"

"What did the judges ask you, Jeanette?"

"I'm not supposed to tell."

"They don't ask political questions, do they? How old does a senator have to be? I keep forgetting."

"They're not going to ask you civics questions, stupid. They want to know how you think about current events. Sorry, Cammie, but it looks like you're sunk even before you've been called."

"Shut up, Laurie. What do you know?" said the chestnut-haired girl.

I looked in the mirror. Green oatmeal streaked my face. A thought as surprising as a wasp sting popped into my head. *You're damaged. You don't belong here.* I believed it.

The chestnut-haired girl turned to me. "Hey, you with the big hair, who are you, anyway?"

"I've seen her at the library," Cammie said. "She's always reading some old book."

"You're the girl who lives at the funeral home, aren't you? You dated H, and you hang out with those dirty hippies.

I stopped smiling.

Mrs. O'Dell called, "The judges would like to see María Amelia Casi . . . Casi . . . meero—"

I stood up. "María Amelia Casimiro Monteiro. That's me."

Besides having flecks of green oatmeal in my hair, the interview went flawlessly. I listed the qualifications I hoped to see in the next president and made the judges laugh when I added, "We should elect someone with a nice, straight fairway shot to safeguard the American people." I enumerated the reasons the Equal Rights Amendment was superfluous, and when asked if art imitated life or life imitated art in

Hollywood, I came down on the side of life imitating art, complete with references to specific films and television programs.

The bank president rose to shake my hand. "Thank you, Amy, you're quite astute."

ALTHOUGH MY MOTHER nearly stroked out, I washed my hair before the evening portion of the pageant and let it dry in the sun. No Dippity-Doo. No hair spray. No bun. I showed up just the way God had made me—the queen of fuzz.

The evening pageant was held in the park. A tangle of electrical cables snaked from generators to carnival rides and food booths. Cotton candy and hot grease. Screams and laughter. Tinny music from the carousel. Thousands of light bulbs twirling and blinking. The bark of booth operators inviting, cajoling, and shaming participants to lay their money down.

I tiptoed over the cables in my jade evening gown. The princess-line dress floated weightlessly over my skin. Carnies turned to whistle, but really, who would consider that a compliment?

Me, that's who.

The pageant stage—a flatbed trailer attached to a tractor—was set up in the rodeo arena. A skirt of crepe paper covered the wheels, and a well-worn backdrop gave the contestants a place to stand unseen to gather their courage before stepping through an arched cutout. Workers were still assembling the runway platform when I arrived.

My gown shimmered like water under the floodlights. The other contestants—and this may sound unkind, but it's the honest truth—looked like Little Bo Peeps with all their eyelet pinafores and dotted-swiss dresses. We stood behind the backdrop until our names were called. Once we walked to the end of the runway and back, the contestants scattered to prepare for the talent section of the pageant.

Mom found me sitting on the trailer hitch tuning my guitar. "You looked gorgeous walking down the runway. Oh, the memories. Just remember to keep your chest up. Think of a puppet—"

"String attached between my boobs. Yeah, I think I've got it."

"What are you going to sing?" she asked.

"I don't know yet."

"You don't *know*? How can you not know? Sing a Patsy Cline song. That will show them what you're made of."

"Too sad."

"Elvis?"

"Too trite."

"Something Motown? 'I Heard It Through the Grapevine'?"

"No Pips."

"Amy!"

"Go sit down, Mom. Something will come to me. In fact, I'm considering a John Denver song."

"Perfect!" She kissed my cheek and spat on her finger to rub away the lipstick. "The judges will love a John Denver song. This is Colorado after all."

Once she left I picked through the chords of "Leaving on a Jet Plane" while Cammie performed "The Star-Spangled Banner" as an interpretive reading. The crowd went wild.

Something patriotic? I strummed through "The Battle Hymn of the Republic" but realized I only knew the words to the first verse. *Be original!*

Laurie dazzled the crowd with her baton twirling. Debbie took her Sheltie through his paces. Sit. Down. Roll over. Play dead. The irritable brunette introduced her piano piece. "It is my pleasure to play 'Waltz in D-Flat Major' by Frédéric Chopin. You will recognize the piece as the 'Minute Waltz,' although Chopin never intended the waltz to be played in sixty seconds, so put away your stopwatches." She paused to allow the audience time to laugh. *A pro.* "Picture, if you will, a small dog chasing his tail, for such was Chopin's inspiration for writing this waltz." Another grateful laugh from the audience. She played the flighty piece flawlessly.

Elvis wasn't trite so much as seasoned, like last year's blue suede shoes. *How about Patsy?* This crowd would love "Crazy."

"Be Thou My Vision."

That's not much of a toe-tapper, Lord.

Sing me a love song, my beautiful sister and bride.

WHEN THE EMCEE slaughtered my last two names, I wiped my hands on my dress and took the stage. I spotted Mom already crying several rows back, and Feather and her family cheered wildly. I closed my eyes to pick the introduction. Tears flowed and my voice caught when I sang, *"Thou and Thou only, first in my heart,"* but I didn't care. The song was a promise and a prayer.

When I finished the song, the audience sat perfectly silent. Mrs. Clancy dabbed at her eyes, but so did Charles. Finally, the emcee clapped beside me, waking the audience to join in. Into the microphone, he said, "Lovely, Miss Monteero, just lovely. Thank you."

I came in third after the brunette and the dog trainer. I won a $50 savings bond that would mature about the time I earned my graduate degree.

Stop-and-Chomp, here I come.

Forty-Three

I sat on the steps reading *Emma*, waiting for Mom to turn the corner toward home after her day's work. The light seemed cleaner, more direct and playful the closer the days moved toward fall. The moon, now waning, hung in the sky most of the day as if something momentous were about to happen. Anticipating such an event left me weary of life. My goal for the day was another nap. I set my book aside to return to the kitchen where I covered the chicken I'd prepared with foil and slid it into the warm oven.

I lay on the couch and pulled an afghan over me. The sound of cardboard boxes being kicked and sliding across the kitchen floor woke me. Mom clicked on the amber lamp. "Amy, your dinner smells wonderful. Are you hungry?"

"You're just getting home?"

"I had plans to make."

I joined her in the kitchen to whisper, "Mrs. Clancy's here. She's preparing for some kind of audit. She's really cranky."

"I'm glad she's here. I need to talk to her." Mom practically marched down the hall toward Mrs. Clancy's office. Where did she get the energy? She tapped on the door and walked in. The door clicked shut. Soon the muffled sounds of Mrs. Clancy shouting at Mom and Mom retorting came from the room. I was about to join them to apologize and pull Mom from the wreckage, but Mom stepped into the hall smiling. She stopped and reached for the doorknob. "I'm glad we see eye to eye, Georgia. We'll be out by noon tomorrow. Good-bye and good luck."

"Good riddance!" Mrs. Clancy said. "And close that door. I've got work to—"

Mom pulled the door shut.

I left the milk jug on the counter to follow Mom into her bedroom.

"Grab some boxes," she said. "We don't have much time to pack our things."

"What's this about? Why are we leaving? How are we leaving? And where are we going?"

"If you'd stop asking me so many questions, I'd be happy to tell you." She smiled broadly, like the last time she'd beaten me at Scrabble. "If you want to be in Santa Barbara for the first day of classes, Charles says we need to leave tomorrow."

"Tomorrow?" I sat on a kitchen chair. "Wait a minute. How will we get there?"

"Charles will take us."

"In his Pinto?"

"There should be plenty of room."

"But Charles has to work. Who will do his job?"

"Why do you think Mrs. Clancy is so upset?" Mom pressed a box into my hands. "This is for your books." She twirled a strand of hair around her finger. "Wait! We should start in the kitchen."

Mom scooped the contents of a utensil drawer. "Is this our can opener?"

"No, ours has a green handle." I opened the towel drawer. "How are we affording this?"

Mom's face was a lake on a breezeless afternoon. "I sold the Pontiac." She tossed tins of spices into the box. "Don't drop your jaw like that, *fofa*. You look simple."

"It's just that I never dreamed . . ."

"Yes, I know. But it had to be done. Charles offered to pay for everything, but it didn't seem right, somehow."

"And Charles? I thought you were just friends."

"Yes, well, I did too. I mean, would you ever imagine Chuck—"

"Chuck?"

"It suits him, don't you think? Anyway, you and I both know he's not my type. At least, that's what I thought. I don't know how he did it, but he won me over. I'm crazy in love with him, and we haven't even . . . well, Chuck is quite serious about his faith, which is a good thing. He's taught me so much. I never knew God counted the hairs on my head. Why didn't you tell me?"

"Are you going to marry him?"

Mom rested her hands on the edge of a box. "We've discussed it. He wants to find a job first and get you up and running at school. Maybe next year." She shrugged. "Who knows? Maybe sooner, if things go well. What do you think?"

"Charles . . . Chuck is great. He's perfect for you."

"There's something you're not saying."

I covered my face with my hands. "I'm two days late."

"Two days?" She pulled me into an embrace. "That's nothing. It could be the excitement of the pageant. *Fofa,* you can't be . . . no, it's emotion. Before we get to Las Vegas your period will come. Amy, no, you are definitely not pregnant."

"Maybe we should wait. There's no sense going to California—"

"We're going."

"But what if . . ."

Mom tightened her grip on me. "Then we'll have a new member of the family to love. We'll get through it. We always do."

"Westmont won't let me attend classes."

"There are other schools."

"But I've always dreamed . . ."

"If I can love a pudgy, bald guy, you can dream a new dream, a better dream for yourself. But until we know what we're dealing with, I say we proceed with the original plan with one minor addition—Chuck the woman slayer."

THE PINTO'S HOOD tilted upward from being loaded to its ceiling. Chuck slammed the hatch closed. "I guess that's it." He offered an arm to Mom and the other to me. "Shall we, ladies? Church is about to begin."

"Leoti is saving us seats," I said.

Leoti waved us into our places. "I'm so excited. I can hardly breathe," she said.

A painter's tarp covered the new windows. The windows were the last thing on earth I wanted to see. Every time I thought of them, a squall of emotion pitched me into the depths. According to the bulletin, the windows would be dedicated after the offering. That gave me time to consider my options, like excusing myself to go to the restroom or fainting as the tarp was removed. But I knew I'd stay beside Leoti. Her friendship meant that much to me.

I stood for the call to worship, and with a comfort that comes from familiarity and consistency, I remained standing for the hymn.

Mom leaned over. "Not exactly Motown, is it?"

Pastor Ted delivered a sermon from the eleventh chapter of Luke, something about the Lord's Prayer. Honestly, I didn't hear much of what he said. The thought of leaving Cordial thrilled and saddened me. *What's with that?* This kind of dissonance shouldn't have surprised me. Wondering if a baby grew within me had kept my thoughts bubbling like a stew on the stove. My recurring nightmare had me waddling to class about twenty months pregnant. When I squeezed through the door, my classmates gasped and the professor stomped his foot and shooed me back out the door. I shook my head to clear the dream from my head in time to sing the "Gloria Patri" and recite the Lord's Prayer. Never had the congregation uttered the words with more conviction. I should have listened to the sermon.

Pastor Ted stood at the pulpit. "Before our closing hymn, I want to thank the anonymous donor who commissioned the replacement windows and the attendee of Spruce Street Church who assisted the artist with the actual repair of the windows. The congregation thanks you."

The congregation clapped politely. Leoti took my hand and squeezed it. A deacon dimmed the lights.

Pastor Ted said, "God's second creation was light. For those of us with only rudimentary understanding of physics and the attributes of light, we may not fully understand the gift God has given us. Light provides warmth and energy for plants to grow. Light allows us to see joy in a child's face when he or she first steps onto a lush lawn or the pain of friends who have suffered a great loss. Our tasks are easier by the light of day. We don't get lost as long as we can see where we're going. Truly, light is a wonderful gift.

"But hear this, friends. Light also brings us color. Imagine if you will the world without color. Words like *dull*, *bland*, and *depressing* come to mind. What would spring be like without the first tender shoots of green breaking the earth and the explosion of color crocuses and daffodils provide? On the other hand, perhaps fewer speeding tickets would be issued for a lack of red sports cars, and wives would no longer have to question their husbands' taste in clothing. Would avoiding a fashion *faux pas* be worth living in a black-and-white world? Our God and Maker says no.

"As Deacon Gartley lowers the tarp from the windows, prepare to receive this amazing gift of color from our good Father."

A collective sigh of appreciation and then thunderous applause erupted from the congregation. The purity of the colors startled me. They were the colors of Cordial—the green of the orchards, the gold of drying hay fields, and the life-rich brown of earth, all at their loveliest during a rosy sunset. Most surprising of all, the light didn't magnify my sin as expected but overwhelmed it. Again, gratitude pushed me to tears. Enjoying God's grace was sloppy business.

FEATHER AND HER family stood in front of Clancy and Sons when we stepped out of church. Feather embraced me. I settled my cheek on her fuzzy little head, content to smell hay and chicken feed and that hint of rosemary that lingered in her hair.

She stepped back but held my hands with a strong grip. "I haven't had one seizure, not one—not even a petit mal," she said. "All of my tests were normal. I don't need the medicine. Jesus healed me."

I looked to Butter.

"She's right. The doctor repeated the EEG, only this time he made us stay up with her all night before the test. Evidently, a fatigued brain gives a more reliable reading, but the test was absolutely normal. Of course, the doctor was careful to explain that a normal EEG is possible for epilepsy patients, but he can't explain why she's asymptomatic. He wants to take a wait-and-see approach."

"As for me," Straw said, "I've waited and seen enough. My little girl is free of epilepsy." I only recognized Straw because he held each twin by the hand. He had shaved his hair close to his head. The scissor nicks had scabbed over, but most transforming of all was a clean-shaven face. "And I want to thank you from the bottom of my heart."

"I didn't heal her," I said, which made the whole family squirm, so I changed the subject. "You shaved?"

"I start at the mine tomorrow," he said, looking at Butter. "All that hair would be awfully tough to keep clean."

Feather gripped me about the waist again. "You have to promise to visit. California is so far away."

I whispered in her ear. "You were the very best part of my summer. I'll never forget you, not ever."

Inside the Pinto I sat in the backseat, pressed to the door by a pile of bedding. Watching Feather skip to keep up with Straw started me crying for the umpteenth time that day.

"Let's go," Mom said. "We're burning daylight."

Forty-Four
The Present

Thirty-six miles to Sleepy Eye

I close the book and snap off the light at 1:15 a.m. I have no idea what happened in the story I was reading, but I'm finally too tired to both dread and anticipate meeting my father. The vacancy sign bleeds red light around the curtains, so I turn my back on the window. Soon after my head sinks into the pillow, a nonsensical vignette plays out in my mind, assuring me that sleep is only breaths away. I dream of losing the orientation students at Knott's Berry Farm when a stampede of footsteps in the room upstairs startles me awake. The travelers drop their baggage, as heavy as bowling balls, repeatedly. I sit up to scowl at the ceiling.

How much luggage do you own?

Children shout to claim a bed, and soon their giggles accompany creaking bed springs. A young girl, from the pitch of her scream, protests not having her own trampoline. "Stop jumping on the beds," yells the mother, and with acid on her tongue says, "I told you we should've stopped in Sioux Falls! You never listen to me, and now the pool is closed."

No more Sleepy Time motels for me.

I reach for the phone to call the front desk, but I remember traveling with Stephanie, Micole, and Graham to attend a family wedding—on Sam's side—in Jumbo, Oklahoma. After being in the car for ten hours, the neatly made beds of the motel room beckoned to the kids like a playground. About an hour later, we were cordially invited to find other lodging for the night. Traveling with small children is torturous.

My upstairs neighbors power up the television and turn the volume to high. An infomercial for the Miracle Broom blares through the ceiling, which reminds me of the Snickers bar I have in my suitcase. It's funny how the mind works when it craves sleep. The rhythmic creaking continues, but under the influence of chocolate and peanuts, I resign myself to sleep deprivation.

Licking the chocolate off my fingers, I run through the list of questions I want to ask Carl—my *father*—like, Why didn't you marry my mother? Did you look for us? Do I have stepbrothers or sisters? Do you suffer from any hereditary diseases? Am I good enough to be your daughter? Can I have a hug?

Enough!

I expect Mom to knock on my door at any second. Her snores, however torturous, would nonetheless muffle the noise from upstairs. I click on the lamp and reach for the remote. No need to turn the volume up. The frenetic announcer is clearly understandable through the ceiling. Besides, I stare without seeing the Miracle Broom draw *oohs* and *ahhs* from the studio audience. I fall back on my pillow. The room flashes with color from the television screen. In turn, I worry that Carl is on vacation, or won't answer the door, or died last week. Most disturbing, however, is this question: What if he doesn't like me? I hug the Gideon Bible to my chest.

I am my beloved's, and his desire is for me.

"My bridegroom, my Savior, you are all I need." At least, that's what I want to be true.

And then there's Mom. I fear she will scold Carl, demand he play his fatherly role, be a grandfather to my children. Or worse, she'll flirt with him. I dig through my suitcase for *Pride and Prejudice.* The triviality of sisters marrying rightly and the ponderous cadence of the story lull me to sleep around three.

MOM STEPS BACK from the vanity mirror, turning to admire her profile from the left and the right. She pats her stomach. It's as flat as a griddle. Mine is rising dough—puckery, pliant, and dimpled.

"Do I look as old as I feel?" she asks and taps the flesh under her eyes. "I slept like a baby. Where did these bags come from?"

"You slept like a baby?" Except for a softness around her jaw and eyes, Mom is ageless. She's mistaken for my children's mother regularly, which she delights in reporting back to me. "You look fantastic, and you know it."

She runs her hand through her hair, giving the crown a tousle. "I'm ready, I think, unless this blouse is too young for me. I bought it at the Gap. Is it too clingy?" She holds a green blouse with ruffled collar and cuffs up to her chest. "This blouse is a bit too matronly, but the color is better, and the slacks have the nicest sheen. Very fallish.

What do you think?" She drops the blouse on the bed. "Wait! Don't say anything until you see this." She holds a bejeweled jacket with a pair of jeans. "This is the real me, right? Give me a minute. I'll change in a wink."

"We have lots of time," I say. "It's not like he's expecting us." I take the jacket from her to hang in the closet. "We need to talk before we do anything."

She pushes her nightgown and a towel onto the floor and sits in a chair upholstered with John Deere fabric. "Did you drink all your coffee?" she asks. "I could use another cup."

"This won't take long."

Mom checks her hair in the mirror and tugs at a curl. "I think there's a coffee pot in the lobby."

"Mom?"

"Yes, Amy, what is it?"

"I'd like to return the car to Carl by myself."

"What? Why? You're afraid I'll embarrass you, aren't you?"

A little. "No, of course not. I'm concerned that Carl will feel overwhelmed if both of us show up on his doorstep. I don't want to intimidate him, and I know you don't either. This is something I should do."

"You *are* afraid I'll embarrass you."

A bubble of anger pops in my gut. I fight to keep my voice even. "This isn't about you. I'm the one with the most to win or lose from this meeting. Please, give me the keys. I want to go." I have a strong urge to stomp my foot.

Mom crosses her arms and narrows her eyes to slits. "Haven't I been a good mother to you? Didn't I provide for you and look after your best interests? And don't forget, I drove you across a whole continent to fulfill your dream."

So, in her eyes, this is about her. "You've been a fabulous mother. I don't know how you did it alone." But I won't lie. "Sometimes you got distracted, but I always felt loved. Now I want to be the woman you raised me to be."

Mom sits with her chin resting on her chest for a long time. I fight the usual urge to acquiesce. Finally, her head pops up, and she removes the tiara's velvet box from the dresser drawer. The velvet is balding.

I press my hands over my beating heart.

"Is it your job to return the tiara too?" she asks, holding the box out to me.

Good question. "Couldn't you mail it?"

"That's cowardly."

"I'm sure the pageant people have replaced the tiara by now. The last time I saw it, the thing was getting ratty. Rhinestones had fallen out. Tines from the combs were broken."

She hugs the box to her chest. "I had it repaired, thank you very much." She sits on the edge of the bed. "I need a clean conscious more than you know. It's my job to return the tiara to its rightful owners. If I don't return it this visit, I'll come again, later, on my own, without you."

I sit beside her. "I need you to understand why it's important that I go alone."

"You don't owe me any explanations," she says with a sigh and lowers her eyes.

"Of course I do. You're my mother. I won't leave you sulking in a motel room."

"I'm not sulking."

She stands to lean against the vanity sink. I wrap my arms around her and talk to her reflection in the mirror. "It's incredibly brave of you to bring the Pontiac and the tiara back to Sleepy Eye. You're an amazing woman, so resilient. And your ministry to single moms makes me so proud of you. Stephanie and I never would have made it without your help. I wouldn't have gone to school, or earned my degree, or met Sam. You are a rock and I love you."

A tear rolls down Mom's face.

For years, my disappointment with God centered on the apostle Paul's assertion that we are new creatures in Christ. For far too long I thought this meant a personality change. It doesn't. Mom is still impetuous and fun-loving and more than a bit self-involved, even though she mentors single moms and shares God's love to anyone, anywhere. Her exuberance is a boon for God's kingdom. She's indulged in his unbridled love, something I envy at times. That doesn't mean I don't fight the urge to change her on a daily basis. Her frequent travels help tremendously. My ability to love her unconditionally skyrockets when she's traipsing through cobbled villages or sandy beaches on foreign continents. The older Mom gets, the bigger her personality becomes. Whoever says people mellow with age doesn't know Mom.

Truthfully, I haven't changed that much either. I still overanalyze everything, balk at unplanned activities, and—although I know this is wrong, wrong, wrong—I tend to categorize people, places, and things into black or white. When something defies categorization, I get a migraine. Grace is an intellectual surety that hasn't quite sprouted in my heart. This will be me until I take my last breath in this world and run splish-splashing across the River Jordan into the next.

I kiss Mom's cheek. "What was I thinking? I can't go to Sleepy Eye without you."

She smiles like a kid given a week-long pass to Disney World. My heart nearly breaks.

Forty-Five

Sleepy Eye, Minnesota

"Was I speeding, Officer . . . ?" I read his name tag. "Holstad?"

He walks around the car and returns to lean on the open window. "Nope, you weren't speeding." He lifts the bill of his cap to Mom. "Ma'am."

I came clean. "I did weave over the line a bit. The statue of Linus intrigued me. 'Peanuts' is my favorite comic strip. I relate to Linus. He's so sweet and wise."

He looks in the backseat. "Are you just passing through or planning to stay a spell?"

"My mom . . . this is Francie Moberly, and I'm Amy Tanabe, a student recruiter at Westmont *Christian* College and mother of three children. I give to the Santa Barbara Policeman's Ball every year, and I don't even dance. Sam, my husband, donates flowers to decorate the tables. He grows the most amazing orchids you've ever seen."

"Amy, you're babbling," Mom says. "Tell him about the car."

Officer Holstad narrows his gray eyes at me. "Ma'am, may I see your license and registration, please?"

I release the seat belt to search the glove compartment. Mom pushes me away. "I can get it." She finds the registration, finally, folded inside the map of Iowa.

"The car is registered to my mother," I tell Holstad, handing him the papers. "We're here on a bit of a mission."

Mom leans over me to talk to Holstad. "Look, policeman, sir, my daughter had nothing to do with stealing this car. She wasn't even born yet."

"That's interesting." He studies my driver's license. "California? Hmm. I'll just be a minute." He saunters to his car where he fiddles with something below the dash, probably a laptop linked to every database known to man. Dread tiptoes up my spine.

"Is there a statute of limitations on car theft in Minnesota?" I ask Mom.

"How am I supposed to know?"

"You didn't check? Oh boy, this is going to be bad."

Officer Holstad returns to the car all smiles. "Ladies, I can't tell you how happy I am you've finally returned to our fair little town of Sleepy Eye."

"You don't understand, I've never—"

"If I had a key to the city, I'd give it to you." He squats to talk to us eye to eye. "You see, I'm retiring next week, and you could say I've been waiting for you to drive into town for, let's see . . ."

"Fifty-one years?" I ask.

His smile disappears. "I would have resigned years ago if I'd waited that long. No, Ole Swenson has been hounding me for twenty years." He rubs his chin. "Yep, he started calling me right after I got my bars. His mind just sort of slipped into neutral, if you know what I mean. He calls every day, mind you, to report this very car stolen."

"I can explain everything," I say. "Mom, tell him."

He stands, his hand resting on his substantial gun holster. "No, not yet you don't. There's a boatload of people at the station house who'd love to hear what you've got to say. Would you ladies step out of the car, please?"

I deeply regret not bailing on this adventure back in Barstow. "Can I call my husband? It will just take—"

"There will be plenty of time for phone calls after you girls have given your statement."

I pull up on the door handle. The officer is nine feet tall. "Our statements? Are we in trouble, Officer Holstad, sir?"

Holstad ushers me to the cruiser with a hand to my elbow. "We'll have to hear your story now, won't we?"

Mom double steps to face Officer Holstad. "I told you, she had nothing to do with stealing the car. It was all my idea."

"This is going to be better than I thought," he says, tossing his pen and catching it.

His cavalier attitude irks me. "You know, sir, I've never gotten a ticket in all the years I've been driving. There was a parking ticket a few years ago, but I'd forgotten to put the juror sticker on the dash. Just a misunderstanding, you see. The defendant got ninety-six years for resisting arrest and endangering a police officer."

Holstad opens the back door of the cruiser and motions for us to enter. A steel mesh separates the front seat from the back, but more troubling are the stains darkening the upholstery.

"Would you mind if Mom and I drove to the station in the car?" I ask, nodding toward the Pontiac.

A wry smile plays at his lips. "It's just a precaution, ma'am."

"Maybe I should lock the Pontiac."

He puts his hand on my head and presses me into the cruiser. "Auto theft isn't all that common here in Sleepy Eye."

I spread tissues on the seat to protect my jeans from whatever unthinkable fluid stains the seats. Mom refuses the tissues I offer. She shifts roles and becomes a tour guide, even though most of the businesses on the main street are empty. "That used to be Peterson's drugstore. My friend, Lynette—and boy, was she a homely little thing—she and I shared Cokes there every Friday after school. Oh, the dime store closed. They had a small fabric department in the back. I bought remnants to make skirts and blouses. I did all of the sewing by hand. There's the butcher shop, and the library, and Larsen's Department Store. I bought my first bra there."

"Mom," I plead.

"What? Every young woman has to have a first bra. I'm sure the fine officer knows that, don't you Mr. Policeman, sir?"

"Not my department," he says tight-lipped.

Officer Holstad turns right and parks in front of a blockish building completely devoid of ornamentation. It seems the people of Sleepy Eye are sensible above all else. I can't open the back door from the inside.

Officer Holstad leads us down a hallway lined with glass-walled offices. "Hey, Hanson," he calls to a woman reading a magazine in front of a telephone. "You gotta hear this. Meeting in the break room. Nelson! Hang up the phone. We got us a couple suspects here. Bring your steno pad, Olson. We're taking a statement in the break room." He turns to us. "You ladies won't mind if I get my wife down here, will you? She works at the nursing home where they put Ole Swenson, Carl's old man."

"The more the merrier," Mom says. "We do have a plane to catch in Minneapolis tomorrow."

"We should be done by then."

"Johnson, get these ladies something to drink. I'm running out to Golden Acres to pick up Helga." He points at Johnson's nose. "And don't you dare start without me."

Johnson weighs about sixty-five pounds. His holster is empty. I could take him if things go bad. Holstad heads back down the hall to retrieve his wife. I follow him. Excuse me," I say to Holstad as he pushes through the door. We stand by his cruiser. "Can I talk to you for a minute?"

He stands with hands on hips. John Wayne was less imposing.

"The disappearance of the Pontiac is related to a rather personal issue for the son of Ole Swenson. Is Carl the kind of person who would want a roomful of city workers and their families to know about his past?"

Officer Holstad sighs heavily and turns to go back inside. "Probably not."

MOM PULLS ME into a stall in the station's ladies' restroom. She whispers, but there's desperation in her voice. "You were right. You have to meet Carl by yourself."

I should be relieved. I'm not. "Wait a minute. You promised—"

"You made me beg."

"Please, Mom, I need you with me."

"I'm not being vindictive . . . to you. To Carl, well, that's another story. My motivation, and I'm not proud to admit it, was to show Carl just what he missed by not marrying me, but that attitude doesn't honor Christ, and it certainly doesn't reflect my love for Chuck. I just can't go."

The restroom door opens and closes. A pair of sturdy shoes and thick ankles stop in front of the stall. "Officer Holstad sent me in here to remind you ladies that your meeting with Carl Swenson is set for three, so you better finish up whatever the two of you are doing in there."

I open the stall door. "We aren't doing anything. We're talking."

Mom pulls the stall door closed. "And I want to pray for my daughter . . . alone." Mom embraces me. Her hair tickles my nose. "Jesus, our precious Savior, give Amy a big, fat portion of your grace to see her through this meeting with her father. You are her sufficiency in all things and her true Father. I pray that Carl won't be a poop. In Jesus' name, amen."

I kiss Mom's cheek. "You're sure you won't come?"

"This is your day, *fofa*."

OFFICER HOLSTAD GIVES me directions to the park where I'm meeting Carl. I park the Pontiac in front of a dapper colonial where I can observe the man who is my father and gather my courage to meet him. I feel myself sliding back through time. I'm seventeen and his absence has eroded a gaping hole in my heart. I grip the steering wheel to steady my hands. "Stay with me, Amy, old girl."

Carl sits on a bench near the bottom of a long grassy slope. Before him, Sleepy Eye Lake is etched by a fickle breeze that leaves the surface both serenely glasslike and racing toward the far shore. There's nothing serene about what's going on in my chest. My heart pounds with the urgency of the rippling water. It's not too late to shift the

Pontiac into reverse and resurrect my fantasies of a nice Portuguese father who died, as young people do, tragically. H comes to mind, and a familiar ache grips my heart. I rest my head on the steering wheel.

I picture myself driving to the Minneapolis airport to leave the Pontiac in extended parking. Clearly, more than a smidgen of Minnesotan sensibility courses through my veins, thanks to Carl Swenson, which explains why Mom and I see things—*everything*—differently. I couldn't leave the car in extended parking any more than I could walk away from an opportunity to meet my father.

Lord, strengthen me by your example to love Carl Swenson no matter what happens.

I feel good about this prayer. Love is the currency of God's kingdom. I'm rich that way, a true gazillionaire. I can meet this man, hear his voice without deflating like a pricked balloon, and walk away knowing I'm loved by my heavenly Father and a whole slew of people who think I'm terrific. Carl is only a man, the donator of twenty-three chromosomes toward who I am. He could be a very nice man. In fact, he probably is. I hear the Minnesotan winters make a man appreciate life. There's a good chance he sings in the church choir. Maybe I got my musical talent from him. Cruel people don't go to weekly practices to stand before a church full of people to sing. Perhaps he doesn't go to church. Maybe he's tone deaf. That's okay. Lauren's tone deaf and she loves me.

Then why am I still sitting in the car?

Carl is a big man—thick around the middle, broad at the shoulders, tall sitting down. The sun glints off his wavy hair. That answers the question about my unmanageable mop.

Thanks a lot, Carl.

He shifts. His right leg bounces. Are butterflies river-dancing in his gut too? Does he think I'll show up at his Thanksgiving table?

That I want a piece of the Swenson legacy? An apology for fathering me? A push on the swings?

I smack the steering wheel with my palm. "Don't overanalyze this. Just get out of the car and be nice to the man."

I can do that.

I open and close the car door noiselessly. Why I think I must surprise him, I'm not sure, although it would be a shame to drive all this way to have him bolt across the lawn into the trees. Or would it? As I near, I see his hair is mostly silver with remnants of blond, and someone has pressed creases into the sleeves of his golf shirt. I don't iron Sam's shirts. I suppose if he played golf . . . no, I would never iron a golf shirt. I like the soft pebbliness of Sam's shirts, of him.

Carl turns toward the sound of leaves crunching under my feet. There are my big nose and eyes right in the middle of his face. Another mystery solved, only *his* head is big enough to do my features justice. He looks great. Fatherly. Very Norwegian.

He stands. "Amy?"

I morph into an Avis counter girl. "There's your car. Mom . . . *Francie* wanted to deliver the car herself, but I . . . well, she's waiting at the police station. Thank you for not filing charges." I hold the keys out to him. "I filled the tank in Springfield."

"Can you sit with me for a minute?" He extends his hand. It's smooth and doughy, yet strong. "I'm Carl." He wipes off the bench with a hankie from his pocket. I thank him and sit on the edge of the bench, rod-straight, ready to flee. I beseech the woman in me to act her age.

"Have you had a good life?" he asks.

"Yes, I have. And you?"

He studies my face.

"I don't look like my mother," I say.

"You're lovely. I suppose you're married and have children."

"I'm a grandmother."

He frowns, doing the math no doubt.

"I was eighteen when my first daughter was born, and no, I wasn't married."

"That must have been difficult for you," he says, squinting into the sun.

"Loving my daughter was easy. Forgiving myself proved much tougher."

"Then we have something in common."

"We do?"

He rubs his eyes with the heels of his hands. "Your mother was a brave girl, Amy. I gave her money and a map to a doctor in Minneapolis who would take care of our little mistake." He raises his eyebrows to emphasize the word *mistake.* "My parents were out of town, so I let Francie drive the Pontiac and face the procedure alone. I told her I had something else to do, probably something terribly important like a lake party or a pick-up softball game. In reality, I can't remember what was so important. Maybe it was nothing at all.

"When she didn't return with the car, I panicked. The Lord knows I ran every conceivable story through my head to appease my father, but I knew I would have to face him and tell him what I'd done. So I did the only manly thing left to me: I ran away to join the army.

"I called my father from my first post to tell him the Pontiac had been stolen from the parking lot." Carl turns his spring-green eyes on me. "Aren't you disappointed that you came all this way to meet a man like me? I'm sure you deserve better."

Anger is not the emotion I'm expecting, but I work to control my voice. "Let me get this straight, you sent my mother to get an abortion?"

"When Holstad called to say you were in town—" Carl's voice cracks. He removes his glasses to wipe his eyes. "I thought your mother had gone through with it, that you were dead. All these years . . . I'm not proud of how I behaved with Francie. I was young, full of myself, and stupid. And she was exotic and so very sweet, but she wasn't of my people. That must sound . . . I don't know . . . yes, I do. I sound like a bigot, don't I?"

The universe tilts for a moment while I adjust the picture I've carried of my mother for most of my life. I was always the reasonable one, the one who shifted ballast to keep our little family upright in the water. Growing up was hard work. But hearing this, I know Mom saved me as surely as if she'd carried me from a burning building.

I've gained more than I imagined from meeting Carl. I itch to return to the police station to see Mom.

"Did your mother marry?" he asks.

"Yes, when I was seventeen, in Las Vegas. Chuck is amazing."

"Was it difficult for the two of you, before she married, I mean?"

I could easily draw blood with a few time-worn memories. "There were difficult times, but most were good. God has been very good to me . . . to us. Mom and me."

School has let out and children ride by on bicycles and carry gigantic backpacks. Carl shifts in his seat. He stands and I join him. "It's been real nice meeting you," he says. "You seem like a good person. I'm very glad you're doing well."

I hold the car keys out to him again. "Enjoy your car."

"I don't want it," he says. "The car would cause more problems than it would solve."

"Yes, I can see that."

He shakes his head slowly. "Sell it. Buy yourself something nice."

I try to memorize the creases of his neck, the burn scar on his hand, how he smells of lemons and tobacco.

He says, "I asked my father for a red Impala convertible, but he held an unwavering loyalty to Pontiacs. Still does." He motions to the car. "That has to be the ugliest car Detroit ever made."

I carry a sheath of photographs in my purse to show Carl. Wedding photographs. Christmases. Birthdays. Graduations. My granddaughter Emily Rose. An aerial photograph of the Westmont campus where I work. I even carry a sales catalog from Coastal Orchids and Flowers where my husband works with his family as a wholesale flower grower. His flowers are gorgeous.

"Listen, Amy, if you're hoping for a relationship . . . that would be difficult. I'm glad your mother didn't follow my instructions, but my wife doesn't know anything about you or your mother. I went to college after the army. That's where I met Jean. We have five kids. Well, they're not kids anymore. None of them live in Sleepy Eye. I was pretty tough on them. We haven't heard from one son in a long, long time. He got mixed up with drugs. He's been in and out of jail so many times . . . it's been hard on my wife."

"I perfectly understand. My life is plenty full. This trip was Mom's idea. She wanted to return the car, to make things right."

Carl hitched up his belt. "I don't have any hard feelings. You can tell your mother that. And tell her I'm sorry. Real sorry."

I finger the ignition key. "I better get going. I'm burning daylight." I'm almost to the car when I remember how reading a Bible story had finally dissipated the shame I carried from my relationship with Falcon.

"Carl! Mr. Swenson!" I call, running to where he already sits behind the wheel of an idling truck. I stand on the running board, and the window slides down. "Don't feel a moment of remorse over your relationship with Mom. That would be a waste of time and of the precious days God has given you."

"I don't think God cares one way or another how I spend my days. I haven't exactly given him any cause to care about me. I've ruined every relationship that came my way."

"Are you familiar with the story of the prodigal son?"

"I think so."

"The son asks for his inheritance, then he spends every last dime on prostitutes and lavish living."

"My wife will be wondering where I am."

"You have to hear this."

He sighs. "Make it fast."

"The son ends up a slave, feeding hogs the food that's denied him. Have you ever noticed that the son never says he's sorry for the hurt he causes? He returns home because he's starving. The servants in his father's house have more than enough to eat. He goes home to survive, Carl, and he is welcomed by a father who runs to meet him on the road."

Carl covers his face with his hands, and his shoulders shake.

"Go home, Carl. Go home to enjoy the goodness of your heavenly Father. He loves you just as you are."

I DRIVE AROUND the lake until I find a secluded place to shed a fifty-five gallon drum of tears. I cry for all the things Carl missed, but this is too long of a list for a post-menopausal woman to recall, so I cry for the guilt he bore and pray he finds his way home to the Father. And then I cry for all the things I missed growing up without a father. The father-daughter dances. Sitting on his shoulders at parades. Having him tear up as I walk down the stairs on prom night. I blow my nose on the last tissue in the box.

"That's enough. Start the car."

Hiding anything in a town the size of Sleepy Eye is impossible, so I drive up and down streets until I find the Golden Acres nursing home. The building is as monotonous as a freight train, white with a red-shingled roof and shaded by ancient maples and oaks. I ask the woman at the front desk for Mr. Swenson's room number.

She removes her glasses. "Are you a relative, hon?"

"Do I have to be a relative to visit him?" *How surprised would she be to know I'm his granddaughter?*

"No, that's just my curiosity talking." She reaches behind her for a sheet of paper to lay in front of me, a floor plan of the facility, and draws a red *X* on a room. "We usually know the people who visit our residents."

"Does Mr. Swenson have a nice view?"

"He can see a field of corn. That's about as good as it gets around here." Her eyes narrow to slits. "You aren't one of those state auditors, are you?"

"No, I'm like you, just curious." I study the floor plan. "So he's on the . . . ?"

"South side of the building."

"The side with the parking lot?"

"Yes, but I don't think that bothers him. He's crazy about cars."

"Good, well, it's nice to know he's so well taken care of. Thank you."

I park the Pontiac outside Mr. Swenson's window. I have either made Officer Holstad's life easier or harder, but definitely more interesting. I walk the two blocks to the police station singing.

Oh, for the wonderful love He has promised,

Promised for you and for me!

Though we have sinned, He has mercy and pardon,

Pardon for you and for me.

BACK AT THE police station, Mom is standing on the break-room table, head erect, shoulders back, wearing the tiara and sash. She spreads her arms wide and says, "When I walked on stage, the audience hummed. Down front, a man asked, 'Who is this dark beauty?'"

The whole Sleepy Eye police department sits enraptured by her. I lean against the wall to listen, for the first time appreciating Mom's ability to capture a crowd with a good story.

"I collected pop bottles to buy a secondhand dress and fabric for a sash and petticoat. My friend's mother loaned me a pair of pumps. They were too big. I had to stuff the toes with tissue paper so they would fit."

"Mom," I call out, "tell them about your talent."

Long live the queen of Sleepy Eye!

Acknowledgments

My name on the cover is a bit misleading. These are the people who made *The Queen of Sleepy Eye* more than an idea buzzing in my head, and my heart sings with gratitude.

Dennis, my sweet husband. Thanks for not mentioning the buildup of dust or the orange ring in the toilet. Your confidence in me is confounding, but I love you all the more for your generous support.

Janet Kobobel Grant, my agent extraordinaire. Thanks for finding *Queen* a "country." You're the best.

David Webb, my editor at B&H. You urged me into deeper waters with your keen sense of story. Thanks to you and Karen and the whole staff at B&H for making *Queen* a much smoother ride for our treasured readers.

The indomitable women of my critique group. You're more than comma cops to me; you encourage me to new heights and point out my flounderings. Thanks Sharon Bridgewater, Muriel Morley, and Darlia Sawyer. I love you! My hearty appreciation also extends to special-appearance critique members Tammy Martin and Brenda Evers.

Sherry Opp, my good, good friend. All I needed to know about stained-glass was a phone call and a lunch date away. You made research a delight.

June Fellhauer, my sister in Christ, my prayer warrior, and my window on small-town mortuary life. Keep the light on!

These generous folks provided me a keyhole look at the North Fork Valley: James M. Gall, Bob Lario, Michelle Cumpston, Marsha Jackson, Paul and Carol Millerman, Ricky and Candy Brodel, and Myrna Westerman and her wonderful staff at the Paonia Public Library.

During research trips, Sharon and Carol Oberholtzer opened their family ranch to me. The room over the tack house is truly the penthouse suite of the North Fork Valley. Their ranch foreman, Red Hughes, is a straight-shootin' cowboy who never left me wondering what he thought. I appreciate that, Red.

Deb Pennington, friend, hairdresser, poultry enthusiast. It was your turkey, Pick, who corralled a vigilant rooster while I observed the hens in your big, red barn. Pick, you're my hero. Deb, thanks for sharing your slice of heaven with me.

Tina Darrah sipped coffee with me for two hours, sharing her experiences and wisdom—and she had never met me before! That's faith. Thanks, Tina. All that you so generously gave made *Queen* a better book. Thanks to your husband, Paul, for introducing us.

Angie Doorenbos, thanks for being my navigator and espresso aficionado on our trip through Sleepy Eye.

Kris Trexler, restorer of a gorgeous 1958 Pontiac Bonneville Sport Coupe, Jubilee Edition. Thanks for answering my "girl" questions about your masterpiece.

Michael Blackburn, funeral director and co-owner of Callahan-Edfast Mortuary in Grand Junction, Colorado. He enumerated the blessings and challenges of his work. Mrs. Clancy is based on the lunchroom lady at my elementary school, *not* Michael whose heart is as tender as his wit is sharp.

John Fischer, songwriter and fellow writer extraordinaire. I sang "Have You Seen Jesus My Lord?" with my college roommate until she wearied of my lackluster harmonies. It's still an all-time favorite, John.

To my readers, I extend my warmest regards. Thank you for reading my little story. I pray you consider the time well spent.

And to my Heavenly Father, thank you for filling the daddy-shaped hole in my heart. I love you.

A Readers Club Guide to

The Queen of Sleepy Eye

The Queen of Sleepy Eye

Summary

It's the summer of 1975, and Amy Monteiro believes it's high time her mother, Francie, the deposed queen of the 1958 Sleepy Eye Corn Festival, lays aside her tiara and grows up. After all, Amy is California bound with a full-ride college scholarship. Studious and focused, Amy is twilight to Francie's midnight beauty. Francie, gregarious as she is impetuous, can't seem to imagine life without Amy. Determined to detour her daughter's push for independence, Francie packs her beloved Pontiac Bonneville Sport Coupe, Jubilee Edition, and together they hit the open road.

While Amy sleeps in a Dramamine stupor through the Rocky Mountains, Francie follows beguiling road signs to Cordial,

Colorado, a town caught between tradition and ideology, where old-timers long for the past and long-haired hippies shelter themselves from an enigmatic world. A failed transmission exiles mother and daughter in this teetering milieu. Before the sun sets, Francie secures them a position as caretakers of Clancy and Sons Funeral Home in exchange for free rent. However, Francie then takes a job at the hardware store to pay the automotive repair bills, leaving Amy to polish caskets and host viewings. Despite a pinkie pledge with Amy to put her love life on hold, Francie begins dating a coal miner and settles into the life rhythms of Cordial, while Amy is determined to get herself to California—with or without her mother.

During one unforgettable summer, values clash, belief sparks, myths fade, and a mother and daughter both come of age when they are introduced to the power of grace.

Questions for Discussion

1. The author lived through the 1970s, but her research led her to fresh discoveries about the people and time. How has the novel compared to your memories of that time? If you are too young to remember the 1970s, what stereotypes did the story challenge for you?

2. Which of the characters makes the biggest impact on Amy and how?

3. How do each of the major characters—Amy, Francie, Feather, H, Mrs. Clancy—change over the course of the story? Which characters demonstrate little or no growth, and why?

4. What do we learn about Amy through her relationship and correspondence with Lauren?

5. What similarities or differences do you recognize from your relationship with your

mother and/or your daughter and the relationship between Amy and Francie? What could you do to strengthen your relationship?

6. Amy believes she is insulated by her faith from making the same mistakes her mother has. How is that true or untrue? What unmet needs are shared by both Amy and Francie? How does Amy's need make her vulnerable to temptation in the apple orchard?

7. Father Raymond says to Amy, "There never lived a perfectly good saint, but true saints learn to enjoy the goodness of God in spite of their imperfections. Let him love you as he made you and lavish you with his grace." How does his counsel correspond with your own view of God?

8. Why does Pastor Ted refuse to come and pray for Feather? What do you think of his dilemma? If you were Amy's pastor years later, how would you counsel her regarding this experience from her past?

9. Amy's dreams of college and independence die hard. What is the source of our dreams? When

is it time to let a dream rest in peace? When is it time to resurrect a dream?

10. Amy tells Carl to rush to the Father just as the prodigal son ran to his. In what ways have you distanced yourself from God?

The Author's Guide to Enhancing Your Book Club Experience

If reading *The Queen of Sleepy Eye* piqued your interest about the places Francie and Amy visited, I suggest a "cyber trip" via the image search command on your Internet browser. Try googling a few of these place names—North Fork of the Gunnison River; Paonia, Colorado (the town and vistas that inspired Cordial); Bogan Flats Campground; Yule Marble Quarry; and, of course, Sleepy Eye, Minnesota—and you'll see why I enjoyed my time in the North Fork Valley and beyond.

I personally found Feather's back-to-the-land family an especially intriguing component in *The Queen of Sleepy Eye* story, especially since the same dissatisfactions that drove mid-1970 families to sustenance farming are now pressing contemporary urbanites toward self-reliance. For a deeper look at family farming in America, I recommend three memoirs. First, *Heathens: Hard Times and High Spirits on an Iowa Farm During the Depression* by Mildred Armstrong Kalish. Not one bit self-indulgent, this memoir reveals the power of family working the land together. *Back from the Land* by Eleanor Agnew follows the back-to-the-land movement full circle from dreamy idealism to biting reality. Finally, for a look at a contemporary urban-family-turned-farm-family, *Animal, Vegetable, Miracle* by Barbara Kingsolver may just motivate you to sharpen your hoe.

When it comes time to plan your book club meeting, consider hosting the event around a royalty theme or even a "hippie" theme. Stop by my Web site at www.pattihillauthor.com for table décor ideas, recipes, and activities to make your book club meeting for *The Queen of Sleepy Eye* your best ever.

Daylight's burning . . .

Patti

An Interview with Patti Hill

Patti, tell us about how you came to write novels.

I really am a most unlikely writer of fiction. During my formative years, reading was limited to the newspaper and *Reader's Digest* until my sixth-grade teacher introduced me to Walter Farley and Marguerite Henry. Horse stories turned me into a voracious reader. If I couldn't own a horse, reading about them was the next best thing. I raced across the desert on the Godolphin Arabian and stretched over the neck of the Black Stallion as he pressed for the finish line. I loved living vicariously through the characters of books.

I first heard I should be a writer from a friend's mother. I was incredulous as I wrote little more than homesick letters from my new hometown. But a college professor seconded the notion, and this felt like a calling to me. I think of Sarah and the birth of Isaac—and this isn't meant to be a disrespectful comparison—but it took God a while to fulfill my calling too. Sarah wasn't ready to be a mother until her ninety-ninth birthday, and I wasn't ready to birth a book for several decades either.

When my two amazing sons were older, I went back to college to earn a B.A. in English Literature and Elementary Education. All thoughts about being a writer—although I wrote constantly, personally and professionally—had been forgotten. And then I got a story idea. I took a hiatus from teaching to write, and, well, the rest is history.

So where were you during the summer of 1975?

I had just finished my sophomore year of college and moved home for the summer to work at Carl's Jr. The French fry cooker made the summer extremely long and hot in my lime-green tunic and brown leotards. I longed to be back in San Luis Obispo with my friends who were taking summer classes and going to the beach to "study."

Did living through that time prepare you to write *The Queen of Sleepy Eye*?

Yes and no. Since I was a teen then, a very young adult in the seventies, I was hyperaware of pop culture. And a quick glance at a J. C. Penney catalog from 1975 reawakened my Seventies sense of style, and I do use that phrase advisedly. I spent that decade strumming folk songs and faith choruses on my guitar. My poor family. I would play for hours on end. Flip-flops were my official footwear from March to December, and during a high school interior design class, my creations included macramé plant hangers and open-weaved draperies. On Friday nights I sat glued to the television for *The Rockford Files*. But I was also a part of the Jesus Movement in Southern California. I attended Jesus People concerts and Bible studies under a circus tent, sometimes three nights a week. My friends and I carried huge Bibles to school every day so we could conduct impromptu Bible studies during lunch or witness to fellow students. It was a very exciting time to be a part of God's family.

All in all, I led a rather insular life in a California beach town. My contact with the counterculture was limited to a few "Jesus Freaks" and those I met street witnessing along Pacific Coast Highway. Many of those witnessing encounters involved people under the influence of drugs, so I wasn't very effective in my mission, and sadly, the experience tainted my perceptions of hippies and long-hairs. I lumped them into one smelly and disoriented group.

During my research for this book, however, I discovered the back-to-nature movement. These people worked extremely hard to provide a safe place for their families to live and grow. The Seventies were a scary time. Fresh-faced boys were being drafted to fight in Vietnam; the Iran hostage crisis made us feel incredibly vulnerable; and the whole Watergate fiasco fostered a distrust of authority. And don't forget acid rain—the world was dissolving all around us! The back-to-nature folks withdrew to become sustenance farmers, aiming toward a cashless society and developing relevant relationships on their own terms.

Quite frankly, I never would have made it as a back-to-nature woman. They lived in cabins built with their own hands—no indoor plumbing or heating or electricity. I did, however, dress the part of an "earth mama" in college—overalls, Birkenstocks, and bandanas. We drank things like linseed oil in potato water, though I can't remember why. I still eat Ak-Mak crackers but consider carob a sad substitute for chocolate.

Are any of the characters in the book autobiographical?

Simply put, they're all me—or you. Unless the characters of fiction resonate with the truth of our experiences, they're lifeless. For instance, Francie hopes her moment of brilliance as the queen of Sleepy Eye portends greater things ahead. A professor's note at the bottom of an essay convinced me I was writer material. How's that for delusions of grandeur? And I walked the periphery of high school society just like H. Would I do anything to fit in? I was the sole member of senior senate to wear a Greek toga on Triton Day. No one remembered to tell me when the seniors voted not to dress Greek after all—or was it geek? Long day. And like Amy, I've stuffed a cavernous hole of loneliness with clothes, ambitions, and faulty relationships. All the while, Jesus stood at the ready to be my Prince. I want to leave a legacy of faith like Leoti. In times of loss, I've been coldly efficient like Mrs. Clancy. But it's Feather I most want to be like—splayed out in faith, watchful and expectant. Take me, Jesus, I'm yours!

As a parent, I gritted my teeth during several scenes with Francie. I wanted to shake her. What made you create a character like her?

I've known women like Francie, and you're right, they're aggravating. Some traumatic event—like early motherhood, abuse, or loss—has stunted them emotionally. They muddle through serial relationships and bear children who end up parenting their mothers, in essence, thereby robbing their children of their childhood. But these women aren't evil. They're wounded and redeemable and loveable. We all are. That's the profound mystery of God's love.

We've talked quite a bit about characters. What came first for *Queen,* the characters or the story?

I wrote this book completely backwards, because it was the title that came first. My sweet friend Margaret announced with great flourish at my second book launch that she had been the queen of Sleepy Eye. I loved the sound of "The Queen of Sleepy Eye," so I wrote the potential title on a napkin and thumb-tacked it to my bulletin board. It stayed there until I started mulling over ideas for a fourth project. A writer must never despise inspiration, even when it shows up out of sequence in unexpected places, but I hope to write all future books after coming up with the story premise or characters first.

Amy's encounter with Pastor Ted over Feather's poor reception at Spruce Street Church is heartbreaking yet insightful. Was this scene based on personal experience?

This is the question I've been dreading, but yes, the scene is based on a lifetime of experience in churches of every shape and size. All churchgoers aren't nice, nor are all churchgoers believers, yet these very folks tend to be among our most faithful attendees. The "tares" volunteer to head committees and are elected to elder boards. I have to tell you, I don't get it. Why would anyone situate themselves in this position unless they are completely sold out to Jesus?

I appreciate that Jesus anticipated their presence by sharing the Parable of the Tares (Matt. 13:24–43). The story serves as a warning to judgmental people like me. Jesus is saying, "Yes, I know the weeds drain resources and compete for nutrition, but culling them out only expands their destructive influence. Let the Holy Spirit do His work, and live out your relationship with Me on a lampstand so they can see My love in you. They may yet become what they are not—wheat."

You're not off the hook yet. Let's talk about Amy's moral fall. Why didn't she just push Falcon away?

That's exactly what I had intended. In my outline and synopsis, Amy did push Falcon away. But when I wrote the scene, her sudden turnaround didn't ring true, not for how Amy had looked to Falcon to satisfy her loneliness, not for how she despised her mother's behavior, and certainly not for her harsh judgment and withdrawal from Lauren. Amy needed to discover that even an egregious fall doesn't exempt her from God's love and forgiveness, that he is more than willing to receive a repentant child with open arms. In fact, he'll run to her when she's still a long way off, just like he ran to the prodigal son. I wanted to portray that kind of exuberant redemption in *The Queen of Sleepy Eye.* It's for all of us.

Besides, it's not enough to face the temptations of this life with one Scripture verse as Amy tried to do. June Fellhauer, a dear and longtime friend, once ministered to unwed mothers on the local and national level. Watching those young mothers struggle to find their one true love broke June's heart. She wanted to equip girls to wait for their prince rather than simply being there to pick up the pieces. Several years ago she started teaching a high school girls' Bible study based on the Song of Solomon. Remember the young maiden of the book who enters a covenantal relationship with her prince? Well, June guides the girls to make the same commitment to Jesus, their true Prince. Participating in her ministry made a huge impact on me—and Amy. For more information, check out June's Web site at www.wakeupministries.com.

Tells us about the car. What part does it play in *The Queen of Sleepy Eye*?

I didn't set out to create deep symbolism with the Pontiac, but the car's purpose grows with the telling of the story. First and foremost, as long as Francie keeps the car, it ties her to her past. She can't move on. It's a big, gaudy reminder of her grab for meaning but also her most heroic moment. And then the car becomes a sort of albatross, limiting her movement with fear. Selling the car finally allows Francie and Amy to build new lives. Only when they're strong enough does the car reappear to carry them back to Sleepy Eye where they have some issues left to resolve.

The ending wasn't what I expected. I wanted Amy to find the father she deserved. What's with Carl?

Carl is a sad man because he doesn't grow from the boy we come to know through Francie's memories. All he's accomplished is adding fifty years to his life. To be fair, there is only one Father who never disappoints. I'm so proud of Amy for directing Carl toward the Everlasting Father.

Let's end this on my favorite topic, food. What are lavadores?

Lavadores are gently sweetened lemon cookies from Portugal. My family loves them, especially during the summer with vanilla ice cream. *Lavadore* means "washboard" in Portuguese, referring to the ridges pressed into the cookies with the tines of a fork. Here's the recipe:

Lavadores (Washboard Cookies)

Makes about 4½ to 5 dozen

½ cup butter, softened
1½ cups sugar, divided
4 eggs
Grated peel of 1 lemon
4 cups all-purpose flour, as needed
1 tablespoon baking powder
Preheat oven to 350 degrees F

1. With an electric mixer on medium-high speed, or by hand, cream the butter and 1 cup of the sugar for about 1 minute. Beat in the eggs, one at a time, blending well after each, until the batter is fluffy and pale yellow, about 2–3 minutes. Stir in the grated lemon peel.
2. In a medium bowl, whisk together the flour and baking powder, stirring to distribute the ingredients evenly. Using a wooden spoon, fold the flour into the egg batter. Mix well. Gently knead the dough in the bowl for about 5 minutes.
3. Place the remaining ½ cup of sugar in a shallow dish. Shape pieces of dough into 1½-inch balls. Roll in the sugar and place on parchment-lined or lightly greased cookie sheets, 2 inches apart. Flatten gently with the tines of a fork to make horizontal lines. Bake for 20–25 minutes or until a light golden color.

About the Author

Patti Hill lives in Colorado with her husband of thirty years, Dennis, a garden center owner, and their pacesetter dog, Tillie. Her grown sons, Geoff and Matt, live and work in the Northwest. Cramming seven years of college into twenty-two, Patti finally earned her Bachelor of Arts degree in English Literature in 1995—only three years in dog years.

Her life's journey has led her through amazing opportunities—teaching Bible studies, participating in puppet and acting ministries, serving as a volunteer in her community, and meeting the most amazing short people as an elementary school teacher. And, of course, she cherishes her years as chief laundress of the Hill household.

Inspired by a writing class with Lauraine Snelling, Patti now lives her dream of being a novelist. Her first novel, *Like a Watered Garden*, was a finalist in the first-novel category at the 2006 Christy Awards. A *Publishers Weekly* starred review said, "Fresh prose, wry humor, an enjoyable protagonist, and strong pacing make Hill a welcome addition to the ranks of inspirational novelists."

Visit Patti online at www.pattihillauthor.com.